"Mamaw," she said, pulling in her focus as tight as a wire. "Sometimes I get just as mad as you do. In law school, they teach us that this anger must be subjugated...." She rethought her words. "Must be conquered. Reasonable men agree to live by reasonable laws. If one of them breaks a law, then he is brought to justice by laws that have been agreed to, not by the feelings of an individual or a mob."

Mamaw listened quietly, her eyes as soft as a doe's. She set the other cup on the table in front of Alma, pulled her wheelchair, and eased down into it. "We Bashears, we don't ask for trouble, but if people do us wrong, and no justice is forthcoming, then there's only one law we'll live by—the law of revenge...."

THE LAW
OF REVENGE

THE LAW OF REVENGE

Tess Collins

AN AUTHORS GUILD BACKINPRINT.COM EDITION

The Law of Revenge

All Rights Reserved © 1997, 2005 by Tess Collins

No part of this book may be reproduced or transmitted in any form or by any means, graphic, electronic, or mechanical, including photocopying, recording, taping, or by any information storage or retrieval system, without the written permission of the publisher.

AN AUTHORS GUILD BACKINPRINT.COM EDITION
Published by iUniverse, Inc.

For information address:
iUniverse, Inc.
2021 Pine Lake Road, Suite 100
Lincoln, NE 68512
www.iuniverse.com

Originally published by Ballantine

First Edition: July 1997

ISBN-13: 978-0-595-36711-5 (pbk)
ISBN-13: 978-0-595-81287-5 (cloth)
ISBN-10: 0-595-36711-9 (pbk)
ISBN-10: 0-595-81287-2 (cloth)

Printed in the United States of America

FOR JAMES N. FREY,
A DAMN GOOD TEACHER

And special thanks to Judy Jones Lewis, Mary Dunn, and Lou Ligouri for help on legal aspects of this story and to my agent, Jane Dystel, and editor, Susan Randol, for their care in shepherding this first novel.

1

Alma Bashears waited for the elderly man to stop sobbing. She turned away so that he wouldn't see her embarrassment for him. It amazed Alma that someone as rich as Mitchell Brenner could be reduced to this level of humiliation. The culprit, who sat a few inches from her father's quivering body, fiddled with a nose ring and adjusted a silver-studded collar around her throat.

Brenner's eighteen-year-old daughter, Lucy, screwed anything that would look at her, shoplifted for the pleasure of accomplishment, and sniffed cocaine until her nose had almost rotted off her face. In thirty minutes Lucy Brenner faced sentencing before the toughest judge in San Francisco and there was no chance that Daddy could buy her way out of this one.

If her father's outburst disturbed her, Lucy didn't let it show. She casually combed her black-lacquered nails through greasy strands of maroon-colored hair. "Look, lady," Lucy said to Alma, "you've upset my daddy. Either you figure a way to get me out of this mess or he'll fire your watusi."

The tone of Lucy's threat sent anxious twists through Alma's stomach. Alma had been a senior associate with the San Francisco firm of Steinburg, Erickson, and Janovic for six years. She intended to be a partner before her thirty-fifth birthday—three years from now, if this case didn't get her canned.

Mitchell Brenner gave the firm a few million dollars' worth of corporate business a year. Now even the senior partners were worried. If Brenner's little girl went to jail, that business would fly south. Alma knew she'd be hanged as the scapegoat.

Brenner wiped his eyes with the palms of his large, liver-spotted hands. "I've made a mistake," he said, sniffing and clearing his throat. "We need a criminal lawyer . . . a big hitter."

"We discussed this at the start," Alma said, praying she would not have to call in a senior partner to pacify him. "Judge Barnett hates rich kids and has no use for high-profile attorneys. One look at a face that's been in the newspaper more than twice and Lucy will be in the Chowchilla Women's Correctional Facility by the end of the day."

"I am not going to jail!" Lucy shot up from the couch—all studs and black leather creaking and clinking. "You might as well buy me a ticket to Asia, old man! I refuse to be locked up like I'm a starlet in a Linda Blair movie!"

"We all agreed, Mr. Brenner," Alma said, ignoring Lucy's outburst. "The senior partners believe this is the best strategy."

"Look at you in your little navy Brooks Brothers suit and Sassoon hairdo!" Mr. Brenner yelled. "If this defense had been handled competently, we wouldn't be in this position now!"

"She's guilty, Mr. Brenner," Alma shot back, even though his attack had her trembling inside. "They have her on videotape—buying, using, and selling cocaine."

"Didn't Joe Elliot hire Dershowitz to defend his kid?"

"Little Jimmy's presently doing five-to-ten in Attica."

"It's not fair," Lucy whined. She dropped to the floor and crossed her legs, showing a good deal of ample thighs. "They're doing this because of who my father is. It's your fault, Daddy. And yours." She glared at Alma.

Alma stared hard at Lucy, wishing she would shut up. "We don't have much time. Mr. Brenner?"

He crossed his arms tightly over his chest and stared at the floor. Alma recognized this as a bad sign. She bit her lip and stared at the phone. If she had to call a senior partner to pacify Brenner, it would make her look as if she couldn't handle it. "Mr. Brenner," she said softly, "if anybody in this town can tug a tear out of Judge Barnett, it's me."

Brenner took his daughter's hand. "Honey," he said to Lucy, "I believe in you, even if no one else does." He turned to Alma and shook his finger in her face. "She's my little girl."

Alma followed Mitchell Brenner to the door, swallowing the responsibility implied in his final words. She watched him until the metallic elevator doors closed behind him. The doors reflected back a distortion of Alma's straight black hair, which hung slightly below her shoulders. She was glad she wasn't close enough to see the expression on her own face. Confidence was what she needed now. Her future hung on a rich, spoiled junkie.

Alma turned toward Lucy and smiled slightly. She reached into a closet and pulled out a size 14 Ann Taylor dress, classic-looking but not too chic. Lucy's painted mouth scrunched up as if she might regurgitate. Part of Alma wished Lucy would spend the next ten years in prison. Alma assuaged her guilt at representing this despicable rich kid by reminding herself of how important Brenner was to the firm. It would be she who saved this account, and she'd remind her bosses of it when the time was right.

Taking the dress off its hanger, she threw it at Lucy. "We have twenty-five minutes." Alma slipped out of her high heels and stood like a fullback guarding the door. "In fifteen of those minutes I intend to have you in that dress."

"You and what army?" Lucy sneered, and stepped toward Alma with a tough swagger.

Alma stood firm. Lucy stopped three feet short of her. She glared into Alma's eyes. When Alma didn't move, Lucy blinked and looked at the floor as if contemplating what to do next.

Alma let one side of her mouth curl into a smile. "You think you're the first rich kid I've tangled with? Personally, I'd sleep better nights if you spent the next ten years of your life in Chowchilla prison. You know how a rich girl like you will look after ten years in prison, Lucy? Let's just say it would make your present appearance seem appealing."

Lucy slowly turned away. She faced the mirror on the back of Alma's closet door. Her mouth was drawn down in a frown, her eyes wide and wild like a rabbit's caught in headlights. As she watched her reflection, she leaned over and picked up the dress, then draped it over her arm. Then she twirled around and faced Alma. Lucy stuck out her tongue as far as she could, revealing a silver stud pierced right through the meaty middle part.

Alma smiled at the girl's attempt to shock her. "How do you talk with that thing in your mouth?"

2

"No family in America, Your Honor," Alma said, "whether rich, poor, or middle class, has remained untouched by this whirlpool of drug abuse that ravages our nation." Alma looked into Judge Barnett's eyes, opening her hands as if soliciting the understanding of a wise old man. "What I can point to is the answer in this individual case and that is Lucy Brenner's family. A family who knew they'd lost their daughter." Alma stepped around the podium, closer to the judge. She knew her next words better be the argument of her life. "Lucy would be dead today were it not for the intervention of her father. This father fought to get his little girl back, and he will continue to fight. More than that, Lucy herself is now fighting. She fights to regain the person that she was. She fights that fight"—Alma paused and emphasized each word—"every day of her life."

Alma asked Lucy to stand. The dowdy-looking girl she'd been transformed into stood up. Wire-framed glasses with lenses as thick as the bottoms of soda bottles blotted out her cheekbones. Her hair was styled into a pageboy and sprayed brown. "In closing, Your Honor," Alma said, "I ask that you look at this girl. You, who have judged many a criminal, can see that this child is not a criminal. This girl is a victim. A girl who has sworn never to be a victim again. We ask that you allow her to prove that to you." Alma returned to the defense table, put her arm around Lucy, and waited.

Judge Barnett's expression was rigid to the point that his loose jaws looked as hard as stone, and his glazed eyes seemed to regard the courtroom as a mural rather than a room with interacting people. Alma turned to look at the spectator section, trying to measure the effectiveness of her strategy. A few reporters were scribbling notes, and when one looked up, the expression was the usual jaded and noncommittal stare. Brenner sat behind Lucy, his hands folded on his lap. A few people smiled at Alma, seeming to offer their sympathy, but most avoided looking at her.

Oh, my God, Alma thought. I've lost. She looked again, hoping she'd misread the spectator section. In the back row she saw a familiar wave of black hair. Jordan McFedries—California State Supreme Court justice, and if Alma had her way, the man she would marry. She turned quickly toward the judge, praying he hadn't seen Jordan. If Barnett thought Jordan's presence was meant to influence him, things could turn ugly.

The judge scratched his temple with an index finger. He stared out the window and did not look at either Alma or the prosecutor as they stood, awaiting his judgment. Barnett tapped his pen against the wooden gavel. The courtroom was silent as a country house at midnight.

Why won't he speak? Alma wondered, and couldn't help glancing sideways. The prosecutor was sneaking a look at her. He was probably just as confused and tense. His eyes narrowed at Alma as if to say her emotional plea had disgusted him. Lucy was pale, and she held on to the table to steady herself. Alma could feel her trembling.

"Well." Judge Barnett drew out the word. "Young lady, you'd better never let me regret my decision." He wrote on the papers in front of him as his bass voice spoke. "Lucy, you are to continue drug counseling for not less than one year, and I'm ordering two years' probation with one thousand hours of community service."

After they were in the limousine, Mitchell Brenner shook Alma's hand. "I don't have words for my appreciation," he said.

Lucy rolled her eyes and pulled a bottle of black nail polish from her pocket. She twisted off the cap and dipped the brush in and out.

"Don't you realize how much your father loves you?" Alma asked her.

Her question prompted Lucy to slouch in the seat. "It's over," she replied, brushing a stroke of black lacquer on her middle fingernail. "You're out of it."

Brenner rubbed his hands over his face. "Maybe you'd better put that away."

Lucy continued painting.

"My father disappeared when I was ten," Alma said. "He was a coal miner when the mines went bust, and it was Christmas. He took a job in a Detroit car factory to earn Christmas money. The police said he was probably murdered for that money and dumped in Lake St. Clair."

Lucy shifted herself until she faced the car door.

Alma brushed the expensive linen of her suit and pushed up a sleeve to check the time on her diamond Wittnauer watch. Mitchell Brenner followed the gesture, and his troubled eyes seemed to acknowledge that Alma had made something of herself while his daughter never would. "I'd have given my right arm if my father could have seen me graduate from law school," Alma said.

Brenner slapped his daughter's hand, knocking the nail polish to the floor. "No more!" he demanded. "No more! No more!" His face flushed a pinkish red as his jaws clamped together like a trap. His eyes reddened and filled with tears that did not fall onto his cheeks. "I said no more, girl."

Lucy's body became a tight wad of muscle attached to the car door. She held her breath, then spat it out. A single tear fell down her cheek. Her father reached over and touched her shoulder. She leaned, inch by inch, until she was in his arms, and he rocked her back and forth.

"Let me out at California and Sansome," Alma said to the driver. As she exited the limousine, Mitchell Brenner looked up at her. His eyes glistened, and his expression spoke more gratitude than words could ever have expressed. Alma realized that, today, she had done more than her job.

3

As Alma walked down the corridor of the deserted thirty-sixth floor in the Bank of America building, the red exit lights lit the hallway with an eerie glow. When she got to her office, she dumped her briefcase behind the desk and stepped out of her shoes, then made her way to the closet mirror. Dabbing at flecks of mascara, she was glad to see that the lines of her face didn't show as much tension as she was feeling. Her gray eyes, so dark a color that they were often mistaken for blue, had a catlike quality that she often used to unnerve hostile witnesses.

She rubbed her shoulders. The tension of the day had her neck in knots. Bringing her fingers up to her jaw, she pressed underneath the high cheekbones that were part of her Cherokee heritage. She inhaled and let her full lips circle around the air to control the breath. The reflection of a man's hand caused her to gasp. The hand circled her neck and pulled her face forward for a deep kiss.

"I could strangle you," she said, breaking free of the kiss.

"Nice back-door job," Jordan said. Before she could respond, he leaned down next to her ear and whispered, "Would you like to see how I do a back-door job?"

"Here? Now?" Alma teased. She pushed away from him and stood in the middle of the office, hands on her hips, leaning forward as if to accuse a witness. "You were there today," she said. "I saw you slip in. You could have blown the case for me if Barnett had noticed."

"I only stopped by to admire my handiwork—in action."

"Didn't you have a death penalty case to decide or something?"

"I sent them all to the electric chair and went home early."

Alma laughed, then circled her desk and dropped into the plush leather chair. "The big boys didn't think I could handle it."

"Nonsense." He waved his hand through the air, then brushed the side of his short black hair.

Alma wished his eyes weren't the same shade of gray as her own with an equal intensity that kept her from looking into them for very long. His square jaw never dropped its set determination, and his six-foot frame was more suggestive of a basketball player than a supreme court justice. "Don't think that just because you're hard to resist that I'll drop this. If the partners have so little confidence in me that they have to send you to the courtroom in the mistaken delusion that they'll hedge their bets with Barnett—"

"You're imagining things," he interrupted. He rounded the desk, pushed some papers aside, and leaned against it. "I simply wanted to see you in action. After all, I don't want Steinburg, Erickson, and Janovic taking all the credit for so well trained an attorney as you."

"Credit you'd rather take for yourself?"

"Let's just say I have things in mind for you."

"What things?" Alma asked.

"Come here," he said, opening his arms.

Alma hesitated. She stared into his eyes, wishing she could read his complex intentions. Jordan always had a reason for doing things. Then she sprang up and melted into him, and he hugged her just tight enough for her to feel the muscles in his chest. She slid around in his arms so that they both faced the window. The sun was setting, and the horizon glared a neon fuchsia. The quiet was like a new experience. She thought that life, for them, always seemed full of too much noise.

Jordan kissed her behind an ear. She reached around and stroked his leg. "We shouldn't do this here," she said. His hands were already on her thighs, spreading them apart and sliding upward, raising her skirt in the same motion. She unzipped his pants and pushed him back onto her desk, letting her body slide on top of him.

"Who sent you today? Steinburg or Erickson?"

"I love it when you wear garters."

"They asssigned me to this case because of the partnership fight. Right? If I'd blown it, it would have given Janovic fuel against Erickson."

"I knew you were wearing them when you stood up to give your closing argument."

"You like it even better after you've seen me in the courtroom. Admit it, it turns you on, doesn't it?"

"If you ever practiced before me, let's just say I'd have you in chambers . . . a lot."

"You can have me anywhere you want me."

"You are a mesmerizing little witch. It amazes me how you always have everything against you and you still come out on top."

"I'm on top now, aren't I?"

He bit into her neck while she straddled his lap. The phone rang, momentarily interrupting them. "Ignore it," Alma said. "It's after hours." She vaguely recalled leaving the answering machine on and cursed to herself. She didn't want anything to spoil the moment. She wrapped her legs around Jordan's and sucked on his tongue with the rhythm of their breathing.

"Alma ... Alma Mae," said a woman's voice to the machine, singing with the heavy accent of the southern Appalachian Mountains.

Oh, God, Alma thought, my mother.

The mountain accent was a mixture of eastern Tennessee and western Virginia, though her mother lived on the state line in Kentucky. "Alma, Uncle Ames is down at the library. He's faxing you some paperwork." She spoke to someone else, and the muffled arguing caused Jordan to laugh.

Alma felt acute embarrassment and pushed away from him. "It's my mother," she said. In the next office the fax line rang.

"It's Vernon," her mother said. "Big troubles, honey."

Alma's younger brother had been arrested a half-dozen times for public drunkenness and disorderly conduct. Not uncommon for Vernon, she thought, and hardly a reason to call her in California. She hadn't been back to Contrary, Kentucky, since she'd left fifteen years earlier. The town of about fifteen thousand seemed caught in a time warp—ten years behind the rest of the world, though when Alma was growing up there it had seemed like twenty. She clenched her teeth, trying to suppress her deep resentment of this phone call.

"He killed a man, Alma. Bill Littlefield. The stuff Ames is sending will explain it all. Well, we just wanted you to know." More muffled arguing, then when her mother spoke again there was a hesitant quality in her voice. "Uh, Mamaw wants you to come back." Another hesitation and muffled talk. "She says we need you. That's all. Let us know if you're coming."

The disconnected line transmitted a series of beeps, then a dial tone, then it was quiet. Alma couldn't break her focus on the caustic tone of her mother's "if you're coming." She turned away from Jordan and fought to control her annoyance.

"Hey, you okay?" Jordan put his hand on her shoulder.

"I have to get to the fax machine." She could feel him following her. She hated that he had heard this, hated his sympathy even, and hated that he had probably figured out that her family was a bunch of crackers instead of the simple country folk she'd described.

She took the pages as they slid out of the machine. An article from the local newspaper; another one from the largest nearby city, Knoxville, Tennessee; an arrest warrant; and, finally, a note from Uncle Ames: "Please, come at once."

"It happened this morning," Alma said to Jordan as she read the local article. Vernon was applying for a job at the Littlefield Hotel and Spa. Bill Littlefield threw a gum wrapper at Vernon and it bounced off his nose. Blows were struck. Vernon ran. Littlefield died at the scene of head injuries.

The Knoxville paper called Vernon a job-seeking drifter. Alma knew the reporter hadn't bothered to check the facts. Vernon had lived in Contrary all his life. He'd certainly been there longer than Big Bill Littlefield, who'd hailed from Ohio. It seemed odd to Alma that a Cincinnatian would seek his fortune in a used-up coal town like Contrary. The local *Contrary Gazette* had gone into more detail, as it had covered Vernon's numerous misdemeanor arrests. He was identified as the son of Esau and Merl Bashears, and readers were reminded that Esau had disappeared more than twenty years before under mysterious circumstances while working in Detroit. Both articles listed the achievements of William J. Littlefield, known to his friends as "Big Bill," and to most of Kentucky as the man who would have revitalized eastern Kentucky's economy.

"A gum wrapper?" Alma said. "It would be funny if it weren't so ridiculous." Anger surged through her. It would be just like Vernon to get into a fight over something so stupid. "My poor grandmother. This is not something she needs."

"Involuntary manslaughter," Jordan said, reading over her shoulder. "If it's his first offense, he won't serve a day." He put his arm around her. "That is, if you're the person coaching his attorney."

Alma pushed his arm off. "I'm not going back there. There's too much to do here."

Jordan's face registered surprise. "After today, your position here is more than secure."

"I hate that town." A rush of heat filled Alma's head. Her eyes and nose burned as if she'd breathed in salt water, and she turned away so that she wouldn't have to look into Jordan's eyes.

"This doesn't have anything to do with the town. It has to do with your family." When she didn't respond, he seemed annoyed. "Well, I'd go back."

"Obviously, I didn't grow up with your family values!" She could feel a heated irritation growing and busied herself by stuffing the papers into a file. "You know, Jordan, we can't keep meeting in offices and hotel rooms between here and Sacramento. It's a totally ridiculous way to live."

Jordan ignored her attempt to change the subject. "After all you said about families today? Not that I'm suggesting you need to believe your own summations, but . . . Just stop it, Alma!" He reached out and spun her around. The papers spilled onto the floor. "Think."

Alma's hands shook. She held on to Jordan's lapels to keep him from noticing. A part of her was revealed, and she hated it. "I'm not going back," she hissed through gritted teeth.

"Alma, you're about to fall apart. What is it?" She tried to pull away, but Jordan held her. "Count," he said. "Remember what I taught you. Law is numbers and numbers are unemotional." He pulled her to him and squeezed her tightly, stroking her hair with one hand.

His touch invaded her muscles, making them feel rubbery and weak. She held her breath to keep from crying.

"One is the law," he said. "Two is the opposition, three is the evidence, four is the plea."

She repeated it with him until she spoke without emotion, her voice calm, collected. "Five is the court, six is the jury, seven is the presentation, eight is the verdict, nine, we win the case or we go back to one and appeal."

"But the best," they said together, "is to win the case before number two."

"Because two," Jordan repeated from his recent speech to the American Bar Association, where he'd unveiled his method of counting out the law, "is a great time for a late lunch." He smiled, holding one hand to her cheek and watching her as closely as a doctor watches a critically ill patient. "Honey, he's your brother." He rubbed her arm soothingly.

"How can I go home? I can't go home."

"Tell me what's wrong."

"I can't. I just can't."

"Alma," Jordan said firmly. "I know you well enough to know you aren't going to sit here on your hands while your brother is left to the mercy of a small-town lawyer." He reached into his pocket and pulled out a small box. "Besides, if you don't go, I can't give you this going-away present."

Alma stepped closer. He held a ring box in his hand and her heart leaped. She took it and snapped back the top. In it was a pair of blue topaz earrings. She turned to the window so that Jordan wouldn't see the disappointment on her face. It's not a diamond, she thought. No diamond. "The most beautiful earrings I've ever seen," she said.

He came up behind her and wrapped his arms around her waist. "I have some things I have to handle this weekend anyway. Before you leave, call Bob Krauss in Knoxville. I'll call him as well." He squeezed her tight. "Your favorite boss, Eric Erickson, went to law school with him. Use that." Turning her around, he held her face between his hands. "You go home, and when you come back, we'll have a lot to talk about."

She closed her eyes and leaned her head against his shoulder. Home, she thought. I'm going home.

As he held her, they watched the sun go down behind the San Francisco skyline. It filled the office with a reddish-pink glow, blinding them to everything but each other's warmth.

4

Alma leaned her forehead against the plane's window. Cold and frosty. Frosty as her bedroom windows used to get when she'd lain in bed waiting for the blare of the alarm clock. Time for high school. Her sister, Sue, had slept beside her in the same bed. Sue's gentle snores had always sent a low vibration through the room.

Covering them were thirty-year-old patchwork quilts that smelled as old and musty as a damp closet. *No need to wash in wintertime, Alma Mae,* her mother would say, *we'll freeze our fingers off.* Alma had hated that smell—a sweaty smell, a dirty smell. Sometimes she'd thought she'd go crazy if she didn't escape the wrinkled hills that seemed to fold in on themselves like a series of prison gates.

The plane vibrated, jarring her from the suffocating memory of home. It soared through a mass of cottony clouds and in seconds was above the snow-covered Great Smoky Mountains. Giant pine trees looked like deep chasms on the mountainsides. Easy enough to slip into and disappear . . . pull in all your dirty secrets behind you, Alma thought. She sucked in a deep breath. As she exhaled, a shiver went through her.

The engines droned loudly like the roar of a lion . . . or of a waterfall. The sound reminded her of Jesus Falls near Contrary. A sick feeling spread through her stomach.

* * *

Fifteen-year-old Alma Mae saw Narly Gentry sitting on the bridge with three other high school boys. She curled the left side of her hair behind her ear. Narly's red-and-white-checked shirt hung out of his jeans, and his sleeves were rolled up to the elbows. The other boys wore white T-shirts, and one had a pack of Marlboro cigarettes neatly flipped in the sleeve. The smell of cigarette smoke colored the fragrance of honeysuckle growing along the creekbank.

The boys were seniors and she was a sophomore at the county high school. Rudy Delmar and Earl Roscoe had been held back because their grades and attendance records were so poor. Jefferson Bingham lived in the same hollow as Alma, just a few houses down. He saw her coming, jumped off the bridge railing, and turned his back to her. His arms waved in front of him as if he was explaining something to the other boys. Rudy leaned toward Jefferson and smacked his cheek lightly. Jefferson looked back at Alma once, then headed toward Slow Man's Market just beyond the bridge.

Alma wondered what Narly Gentry's business was in her part of town. He was a downtown boy and they never ventured way up there in the hollows. Only Sue had known of her crush on Narly until she told their mother. "Now, Alma," her mother teased, "yer a girl from the hollows, and Narly Gentry is a downtown boy."

Alma looked down at the ground as she walked, but she couldn't help flicking her eyes upward at Narly as she approached. His bushy brown hair waved back from his face, making him look like a young Elvis. A tingling excitement spread through her as she hoped he would notice her.

She stopped at the opposite end of the bridge and bent

THE LAW OF REVENGE

down to retie her new brown and white oxford shoes. She'd saved the whole year to buy them. All the downtown girls wore them and no one in her hollow yet owned a pair.

Narly's family was rich. He drove a restored Thunderbird to school every day. His father was campaigning for a seat in the State House of Representatives. Narly mostly dated cheerleaders and majorettes, but right now he didn't have a girlfriend. She peeked up at the boys as she double-tied the bows of the shoelaces. Below, the creek water bubbled over the rocks like a baby gurgling, and the sound tickled her insides.

Alma imagined what it would be like to date a downtown boy. Taken to the Burger Hop . . . to dances . . . bought presents on Valentine's Day . . . someone to sit with at church . . . good-night kisses . . . all the girls staring enviously at her . . . Alma wasn't allowed to date yet.

As she passed the boys, they turned their backs to her and looked at the ancient willow tree that overhung Crawdad Creek. Narly didn't even speak. As Alma went into Slow Man's Market, her stomach was heavy, as if full of rocks. She bought a box of salt, a pound of butter, and fifty cents' worth of baloney as instructed by her mother. Maybe I'll speak to them on the way back, she thought, and her mood lifted.

"Alma?" In the back of the store Jefferson Bingham hid behind a black potbellied coal stove. "Can I talk to ye?" he said, sounding unsure of himself. He shifted from one foot to another like a schoolboy waiting to see the principal.

After Alma paid old Mr. Hanson, she picked up the bag of groceries and turned toward Jefferson.

"Go home by way of Reed's Junction," he said.

"Reed's Junction? Why, I'd be goin' a half mile out of the way." She looked over at Mr. Hanson as if he might explain it, but the elderly man swayed in his rocking chair, one finger scanning the words in his black leather-covered Bible. His hearing aid was half out of his ear.

Jefferson swallowed, his Adam's apple bobbing up and down, and said, "I know, but—some of them yellow daffodils grow out by the railroad track there. I know ye like 'em." His blond bangs fell into his eyes and he stared through the spikes of his hair.

A surge of annoyance shot through Alma. They'd grown up in the same hollow and she knew better than to think he was flirting. More than likely, she thought, Narly had said something about me and Jefferson is just devil enough to try to send me in another direction. Probably thinks I ain't good enough for Narly. "Jefferson Bingham, I never told ye I liked daffodils and as a matter of fact, I don't." She turned on her heels and headed toward the screen door.

"Then go by way of Turner's Graveyard or the Phillip's station—" he said as she slammed the door, cutting off his words.

A warm breeze blew Alma's hair back from her face, and she fluffed out her white linen blouse with her free hand to cool the sweat on her back. Narly straddled the bridge rail. Rudy had disappeared, and Earl leaned out over the water as if looking at something below. She would speak to Narly, she decided. It couldn't hurt to say hello to him.

As she approached, he turned around and looked right into her eyes. Alma's heart pulsed until she thought it might pop up into her throat. "Sure is hot today, ain't it, Narly?"

"Why don't ye come down and cool yer feet in the

THE LAW OF REVENGE

creek with me?" Narly said, and smiled, showing straight white teeth with silver braces across them.

Alma's breath caught in her throat. Swarms of thoughts flitted through her mind like bees. Her mother was expecting her home, the butter would melt if she tarried, and she didn't want to seem overeager. Narly was interested in her! "Narly, I'd just love to, but my ma's expectin' me home."

"Aw, live dangerous. We'll let you look at the gopher Rudy trapped in a hole under the bridge."

Alma stepped up onto the bridge and looked over. A cool rush of wind came off the water. "A gopher," she said. "Now look at that creek. I'd get my new oxfords all muddy." She balanced on one foot and looked down at her shoes, very much aware that Narly was looking, too.

"You can walk on the rocks," Earl said. "Rudy'll bring 'im out once yer down there."

"Yeah." Rudy's voice called out from underneath the bridge. "Come on down, Alma Mae."

"My butter will melt, if I take too much time."

Narly's smile, frozen around his braces, made his upper lip protrude like two bumps on a tree, hence his nickname, Narly. He held out his hand to help Alma down the creek bank. Earl followed them, holding Alma's groceries and promising to catch her if she fell backward.

The cool wind from underneath the bridge was as inviting as the smell of supper. Her oxfords slid on the brown and gray pebbles until she stepped onto the large, flat creek rocks. "Good thing this water ain't deep, I can't swim a lick."

"I took swimming lessons last year, Alma Mae. I'd rescue ye, if ye fell in." Narly's hand tightened around hers as they jumped from rock to rock and crossed the creek.

Alma's stomach filled with butterflies. She could hardly believe she was holding Narly's hand. "Where's Rudy?" she asked.

"Yonder he is." Narly pointed under the bridge.

The harsh sun made the underside of the bridge appear even darker. She squinted and shaded her eyes with her hand. "It's awful dark under there."

"Go on," Narly said. "I'll be right behind you."

Alma stepped closer to the bridge. "I can't see nothing under there," she said. A shiver went up her spine. She shook off her nervousness and told herself she was being silly. Narly stayed behind her. She smiled when his hand brushed across her shoulder. "Okay," she said. "Here I go." She touched the cool concrete edge of the bridge and ducked underneath it into the darkness.

The plane bounced as it landed. Alma squeezed her hands together. She could feel her facial muscles tightening. Here she was, going to a place she'd vowed never to see again. Her shoulders felt stooped and her lower back spasmed with tension.

The Knoxville airport was the nearest to Contrary, and as Alma walked through the passenger gate, she wondered who would be there to meet her. Well, this time, they would meet a different Alma Bashears. She pulled herself up straight and stepped into the airline terminal.

Uncle Ames's high nasal tones called out over the airport noise. "Lordy, lordy, it's little Alma Mae." He grabbed her in his long arms and kissed her on the cheek, squeezing her so tightly, she exhaled a small grunt. She could feel herself distancing her emotions and concentrated on all she needed to do.

Trading hugs continued with Uncle George, Aunt Joyce, Cousin Rodney, her sister, Sue, and the two

preschool nephews Alma knew only from Christmas pictures.
    Within a second she felt fifteen again.

5

Alma got carsick even before they started across the winding roads of the Jellico Mountains. Somehow she knew she had to calm her stomach and use the time to find out about Vernon. She hated walking into a case with only a few hours' preparation. Uncle Ames's old Ford station wagon smelled of hunting dogs and cigarette smoke. He and Rodney shared a Camel cigarette about every twenty minutes. As Alma shifted her position in back to avoid a stream of smoke, her fingers slid into the shredded upholstery and caught on straw padding and springs. When she thought she'd throw up, she cracked a window, only to have one of her nephews roll across the bed of the station wagon and stare at her oddly.

"Momma, I'm cold," the boy objected. He continued to stare at Alma as she cranked the window closed. "Are you the one who robbed a bank?" he asked, his eyes wide as if he were looking at Jesse James.

"Larry Joe, hush up," Sue said, smacking the little boy lightly on the arm. "We have to talk about adult things."

"It's all right," Alma said, then turning to Larry Joe, "No, I've never robbed a bank."

"That's not the story as I heard it told." The brown-haired little boy pressed his lips together and rubbed one index finger across the other in a shame-shame gesture. "You robbed a bank and went to college."

"Well, sometimes, you just can't believe everything Uncle Vernon tells you." Alma could hear Vernon in the little boy's exaggeration and almost giggled. If she'd been younger, she might have told Larry Joe an equally outrageous lie about Vernon just to get back at her brother. The quiet in the car told her that everyone else was wondering the same thing. "Just how did you get your college money?" Narda Hollings used to ask her repeatedly. "I got that scholarship you had your heart set on. So what did you do . . . rob a bank?"

The wind whistled through a front car window that wouldn't completely close. The sound disturbed the uncomfortable quiet. No, she thought, I'd never tell any of them how I got my college money, even if it means Vernon will blab to the whole town that I'm a bank robber.

Alma stared at the bare mountainside: half-melted snow muddied the ground and leafless trees were indistinguishable from one another. Once she could tell the difference between an oak, maple, tulip, and dogwood. Now they all looked the same. Her family reminded her of a faded black-and-white photograph. Their faces were as she remembered them. Their expressions awakened a host of childhood memories. Their voices carried the same familiar tones and inflections. Only the signs of aging were added. Ames and George had turned white-haired, and like Aunt Joyce, the skin around their brows had loosened to hood their eyes. Rodney could have stepped out of his high school yearbook, a rounded pot-belly the only evidence of his age.

It was her sister that Alma had a hard time looking at for any length of time. A year younger then she, Sue had spread through the hips, and her neck was ringed with a double chin. As children, people had often thought they were twins. When their gazes met, Sue quickly looked away. Alma turned to Eddie and Larry Joe. "You boys sure look a lot like your mother," she said, hoping Sue would acknowledge it as a compliment. She did not. Alma sat silent for the next hour.

"Are we going to stop for gas in Fonde?" she asked as the car rounded a hairpin curve, sending a nauseous gulp into her throat.

"The Fonde filling station closed down," Aunt Joyce answered, twisting around to look at her. "Ain't much of nothing left of Fonde anymore. Just a few old houses and a Holiness Church."

"We got enough gas to make it home. Don't ye worry, honey," Uncle Ames said, lighting another Camel and passing it to Rodney.

Aunt Joyce pushed back a lock of salt-and-pepper hair and leaned her forehead against the window. The smoke was probably bothering her just as much, Alma thought, but she wouldn't say anything. Alma saw her grandmother's face in her aunt's reflection in the car window. Her blue eyes darted around as if she were carrying on a conversation inside her head. Her skin, browned from years of gardening under a hot summer sun, was still tight across her cheekbones, and her features mirrored the same sad expression on Sue's face.

Sue's eyes were red-rimmed, and occasionally she turned toward the window and dabbed a tissue at them. Uncle Ames squeezed the steering wheel so tightly that his knuckles were white islands in his weathered brown hands. Beside Alma, Uncle George seemed intent on trying to hold himself still. Once he reached over Rodney's shoulder for the Camels on the dashboard, but after shifting the pack from one hand to the other for several seconds, he handed it back to Rodney. Only the giggles and mutters of the two little boys playing in the back of the station wagon marred the silence.

THE LAW OF REVENGE

As the car rolled onto the top plateau of Fonde Mountain, a blast of sunlight consumed them and Alma shaded her eyes. They crossed into Kentucky and the familiar landmarks: the falcon-shaped rock formation high on the hill above Quinntown, the meandering Choctaw Creek, a row of log houses fastened on to the mountain with the front porches propped on narrow poles. Midnight Valley lay ahead, shrouded in gray fog. Crimson County anchored its southern end. On the Kentucky-Tennessee border was Contrary.

Alma cleared her throat. She knew they'd be reluctant to talk, but it had to be done. "I don't recall the name Littlefield," she said. No one answered her, and the steady whine of the car's wheels as it rounded down the mountain continued for about a minute. "I take it he's a newcomer?" She purposely fashioned her word choice to match her family's.

Aunt Joyce rubbed her chin, casting a backward glance at her husband, George. "He came to town just after you left for college, Alma."

Uncle George shook his head as if disgusted. " 'Bout the only people he got along with was the bootleggers, and that's 'cause he'd let 'em use a room on the Tennessee side of his hotel when they was expecting a raid."

Rodney laughed out loud. "Which was a funny thing since he had a gaggle of policemen in his pocket. A bunch of 'em got to be known as the Littleafia. They'd do anything from fixin' tickets to roughin' up somebody he didn't like. And, of course, they'd always let Bill know when they were ordered to raid the bootlegger."

"Started throwing his weight around right up-front... even the Gentrys couldn't stand him," Uncle Ames said through clenched teeth. "Nobody paid him any mind... till he bought an interest in the utility company. Used to walk up and down the street threatening to turn off anybody's electricity who didn't give him . . . oh, a free haircut . . . lunch on the house . . . always with a smile, so you never knew if he was serious or not. In time, he made himself a place and there weren't many who'd take him on."

The name Gentry caused Alma to lose her focus for a moment. Her chest muscles twitched, and her heart beat with the rhythm of the twisted road. "Is Charlotte Gentry still alive?"

Uncle George laughed aloud. "Reckon she was the only one who ever put Bill Littlefield in his place."

"Not surprising," Alma said, trying to keep her throat muscles from constricting and cutting off her voice. "She must be seventy by now."

"Seventy-two," Aunt Joyce volunteered. "Littlefield wanted to change Contrary's name to Littlefield—Littlefield, Kentucky. Well, Charlotte left that monstrosity of a house she lives in and went down to address the city council. Let me tell you, when she was through with them, any councilman who'd had the nerve to vote for Bill Littlefield's proposal would have found hisself on the hook of a fishing pole hanging over a dry creek."

Alma felt herself shifting into her lawyer mode. It was a good feeling, and she valued the technique Jordan had drilled into her. It gave her emotional distance from the situation, and that was definitely what she knew she needed right now. "The Littlefield Hotel must have employed a substantial number of townspeople."

"Yeah, he had plenty of bluegrass money and too much bluegrass attitude." Uncle Ames began to snicker. "Reckon all them thoroughbred investors'll pull out now."

"Hmmm. So that means all his employees face unemployment?"

"He had it comin'," Sue said. "It's a wonder nobody ever killed him before this."

"Maybe so," Alma said, leaning forward so that she could look at Sue, "but you can't just go around killing people because they're despicable."

"Killing!" Sue's voice grew loud and even the two little boys stopped their playing and looked at their mother. "Just whose side are you on, Alma Mae?" Her eyes watered and threatened to spill over.

"Vernon's side. But Vernon is going to be charged based on the law, not based on his family."

"Oh, hell, you sound like a damn California yuppie." Sue's hand flew up in the air and landed on her lap with a loud slap.

"Sue . . ." Uncle Ames said. "Now, you stop that."

"The reason I ask is to find out what the community sentiment is. We may have to get a change of venue if the only jury we can get are those whose livelihood was dependent on Littlefield."

"Momma, why does Aunt Alma talk funny?" one of the boys asked.

Sue's voice began to quiver and then ended in sobs. "Well, all I hear you doing is criticizing our brother. He needs us now, and all you're doing is dragging him down. She talks funny because she's been gone too long from the mountains, Eddie." Sue hiccuped for air. "I don't even know why you're back here, Alma Mae. You should have just got back on that plane the minute you saw us hillbillies. I saw that look on your face."

Sue's crying was as infectious as a cold virus, and Alma fought to keep her ragged emotions deep inside. She liked to think of herself as unreadable, but inevitably no one could read her as well as her sister. Her family's emotional outbursts were something Alma might use in the courtroom, but she'd have to control them in herself.

She could have kissed Aunt Joyce for turning back to give Sue a handkerchief and to look at her so sternly that Sue managed to quiet herself.

Alma parted her lips and slowly inhaled air stale with smoke, but it steadied her enough to speak. "I think I should let everyone know.... I won't be defending Vernon. I'll coordinate getting him a criminal attorney—in fact, I've already made some calls about an attorney. I'll assist with the case, but because I'm his sister it would be wiser for him to have representation that is more detached."

"Mamaw might have a few things to say about that," Uncle Ames said, annoyance in his voice. "She's the one who made your momma call and get you back here." He looked over at Aunt Joyce, then back at the road. Both of them were clearly upset.

"Whoever defends Vernon will be up to him, not Mamaw," Alma said firmly, putting on her best attorney front and feeling more in control and less likely to be manipulated. She wasn't surprised that Mamaw had been behind her mother's call.

"I don't understand you," Sue said. "You talk about Vernon like he was a character on some television show. This is serious, Alma Mae! You need to start being part of this family, and you should be proud of your brother."

"For what?" Alma's anger rose in her. "Did he cure cancer? Did he rescue an infant from a burning building? Did he give to the United Way? He killed a man, Sue!" Alma sat up straight in the sinking cushions of the car. Heat flowed through her like the blood in her veins. "I know how serious this is."

The car swerved on the slick pavement, causing the children to scream and the adults to lean into each other to keep from falling forward.

"Do it again, Uncle Ames," Larry Joe called out. He began tickling his brother.

"You children hush yer mouths," Alma said. She hardly realized what she had said until she noticed Sue glaring at her. Her accent was that of a mountain woman yet she maintained her stance as an attorney. Aunt Joyce glanced sideways at her, her mouth forming a crooked little smile. Alma knew she could handle her family, and from what she'd heard so far, they were most in need of protection from themselves. In a land where they always believed themselves the victims, it would be too easy to give in and say it was God's will or their lot in life. Mamaw was smart to bring in someone from the outside who was from the inside.

They turned from the mountain route directly onto Contrary's main street. Except for their worn look, few of the buildings had changed. Redbrick from the turn of the century made the town look like an old English village. The JCPenney clothing store on one corner of the town square with a Woolworth's kitty-corner to it made up the main stores. Sandwiched between a Piggly-Wiggly and a Wal-Mart were a smaller drugstore, a jewelry shop, and a video arcade.

The town seemed smaller, toylike, to Alma. She fought the temptation to soak in a flood of memories. She, Sue, and Vernon splitting one cherry Coke at Woolworth's food counter. Her father looking down at her before they crossed the street, saying, "Take my hand, Alma." Her mother and Aunt Joyce arguing in front of the JCPenney's about whether Alma was old enough for her first bra. And there were other memories: Narda Hollings, the drum majorette, telling her friends to make sure Alma was not invited to join the girls' club. The boys whispering that maybe Alma had done it—but unsure about it, none of them ever approached her. She always knew when people were talking about her and had developed a sixth sense for it: the lowered eyes with the flat smile that seemed to indicate they'd been caught; the awkward turning away; the eyes staring too deeply into hers as if they were trying to read her, to figure out what made her work. And Alma, repeating to herself over and over again: *Show them nothing, don't let them see anything of you.*

"Where's your gopher, Rudy?" Alma asked.

"Come on over and see." Rudy's voice echoed from a dark corner at the far end of the bridge.

Narly let loose Alma's hand. A few feet away the ground dipped, allowing her to stand upright. She reached up to guide herself but couldn't feel the bridge. "I can't see nothing," she said, standing still to let her eyes adjust to the darkness.

"Over here," Rudy said. "He's real pretty, Alma. I'll even let ye pet him."

The tone of Rudy's voice sent another shiver up Alma's spine. She looked over her shoulder for Narly. The brightness of daylight was like a wall at the end of the bridge. "Narly, did you follow me?"

"Here!" Rudy said, jumping in front of her and grabbing her hand. "Pet my gopher!" He forced her hand onto something warm and hard. His pants were bunched around his knees.

Alma jerked back and bumped into Earl. He pushed her forward so that she fell to her knees. She struggled to regain her balance.

"Well, then pet my gopher," Earl said, laughing and pointing his finger at her. He also had his pants and underwear pulled down, exposing himself.

Alma picked up a handful of gravel and threw it at him.

"Hey!" he yelled, unable to dodge the biting sting of the gravel. "Don't do that!"

"How dare you!" Alma shouted, attempting to get up but sliding again in the loose pebbles. Her heart fluttered like a trapped bird trying to burst out of her chest. How could Narly have done this to her? She liked him. Her mother's words came to mind: "Alma Mae, yer a girl from the hollows and Narly Gentry is a downtown boy." Earl stepped toward her. Alma threw another handful of gravel. "I hate you!"

"Stop it! We ain't hurtin' ye!" He went down on his knees beside her to avoid the rocks and grabbed one of her arms to prevent her from throwing a third handful. "You bitch!"

Alma slapped him. "Get away from me!" Her nails scratched deeply into Earl's exposed leg.

He smacked her hard across the face. "Grab her other arm, Rudy," he yelled. Rudy hesitated. "Narly! Grab her arm! Grab her, or she'll scratch the hell out of ye!"

Alma struck out at Earl again, catching his inner thigh and digging in her nails as deeply as she could. He screamed and called her another dirty name. She twisted to escape from his grasp. Her wrist pulsed painfully. "Help me, Narly!" she cried out.

"Damn it! Grab her other arm!" Earl yelled.

"Just let go of her!" Rudy yelled back.

Narly moved forward at the harshness of Earl's voice. "Stop scratching him," he said to Alma, trying to get ahold of her arm. "It's just a joke."

She began to cry and wildly struck at anything she could. "How could ye do this, Narly?"

"It ain't no damn joke to me!" Earl said. "She just sliced the hell out of me!" He forced Alma against the ground, knocking the breath from her. "Come on, Rudy, you first."

A rock cut into Alma's back and she shouted, "Let me go!" Narly held her arms above her head, pulling them so that she thought they'd rip from their sockets. "Don't!" she screamed.

"Earl, what are you doing?" Narly asked when Rudy hadn't moved as Earl demanded. "Alma, just stop fightin'!"

"She's gonna pay!" Earl promised, his dark features scrunched up like a dry sponge.

Alma kicked as he came at her. Earl caught one ankle and twisted it so hard she screamed. Why doesn't anybody hear me? she thought wildly. Why doesn't anybody help me? "Yer a girl from the hollows, Alma Mae . . . a girl from the hollows." Her mother's words kept repeating as Earl dragged her panties down around her thighs, then ripped them off with one jerk. She smelled liquor on his breath as he lay on top of her. His hand across her mouth tasted like dirt. He squeezed it tight, mashing her lips into her teeth.

A car drove over the bridge, causing a deafening roar all around them. Alma's scream mixed with it.

Earl's thighs pressed against hers, stretching the small of her back. "I got her," he said, and Narly let go of her arms. Earl crossed them above her head, pulling her forearms down behind her neck so that she couldn't move them. He tried to kiss her, but she turned her head, wishing she could twist her neck enough to bury her face in the dirt.

He lifted his torso, but when he rammed down, he struck the side of her leg. He tried again, his face coloring an angry red each time he missed.

"Noooo!" she cried out, and squirmed to get loose.

He hit her on the cheek. "Come on!" he yelled in her ear. He reached down between her legs and rubbed his whole hand against her.

"It hurts," Alma whimpered.

He inserted a finger in her. "There," he said, and stretched her open. He pressed into her, pulled her legs up, and held them with his arms.

Alma felt folded into herself. He bounced against her and paid no attention to her crying. She could hear her voice, but somehow it no longer seemed to be hers. "My bones are breaking."

"Yeah, yeah," he said, his voice almost a growl and rising a pitch every time he said it. "Yeah, yeah." He pulled out and ejaculated on her stomach. As he rolled over beside her, she tried to get up. "Oh, no," he said. "Rudy."

Alma raised an arm to prevent Rudy from getting on top of her, but he shoved her arm aside so that it fell like a broken doll's.

"It'll be over soon," Rudy said. Earl laughed and slapped him on the rump. "Hey! At least I won't have any trouble getting in. You broke her in good, Earl!"

Alma reached out to fight Rudy, but his enormous weight nearly covered her. He crushed her into the dirt and rocks, grunting with each thrust. Alma gasped for breath and squeezed her eyes closed, waiting for him to finish.

"Uncle Ames," Alma said. "Let me off at the town square. I'll just walk over and check in on Vernon." Uncle Ames pulled the car over and she stepped out into the crisp mountain air, her briefcase under one arm and a *New York Times* under the other. She waved good-bye.

Aunt Joyce called out as they pulled away, "You call us when you want to come home. We'll come and get you, no matter how late."

Alma turned around and stared in the window of Belinda's Boutique. The store where all the town girls bought their clothes. Mannequins, outfitted head to toe in Calvin Klein clothing, were posed on a Twister board. Inside, a teenager paid for a pair of blue jeans by dropping a credit card on the counter.

Alma heard coins dropping on that same counter . . . *counting out sixteen dollars and fifty cents for the brown and white oxford shoes that all the town girls were wearing. Miss Belinda scooped up Alma's money with one swipe of her hand across the counter. She stared down at Alma's clothes over a pair of bifocals that hung on the tip of her nose. With two fingers she handed Alma each shoe, never offering her a bag. . . .* Alma looked down at her Bottega Veneta pumps and smiled.

She walked up Carlton Street and crossed the bridge over Moccasin Creek. Patches of ice clung to the frozen banks. The water flowed steadily over brown rocks that looked like they were covered with sludge from the mines. Her eyes followed the creek till it disappeared behind city hall. Farther on, it wound around the part of town called Reed's Junction, then to Silver Lake. Small tributaries ran into it, including Crawdad Creek, which was fed from Jesus Falls. Alma's breath furled around her like a puff of cigarette smoke and whipped behind her as the icy wind blew. She pulled the collar of her coat closed.

As she walked on, she hoped she'd still find Lolly's Drugstore around the corner. As a teenager Alma watched sixty-year-old Lolly turn out hamburgers and milkshakes just as she had for Alma's parents a generation before. Lolly always went out of her way to thank Alma for the nickel tip she left, even though Alma knew the other kids left larger tips. She turned the corner and there it was. The scripted red letters "Lolly's" across the window, still shaded with black. "It's too much to hope," Alma said to herself as she peered in the window. Two teenagers worked behind the counter. "Poor old Lolly's probably dead by now."

As Alma walked the next two blocks toward the jail, the familiarity of the town returned like turning a page in a childhood storybook. She hadn't expected to feel such comfort with the place. Perhaps her anonymity gave her the perception of safety, she told herself. This was the place of which she was a product, and she had returned, having taken that base material and refashioned it into something new. Well, Contrary, she thought, how does a corporate attorney from San Francisco's most prestigious law firm look to you?

A young woman of about twenty struggled to get a pink baby carriage over the street curb. Alma reached down to pull up the bottom of the carriage. "Thank ye so much." The woman smiled, her teeth crooked on one side and her face so covered with freckles, her milky skin was hardly visible.

Alma couldn't remember ever seeing anyone in San Francisco who looked like this woman. Her plain beauty flowered so simply that most would have missed seeing it. And yet it wasn't her looks that contributed to her uniqueness, it was more the manner in which she walked, pushing the carriage ahead of her as if inside it lay a crown prince. Nothing about her suggested the cocooned look of a city person. Fonde Mountain towered ahead of her, as heavy as an Egyptian pyramid, and Jellico Mountain curved up in the west with all the dark animosity of a Disney villain. Yet she walked forward, probably on her way to JCPenney, with no notice of the towering giants that framed her world.

She's so typical, Alma thought. Oblivious. And here I am, right back in the middle of it. Yes, if there's any place on earth between a rock and a hard place, its name is Contrary, Kentucky. And the only way most natives remained sane was to live life in blissful ignorance.

Vernon was like Alma. Even if he hadn't left Contrary, he didn't live life with illusions. Vernon always lived life for its pleasures. *Prison . . . no, not Vernon's idea of a future.* So why had he killed a man over a gum wrapper?

6

An officer blocked the doorway. As Alma stepped up to the police station, she moved to the opposite door and he shifted with her. Standing about six feet, he had the beginnings of a belly hanging over his belt. His black hair, slick against the sides of his head, looked wet with hair cream. He smiled a crooked grin. "Whooowee!" he said. "You look like something out of a magazine."

Alma did not smile back. She moved around him again and flung open the door so hard that it hit the wall. Then she looked back at him long enough to let him know that she was not amused or impressed or afraid. One of the Littleafia? she wondered. If so, who would his loyalties go to now?

The Contrary Police Station smelled like disinfectant. In the few seconds that it took Alma's nose to adjust, a drunk woman threw up in a trash can. The woman's wrist was handcuffed to a bench so rickety that with any effort she could have broken free. A few policemen sat at desks that looked like army-surplus furniture. The woman at the information desk buzzed Alma through a gate and told her to continue down the hallway until she came to the main part of the jail.

The hallway was chilly and had the feel of a chamber that would echo if she spoke. She hated thinking of Vernon in this place. It seemed so removed from the mountains he loved that being in there must seem like . . . She thought helplessly of the word *jail*. A sign-in desk wedged behind a too-small doorway was manned by a black policeman. His nameplate read OFFICER FRED WALKER. Alma signed her name on a paper that looked as if it had been crumpled up several times that day. "I'm here to see Vernon Bashears," she said.

"Take a seat," he replied, pointing to a bench.

It squeaked when she sat down and weaved to the left side. Alma had never felt comfortable in jails. Her California corporate cases kept her far from such institutions, and her few convicted clients were usually sent to spalike federal prisons. She sifted through her *New York Times* but couldn't focus on any story. After she tossed the paper in a wastebasket, it surprised her to see Officer Walker retrieve it and begin working on the crossword puzzle.

Twenty minutes passed. Officer Walker looked up at her, then made another phone call just as she started to speak to him. Alma reviewed what she had to discuss with Vernon: why he had fought Bill Littlefield and every detail of his and Bill's history. She inhaled deeply. No, she thought, nothing heavy today. I'll have to talk about our family and get him out on bail, then go in for the tough questions.

A gate slammed, jarring Alma from her thoughts. Vernon was her baby brother, she decided, and he wasn't going to spend a minute more in there than he had to. She owed him. She owed him at least that much.

Alma's teeth chattered, and she clamped her lips together, trying not to make a sound. If she could just be quiet, maybe the boys would stop hurting her . . . maybe they'd go away. Her stomach throbbed as if someone were continuously punching her from the inside. A sticky wetness covered her thighs and belly.

The boy's voices blurred together. "What are we gonna do now?"

"She'll tell."

"What are we gonna do to make sure she don't tell?"

"You're next, Narly."

"Go on, Narly. Go on now, we both did it." Earl and Rudy moved off toward the creek and splashed water on themselves.

"Are you cold, Alma?" Narly asked.

His face swung in front of her like a pendulum. His hands stretched in size, reaching out for her like giant claws trying to clamp on to her shoulders. They're going to kill me, she thought. They'll kill me. Narly's braces caught a gleam of daylight. Alma followed that gleam as if it were a bridge to the outside. Daylight . . . bright as early morning coming through her window. Her father's words like a soft blanket around her . . . "Yer different, Alma Mae. Yer better than the hollows."

Alma swung forward and butted her head into Narly's stomach, knocking him off balance. She ran for the daylight, jumping feetfirst into the creek.

The boys all yelled at once and tripped over themselves as they scrambled to pull up their pants. "Catch her!"

"Don't let her get away!"

"Grab her, Narly!"

"She's in the creek, crazy! I'll get my shoes wet!"

Splashes of water echoed behind her as she heard them chasing her. The thick briar patches overhanging the creek bank ripped her dress and mud squished out the sides of her new oxfords. The walls of the bank were getting higher. Alma had never been this far up the creek. Around a bend the water almost reached her knees and rushed faster than a river. The hard sound of splashing roared back at her. Jesus Falls! Trapped!

"Circle 'round, Rudy! Get her at the top!"

Alma plunged toward the bank and grabbed a handful of vines that hung from the top. She climbed the rocks beside the waterfall, scraping her hands and knees. The boys' shouts nipped at her feet like pursuing hounds. Halfway up, her breath wheezed out of her throat. Her arms trembled as she struggled to hold her weight.

One of them would be at the top waiting! She looked down. The waterfall fell about ten feet into a deep pool. No one knew how deep. Alma couldn't swim. She held on to a vine and looked up at the cloudless blue sky. If they caught her, it'd be more of the same. Rudy might get to the top before she could climb the rest of the way. Narly and Earl were already below her shaking the vines to try to make her fall.

"That's it, boys!" Earl yelled. "We got her cornered!"

The pond below was calm except for where the waterfall entered it. There, the water billowed out like frosty clouds. Alma let go, falling and slamming into the water so that the breath was knocked out of her. She thrashed, gasped for air. As she floated in the water, her movements became slow, the water velvety. Slowly, she sank to the bottom, holding on to her last breath. The loose sandy bottom was soft against her. From the surface, the boys' faces stared down. *Pull yourself along the bottom to the other side*, said a voice inside her.

A splash erupted into a whirl of sand around her. They were coming in after her! Alma hooked her arm around a half-embedded log. She'd grab on to all three of them and hold them all down with her. Drown them all!

Her lungs ached, her breath finally bursting through her throat in a cascade of bubbles. She reached out for the body coming toward her. The face . . . the face . . . it was her brother, Vernon. He couldn't swim! He'd drown! Her baby brother would die and she'd be to blame. Vernon grabbed Alma, pulling her loose from the log, and kicked his feet off the bottom of the pond.

They flailed in the water, both of them under at different times. Pulling each other up. Swallowing mouthfuls of the metallic-tasting water. Slapping at the pond as if shoveling snow behind them.

Vernon anchored his feet on the ledge of an upward slope. He pulled Alma toward him. They inched themselves up out of the water. She crawled up the rocky bank and fell once she was on land. She tried to get up but fell again. She couldn't walk. Her inner thighs stung with raw irritation, and the muscles trembled. Her scraped knees were full of grit. She'd bitten into her bottom lip and could feel the swelling against her tongue. She tried to talk, but only a wailing sob came from her throat.

Vernon sat beside her, staring into the pond. His arms and chest shook and water dripped from his nose. "Jefferson said I should come," he said, unable to look at her. "Jefferson said I should come," he repeated.

Alma couldn't look at him. She wailed until her hoarse voice scratched her throat. Then Vernon put his arm around her waist and helped her walk home. The sun dried their clothes, and they smoothed each other's hair before entering through the back door. Only Alma's swollen lip showed evidence of any violence.

Their mother ironed. She barely glanced up and seemed to have forgotten that she'd sent Alma to the store. Her face looked weary and lined from working a twelve-hour shift at the paper factory. She touched the side of Alma's lip. "You two been fightin' again."

Vernon watched Alma, taking his lead from her. Alma moved over beside her mother and took the iron. "I'll do it, Momma," she whispered. She looked up at Vernon's *tightly fixed face, and for the rest of the day she acted as if nothing had happened.*

Alma's next memory of Vernon was again of his face, but this time his gray eyes stared at her from behind bars. The beating he'd given Narly Gentry had put Narly in the hospital for three weeks. Vernon had looked for the other boys, but Narly was the only one he caught.

"I'll tell," she said to Vernon. "I'll tell what happened and get ye out of here."

"Don't ye say a word, sis." He shook a finger at her. Looking at the concrete floor of the Crimson County Juvenile Detention Center, he inhaled a deep breath. "The other boys . . . they already bragged some . . . but what happened to Narly shut 'em up. If ye talk . . . they'll say it wasn't . . . you know."

"They said I was willing!" The urine odor on the floors and walls nauseated Alma, and she thought she'd vomit.

"Hey, sis, it ain't so bad here. 'Sides, the food's better than Momma's cookin', anyways." Vernon blinked and tried looking under her downturned face. "It's only a year. What's a year?"

So Alma had lived with the secret, and her life became a whisper of dark and dirty rumors told at teenage parties and in steamed-up cars. When she left Contrary three years later, she swore she'd never return.

"Will it be much longer?" Alma asked Officer Walker. "Bashears, I'm here to see Vernon Bashears."

His eyes looked at a level just above the newspaper, staring at her hard. "His attorney is with him."

"I'm his attorney," Alma stated clearly and impatiently. "You must be thinking of the wrong inmate. Why don't you check again?"

Fred Walker dropped the paper on the desk and stood

up. He was a good three to four inches over six feet. The chair scraped the floor as he pushed it back with his foot and stepped around the desk in front of Alma. His skin, a chocolate brown, looked yellowish under the bare lightbulb that hung above him. "I am not mistaken about the man who did this to me." He unbuttoned the cuff of his shirt and rolled it above his elbow. "I've arrested bootleggers, bushwhackers, marijuana growers, sots so drunk they couldn't stand up, and Vernon Bashears is the meanest codger I ever run across." On his forearm, a ring of teeth marks broke into his skin. "It took four men to arrest him."

Alma laughed.

"What the hell are you laughing at?" he demanded, suddenly looking down at the sign-up sheet. "Elly May?"

"Alma . . . just Alma." She pushed up the sleeve of her sweater and held her arm out next to Officer Walker's. Faded white scars on her inner arm matched the bite on his arm.

Officer Walker rolled down his sleeve. "So you know him?"

"I'm his sister."

"So why'd you say you were his attorney?"

"I'm also his attorney."

Walker's eyes narrowed. "That's a new one. You should have stuck with the sister story."

Alma's mouth dropped open. "I beg your pardon?"

"Look, Miss Elly May Clampett, or whatever your name is, it's getting a little tiresome having all Vernon's bimbos come and go like this was some island resort." He waved a half-wadded-up sign-in sheet. "Might as well know, five sisters already visited him this morning. Hate to bust your bubble, Elly May, but you might as well start looking for a new boyfriend 'cause this one's going up the creek for a long time."

A door slammed to the far left of them. A blond-haired man with glasses and a brunette woman dressed in a gray suit, vigorously writing on a notepad, stopped to watch them. "That's a decision I'm willing to leave to a judge and jury," Alma said, "not the Midnight Valley Mounties."

The man and woman approached the side of the desk. "Now, Fred, you'll get one of your headaches," the woman said.

"Not me, Ellen," Officer Walker replied as he pressed a thumb to the side of his temple. "My headache is just on her way out."

Alma glared at him. "You're going to be pressing out a migraine before I step one foot away from this building." She slapped a folded section of the newspaper on the desk, and it fell to the floor. "I'm here to see my client, and to deny me access to him is in violation of his civil rights. Does that phrase ring a bell with you, Officer Walker?"

"Fine, smartypants." He smiled wide and pointed at the man and woman. "Meet Mr. Bashears's real attorney, Jefferson Bingham, and also Ellen Farmer, the assistant commonwealth attorney who's going to put ole Vernon where only the rats will talk to him." Officer Walker crossed his arms on his chest, looking down at Alma with a scowl that made his upper lip overlap the lower one.

"You're Alma Bashears." Jefferson Bingham stepped forward and shook her hand. "You and Vernon have the very same eyes."

"It's been a long time, Jefferson," Alma said, smiling and noting that Officer Walker had dropped his arms and was standing in a less defensive position.

Jefferson's hair was shoulder length in the back, and

he'd tied it into a ponytail, which had curled around his collar. He brushed the ponytail back, taking in her full body the way an old flame at a high school reunion might. "You look terrific," he said.

"Perhaps you can enlighten me?" she said, motioning toward Walker. She exchanged a firm handshake with Ellen Farmer, who looked to be a little younger than herself and had a definite midstate accent in her "How do you do?" She sported the stiff, bubble-capped hairstyle Alma remembered as common to most mountain beauty shops, and she studied Alma with the attentiveness of a woman, not a lawyer. "I seem to be unable to get in to see my brother," Alma said, with an emphasis on "brother."

"To be brief," Jefferson started, speaking with a flattened accent Alma knew he'd probably developed in a northern law school, "the commonwealth's attorney has offered Vernon a deal. Second degree."

"Second degree?" Alma tried not to show a reaction, but her voice had cracked. "It is my understanding that the circumstances were more in line with manslaughter." As often as Alma had been in a courtroom, only hearing the verdict outweighed the tension of hearing an unexpected charge. Her heart raced, and her shirt stuck to her underarms. To regain her composure, she tapped the heel of one shoe on the linoleum as if considering their words.

"We've discussed it with Vernon," Jefferson said, "and—"

"Since he's refused the offer," Ellen interrupted, "you should know that the commonwealth's attorney intends to ask the grand jury for a first-degree murder indictment."

"You've discussed it with Vernon without me present?" Alma looked directly at Ellen Farmer, who let her gaze drop to the floor. As if she'd read her mind, Alma knew what this prosecutor was up to. It shocked her that Jefferson didn't see it. He'd probably been appointed by the court, she figured, and the extent of his legal abilities was real estate contracts. "Not only are you violating my client's rights to an attorney of his choice," she said to Ellen, "but you're trying to push him into a plea before I've even talked to him. It's a dirty trick not worthy of competent prosecution."

Ellen Farmer responded quickly. "We don't have to push, Ms. Bashears. We have the evidence we need to convict Vernon."

"Then why the deal?"

Ellen wet her lips by sucking them inward. "Those were my instructions."

"Is there a little problem with your case, counselor . . . maybe Fred Flintstone here didn't read my brother his Miranda rights?"

"Hey," said Officer Walker, stepping forward to defend himself, "I read him his rights! Can't say he listened much."

"Jefferson, how could you let this happen?" Alma demanded. "Even a court-appointed attorney should have better sense than to entertain deals with the prosecution this quickly."

"Alma . . . There's something you don't understand." Jefferson looked at Ellen and then back at her.

"I understand a little too well. It's a small town, everybody knows everybody. It's too easy for local attorneys to be in bed with the commonwealth attorney's office. Justice is too often a matter of opinion in the mountains. But this is my brother, Jefferson."

"I'm not court-appointed."

"You're also not doing a very good job of representing my brother's interests."

"Your mother hired me."

Alma's chest constricted, as if someone had sent a volt of electricity through her. "My mother..." she echoed.

"Look, now that you're here..." He stopped and turned to Ellen. "I need to confer with Alma."

Ellen opened her hands in a "whatever" gesture, then said good-bye in an icy but professional tone. As she opened the door, a gust of air blew her hair back from her face, but its bubble shape held.

Jefferson waited until the door closed and then removed his glasses, wiping the lenses on the front of his coat. "There's a vacancy in the state assembly, Alma. The assemblyman from this district died, and the governor is going to appoint someone, probably within the month. You know the kind of publicity a case like this can get an ambitious prosecutor. It seemed best not to give them the opportunity to turn it into a political bonanza."

Alma considered the merits of Jefferson's way of thinking. Kentucky politics were emotion-ridden and double-dealing. A campaign based on a heroic prosecutor protecting the common man from a heinous murderer was tempting... it was too tempting, too good an opportunity to lose. "There was no deal, Jefferson. Can't you see they were bluffing? It's a quick, easy way to get their hands on Vernon."

"I've done nothing to compromise his defense."

"And she," Alma said, pointing in the direction Ellen had gone, "should never have been in there. You allowed yourself and Vernon to be used."

Officer Walker threw his head back with a deep, satisfying laugh. Probably to show he knows I'm correct, Alma thought. He leaned against the desk and looked over to see what Jefferson would do.

"Ellen is really not that way," Jefferson said to Alma, then drew her out of Walker's hearing. "Better her than the commonwealth attorney." He put his glasses back on and pushed blond bangs to one side. He held his hands in front of him, pressing his lips into a thin line. The intensity of his eyes showed his annoyance that she wasn't more grateful for his efforts.

"We've known each other too long a time, Jefferson," she said with sincerity. "Sometimes we say things we don't mean, sometimes it's hard to say other things. I understand the bail hearing is at ten A.M., so let's meet in your office at eight." She waved a hand for the hovering Officer Walker to take her to a conference room. "Let's forget this and start all over tomorrow."

Jefferson stood there, looking down at his shoes. "You know, Vernon is not the easiest of clients to represent."

Alma turned around and winked at him. "See you early. And don't bring that commonwealth attorney with you." Jefferson's cheeks seemed to drain and colored to a pale white. For only a second Alma wondered why.

7

Officer Walker's head nearly touched the ceiling, and he leaned down as he entered the conference room and looked around. "What he didn't tell you about the commonwealth attorney wanting to be in the state assembly is that he's already got the clout behind him to do it. Now all he needs is the public support." Officer Walker spoke matter-of-factly, as he moved around the room. He shook the bars on the windows as if to test their strength. "It don't take a genius to realize this case could give him just that."

"Is any of that clout Littlefield money?" Alma asked.

"Money is money to rich folks. How would a small-town cop like me know where it came from?"

"Thank you for telling me that," Alma said sincerely, almost wishing Littlefield money was behind the prosecutor's bid for the assembly seat. That she could make use of.

"Don't thank me." Walker ushered her toward a pine table and a set of six chairs. The uneven tabletop was carved with autographs, and the room smelled of the same disinfectant, only stronger. "I just wanted to see what you'd do." His mustache curled up on one side, so half his front teeth showed.

It wasn't a smile, Alma realized as she waited for Vernon. No, Officer Walker was amused . . . with her, with this town, with life. He didn't really care what happened, and had probably spent his life teaching himself not to care. If she'd grown up in a city, she might have thought it was just one of the survival skills of a policeman, but she'd grown up in this town—in the poor white hollows, and he, no doubt, had grown up in the Junction, the black part of town. Walker's attitude was clearly one of noninvolvement for purposes of self-preservation. If he got to watch a bunch of white people trip over themselves from time to time, it was more interesting than an evening in front of the television set.

"Yeah, I know how you feel, Fred," she whispered to herself. She rolled her shoulders, trying to press the tension out of them. Hunching forward, she let her head hang until her chin touched her chest. She slipped her feet out of her shoes and massaged the ball of her left foot. Through the wall she heard a man and a woman walking into an adjacent room. The sounds of the drunken woman she'd seen cuffed to the bench played like a soap opera. Her husband shouted recriminations. In reply came dry heaving and bouts of tears. Alma jumped at the sound of a slap. Another slap sounded between the woman's pleas for forgiveness.

Someone entered the room and stood behind Alma. Before she could turn around, he spoke. "Oh, God, what'd they go and get you for?"

Alma stood up. Her hands trembled. She wasn't sure she could turn around. Breathe, she thought. She twisted her head and somehow her body followed. "You look a lot different from what you sound like on the telephone," she said.

Her brother: Vernon, his face as round as the moon, tanned even now in February; his body shaped like an inverted triangle, wide shoulders that tapered down to his hips. The looseness of the county-issued gray jumpsuit prevented any further distinction of his body. He walked over with a familiar swagger, his shoulders slightly hunched. Dropping down into a chair opposite her, he propped one foot on the chair next to him. His eyes squinted as he took in the length of her, seeming to assess their likenesses and differences. He nodded as if to indicate approval. As their eyes linked like clasped hands, his features jelled into a guarded expression. He chewed his gum and stared out the window, looking down occasionally to the carved names on the table. "You know, I never measured up real high on the yardstick of good."

"Look at me," she said, wanting to forget the case and just talk to her brother. He continued to stare out the barred window at Moccasin Creek. His irises were gray, and the sunlight made the color clear and deeper against the bloodshot red webbing the whites of his eyes. On each side of his upper forehead he'd started to go bald and the center shock of black hair looked wet. "You're starting to look like Daddy."

Vernon glared up at her and turned away quickly, as if too embarrassed to sustain a visual connection. "You seen the newspapers?"

Alma nodded. "Why don't you tell me what happened?"

"I did it. Ain't no doubt about that."

"I want you to listen to me, Vernon." Alma leaned forward over the table. "This man Littlefield, in the rest of the state he's the savior of Appalachia. We need to build sympathy for you."

Anger filled the lines of Vernon's face. He turned squarely toward her and tipped his chair back so that it balanced on its rear legs. "I ain't sorry."

"That's not the image we want to give a judge and jury."

"Dern fool deserved it, and I'd do it again!" Vernon

aimed his voice at the door, where Fred Walker and a guard stood outside sharing a cup of coffee. "I said I'd do it again!"

"Vernon, would you shut your big mouth!" A surge of anger that seemed left over from adolescence rumbled in her stomach, and her voice rose in pitch as she ordered, "I don't want you to speak to anyone but me."

"It's too late. I already confessed."

Alma sank in the chair and dropped her face in her hands, which were almost at the level of the table. She groaned, trying to think of Kentucky statutes she might cite. "Jefferson and that Ellen Farmer had no business talking to you. . . . I'll try to get the judge to believe you confessed under duress."

"I am not under duress!"

Alma balled a fist and swung it, striking Vernon on the jaw so that he flipped backward, landing on his side as the chair tipped over. "Now you're under duress!"

The guard started to run in, but Walker stopped him, patting his shoulder and steering him back to the coffee. Vernon stared up at Alma. A drip of blood colored his lip and he licked it with his tongue. Against the wall an old silver-painted radiator hissed out a line of steam and its pipes knocked in the wall.

Alma opened her briefcase and pulled out a pair of glasses and a yellow notepad. "Now," she said, looking down at Vernon, who was still on the floor. "Before I left California, I talked to an attorney named Robert Krauss and asked him to consider representing you. He's from Knoxville, and I'm trying to convince him to drive up tomorrow. He can practice in Kentucky and has plenty of experience in criminal law. You may recall reading that he defended that senator's wife a few years back when she killed her lover."

"Uh-uh." Vernon shook his head, propping himself up on his elbows. "I want you."

She blew out a breath. "I'm not that familiar with Kentucky statutes any longer."

"Jefferson can help you." Vernon stood up and dusted off the seat of his pants. "Wouldn't be the first time."

"What do you mean?"

Vernon picked up the chair and straddled it, crossing his arms on the back. "You mean you forgot?" He leaned back, holding on to the chair seat so that it creaked in concert with the banging radiator. "And I always thought you were such a smart girl."

"Vernon, don't play games with me. Jefferson isn't up to this case." She took a pen from her briefcase and began numbering the lines on the notepad.

"It was him that come and got me that day." Vernon licked the split in his lip and rolled his eyes upward to the fluorescent lights. "I'd never've knowed to go toward Jesus Falls if he hadn't come and told me about the little joke them fools planned on pulling."

Alma stopped writing. Her skin flushed as if she had just stepped from a sauna. She walked over to the radiator in her stockinged feet. The handle at the side was hot, but she barely felt it as she twisted it closed.

" 'Sides, he needs the work. You know, he run for commonwealth attorney and lost." Vernon stared at Alma intently as she sat back down. The skin around his eyes pulled tight and wrinkled into his hairline.

Alma felt he was waiting for her to ask him something. "Jefferson . . ." She could hardly speak. "Jefferson is too honest for politics, anyway." She could tell from the way Vernon stared at her that he wanted to say something else, but if it was about that day, she couldn't—she wasn't ready to discuss that day with him. In all these years they'd never spoken of it except for the day he went to reform school. One part of her was surprised that he brought it up now. Another side of her fought the humiliation and the fear that it had all been her fault. "Okay, Jefferson can help." She felt part of her resolve give in under Vernon's stare and hated herself for it. "But he works for Robert Krauss. I only have experience in corporate law."

"Shhiiit!" Vernon spit on the floor. "It's a wonder you didn't work for old Littlefield hisself." He turned away as if disgusted by the sight of her.

"I've worked hard for what I have, Vernon. You could've had the same if you'd worked half as much as I did. I'm getting more than a little tired of apologizing to my family for it." She threw the notepad in her briefcase.

"Still be better if you defended me."

She shut and locked the briefcase, slid her feet back into her shoes. "How so?"

"Well," he said, locking his fingers together and pushing them out so that the knuckles cracked. "The way I see it, if kin defends me, then I can pay the bill on time." He looked up at her, eyebrows peaked, and smiled a half smile. "If at all."

Vernon pointed an index finger up at her. Alma rolled her eyes and laughed loud enough to draw Fred Walker's attention. "We're finished," she said. "Is the cab stand still at the corner of Main and Washington?"

"Sure is," Vernon answered for Walker. "Have 'em take Uncle George a case of Schlitz while they run you home."

"This is a dry county," Walker fussed. "We don't have bootleggers."

8

As Alma walked toward the cab stand, she realized how much she'd forgotten about this town. What other area of the country would continue to vote itself a dry county but allow the cab stand to double as a bootleg operation? One call and the alcohol of your choice was delivered right to your front door. The crowning hypocrisy was that the cab stand was positioned across the street from the Methodist church. "Mountain service industry," she sneered.

On the corner, Alma stopped at a phone booth. As she dialed Robert Krauss's phone number, she thought that she must now deliver what she'd promised. She was surprised when the man answered the phone himself. "Bob Krauss." A deep voice, resonant with a treble that made him sound like a trusted minister.

Alma introduced herself, then said, "Mr. Krauss, have you made your decision?" There was a pause, a shuffling of paper. She wasn't sure if that was good or bad.

"Jordan McFedries called to continue pleading your case, Miss Bashears."

"Call me Alma," she said, hoping to move their relationship toward a more casual one.

"Just because you work for Eric Erickson, don't assume I can be manipulated. Eric may have been my old moot-court partner, but law school has long since disappeared in my rearview mirror." Alma started to speak, but Krauss continued. "I take cases because they interest me or because they need me, not because someone's boyfriend is a state supreme court justice. I'm afraid I must turn you down."

Alma stared up into the cloudless blue sky. Just above the treetops rose the sharp roof of a gray and white house. "Make no mistake, this case needs you." She inhaled, hoping he'd wait for her to finish. "I made a mistake by asking Jordan to call you. Please understand that I feel very much alone here, and when I asked for a recommendation of the best, your name came up more than once." Alma's eyes traced the pointed roof of white tile. Its steeple shape angered her. She hadn't seen that steeple in over fifteen years and seeing it now felt like a burn on her skin. The last time she'd stared up at it she remembered thinking that it was the final stake this town had plunged into her heart.

She could hear Krauss moving papers and suspected he was packing his briefcase. "What I'm facing is a status quo rooted in the 1930s," she said. She waited. He did not speak but also did not hang up. "The forces I will face are ... my demons in the night, Mr. Krauss. I'm facing my hometown, and I'm afraid to do it alone. Won't you please help me?"

Silence. "I'll drive up tomorrow," he said finally, "and decide after I talk to your brother."

Alma felt the tension lift from her shoulders. "Thank you."

She hung up the phone and stared again at the gray steeple piercing the sky over the tops of trees as if proclaiming its dominion. She walked down the street toward the huge house, then stopped at the corner of Washington and Kirkland. The three-story gray mansion with the solitary steeple belonged to Charlotte Gentry.

The windows were murky and the lawn was clear of snow. In an upstairs window the curtains moved, and in the darkness behind them someone peered out at her.

Alma continued walking and didn't look back until she had reached the corner. The curtains closed, and Alma wished she could control the trembling in her chest that threatened to become hyperventilation. What little warmth toward the town her memories had awakened evaporated behind the swarthy curtains of that house. Alma breathed through her mouth, and the words cracked out of her throat, "I'm not afraid of you, Charlotte Gentry. I'm not afraid of you."

9

About a quarter of a mile from her grandmother's house, Alma climbed out of the taxi. She had a sick feeling in the pit of her stomach. The air had the familiar smell of earth and even the icy chill could not cover it. She checked her watch. Four o'clock. First-degree murder, she thought. How am I ever going to tell Momma and Mamaw? The charge didn't make sense. Even for a victim as wealthy and influential as Bill Littlefield, the facts were not in favor of a man who had provoked a fight and was killed when the accused defended himself. Vernon had only defended himself. They'd never win a first-degree charge and would lose Vernon for good. Alma wondered what else the prosecutor could have. Ellen Farmer had seemed too confident.

She gave the cab driver a ten-dollar bill and told him to keep the change. His eyes opened wide, as it was only a seven-dollar fare, but he didn't argue and drove away. Alma had forgotten that fifteen percent was a concept that had never taken hold in the mountains, where gratuities rarely exceeded a dollar.

She watched the red taillights disappear over the hill, rounding through a grove of pine trees, across a ragged plank bridge, and onto the paved road. *Same route I used to walk to school. Caught the bus at the mouth of the hollow.* For a second she saw herself, Vernon, and Sue trotting down the road. Pulling Vernon between them because they were afraid they'd miss the schoolbus and have to walk. His shaved head barely spouting black hair, her and Sue's pigtails flapping in the wind. Could they have been more than eight and nine years old? Vernon must have been seven. "You were such a sweet little boy," she said aloud. "What kind of man have you grown into, brother?"

Vernon's arrogance bothered her. His disdain seemed calculated, as if he didn't comprehend that he'd taken a life. Could he be that coldblooded, she wondered, or did he just lack awareness? The latter she could understand. When she'd first left the mountains, it had taken her awhile to become conscious of the effect of her word choice, her accent, or even her thought processes—so different from the outside world. If I grew into anything, she thought proudly, it's worldly wise.

Maybe she was being arrogant. Vernon chose to live in this town. Why should he be any different from the other people in it? This part of the country had a violent history—Indian wars, the Civil War, Prohibition, coal mining, and unionizing wars. Every individual in Contrary mirrored it. Only the single deaths didn't get written about in history books. Unless you're as rich as Bill Littlefield, Alma thought, and are about to save the town from economic destruction.

Across the road a porch light flipped on at Uncle Ames's house. The windows were dark, which probably meant he was in his basement, where he tinkered and—though he didn't realize it—invented. He'd made the porch-light timer long before they were available in any hardware store. The redbrick chimney on the side of his house puffed out gray smoke, filling the cold air with a burned scent.

Next door, Aunt Joyce and Uncle George lived in a

gray tile house. Alma could see them through the kitchen window, sitting at the dinner table, her aunt pouring milk from a half-gallon Pet's Dairy carton into her uncle's glass. Sue and her husband, Jack, lived about a quarter mile down the hill. Their mailbox was painted fire-truck red, and Larry Joe's and Eddie's names had been added at the bottom in green and purple paint. Jefferson's parents had a house on an acre of land down by the plank bridge that crossed onto the main road.

The hollow was once populated by twenty families, but now only a few were left: the Fletchers, the Binghams, and the Gilberts. These occupants were old, their children long gone to the cities, returning only for the occasional holiday. Alma remembered a time when two dozen children had played on the mountainside. It seemed every time she called home, she was told of another hollow family who had died out or moved away.

Mamaw's house dwarfed those of the neighbors. Ten rooms total, five downstairs and five up, the house had been built by Alma's grandfather, who had worked double shifts in the Pruden mines to pay for it. Mamaw had raised nine children in this house—two had died of polio before they were ten, two more had given up their souls to the cold Pacific under a burning, tropical sun when the U.S.S. *Chicago* and the U.S.S. *Rockcastle* sank during World War II, another son had died in a mining cave-in, and a daughter in childbirth.

Then there was the mystery son.... Alma's father, who'd left for Detroit to work in an auto plant for Christmas money and disappeared. "He must've been kilt, else we'd've heard from him," Mamaw had said over and over. Alma still thought it was equally likely that the city had just swallowed him up ... given him a life so different from Contrary that coming back had been impossible. Even as a child she had understood and never blamed him for not returning, while her mother's eyes had grown harder and harder with each passing year.

Alma stepped over ice patches frozen in the cracks of the concrete sidewalk and walked up toward the redbrick house with the blue swing and the peach-colored porch chairs where her grandmother lived. A million memories exploded: of Christmases and cousins, Thanksgiving feasts with so much food it hid the tablecloth, fifty rainbow-colored eggs to hunt at Easter, hide-and-seek with all the kids in the hollow, her first kiss under the dogwood tree, tears sliding down Mamaw's face as she closed the coffin over Pappa's shrunken, cancer-ridden body. Yes, Alma thought as she stepped up onto the wooden porch, good people live in this hollow. All the same, she knew that if she was going to protect her family and do her best for Vernon, she'd have to keep them out of the trial process. The image they would project would be too . . . *contrary*, she decided, and laughed.

Through lace curtains Alma could see a man tapping his pipe into a table ashtray. He looked to be about fifty, balding at the crown, with an impatient disposition, as he crossed and recrossed his legs. Alma didn't know him. She inhaled a deep breath and held it as she turned the doorknob. The image of an ancient messenger popped into her mind—the bearer of bad news.

10

A gust of warm air made Alma aware of how cold it was outside. She stepped into the smell of pipe tobacco and squirrel gravy. The stranger she'd seen through the window stood. "Quick Jackson," he said, "friend of your momma's." He smiled and reached for Alma's briefcase.

Before she could express her thanks, voices came from the kitchen like an old and too-telling story. "I don't give hog's piss what you think." Her mother's voice stretched like taffy in spite of the vindictiveness of her words.

"Now, Merl, let's let Alma do what she's trained to do," Mamaw said. A chair scraped against the floor, and Alma thought her grandmother must have knocked something over. "She'll know what we ought to do."

"I should never've let you talk me into calling her," Alma's mother said.

"Ladies . . ." the man said toward the kitchen, then turned back to Alma, trying to hide an embarrassed expression. "I recognize you from your pictures," he added, extending one hand to her and heaving the briefcase beside a flowered couch with the other.

Alma shook his hand, then he stepped aside as her mother swooped in from the kitchen. Jefferson Bingham's hiring popped into Alma's mind, and she bit her tongue to keep from immediately starting an argument.

"Honey, honey, honey." Her mother wrapped her arms around Alma's neck. "I didn't think you was ever gonna get here!" Her mother kissed her on the cheek, then pushed back from her, studying her features as if trying to see herself. "If you'd been a second longer, I'd been gone out to supper."

"Momma," Alma said, feeling as awkward as a teenager. "I guess you were just talking about me."

Her mother's smile faded, then jerked back into place. "Mamaw, get in here," she called out to the kitchen. "I see you met my new boyfriend, Quick."

Alma tried not to stare at her mother's platinum hair with its dark roots, the thick azure eyeshadow and red lipstick that made her look whorish. Obviously dressed up for a date, Alma thought. Tight blue jeans clung to her mother's petite thighs and a pink angora sweater rounded out her overly endowed chest. Alma couldn't help feeling annoyance budding inside her and wished she had the courage to ask what had possessed her mother to hire Jefferson Bingham.

A humming noise from the kitchen grew louder. Alma's grandmother maneuvered through the door in a motorized wheelchair. "Mamaw!" Alma cried out. She hurried over and leaned down to hug her. The fragile body rose up and squeezed her with a strength that didn't seem possible. "What is this thing?" Alma tapped the wheelchair. "Why didn't anybody tell me?"

"Honey, I can get around just fine when I have to. This ole thing just makes it a little easier on days."

"You ought to see her. Why, she runs it up and down this hollow ordering all her relatives around." Merl Bashears fluttered around her mother-in-law as if both were actresses competing for center stage. She turned to Alma. "Honey, you look so good." She pressed her hands to both of Alma's cheeks. "Don't she look good, Quick?"

"Sure does," he answered stiffly, shuffling from one foot to the other.

Merl stared at him peculiarly, then turned to Alma. "You've done a good job of keeping your weight down, and your face don't break out no more."

Alma rolled her eyes, but she ignored her mother's comment. "Momma, you should have told me about Mamaw being in a wheelchair."

"Vernon even smoothed out the step off the porch for me," Mamaw said. At the mention of his name Alma felt the discomfort they all shared surface in a prickly quiet. Mamaw leaned forward and motioned that Alma sit in the chair next to her. "How did he seem to you?"

Alma cleared her throat and stared up at a wall of pictures. "There's a lot of work to do." I've got to tell them, she thought. She couldn't take her eyes off the photograph of her father, Esau Bashears, at age thirty: smooth-shaven, round face, flared nostrils, and raven hair that curled just above the ears. He could have been Vernon's brother. Alma's mouth tasted cottony as she started to tell them about the impending charge against Vernon. The words would not come out. Instead she said, "Tell me what you know about Bill Littlefield that hasn't already been in the newspaper."

"Not married," her mother replied, "so all the girls had eyes for him." Merl looked over at Quick and winked as if to tell him not to be jealous.

"Did he have any other fights, physical or verbal, with local people?"

"Not that I know of . . . well, unless you count that Silver Jenkins, but he'd fight with a hound dog if it'd put up with it." Her mother dabbed a long, red fingernail underneath her eyelashes to dry a tear.

Alma noted her grandmother's quietness. Mamaw obviously had an opinion but probably didn't want to express it in front of Merl. Alma decided to try to draw her out when they were alone.

"Do you think they'll let him out tomorrow?" Mamaw asked. "We've all been trying to think of ways to raise bail money."

"A lot depends on the prosecutor." Alma licked her lips, running her tongue on the cracked skin at the corners of her mouth. Time to pay the piper, she thought. "I have some distressing news. It looks as if Vernon is going to be charged with first-degree murder." She cleared her throat and waited for an outpouring of emotion.

"I feel so bad that we got you to come all the way back here," her mother said. She squinted and shook her mane of shoulder-length hair to one side. "I told Mamaw we'd probably just get you in trouble with your bosses for taking off time."

"Momma, I wouldn't have been anywhere else," Alma said. "Now I don't want to hear you talk to Mamaw like that."

"I don't want to cause ye trouble with your work, Alma Mae." Mamaw rubbed her arm, the liver spots moving as the skin stretched.

"Mamaw, I'm a valued associate at my firm. Trust me, I'm not in trouble."

Mamaw's smile showed more than a side of gold teeth. Pride sparkled in her eyes. It had sparkled there when Alma won a history award in eighth grade, a savings bond for a Labor Day Speech Contest, when she graduated from high school, and that last day . . . when she stepped up onto the bus that took her away to college. It was an expression of acknowledgment that had never crossed her mother's face.

"Anybody who thinks they're indispensable should see how much moss grows on a rolling stone," her mother said, reaching to roll a strand of Alma's black hair between her fingers.

"The distinction I'm trying to make," Alma said, standing up and moving away from her mother, "is that the prosecutor doesn't believe Vernon caused an accidental death, which would have a set of penalties ranging from probation to a few years in jail with good behavior." Alma slowed her speech, wanting to make sure they followed what she said. "Since Vernon has no felony record in his adult life, we'd have his attorney petition for probation."

Mamaw smiled. "So Vernon might not have to do any time?"

"Well, I watch *Perry Mason*, too, Mamaw." Merl cackled and slapped her thigh. "I reckon that son of mine is slippery as a snake." Quick's tight expression seemed to tell her she was wrong, and Merl took his hand and wrapped his arm around her shoulders. "Well, we all know it was a fight in self-defense, so Walter Gentry can just get used to it."

Walter Gentry? Alma thought. Why would her mother mention Walter Gentry? She swallowed, wishing she had a glass of water. Going through this had to be worse than facing any judge she'd ever argued before. "We have to have evidence, Momma," she said, then looked at her grandmother. The thought flashed through Alma's mind: Will she be strong enough to hear this? "The prosecutor will say that Vernon murdered Bill Littlefield deliberately . . . with malice aforethought."

Mamaw's voice dryly frosted the air. "What could his possible penalty be, Alma Mae?"

Alma noticed Quick's arm tightening around her mother's shoulders. He obviously knew of Merl's propensity for hysterics. "Whatever the judge decides, Mamaw. Let's not think the worst until we see what happens."

THE LAW OF REVENGE 69

"I don't mean to interfere," Quick said, his bass voice strong enough for a church choir. "But I think you ought to tell them." Quick's bushy eyebrows moved toward each other, making his expression almost fierce. "It'd be better than them hearing it from one of those town gossips."

Alma rubbed a hand across the burlwood of the chair arm. How often had she thought of this chair . . . the only place she'd ever fallen asleep where she'd felt perfectly safe. Her grandfather had built it. "As I said, it's up to the judge. The absolute worst would be life in prison or . . . the death penalty."

Mamaw's hands flew to her mouth. "My poor baby."

Merl cried out like a bird winged by rock pellets. She turned her head into Quick's shoulder, held it there for a minute, then pulled away. Mascara smeared underneath her left eyelash, and she patted her upper chest as if trying to soothe heart palpitations. "I have to go . . . I have to get out of here. I'll suffocate if I stay here a minute longer." She glared at her daughter. "You been in town two hours and you manage to get my son the death penalty."

Quick jumped to Alma's defense. "Honey, it ain't her fault. She don't have nothing to do with how he's charged."

"A lot you know . . . you're a damn car salesman." Merl hunted through a pile of coats lying on the couch until she found her purse and a raccoon jacket. "We'll be at the steakhouse and then we're going bowling. Don't you say nothing to nobody about all this, Alma Mae." She slowed enough to shake a finger at her. "I'll figure out how to fix it tomorrow." Merl opened the front door but stepped back and said quietly, "I ought to have known it'd be me to settle this mess for Vernon. He ain't gonna be charged with no first-degree murder."

"Momma, it's a matter of public record. It'll be in the papers by tomorrow morning."

"She's just trying to prepare you for what's going to happen, Merl." Quick tried to help her on with her jacket, but she jerked away from him and strutted ahead to the door.

"Just what do you think you could do that ain't been done?" Mamaw asked, and shook her head as if she didn't really expect a reasonable answer.

"He's my son, and I love him!" The whites of Merl's eyes were streaked red and blurred with tears that did not fall. "I'll be fifty years old next month, and it'd be the worst birthday of my life if something like this happened." She sniffed and the expression in her eyes seemed to indicate that she hadn't intended to reveal her age.

Alma's insides felt squished up like the mud pies she'd made as a child. She hated when people became emotional. Alma decided she might as well stir the kettle to its limit and get everything out at once. "Momma, tomorrow morning I'm firing Jefferson Bingham as counsel of record. If I can convince him, Robert Krauss from Knoxville will be defending Vernon. I'll agree to let Jefferson help."

Her mother whipped around. "Krauss . . . I think not!"

"It's already done."

"Jefferson Bingham wouldn't let Vernon get the death penalty."

"Neither will I."

"So you say. I don't know no Robert Krauss. He don't know my boy like I know him, and he won't protect him the way I'll see to it that he's protected."

"It's too late. You called me here to handle this and Vernon will do what I tell him to do. Bob Krauss will be here tomorrow afternoon."

Her mother's lips curled up at the edges, and she slowly lowered a manicured hand into her jacket pocket and pulled out a pack of Marlboro cigarettes. "Have you ever dated a Jew?" She bit the cigarette between her lips. "An African American?" Her voice stretched out the vowels in a sour mispronunciation.

"Merl!" Mamaw said. "You stop talking that way."

Alma knew her mother was regarding her as a target. In her mother's mind, Alma's opposition was as menacing as another woman chasing after Quick. It was an unaccustomed kind of fighting for Alma, but something inside her responded on a primitive catlike level and she imagined reaching out and clawing both her mother's coral-colored cheeks. Instead she said, "I have to get to bed. I have a busy day tomorrow."

"I bet you do," her mother said. "I bet there's a bunch of things you learned in that city that you think will help you here. A bunch of things that your family don't know about."

"Now, Momma. I can't imagine anyone has more secrets than you."

"We'll see about that." Merl flicked the cigarette out the door without lighting it. "When Mr. Krauss meets up with Walter Gentry, be sure to introduce him to Walter's mother, Charlotte."

"Why do you keep referring to the Gentrys?"

"You mean nobody's told you?" Her mother raised her overdrawn eyebrows. "Why, Walter Gentry is the commonwealth attorney. I can't believe you didn't know."

Alma was chilled all over. An adrenaline rush hit her bloodstream. To keep from trembling, she crossed her arms over her chest.

"Come on, honey," her mother said to Quick. "I'm gonna show you the time of your life."

Quick nodded to Alma and gave what was probably

a familiar roll of his eyes to Mamaw. The sound of the door closing seemed to Alma as loud as a boxing-ring bell.

11

"That Merl, she sure does enjoy life," Mamaw said.
Alma knew it was about the closest her grandmother could get to saying anything bad about her colorful daughter-in-law. One, Alma counted to herself to maintain control. *One is the law. Two is the opposition.* She wouldn't let Mamaw see her upset, but she couldn't believe it—Walter Gentry was the commonwealth attorney. That certainly explained the odd reluctance she'd sensed in Jefferson and Vernon. "Mamaw, don't you worry yourself about Vernon. I don't think the worst will happen. It could be years before we get a sentence."

Alma followed the motorized wheelchair into the kitchen, where a pan of biscuits and a bowl of gravy sat on the table. "I could smell all this and it was the only reason I didn't walk out on Momma." She sat and dished gravy over a biscuit, knowing she had to reassure Mamaw. "I think you know I'd never let Vernon be convicted of first-degree murder under these circumstances, even if I had to go all the way to the Supreme Court. And I would, too."

Mamaw poured tall glasses of milk for both of them. A worried look hardened her features despite Alma's assurances. "I don't know if I should tell you." She stared into the milk as if she might see tea leaves that would give her an answer.

"Mamaw, don't hold back anything. You never know what might help Vernon. Lord knows he doesn't seem very intent on helping himself."

"I don't want Vernon to think I'm telling tales on him." Mamaw pointed out the kitchen window. In the backyard was the two-toned brown and white trailer in which Vernon lived. A black Jeep Cherokee was parked beside it at a right angle. "It's all that girl's fault." Mamaw's eyes darted back and forth as if she were reliving the scenes in her mind. "I just know she had something to do with all this."

"Her last name Littlefield, by any chance?"

Mamaw nodded. "Bill Littlefield's daughter." Her cheeks blushed a fiery pink as though recalling unpleasant memories about a woman she obviously didn't like. "Always calling him all hours of the night. Showed up on his doorstep whenever it suited her fancy."

"Somehow, I thought this was all a little more complicated than a fight over—" Alma caught herself. She'd almost said "cock size" in front of her grandmother. "Over . . . what do you think it was over? Her, maybe?" Alma patted Mamaw's hand, thinking she'd have to be more careful with her language.

Mamaw shrugged. "They just didn't like each other. Two roosters in the same henhouse." A timer on the stove buzzed and Mamaw reached for a small vial beside the salt and pepper shakers. She swallowed two pills. "One night she come here all beat up. Vernon cleaned her up and was gonna call the law, but she begged him not to."

"Do you know who beat her up?"

"No . . . she hardly ever talked to me. Vernon kept her out in the trailer and would just try not to worry me 'cause of my high blood pressure." Mamaw showed

Alma the bottle of pills. "But I knowed it kept him all tore up inside."

"Had they been seeing each other lately?"

"I don't believe they'd dated each other in almost a year or so. She got engaged to be married."

"Vernon still in love with her?"

"Naaaw." Mamaw's lips pursed, showing her complete disapproval of the woman. "He never was."

"If so much time passed and Vernon didn't love her, what makes you think she might have had something to do with her father's death?"

Mamaw looked at Alma as if she'd questioned the truth of her statements. "I never said that." Mamaw's cheeks flushed again, this time in embarrassment. It took her a second to recover, then she chuckled. "You're a crafty ole lawyer, ain't you? Don't apologize, honey. I just wish your daddy could see you now."

Alma cringed, realizing she'd been questioning her grandmother like a hostile witness. "Why don't we wait and see how the bond hearing works out before you say that, Mamaw."

"Now, don't you let your momma bother you none. She's just as worried . . . Vernon's always been special to her. I think he reminds her of Esau. You know, Vernon almost moved to Detroit to look for work. Your momma got so upset, she called every person in this town until she found him a job."

"At the tannery?"

"Lord, no, he got laid off there two years ago. He just bounced around . . . couldn't seem to find anything that satisfied him. . . ." Mamaw stared out at the trailer as if it somehow personified Vernon. "Worked at the newspaper, Harry's Restaurant, the mines off and on. He was working in the video store when all this happened."

Alma looked out at the Jeep. Something that she

couldn't quite focus on was bothering her. The Jeep was the current model, even had a telephone antenna. "How did Vernon get the money for that Jeep?"

"That girl give it to him . . . for his birthday."

"That didn't offend his sense of . . . what . . . what does Vernon have . . . machismo?"

"Well, lord, Alma Mae. I don't know what they did in bed!"

Alma laughed and did not correct Mamaw. "Speaking of bed . . . I'm ready for one. Can I stay in the lavender room?"

"I should never have painted it that ugly color." Mamaw steered her wheelchair to a hall closet and pointed to where Alma could find towels and extra blankets. "Everybody that visits wants to sleep in that room, and it's so far away from me, nobody would ever hear me if I got sick."

"Don't you go sounding like Momma." Alma took some towels but refused extra blankets. "I think I remember my way around. I ain't . . . I've not been gone that long, Mamaw." Alma waved and watched as her grandmother maneuvered the wheelchair into a ground-level bedroom.

The lavender room had been her father's room and that was the only reason Alma liked sleeping in it. She opened the door and faced a queen-size iron-bed frame with white sheets on the mattress. Pictures of her father as a boy lined one wall. A wedding picture was on the pine dresser. Black and white. Alma's mother, in what was probably a gray suit, and her father in a navy uniform. He'd borrowed it from Uncle Ames, thinking it would be funny to get married in it, or so Alma was told. "You must have passed your sense of humor to Vernon," she said, "that's for sure, Daddy."

Alma opened her suitcase and pulled out a silk gown,

realizing she'd have been smarter to bring something a little warmer. She'd barely pulled it over her head when the energy seemed to empty out of her body like milk being poured from a pitcher. Her bare feet stuck to the chilly floor, and she moved quickly to open the curtains so that she could go to sleep looking at the clear, starry sky.

The isolation of the room wrapped around her like a blanket. This is a bad joke, she thought. *Walter Gentry. Walter Gentry is the commonwealth attorney.* Alma dreaded having to close her eyes.

Jefferson Bingham tapped his finger on Alma's window. Across the room came a loud rap on her door. Jefferson motioned for her to stop. "Don't open the door," he yelled. His voice stretched out, like the slow tearing of a sheet. "Don't open the door!" She got out of bed and pulled the curtain closed. From the other side of the door a man's voice softly whispered, "Open the door, honey. It's your daddy." Alma was filled with happiness. She thought she'd burst and ran toward the door. Lightning struck, shattering the glass behind her. She was blown through the window, into the cornfield . . . running. Cornstalks tripped her, and hounds bayed in pursuit. If they caught her, she'd be ripped to shreds. She twisted around. The dogs' eyes reflected iridescent red as they surrounded her in the darkness of the cornstalks. She screamed at the top of her lungs, "Daddy, help me! Daddy, please help me!" The red eyes opened and closed, waiting for her. Alone. Completely alone. No one to help her. No one to witness her pain . . . her death. The dogs growled. She hated them. Anger replaced her fear. "I hate you!" She plunged into the center of the pack. They weren't dogs. They were roosters. An electric shock jarred her body as they flew at her . . . flogging her. A man's soft voice answered, "Daddy can't help you, honey. Daddy can't help you."

Alma woke from the nightmare with a jerk and sat up in bed. "God," she said, "I hope I didn't scream out loud." She held still, waiting for the electric pulse in her skin to tone down. "Thank God this room is far away from Mamaw's." The patchwork quilt had twisted around her legs and she straightened it out. Her nose was cold, and she regretted not getting an extra blanket. Her chest muscles trembled. She knew it was not from the cold. Who the hell did she think she was, coming there, trying to take charge? She was a corporate lawyer. What if she did something to cause Vernon to get a life sentence? What if . . .

She struggled to get ahold of her late-night insecurities, but they screamed at her like accusers. What if she saw one of them? What if one of them came up to her, spoke to her? What would she say? It was too late to back away. She was there, and Walter Gentry was the commonwealth attorney. These were facts. She had to face him.

Alma grabbed fistfuls of hair from the sides of her head and shook herself. "Come on, Alma. You can't fall apart. Not now! The past don't matter." She half laughed. "It doesn't matter either," she cajoled herself. She had to put thoughts of what had happened to her all those years ago out of her mind. She would think only of Vernon and winning this case. Repeating to herself over and over that tomorrow she would wake up more a lawyer than a Bashears, she closed her eyes, only to open them again. Out the window the black sky poured whiteness. It was snowing.

12

"Remember now," Alma whispered to Jefferson as they stored their briefcases underneath the defense table, "when Judge Dulaney taught us ninth-grade history, she was a Napoleon freak."

"I think I was sick the day we studied that century," Jefferson said, rubbing his belly and twisting uncomfortably in his chair.

"Never hurts to compare your client to your judge's hero. How we'll link Vernon and Napoleon is something I'll have to figure out."

"I always assumed Napoleon was Judge Dulaney's mentor."

Alma smiled. It was Jefferson's first attempt at humor, and she felt it indicated that he needed a boost in confidence. Her stomach was bouncing up and down like popcorn over a hot fire, but she hid her nervousness with all the expertise of an experienced attorney. Walter Gentry was about to meet his past, and Alma was going to make it as difficult for him as she could.

Contrary City Hall had been built the year before, so the courtroom still smelled of paint and sawed wood. The walls were still clean, the jury box and the spectator section as comfortable as a movie theater, the defense and prosecution tables large enough to accommodate a team of attorneys, if necessary. Alma was impressed.

During breakfast she and Jefferson had pored through arrest reports, warrants, and witness statements. Neither found anything they could point to as improper. Officer Fred Walker had even scrawled a note that he'd read the Miranda rights to Vernon twice—once before Vernon bit him and once after, when an additional charge of assaulting an officer had been added. The prosecution was obviously taking no chances.

Alma had had to hurry Jefferson along to the courthouse. His hesitant steps in the newly fallen snow were as timid as a child's who'd never experienced winter. All morning his left eye had twitched nervously, but when she'd asked him if he was okay, he'd stared down into his black coffee and hadn't answered. She'd wondered if going up against Ellen Farmer was worrying him.

Jefferson twisted in his chair for the second time and Alma hoped that no one noticed. The spectator section was already half filled with a few reporters, a half-dozen friends of Vernon's, and the merely curious who had nothing better to do that day than attend a bail hearing. She wondered if one of the women was Johanna Littlefield. She could hardly wait to get Miss Littlefield on the stand. Somehow, Alma figured, that deadly fight rested on Johanna Littlefield's shoulders. There's more to this than a gum wrapper, she thought. Uncle Ames and Rodney sat in the first row behind her. The other family members had elected to stay home and wait with Mamaw. Alma smiled at Uncle Ames and winked.

Alma's mother entered the courtroom, pushing both swinging doors inward and letting them fly closed behind her. Her wide-eyed look at Alma was pointed, as if she were telling her to wash the dinner dishes now and not a minute later. She plopped down in the last row. Obviously wants to avoid having to talk to me, Alma thought. Her mother had probably talked to enough people by now to know that all Alma had told her the night before was true. Momma never could stand being wrong.

Jefferson didn't bother turning to look at the spectators. His left eye blinked several times, as if trying to control the twitch. Alma wished he would stop acting so nervous. He was making them look unprepared and guilty. "If you were Superman," she said, "your X-ray vision could burn a hole in that table."

"I got to tell you about the commonwealth attorney," Jefferson blurted. He kept staring at a triangle of desk between his hands and bit his lower lip until his teeth left an impression.

"You mean Ellen Farmer isn't going to handle the bail hearing?" Alma leaned back in her chair and glanced across the aisle, acting as innocent as she could. "Why would the commonwealth attorney waste his time on a bail hearing?" Ellen Farmer sat at the prosecution table beside an empty chair, a stack of files in the center of the desk and a brown luggage-size briefcase at her feet. She'd obviously lugged Walter's heavy briefcase without any help, Alma thought, reminding her of herself in law school, always refusing help that she now readily accepted. "Car doors," she said to Jefferson.

"Huh?" He looked over at her. The muscles around his left eye twitched like the leg of a can-can dancer.

"I always let men open car doors for me these days, even a prosecuting attorney. Keeps them a little off balance."

Jefferson looked down again. The bailiff emerged from a side door with Vernon and led him to their table. Ordinarily, Alma would have seated him between herself and Jefferson, but Jefferson was acting so nervously she thought it best that she stay beside him in case she had to take over.

Jefferson and Vernon nodded to each other. "You say

anything?" Vernon asked him as he situated himself in his chair. Jefferson shook his head, his eye still twitching like a drum beat.

"What are you two whispering about?" Alma asked.

Jefferson, looking trapped, nodded toward the door behind the bench. The court clerk, peeking out from the judge's chambers, noted the empty chair at the prosecution's table and wrinkled her brow.

Alma smiled and whispered loud enough so that both Vernon and Jefferson could hear, "Remember in high school if you were late for Mrs. Dulaney's history class, you always got a letter grade lower on the next test?" The clerk peered out the door again. "Well, Walter Gentry is down to a C."

Vernon looked at her. "You know?"

"It was a good day when Mrs. Dulaney retired from teaching and became a judge." Alma looked back and forth between them. Neither would look at her. "Score one to Alma Mae." She snickered. "Let's just hope I have the same effect on the commonwealth attorney."

Behind them the honey-colored partition squeaked. Alma looked around. She hadn't expected what she saw. A tall, bald-headed man with a full beard entered and sat in the empty chair at the prosecutor's table. She slowly leaned back to look at him without drawing attention to herself. There he was in front of her—high school baseball star, president of the senior class, Mr. Most Likely to Succeed—Narly Gentry. She came forward in her seat. Vernon and Jefferson turned toward her, eyes round as nickels. "What's wrong with you guys?" she asked.

"All rise!" said the court clerk. "Judge Mary Dulaney presiding."

Judge Dulaney wasted no time. "Be seated. Court is in session. Let the record show this is a bail hearing for

Vernon Bashears. The charge is homicide. How do you plead?"

Vernon stood and said, "Not guilty, Your Honor."

"For the record, counselors, please introduce yourselves and spell your names." She pointed toward Jefferson.

His voice is clear, Alma thought, and at least he didn't misspell his own name. She was relieved that Bob Krauss was at this moment driving from Knoxville to Contrary. It'd be good to get this case in the hands of a more confident attorney.

The commonwealth attorney leaned forward, resting his arms on the table. "For the commonwealth," he said, his voice a baritone mix of high and low, "Gentry . . . Walter Gentry. W-A-L-T-E-R G-E-N-T-R-Y."

Alma's eyes fixed on him. She parted her lips, breathing slowly through her mouth. Every muscle in her body ground tightly, like a metal fender against the spinning wheel of a wrecked bicycle. Her brain spun the wheel, faster and faster. The sound of his voice triggered something inside her. *I was doing fine. What's wrong with me?* She blinked and held her eyelids closed. Disneyland fireworks exploded in her mind's darkness. Walter Gentry. Walter Gentry. Walter Gentry. The name echoed in her brain and she almost said it aloud. Narly Gentry.

What was strangest was that she'd never envisioned him as an adult. In her mind he was still that gangly, bump-lipped boy with the center shock of hair that rivaled Elvis's. Narly Gentry. *Two is the opposition,* as Jordan would have said.

Walter cleared his throat. "The state requests that Your Honor deny bail. We present for your perusal an arrest record that goes back to when the defendant was thirteen years old."

Alma reached over and wrote on Jefferson's pad, *He's only a downtown boy,* and underlined the last two words, almost as if telling herself.

"Do you have a response?" Judge Dulaney asked, looking at Jefferson.

He stood. "Yes, I do, Your Honor. I object to the defendant's juvenile offense being presented to the court."

Alma concentrated on focusing her emotions on what she wanted to accomplish today. Silently she repeated the words, "Plan and execute," as if willing her subconscious to issue a defense.

Vernon tilted his chair back and rocked on its rear legs. His eyes had a defiant edge to the crinkled skin around them. He whispered, "You're the blamedest thing I've ever seen."

She leaned over and put her lips near Vernon's ear. "If you'd had any guts you'd have told me about Narly yesterday."

"Hell, I lost a good four hours' sleep trying to figure out how to tell you."

"Is there anything wrong?" Judge Dulaney interrupted the proceedings and stared at the defense table.

Jefferson quickly responded, "My associate was just explaining the meaning of some of these legal terms, Your Honor. We'll be quieter."

"Mr. Bashears, do you feel you need to confer with your attorneys?"

"Not if I can help it," Vernon said, looking down at his lap like a boy in the principal's office. Alma touched his arm and nodded toward the bench. "No, Your Honor," Vernon corrected himself, looking up at Judge Dulaney.

"May I have a moment, Your Honor?" Jefferson leaned over and the three of them huddled like football players. "We'll throw mud pies at each other later, gang.

How about we just try to look like we have some semblance of unity for today?"

Alma peered over Jefferson's shoulder at Walter. He stroked his beard, looking casually out the window as if he had something on his mind. He doesn't recognize me, she realized. I'm the last thing he'd ever expect. Probably thinks I'm Jefferson's assistant. "What bail is the prosecution asking?" she whispered to him.

Jefferson rolled his eyes. "If you'd been listening, he wants Vernon held without bail. I've asked that he be released on his own recognizance. Prosecution keeps pointing out Vernon's previous incarceration in the juvenile system."

"Perfect."

"Perfect?" Jefferson tightened his mouth with forced naturalness, as if trying to show everyone watching that all was well with his team.

"I want to address the court," Alma said.

"What are you going to do?" Worry lines shot across Jefferson's forehead.

"Are you ready, Mr. Bingham?" the judge prompted, sounding impatient.

"Do it," Alma said.

Jefferson straightened up and cleared his throat, as if stalling and thinking at the same time. "Your Honor, at this time, I'd like to allow my associate to address the court."

"Is this relevant to bail, counselor?"

"Yes, Your Honor."

"Any objection, Mr. Gentry?"

Walter barely looked up from the 8 x 11 sheet of paper he held between both hands. "We have no objection, Your Honor."

"Proceed. Introduce yourself and spell your name for the record."

Alma slowly pushed back her chair and stood up, resting the tips of her fingers on the table. A nervous rumble erupted in her chest, but she consciously pushed it down. She wouldn't feel. She wouldn't feel anything right now. Walter Gentry did not look up at her, and from her standing position she could see that the paper in his hand was a flyer that read GENTRY FOR STATE ASSEMBLY sashed over a picture of himself. She was going to enjoy this.

"Your Honor," she began. "I have relevant information regarding Mr. Bashears's incarceration as a juvenile. I believe when you hear what I have to say, the court will agree that Mr. Gentry's view is biased." She looked over at Walter. He stared at her just above the level of the flyer, which he still held with both hands.

"Your name, please," the judge interrupted. "Spell it also."

"Of course, excuse me, Your Honor." Alma turned toward the stenographer in front of the prosecution's table. "B-A-S-H-E-A-R-S, A-L-M-A. Alma . . . Alma Bashears."

Judge Dulaney leaned forward and wrote on a notepad. "Sister, I believe. Correct?" Alma answered yes. "Are you a licensed attorney?"

"I am, Your Honor, in California. I'm here in an advisory capacity."

"Proceed, for now."

Before Alma spoke again, she looked over at Walter. His facial expression was as blank as if he were playing world-class poker. That might have undermined Alma's confidence except that the flyer was crumpled in his tightly clenched fists. "Your Honor, the incident for which Mr. Bashears served time took place over fifteen years ago. More important, the incident that initiated Mr. Bashears's trouble with the law was a fight, a fistfight."

Walter's eyes were fixed on her as if she were an opposing quarterback. "Many teenagers get into fights. Napoleon had his Waterloo, and this fight was Vernon's time to be defeated. Not by a worthy opponent, but by a town's social system that defined the worth of its people by the area in which they lived. It was a class struggle, Your Honor, because this fight was with the only son of a prominent Contrary family."

"Objection." Walter was on his feet as fast as a hooked fish jerked from the water, then he sat back down. Probably hoping to keep from seeming distressed, Alma thought.

The judge shushed him with a hand. "I'd like to hear what she has to say."

Alma continued. "A family whose influence made a jail sentence for Mr. Bashears mandatory. The person with whom my brother fought was none other than—"

"Objection, Your Honor." Walter nearly knocked over his chair as he stood again, but this time he was more in control. Ellen Farmer reached out to catch the chair and nearly toppled out of her own.

"Grounds?" Judge Dulaney finally asked when Walter stood silently, staring at Alma.

"Relevance," he replied. "Who the defendant fought with and why is of no consequence. That he was convicted is."

Jefferson stood, catching on to Alma's line of thought. "In this case the identity of that person is relevant, Your Honor."

Walter stepped over to the defense table. "Just what are you trying to prove?" he whispered.

Judge Dulaney's gavel cracked. "You will address the court, not each other." She inhaled a deep breath and looked back and forth between the defense's and prosecutor's tables. "Mr. Prosecutor, your intention of pursuing a first-degree indictment is obvious. I don't see that you have the evidence to warrant that indictment, and unless the juvenile conviction sheds some light on—"

"I'd rather leave the indictment to the grand jury, Your Honor," Walter interrupted.

Judge Dulaney's lower lip stiffened. "I'd like to see all attorneys in chambers."

Great! Alma thought. Keep insulting the judge, and we'll have no bail before you can shine your shoes.

They followed her single file into an unpainted room with two desks and law books stacked on the floor in front of unfinished bookshelves. "You'll excuse the condition of my chambers," she said. "The treasurer ran out of funds a mile short of the runway."

Alma smiled and looked as daughterly as she could. She could smell Walter's musk-scented cologne. Being this close to him caused her skin to prickle. She steeled herself. *My muscles are concrete, my spine is iron, my mind twice as smart, twice as fast, as his. I read his mind. I counter him at every step. This is a game. This is a game. And I will win.*

"What is going on out there?" Judge Dulaney asked. She sat at her desk and crossed her hands in front of her. "May I remind both lead attorneys that this is no longer high school. This court expects professionalism, not schoolboy bickering."

Jefferson spoke up first. "We don't understand the objection. We have relevant information and we're presenting it to the court."

"And to the reporters." Walter pointed a finger in Jefferson's and Alma's direction without looking at them. "This cheap trick, Your Honor, is for no other reason than to try to blackmail the prosecution."

"I'm afraid I don't understand." Judge Dulaney

waited. No response. "I don't intend to wait here all day."

"Mr. Gentry's response indicates to me that he is afraid of the publicity this information will bring to this trial." Alma sat forward in her seat and spoke as if she were addressing a teacher, not a judge. "It also suggests to me that Mr. Gentry is afraid of the truth. Regardless of our information, to bring up a juvenile conviction is irrelevant, if not illegal, in this state." She looked over at Jefferson, wishing she could remember Kentucky law.

"Nonsense," Walter said. "Vernon Bashears is a violent man. He has scores of disturbing-the-peace violations against him. His drunken brawls are well known in many a Tennessee pub. The juvenile conviction underscores that history."

"We are not presenting any information that is not already part of public record," Alma shot back. "Those reporters could find it themselves, if they cared to." She knew full well the newspapers were local and wouldn't bother to investigate further, and Narly knew that, too.

"It's the way they are presenting it, Your Honor. These people have no right to invasion of privacy." Walter gestured in what looked like a practiced imitation of JFK. "They'll draw attention to a little-known fact about the juvenile conviction that lacks relevance to this present case."

"The juvenile conviction has no relevance in this case," Jefferson reminded the judge.

"And if you think it does," Alma said to Walter, slowly stroking her chin, "then why don't you tell Judge Dulaney and let her rule."

Around his beard Walter's cheeks flushed a cherry pink. "You're so damn eager, why don't you tell her!" He slammed his hands on the desk.

Alma slammed her hands down opposite his. "Why

don't you tell her, Naaarrrly!" Her gaze bored into his face-to-face, like a pit bull unwilling to release an opponent.

"Enough!" Judge Dulaney said. "This is not high school, but if I have to reprimand you like children, you are not going to like the punishment. Now, either tell me what is going on or I'll cite both of you for contempt."

Walter paced to the window and stared out through the melting icicles. "I was the boy Vernon Bashears fought with," he said slowly and deliberately.

"I see." Judge Dulaney's eyebrows rose, and she nodded. She wrote some notes on her yellow pad and made marks by them as she spoke. "A fifteen-and-some-odd-year-old offense is weak—and the fact that he was a juvenile carries weight—considering all these facts, I will rule in favor of the defense. Is there anything either of you wishes to say?" She looked over her glasses at Walter, as if daring him to confront her.

Walter held his hands behind his back and pulled back his shoulders as if to show he'd accept the ruling like a professional. His eyes focused upward toward the left, then the right, and Alma felt his expression said it all: This information might endanger my chance to be selected for the state assembly. "The commonwealth," Walter said, "will not object to the court ruling for a release on recognizance."

"I haven't made that ruling yet, Mr. Gentry." Judge Dulaney stood and indicated for them to return to the courtroom. "But I will."

While waiting for Vernon to be released, Uncle Ames and Rodney smiled and patted Alma and Jefferson on their backs. "I always wanted to be a lawyer," Rodney said, shaking his head, "but after seeing you today, I'd never be able to do it."

"Sure you would," Jefferson volunteered. "You know I've been waiting a long time for you to be my partner."

"Alma," Uncle Ames said, "Jefferson, you two did a fine job."

The policeman who had blocked Alma's way the day before shuffled by them. Everyone stopped talking. The man swaggered from side to side as he balanced his gun, nightstick, walkie-talkie, and handcuffs around his waist. "Is he somebody?" Alma asked when the policeman was out of hearing distance.

"Part of the . . ." Uncle Ames paused. "Littleafia."

"About six of them," Rodney said. "They'd do anything Big Bill wanted them to."

Out of Uncle Ames's hearing range Jefferson whispered to Alma, "If Fred Walker hadn't arrested Vernon when he did, they'd have caught up with him and—"

"I get the picture," Alma said, looking after the man as he turned down the hallway.

The door of the courtroom swung open. Walter Gentry stepped out, then Ellen Farmer followed, lugging his briefcase. Alma turned toward Rodney. She felt Jefferson moving along at her back, shielding her from Gentry's view. Her insides were on a slow boil, growing hotter. She spoke loudly enough for Walter and Ellen to hear. "By the time the grand jury hears this case, they'll laugh this ridiculous first-degree murder charge out of the room."

"Jefferson, Miss Bashears," Ellen said as she passed.

"We will entertain any reduced charge you want to submit," Alma said before they were out of range. "The judge's bail ruling should point out your error in attempting a conviction on first degree." She kept herself at an angle to them, never looking at them directly.

Walter turned around and said, "We don't intend to ask for a reduced indictment."

"You thought you had the argument for an outrageous bail. Do you intend to delude yourself that you can get a conviction on this charge?"

Walter cleared his throat and spoke in a soft, low voice. "To delude oneself is to not recognize the truth of a situation. On that count I'd say you have held the scoring point for many, many years."

She heard the click of his shoes against the floor and Ellen's quick shuffle after him. Alma could feel her face flushing. The deep injury she thought long closed opened up like an erupting volcano, tearing through the center of her body. No one could see it. No one knew what she was feeling. She was the only one who knew she was afraid. She was the only one feeling this gash splitting her apart. All Alma could think of was to get as far away from Contrary as fast as she could.

"Odd thing to say," Rodney said, staring after him with a confused look.

Alma excused herself to go to the ladies' room. If she couldn't leave Contrary right this minute, then she had to be away from everyone—just to regain control. Her nails bit into the palms of her clenched fists. Delude myself, she thought. The words *scoring point* ricocheted in her head.

She walked to the farthest stall, noting that all but one were empty. Latching the door, she leaned against the cold tile wall and began to shake. She dropped her briefcase, letting it hit the floor with a loud thud. Wrapping her arms around her chest, she rocked back and forth. The tremor would not stop and she sank to the floor, unable to keep her balance. She pressed her lips together, trying not to make any noise, wishing the woman a few stalls down would leave.

The coffee and Danish from breakfast rose in her throat. She reached for the purse shelf and pulled herself up, balancing between it and the toilet. A flush, then the sound of the woman washing her hands and leaving. When the outside door closed, Alma grabbed her briefcase and slammed it against the wall of the stall. Again and again and again, grunting with rage each time she slammed it. Harder and harder until finally the handle broke.

Her papers and files scattered on the floor; saliva beaded at the corners of her mouth. She clenched her teeth so tight that her panting breath could barely hiss through. Her heartbeat raced, and its pulse sent a painful tingling through her chest. On the back wall her face was reflected in the stainless-steel seat-cover dispenser— twisted and disproportional, but pale, dry-cheeked, and without a trace of suffering. As if nothing had happened. As if she could walk out of this stall and be ready to address the Supreme Court.

13

Uncle Ames beeped the car horn as he drove up to Mamaw's house. A half-dozen faces popped into all the front windows: Merl, Aunt Joyce, Uncle George, Sue and Jack, Larry Joe, and Eddie, all waving their hands, their bright smiles as animated as Christmas tree lights. Alma couldn't help thinking of her father. As a child, she'd planned his homecoming many times, and oddly, this seemed to be it—except this reception was for Vernon.

Vernon leaped from the car and held his arms up in a V like a boxer who'd just won a title. Merl sprinted from the house and was immediately beside Vernon, pointing at him with a gesture like that of an awarding referee. Sue and Jack, Uncle George, Aunt Joyce, and the two nephews came out on the porch, clapped their hands, and shouted encouragement.

Determined to maintain her calm and remain in charge, Alma did her best to smile and seem unaffected. Deep inside, she realized that Walter's comment had made it impossible for her to stay. He held too much over her head. She'd never be able to face him every day.

"Come on, Rocky," she said to Vernon, "that tan BMW over there most likely belongs to Bob Krauss. You've got a lot to do before you can celebrate." Alma had never felt such relief as she did at seeing that car.

Merl inched back between her and Vernon, pushed Alma on the arm, and said, "You're such a worrywart." She escorted him up the steps to slaps on the back and a chorus of "We was worried to death about ye."

Alma followed them into the living room. She held her briefcase under one arm, the broken handle tucked toward the inside. The house smelled of creamed corn, mashed potatoes, biscuits, fried green tomatoes, and deer steak with gravy.

Vernon headed straight for Mamaw. He leaned down to hug her, and tears brightened her eyes. "You sprung me from the joint just so I'd clean up my trailer and feed the dogs, didn't you?" Vernon said, causing Mamaw to giggle like a young girl.

The phone rang, and Sue leaned over the couch and Uncle George to answer it. "Vernon, honey," Sue called out, "it's Lizzy Kay."

"Word travels fast in these parts," a stranger's voice said. Alma turned to see a fiftyish-year-old man, distinguished and well-dressed even in casual clothes, step out from the kitchen. She recognized Bob Krauss from the TV interviews she'd seen on some of his better-known cases. A leonine shock of white hair was combed straight back, giving his heavy eyebrows and intense stare an eaglelike presence. "Mr. Krauss," she said, extending a hand. "I'm glad you came."

"I'm glad, too," he said, and licked crumbs from his thumb. "Your family has been pumping me full of food." He indicated for her not to disturb Vernon, but to come with him. They moved to the foot of the staircase, far enough away from the family so that their conversation would be private. Alma was relieved when Mamaw asked Sue to push her wheelchair into the kitchen and most of the family followed.

"The bail hearing obviously went well," Krauss said.

"I used an old trick Eric Erickson taught me," Alma said. God, I hope he'll take this case, she silently prayed. So far, he was not displaying any of the reluctance she'd heard on the phone.

"Eric approached moot court with strategies that could have rivaled Napoleon." Krauss nodded admiringly.

"Yes," Alma agreed. "The judge is a great fan of Napoleon."

The phone rang again, and her mother jostled Uncle George from the couch to reach the side table. "Vernon, it's for you."

Alma leaned in toward Krauss. "I'd like to get you, Jefferson, and Vernon together and bring you up to speed. It appears that I must return to California tonight."

"I'm sorry to hear that. Eric's good words about you have made me eager to see how you work."

"I'll hold that over his head." She smiled. "I'll get Vernon off the phone and we can meet in one of the upstairs bedrooms, then you and I can go downtown to Jefferson's office."

Vernon no sooner hung up the phone when it rang once more, and once more it was for him. Alma left Krauss standing at the foot of the staircase and motioned for Vernon to follow them upstairs. He shifted away from her and continued his conversation. She tugged on his arm.

"Yeah, baby," Vernon said to the caller. "Missed you, too. How 'bout you juice up that Jacuzzi of yours and we'll pop in it for an hour or two."

Alma began shaking her head. "No. No," she whispered to him. "You're not going anywhere."

Vernon turned his back to her. "Hey, baby, you give me a little time to visit with my people and I'll see you between six and six-thirty." He hung up the phone. Merl bounced down on the couch and whisked her arm through his and he said, "Momma, I'm hungry as a dog."

"There's food enough for an army and it's all for you, precious." Merl smiled sweetly at Alma and pinched her cheek just at the side of her mouth. "You looked so important in there today, Alma," she said in a high singsong voice that Alma recognized as fake sincerity. "I was real proud."

The phone rang and Vernon jumped for it. "Well, Bonnie June. Sure is good to hear from you. I sure did get that chocolate cake you left for me."

"Mother," Alma said, ignoring the sarcasm in her mother's voice. "I've got to get Vernon in with Mr. Krauss. He drove from Knoxville, and the day is half over."

"Honey, you want to go to meetings with your Jewish friend, you go right ahead, but we're celebrating."

"Will you speak with a little more respect," Alma cautioned her mother. "Mr. Krauss is standing ten feet from you!"

"I told you Jefferson could handle the case and he did."

"I'd be glad to stop by and set up your VCR," Vernon said, switching the phone to his other ear and standing to get away from the two women. "Ten o'clock okay?"

"No, you're not," Alma told him, smacking his arm so that he turned to face her.

"Will you stop this, Alma Mae?" her mother said, shaking her head as if Alma were a teenager picking on her younger brother.

"Will y'all be quiet," Vernon said loudly, holding one hand over the receiver. "Yeah, honey," he said into the phone, "a back rub sounds good."

Alma pushed the disconnect button.

Vernon slammed down the receiver. "Damn it, Alma Mae! Who made you queen of my social calendar?"

"This is not the time to be stroking your libido," she replied as quietly as she could, hoping Bob Krauss wouldn't hear. "Why don't you and Momma make a conscious effort to live in the real world?"

Her mother raised a hand as if she were going to slap Alma. "Don't you sass me like that."

"Momma!" Larry Joe stood in the doorway and hollered toward the kitchen. "Grammy's gonna whip Aunt Alma!" He bit into an Oreo cookie, chocolate crumbs dusting the side of his face. The kitchen emptied, and the family, all balancing plates of food, wedged themselves into the living room and stared. No one spoke. They just kept gobbling their food and waiting to see if anything was going to happen.

Alma felt as if she were starring in a Fellini movie. Her mother shrank down, embarrassed, and busily brushed crumbs off Larry Joe's mouth. "You can sometimes be the dirtiest little boy," she said, and kissed his cheek.

"Well, guess what, everybody," Vernon said in a jolly voice as though hoping to ease the tension, "I been out of the pokey for less than two hours and I already got four dates."

"That's real good, Vernon," Uncle George said, "we're glad to hear that."

Vernon looked over at Alma and Bob Krauss, who leaned uncomfortably against the wall. "But I'll tell ye what . . . I think I'll hang around here tonight and keep you all some good company."

"Yeaaaa!" Larry Joe yelled, and swung himself on Vernon's legs. "Can I play on your car phone, Uncle Vernon?"

"When you're thirty."

Everyone laughed. Mamaw called out from the kitchen, "This food is getting cold. I don't know what's so important in there, but if you want any of it, you better come and eat it now!"

Everyone moved at the sound of Mamaw's voice. The phone rang, and Alma answered it this time. Another female caller. She held out the receiver for Vernon. Krauss put an arm around her shoulder and motioned for them to go out onto the porch.

The cool air coated Alma's warm skin. She realized she'd been sweating and wiped the bridge of her nose. To her surprise, Krauss chuckled. "Alma," he said quietly, "maybe you should back off a little bit . . . for today."

"I'd consider it kind, after seeing that little scene, if you want anything to do with this case. I'm terribly embarrassed."

He waved a hand, his breath coming out in long streams of white air. "Something that is extremely hard for us attorneys to learn is that we can't control what people do. We spend our days manipulating testimony, finessing judges, outwitting other attorneys—all to get the outcome we want."

"This is my family, Bob, and they don't have a clue what they're in for. This isn't a case, it's a stepping-stone for a politically ambitious prosecutor."

"Key words . . . it is your family." He leaned on the arm of a rusted peach-colored porch chair. "You can't manipulate your family the way you can a hostile witness. They know you too well. They know what buttons to push."

"Obviously," she said, pointing to the house, "but they're not the only ones who push buttons in this town."

"I have mixed feelings about your leaving."

"I have every faith in you, Bob."

"On the one hand, you just might be the only person who can control Vernon."

"And then only when the moon is full." She laughed nervously.

"On the other hand . . ." Krauss paused just long enough to button up his jacket. "Alma, two years ago I had a nephew arrested for selling a kilo of cocaine in Michigan, where I'm from."

"Oh, no," she said, "that's a mandatory life sentence if convicted."

He nodded. "Like you, I flew back, tried to help coordinate a defense . . . staying out of the way when I should and all. By the time the trial began, I had a bleeding ulcer and heart palpitations."

"It's hard to believe that happening to someone like you."

"Don't let it happen to you, Alma." He took one of her hands in his and rubbed the red coldness from it. "This is ultimately Vernon's problem to deal with, not yours. A guilty verdict is not your fault and a not-guilty won't get you a thank-you."

Alma wanted to respond in some way, but she didn't know what to say. His words were logical, yet as humiliated as she'd felt at the hands of Walter Gentry, if she left Vernon now, would she be the rat deserting a sinking ship? San Francisco beckoned. Thoughts of plush green carpet, the still silence of the private law library, her corner office, just a floor below the partners—her world, so foreign from this one.

"I think . . . perhaps you're making the right decision to leave." Krauss pointed toward his car and she walked to it with him. "I'll go meet with Jefferson Bingham this afternoon. Vernon and I don't need to talk until tomorrow. Now, young lady, go back in there and be

Vernon's sister, not his lawyer. I'll call you weekly with reports and every day once the trial starts."

She shook his hand, thanked him, and then watched until his car disappeared out of the hollow. Thank God for lawyers like Bob Krauss, she thought. Attorneys like him fostered a balance in the profession that made being a lawyer more meaningful than just earning a paycheck. He could sift out reality like wheat from chaff. He understood exactly what this case was about. In many ways he was an older version of Jordan.

Jordan . . . How she missed him. *I'll be in your arms by tomorrow night, my love.* Alma touched her earlobes and the blue topaz earrings, squeezing them as she inhaled a deep breath of cold mountain air. She remembered Jordan saying that he had plans for her—had he wrangled her a partnership? Would he go into politics and run for governor next term, and would she help him campaign as his assistant, his wife? Questions that needed answering. Everything here is in place, she thought. No one needs me. She did not have to face Walter Gentry again. For the first time since she'd arrived, she relaxed. She was leaving . . . leaving for good this time.

14

When Alma returned to the house, Vernon was still talking on the telephone. She smiled at him though she felt like slapping him and stopped to pick up a peppermint from a bowl on the coffee table. She popped it in her mouth, then threw one at Vernon. He caught it but did not get off the phone.

Alma looked back toward the kitchen. Uncle Ames and Rodney were taking turns telling the family about the bail hearing that morning. From the little she could hear, embellishment was an understatement. She slipped upstairs and began packing her suitcase. Her eyes kept wandering back to the two walls filled with family photos and the pictures of her father. "You know," she said softly, "if you'd been here, this might not have happened to Vernon." She touched one frame, aligning it with the pictures on the adjoining wall. A sadness welled up in her chest. "Many things might not have happened."

A few minutes passed, then there was a tap on the door and Vernon asked, "You busy?"

"I'm conferring with the Pentagon."

He opened the door. "I guess you sometimes need the Thirty-eighth Infantry to deal with Momma."

"And you."

He looked down at the bed, then realizing she was folding and packing a shirt, he pulled her suitcase toward him. "You just got here." He touched her clothes as if that would keep her from leaving.

"I'm a liability to this case, Vernon." She pulled the suitcase back toward her. "And you know why."

"I'm sorry. I should have had the guts to tell you about Narly. Don't blame Jefferson."

"I nearly fell apart this morning. I can't do that. I can't do that to this case, and I'm not going to do it to myself."

"Put on your coat." He opened the bedroom door. "Hurry, I got something to show you."

"I'd much rather be in a Knoxville hotel waiting for the next flight anywhere."

"Fine, I'll drive you."

"You can't leave the state."

"This town is on the state line!" He anchored his hands on his hips, one leg jacked up on the bed frame. "All I have to do is cross the street and I'm in Tennessee."

"Vernon, you look like you're about to pout."

"Sometimes I can't stand the sight of you, Alma Mae." He waited and huffed out a breath of frustration when she closed the suitcase. "Please let me show you something."

She snapped shut the locks and set the suitcase at the base of the bed. Vernon stood in the doorway, his lips puckered as they had been when he was a youngster and Alma took him to Woolworth's department store to look at the displays of chocolate-covered raisins and peanuts they couldn't afford to buy. "Oh, all right."

Vernon grabbed her hand and pulled her downstairs past a doting Merl, who was coming up to look for him. Outside, he started up his Jeep Cherokee and Alma jumped into the passenger seat. As Larry Joe and Eddie ran out onto the porch shouting demands to go with them, Vernon pulled out onto the road. Speeding faster than was wise on such an icy road, he plowed through ponds of water that sprayed the Jeep's windshield with an icy glaze. They passed their deserted redbrick high school. Alma thought the broken windows and unhinged doors made it the perfect setting for a teenage slasher movie. The road curved like a bracelet on the sloping hills, past dangling charms of brick and wood houses. Near the edge of town, where the road split to enter Tennessee, Vernon turned onto a gravel road and entered Rose Hill Cemetery.

"A graveyard." Alma looked at him as if he'd lost his mind. "You want to show me a graveyard."

"A grave. Actually, two graves." He gunned the gas and pulled the Jeep up on a hillside.

"Vernon, you're driving on graves!"

"It's all right, they don't know it." He gargled the harsh laugh of a cartoon villain.

Alma put her hands over her face and prayed that no one had seen them. That was all she needed—an arrest for knocking down tombstones and desecration of graves. She'd be in jail herself before the day ended.

"It's too cold to walk all the way out here," Vernon said. He pulled back onto a snow-covered road, stopped the Jeep, and jumped out.

Alma followed him a short way to a gray tombstone.

"There," he said, pointing at it.

" 'Earl Roscoe,' " she read aloud, then covered her mouth with a hand and pulled her scarf tighter. The same shaking that had consumed her that morning at the courthouse began in her hands. She tried to make it appear as if it was due to the cold.

Vernon averted his eyes. "The other one is over yonder." He pointed west where a statue of a winged cherub, grayed with age, sat atop a pinkish headstone carved with the name "Delmar."

"Oh, God, Vernon, you didn't—"

"Of course not!" He regarded her like a city cousin

who always suspected mountain folk were meaner. "Car wreck on Cumberland Mountain. They were drinking at the Holiday Inn, skidded out on the mountain, and hit a truck. Truck jackknifed. Killed the truck driver, too. He . . . he had two kids about Larry Joe's age."

Alma stared at her footprints in the snow. She was standing at the base of Earl Roscoe's grave and didn't even feel the cold. "I'm glad they're dead," she said without the least apology.

"Bet you'd like to get back at Narly, too, wouldn't you?"

She stared at the tombstone. "Attorneys don't think that way about their cases."

"Here's your chance, Sis."

She turned toward him. "You make mistakes when you think like that."

"This is your chance to get back at Narly."

"There's too much at stake. You let emotions get in your way and you're sunk as a litigator."

"But admit it, you'd like to get back at him, wouldn't you?"

"I'd like to twist that Armani tie around his throat and squeeze till his eyes pop out!" She slid unsteadily on her feet down the hill toward the Jeep.

"Now maybe you understand why I killed Bill Littlefield."

His answer stopped her. She turned to stare at Vernon. It was as if she were looking at a different man. She now understood him as a client, not as a brother. Yes, the reasons and circumstances might have been different, the situation turned on its side, but the rage that caused him to do it, that she knew like the process of her own thoughts.

They were both quiet as they drove back to the house. After a while she said, "Tell me about Johanna."

"Just a girl I dated."

"One who gives you a Jeep for a birthday present . . . and a car phone." Alma picked up the receiver and admired the multifunctional design.

"She offered, I took . . . You know me."

"Did Bill Littlefield want the Jeep back? Is that why you fought?"

"No."

"It's not hard to figure that he probably did not want his daughter involved with a hollow boy." She waited, but her brother did not respond.

Vernon patted his stomach and belched loudly. The Jeep swung into the hollow, climbing the icy road with all its four-wheel drive could give. "Don't go," he said, after pulling into the driveway and killing the ignition. "I thought you were crazy to come back, but now that you're here, I feel better."

The outside chill slowly ate the warm quiet of the Jeep. Alma held her hands together. She had to control the shaking. "I can't face him again, Vernon. Do you understand how those boys humiliated me? Narly is a man now. And what happened all those years ago still gives him power over me. Even if I stayed—for revenge—look at this situation." She pointed at the house. "It's ridiculous. I can't handle it. Momma will drive me crazy. And Mamaw . . . I can't stand the thought of disappointing Mamaw. What if I lose the case, Vernon? You'll go up for twenty years and everyone in the family will hate my guts."

Vernon opened his hands in a "so what" gesture, then dropped them in his lap and interlaced his fingers. He looked down at the steering wheel. "How come you and Momma fight like you do?"

"Guess we were just born under opposite stars."

"She and Sue used to fight. But not like the two of you.

It's like there's something more there, something the rest of us don't know."

Alma stared straight ahead. Jack, Eddie, and Larry Joe came out the back door with a slop bucket and headed toward the dog shed. That meant the women were in the kitchen cleaning, Uncle George and Uncle Ames napping, and Jack would have to watch the kids—a perfect time for her to sneak away. "It's tempting, Vernon. But I've made a life for myself in San Francisco. I just want to forget my past."

She slid out of the Jeep, ready for the warmth of the house. From now until the end of this situation, she would only be a relative who offered support . . . from three thousand miles away. "You may not want to talk to me, but don't hold anything back from Bob Krauss. He's not afraid of anybody, and he'll fight for you, Vernon." She closed the car door and wished with all her heart that she could do more for him. But she could not.

Entering the house, Alma heard the phone ring and picked up the receiver. "Hello?" she said, expecting to hear the sugary voice of another of Vernon's empty-headed bimbos.

"Is that you?" a woman asked.

Alma listened.

"I want to see you." Silence. "Do you know who this is?" Silence. "I want to see you now!"

Alma hung up the phone and pressed her hands into her stomach to soothe the knot tightening there. Yes, she knew the caller. She may not have recognized a bald and bearded Narly, but even after all these years it was impossible not to recognize the acrimonious, witchy voice of Charlotte Gentry.

15

Alma began to feel like a gunfighter who'd been given a six o'clock deadline to get out of town. I don't need this, she thought. I just don't need this. I have a life, and it doesn't include anyone named Gentry. Still . . . she imagined what Charlotte Gentry would think if she could see this hollow girl now.

On top of Alma's suitcase lay a white handkerchief bound with a pink ribbon tied in a bow. She tossed it in her hand, judging its weight. A notecard with a border of gray tabby cats lay on the bed. She picked it up.

Alma, your father gave this to me. I always wanted you to have it after I'm gone, but having seen you after so long a time, I'd rather you have it now, so I can rejoice in seeing you wear it while I'm still among the living. Jesus loves you, and I do, too. Love, Mamaw.

Alma pulled the ribbon and out fell a gold pin. A rooster with the birthstones of her father, mother, herself, Sue, and Vernon aligned on the tips of its tail feathers. It wasn't exactly to Alma's taste, but the heartfelt message left an uncomfortable yearning inside her. She pinned the rooster to the left side of her dress, then called a cab.

When she started repacking her briefcase, she found another note taped to the front.

Alma, Me and Larry Joe fixed the handle. Let it set overnight. It was broke. Uncle Ames.

She should go talk to them . . . explain why she was leaving . . . tell a lie about having to be in a California court next week. That's stupid, Alma Mae, she told herself. They'd just ask what's more important than Vernon and they'd be right. She should just say good-bye. Part of her wanted to hug each of them as hard as she could—even her mother—but she didn't want the feelings that would come with touching or to struggle with the emotions that speaking to her family would evoke. The picture of her father as a teenager looked down from above the bed. A ripple of sadness wove through her. She decided to leave a note. We're a family of note-leavers, she thought as she silently maneuvered downstairs, holding her suitcase so it wouldn't knock against the walls.

Alma peeked into Mamaw's bedroom. The old woman was sitting in her wheelchair facing the window. Her head was tilted to the left and nodded in sleep. Relief flooded through Alma's chest, and she sniffed back a wave of anxiety. She studied her grandmother's profile, seeing the resemblance to her own. She left her note by the phone.

Had to go back to California . . . will call soon. Alma.

As the cab turned out of the hollow, in the rearview mirror Alma saw Vernon standing in the middle of the road, watching her leave. Past the high school, down a street lined with oaks and brick houses, into the town. Past Jefferson's office, where he and Bob Krauss were probably talking. Past the First Baptist Church. Past the cab stand that hid this dry county's largest bootleg concession. Alma began to feel as if her body was numb with sleep, pins and needles in her calves, her fingers stiff and cold even in her gloves, her head achy and her eyes so dry she had to blink continuously. "Can't you turn up the heat?" she asked the driver.

"It's up as high as it'll go, Miss Bashears." He looked at her in the rearview mirror, his eyes seeming to consider something. "I got a bottle of bourbon in the glove compartment, if you think it'll help."

Alma reached over the seat, took the bottle, and swallowed a deep gulp. Then another. "I have to make a stop," she said, hardly feeling the burn in her throat. "Washington and Kirkland." Her heartbeat rose, and even before she stepped out of the cab, she was warm and felt a slight sweat on her upper lip. "You'll wait for me, please."

Someone had built a snowman in Charlotte Gentry's front yard. The de-iced sidewalk and the front porch lined with potted miniature evergreens—probably left over from last Christmas, she thought—made the yard look as manicured as if it were summer. Alma moved without thinking as the bourbon flushed through her veins. She knew she should have a reason for being there—a focus to concentrate on. But then, why should she? Charlotte Gentry had called her. Better to know what she's up to, Alma rationalized. She knocked hard on the door and waited.

"In the kitchen!" a voice answered.

Alma recognized Mrs. Gentry. She opened the door and stepped into a stuffy, musty-smelling hallway. A yellowish fluorescent light beckoned from the end of the hall. She passed the living room, slowing to look inside. It hadn't changed in twenty years—a quiet decor of maroon and hunter green. A scent of violet and talc permeated the room. It smells like an old lady, she thought. To the left, the clatter of dishes came from the kitchen.

"You have a terrible habit of arriving just in time to ruin my dinner," Charlotte Gentry said. She sat at a clear, glass table, jars of mustard and mayonnaise were open in front of her, a package of ham and Wonder bread pushed off to the side. Her hair, once the color of gray steel, had turned white as goose feathers, styled in the same back-combed wave that ended at the nape of her neck. She continued to spread mustard on the white bread, licking the excess off the knife. Her eyebrows raised over hooded eyes with puffy bags underneath, and she gestured for Alma to sit and fix herself a sandwich.

"I'll stand," Alma said.

Charlotte Gentry bit into her sandwich, showing a side row of teeth capped in gold. "I thought we had a deal," she said while chewing.

"You made a deal, but not with me." A hot flare shot through Alma. She told herself to stay in control and beat the bitch at her own game this time. *"You white-trash slut." Alma heard Charlotte Gentry's voice in her memory.*

"A lawyer . . ." Mrs. Gentry drawled. "You did better than I would have ever guessed." From under the table, she pushed a stool out with one foot. "You're making me jittery."

"You hog! You fat pig!" A gray-haired Charlotte Gentry had once screamed in Alma's face. She bit her lip and sat down, but only because it kept her higher than the woman opposite.

"It's a shame about your brother." Mrs. Gentry dusted crumbs off her skirt. "Bill Littlefield was Ohio scum—no better than the Carnegies. Came into my town, bought land and businesses, sent all the profit north." She looked Alma up and down. "Most of these local fools are too stupid to figure that out, or as long as they get their monthly pay they don't care what deviltry their employer is up to." Alma figured Mrs. Gentry was taking her time while she assessed the adult Alma. Perhaps the result was not expected. "But you know that, don't you?" Mrs. Gentry asked.

"Did you bring me here to discuss Appalachian sociology?"

"No, I did not." Her voice was sharp and crisp. "As I said, it is a shame about your brother . . . but you might as well write him off. There's no doubt he'll be convicted, so if you believe your being here is going to change things, do yourself a favor and leave before the trial starts. If you try to prevent a conviction, you'll only get yourself hurt."

"It's too kind of you to be concerned for my well-being," Alma said in a soft voice. Then she launched an equally sharp tone. "But my family is in need of a little more protection than the locals can provide, and I'm more than qualified to see that they get it."

Mrs. Gentry let out a curt laugh. "Why?" She pressed her lips to a napkin. "What has your family ever done for you?"

The remark stung. Alma hadn't expected it.

"They didn't even pay for your college education."

"I don't need you to tell me about my family."

"You've proved you're better than they are. You don't owe them anything."

"Perhaps I should point out a few of the more outstanding achievements of your own family."

"At least we're not carpetbaggers like the Littlefields. We put more into this community than we take out."

"But at what cost?" Alma fought to keep her voice calm. "Your view of giving to the community includes stepping on anyone who gets in your way—not much different from the Carnegies . . . or the Littlefields."

She took her time with a throaty chuckle. "I'm sure your education familiarized you with the concept of the end justifying the means. I have the means, you benefited in the end."

"Let's see," Alma said. "The last time I was in your house, it was just before dinner. Your husband was running for the state assembly." Alma reached out and deliberately pinched off a small piece of bread, trying to invade Charlotte Gentry's space. "So, little Narly is going to follow in his father's footsteps." Alma gestured with the bread as she spoke, then bit into it and chewed slowly. She could sense the old woman's spine stiffening. "And here I am . . . the same old blot on your family's honor."

"To be honest, I don't know what you are on my family's honor, but many years ago I didn't like taking chances." Mrs. Gentry took a gulp of milk directly from a pint carton. "Times have changed. My husband's dead. All I have is my son. Anything you could say about him, after all these years, could make you look awfully foolish."

"Mrs. Gentry." Alma inhaled deeply, figuring that the old woman must be clutching her chair to keep from losing her temper. "Narly is a spineless momma's boy, and if you can put him in the state assembly, I could care less. I don't have to live in this state. But my brother is not going to be paving the road for him. Do we understand each other?"

"Don't make the mistake of taking me on. I know how your mind works, little girl. You're not as far out of the hollows as you believe." She picked up the bread slice Alma had pinched and spread a knifeful of mayonnaise across it.

Alma slid off the stool. "You're right about one thing. Times have changed."

"Have they now?" Mrs. Gentry pointed the knife at a covered silver tray.

Alma's throat knotted. She wouldn't, she thought. Charlotte Gentry wouldn't be that stupid ... that insulting. Alma hesitated. Her hand burned like fire as she reached for the silver cover and lifted it.

Underneath she saw money in neat stacks. Years ago she remembered Mrs. Gentry throwing similar stacks of money in the air. Bills had fluttered through the air like butterflies. Charlotte Gentry's voice still rang in Alma's mind: *"You want my money, you get down on your knees and pick it up!"*

"Seventy-five thousand," Mrs. Gentry said, whispering the amount.

In disbelief, Alma watched Mrs. Gentry's bony hand caress the tops of the stacks. Her steely blue eyes aimed arrows at Alma, and the left side of her mouth curled into a cruel grin. Alma rested her hands on the cool silver handles of the tray and looked down. The rooster pin seemed to stare up at her and her father's face formed in her mind.

I tried to walk away that night, Daddy. I didn't want her stupid money. I kept hearing the last words you ever said to me: "I'm going to Detroit to earn some money. We're not going on welfare. We have more pride than that. You always have pride, Alma." I had pride, Daddy, that's why I tried to leave. If only Momma hadn't held me.

Alma lifted the tray and threw the money into the air. It fluttered this way and that, scattering to the far ends of the kitchen. She turned and marched out.

"Well, thank you for saving me the trouble!" Charlotte Gentry shouted.

Alma barely heard her as she stormed through the hallway. At the door she took an envelope from her coat pocket and slid it under a vase. In the envelope was a check for twenty-five thousand dollars. I did have pride, Daddy, she said silently. I didn't forget what you told me.

Once outside, she saw that the cab was gone. "Damn!" she exclaimed. A car door slammed and Alma looked down the street. Her mother. She'd parked a few inches short of blocking the Gentry driveway. The two of them looked at each other without speaking. Her mother stood beside her red and white Plymouth, her rabbit jacket and matching hat as white as the snow.

"Honey?" She clung uncertainly to the car door. "Alma, you can't leave like this. You'll make Mamaw sick." In the backseat Alma saw her suitcase crammed in with bags of groceries. "Now, come on, get in."

"She had the money in nice neat piles this time, Momma," Alma said. She stepped toward her mother. "On the same silver tray as last time. She didn't throw it up in the air. You remember when she did that, Momma. Well, I did it this time. Nobody was there to make me get down on my knees and pick it up this time. She didn't call me a fat pig like she did last time, but then I have lost about twenty pounds since I was seventeen. You remember holding my arms behind my back and letting her call me them names? You remember her flinging those bills in my face? It's amazing how twenty-five thousand can look like so much trash blowing in the breeze. It was seventy-five thousand this time. Think how that looked, Momma. It flew under the refrigerator, on the stove, in the cracks between the cabinets, underneath the glass kitchen table. Remember me on my hands and knees picking up every bill in that room? I'd have walked out of that room if it hadn't been for you . . .

standing there behind me, saying, 'Pick it up, Alma. This is your chance. It'll get you out of the mountains. Pick it up now!' I never knew how you scared Mrs. Gentry into doing what she did. But Charlotte Gentry's still scared, Momma. You must have made up a real good lie."

Her mother opened the car door, her lips pressed tight together, and her eyes so squinted that her mascara-covered lashes appeared interlaced. Before she got in, she turned to say, "You just don't understand anything, Alma Mae!" She slumped into the seat, ground the ignition, lit a cigarette, then put the car into gear and drove past Alma without looking at her.

Leave, Alma thought, like hell I will.

16

The clock in the lavender bedroom showed a little past one in the morning. Alma stared at the maze of papers before her: arrest reports, witness statements, warrants. She'd read them so often, the type began to blur. Everything was so pat. Every *i* dotted on the warrant, every *t* crossed on the arrest report. If she could find a mistake, then she'd have a potential mistrial. If she couldn't find a mistake, then she had to find a pattern to structure a defense. If she couldn't find a defense, then she'd have to force the prosecution into an error. Errors ... She couldn't afford to make one herself. Exhaustion made her muscles limp.

On the wall above her was a family portrait of her father, mother, Sue, and Vernon. Alma had had the chicken pox that week, and her mother hadn't allowed her to be in the picture. Feeling sorry for her, her father had taken Alma to Happy Jay's drive-in to order anything she wanted. "Hot dog with chili and onions and a chocolate shake," she said aloud as if it were yesterday. She stared at her father's movie-star smile and half-moon eyes. "I'll find it, Daddy," she said, turning back to the papers. "If there's something here, I'll find it."

The two witness statements matched almost to the word. Almost too perfect, Alma thought, wondering if they'd been coached. Jim Ralston, a housekeeping attendant, was delivering soiled sheets to the laundry room when he overheard the voices of two men arguing in the private suites of Bill Littlefield and his daughter, which were in the hotel basement. Ralston slowed to listen, then the elevator opened and Clark Winchell, the general manager, emerged. Ralston delivered the laundry and on his way back to the elevator heard Mr. Winchell ordering someone out of the hotel.

Then Littlefield's voice intervened, saying he would handle it and asking Winchell to leave. Winchell rode up in the elevator with Ralston. Hours later, when Winchell found Littlefield over his desk, unsure if he was alive, he and Ralston carried him to the business office, where the paramedics could get to him easier. Shortly thereafter Littlefield was pronounced dead by the coroner.

Clark Winchell's statement identified the man arguing with Littlefield as Vernon Bashears, but he admitted no knowledge of what they were arguing about. He believed that Bashears had been applying for a job. He's lying, Alma thought. Littlefield wouldn't be interviewing employees, especially in his private living quarters. She leaned back to ease her spine. What's one good reason why Vernon was there? she asked herself. Not employment. Johanna Littlefield, she answered.

Alma fought a yawn and jotted down notes. No paper error, she reminded herself. Manipulating Walter Gentry wouldn't be easy. She wasn't even sure she could stand being in the same room with him. "One is the law," she said. "Two is the opposition." She was somehow lost between two and five. The case was about more than Vernon now. She hated the Gentrys and she wanted them to suffer her hate. As much as she tried to force that desire out of herself, it sprouted like a weed and grew stronger every minute she stayed in town.

She rested her head on the desk and stared at the gold

rooster pin. Pressed it to her lips. One is the law. Two is the opposition. Three is the evidence. Four is the plea. . . . "Jordan, I wish you were here," she whispered before falling asleep.

17

"We have to force him into a mistake," Alma told Bob and Jefferson the next morning. "Walter Gentry wants to be in the state assembly, and he thinks this case will impress the governor enough so that he will be selected. What he doesn't know is that I can make this case his biggest nightmare."

"Setting up the prosecutor?" Bob looked questioningly at Alma.

"He'll back off.... The damage for him is bad publicity."

"That doesn't help us defend Vernon." Bob Krauss took his glasses off and cleaned them on his shirtsleeve. "Concentrate on Vernon's defense, Alma—not Walter Gentry's bid for political office."

"But they're related!"

"I understand all too well that there is a time to be aggressive, but this is not it!" Bob's voice vibrated through the room. "Let him show us his cards. If we wait him out, he will."

"But," Alma insisted, "they won't be expecting a frontal attack! If we shoot first, making the press aware of Gentry's hidden agenda, we can keep him squealing like a stuck pig."

"And after that, what?"

THE LAW OF REVENGE 121

Alma was silent. Bob had made his point. She didn't have a backup plan.

"Well . . . we'll . . . we'll do something!" she said after a moment. Jefferson and Bob stared at her as she drained the last bit of coffee from a paper cup. She looked out the window at the slush-covered street, hoping embarrassment wasn't showing on her face. Both men seemed confused by her decision to stay, and their defensiveness was annoying.

"I'm totally overwhelmed by all this legal maneuvering," Jefferson said with all the sarcasm of a standup comic. He opened the office door, jerking it so that the glass window rattled in its frame. "I'm going to the drugstore to get us some lukewarm coffee to clear our brains."

Alma sensed Jefferson's hostility was about more than her decision to stay and participate in the case. Bob was more subtle. He took the approach of a law professor making a fool out of a first-year student. And Alma felt like an L-one student in front of him. "Seems I'm ignoring the advice I gave to Vernon," she said. "To listen to you in all things."

"What is it that you're afraid I'm not seeing?" He slowly twirled a large paperclip between his fingers, waiting for her response.

Alma couldn't focus on what she wanted to say. If she spoke, she'd only babble and maybe say more than she wanted to. Bob sat firmly in his chair, not moving his gaze from her. "Do you trust him?" she asked, and pointed toward the door to indicate Jefferson.

Bob stared up at the door, where the backward words JEFFERSON BINGHAM, ATTORNEY-AT-LAW were visible through the thick plate of milky glass. "You mean because of Ellen?"

Alma's mouth dropped open without her realizing it.

"I guess that's the last time I'll assume I'm keeping secrets from you." She had never underestimated Bob Krauss's legal skills, and any doubts about his perceiving relationships had just been erased.

"Jefferson has much admiration for you," Bob said. "He told me he had a crush on you when you were tots." Alma suppressed a smile. "Don't forget that we might make use of his former relationship with Ellen Farmer. He tells me they parted on good terms."

"I don't trust the commonwealth attorney to do the same thing."

"Exactly. I think we should count on it."

"What do you have in mind?"

"How do you say it in the hollows.... Let's let the compost sit awhile."

Alma stared at him for several seconds before what he meant finally registered. "No, that's not how we say it, but you're close enough."

Jefferson opened the door and let it swing inward until it hit the wall. The paleness of his face suggested that something was wrong. He stepped in and held up the *Contrary Gazette.* A double-decker headline slashed across the top: ALLEGED KILLER RELEASED, BIG CITY LAWYER HIRED FOR BASHEARS, and in smaller script underneath it read: GENTRY VOWS JUSTICE FOR LITTLEFIELD.

"This is what you're not seeing, Bob!" Alma said. "The Gentrys will stop at nothing!" She grabbed the paper from Jefferson and huddled with Bob.

Jefferson picked up the phone, dialed, and asked for Willie George. Bob and Alma consumed the article. The more Alma absorbed the text, the angrier she became. "It reads like we're defending Charles Manson," she said. The article pointed out that Robert Krauss would take over Vernon's defense and likely use the same military tactics that had made him famous for springing his more suspect clients out of jail: a senator's wife who'd killed her lover; a South American drug lord captured in a DEA sting while vacationing in Miami; a rock star accused of bigamy.

"Obviously," Bob said, "someone at the paper is in bed with the commonwealth attorney." He continued reading as Alma hung over his shoulder.

"Willie George!" Jefferson said into the phone. "When did you start writing for the *National Enquirer*? Don't jerk me, Willie, I'm the one who rescued you from that 'inciting a riot' charge at Duke Lindsey's monthly chicken fights." While Willie talked, Jefferson listened. He tapped his fingers on the desk, his eyes focused on Alma.

Alma sat back, troubled. When Bob Krauss arrived in town the night before, he'd registered at his hotel under a pseudonym. No one except the family knew he'd been hired. Someone had leaked that information to the newspaper—and most likely to the commonwealth attorney's office. Now who would have told them? Jefferson, she thought. Jefferson told Ellen.

Jefferson spoke briskly into the phone and then, almost as an afterthought, punched the button for the speaker phone. "It's like this," Willie George said, "the word comes down from the old man. I write it like he tells me."

"Whatever happened to journalistic integrity?" Alma asked.

"Who is that?" Willie's voice rose in pitch. "Look, Bingham, anybody ever finds out I talked to you, my butt is in a sling."

"Trust me, Willie," Jefferson said. "Are there any more surprises in the works—big ones, not just innuendo?"

The sound of Willie punching computer keys mixed with the phone static. "They have to assign the story to either me or Joe Walsh. I don't know . . . this looks strange. Tomorrow's paper has the whole top front section blacked out. The only reason they'd do that is if they have something big to go in." A few seconds of silence. "Bastards . . . they must be letting Joe write it."

"If you hear what it is, will you call me?"

"Yeah, but then I don't owe you anymore." Willie hung up.

Alma, Bob, and Jefferson sat quietly in thought, looking in different directions. "It could be the governor's decision on the state assembly opening," Jefferson volunteered.

"Too soon," Bob said.

"Another personal attack on you?" Alma speculated.

"Possible." Bob rubbed his chin.

"They shouldn't have known about you. Someone had to have told them." She looked directly at Jefferson.

He lowered his eyes to the desk, swallowing so hard, his Adam's apple bobbed up and down. "Ellen asked me out to dinner last night. I didn't think it was a secret."

"It doesn't matter that it wasn't a secret! Can't you see how they make use of the information you give her?"

"How was I to know?" Jefferson could hardly look Alma in the eye.

"Damn it, Jefferson," she said. "That was stupid!" Bob raised his hand to shush her, but she couldn't control her temper. "You walk around here, rolling your eyes every time I speak, acting like I'm overreacting, and when the shit hits the fan, all you can say is 'How was I to know?' You should have known! Why else would Ellen Farmer ask you to dinner?"

Jefferson stood up. Anger flared in his eyes, but only a

slight tremble came out in his voice. "Thank you, Alma. Thanks a lot." He stalked out the door.

She turned to Bob. "Are you about to slap my hands?"

"No," he answered with more spirit than expected. "I think you taught him a good lesson."

Alma looked out the window at Jefferson crossing the street. "I wish I hadn't said that about Ellen," she said. His blond hair whipped around in the wind. She'd had a crush on him, too, for a while, until he'd used her pet frog in a sixth-grade biology experiment. Alma seemed to recall him using a similar excuse about not knowing it was a pet. For the few seconds that it lasted, the memory was warm.

The phone rang and Alma punched the speaker button. "Law office," she said.

"Jefferson . . ." a distressed Ellen Farmer said. "I have to talk to Jefferson."

"Not here," Alma answered, wanting to give her as little information as possible.

"You have to find him! Merl Bashears is over here banging on Mr. Gentry's door. He's locked himself in the office. She's screaming at him! If Jefferson doesn't do something fast, I'll have to call the police. I don't want any more trouble. Just find him!"

Alma slapped a hand to her forehead.

"Greta?" Ellen asked, then realizing that she was not speaking to Jefferson's secretary, she hung up.

"You better not come," Alma said to Bob. "Tomorrow's paper would only say you started it."

Bob nodded agreement. "Your mother I leave to you."

Alma stopped before she bolted down the stairs. She turned and looked at Bob, who was staring out the window, rubbing his hands together. He closed his eyes and leaned his head forward, almost in a bow. For the first time since he'd been there, it seemed to Alma that he was troubled. His fear infected her. They were a team out of control.

18

A truck honked at Alma as she dashed across the street. The splash of slush barely missed her as the vehicle skidded to a stop to avoid hitting her. She waved a hesitant thank-you to the driver, who screwed up his face and shook his head. Anger choked her throat as she came in sight of the courthouse. Her mother was determined to make some mighty stand, and all it was accomplishing was more trouble.

Aunt Joyce sat in her Buick in front of the courthouse, the motor running for warmth, a newspaper spread out across the steering wheel. Alma ran up, tapped on the window, and asked, "Do you know what Momma's doing?"

Aunt Joyce's face was calm and expressionless. "She's filling out some papers for Vernon, honey."

"No, she's not. She's storming the Bastille."

"Lord, lord," Aunt Joyce said, opening the car door. "Her car had a flat and she asked me to drive her here. Alma Mae, I had no notion what she was up to."

They hurried into the building through cold, rigid corridors toward the back wing. Workers in a series of front offices seemed calm. Secretaries and legal assistants worked as if nothing special was going on. "Maybe it's not as bad as I think," Alma called back to Aunt Joyce.

They walked swiftly toward the back offices, trying not to draw attention to themselves.

Alma opened the oak door to the commonwealth attorney's suite and saw a flurry of nearly hysterical assistants. As quickly as she could usher Aunt Joyce inside, Alma slammed the door behind her. "We should call the police!" one secretary was telling another.

"Ellen said not to."

"Don't call the police," Alma said in her best authoritative voice. "Where is Mrs. Bashears?"

They pointed toward an office with WALTER GENTRY across the door in gold lettering. Inside the office loud hammering was accompanied by her mother's voice: "You sorry scoundrel! You open that door and come out here and explain this to me."

"We believe he locked hisself in the closet," a secretary said, calmer than the half-dozen assistants huddled like a football team.

Alma stepped up to the door and rapped on it. "Mother, open this door now."

Her mother answered, "I ain't a-coming out till this rascal takes back every bit of this newspaper crap that his momma had printed in the paper."

Walter said, his muffled voice barely audible, "I had nothing to do with that article!"

More hammering. Alma thought her mother must be beating the closet door with a heavy object. "The hell you didn't!" her mother yelled. "Charlotte Gentry's been half-owner of that paper going on ten years! Don't you think you can lie to me, Narly Gentry! I see her car at old man Parker's house Monday mornings. You think I don't know that's editorial day!"

"We've got to call the police," said one secretary.

"I'll handle this," Alma said curtly. "It'll be over in a minute."

"This is just like a post office massacre," another secretary said, causing several assistants to gasp and shake their heads in distressed agreement.

"This is not a massacre!" Alma shouted.

"No, but I'll sure skin his hide when he comes out of that closet," her mother yelled, banging again.

"You're not doing us any good, Mother," Alma said. "Please."

"Oh! Such surly cowards out there that they have to call my little girl to come and calm me down! Well, screw you all! Especially you, Alma Mae!" The viciousness in her mother's voice cut through the wall like a buzzsaw.

Aunt Joyce patted Alma on the shoulder. "Let me try, honey." She stepped up to the door and tapped on it gently. "Merl," she said in a steady voice, "you open this door right now or I'm gonna have to break it down."

Alma covered her face with both hands. A headache pulsed in her temples. Frail, little Aunt Joyce speaking to the solid oak door was a pitiful sight. The police would burst in any minute. There'd be two Bashears with charges against them.

Instead the knob turned and the squeaking hinges whined as the door inched open. Alma and Aunt Joyce entered. Her mother stepped back and leaned against a large oak desk, staring at a closet door with several gashes in it from the golfing trophy she'd taken from a bookshelf. "Well," she said, looking over at Aunt Joyce, "I couldn't see you in jail for destruction of public property."

"Let's get out of here," Alma whispered, not wanting to be present when Walter emerged from the closet.

The secretaries and assistants gathered around the closet door. One told Walter it was okay to come out. Another secretary, obviously raised in the hollows, stood beside Alma's mother with a crooked smile on her face. "Merl Bashears," she said, "I thought when you painted your skin green to win that 'Martians are coming' radio contest that you'd done the craziest thing I'd ever seen a human being do—but this beats all."

Merl stared dejectedly at the floor. She handed Alma the newspaper. "Have you seen this?" She pointed to a paragraph where Walter had described Vernon as deranged and possibly psychopathic.

"These things prejudice a jury, Mother. I can make them work in our favor." Alma took hold of her mother's arm and steered her through the crowd. "You've got to start trusting me." Behind her, Alma sensed the presence of someone taller. Anxiety shot through her like the burn of swallowed whiskey.

"I need to speak with you," Walter Gentry whispered.

Alma looked over her shoulder. He was closer than she'd thought and her back muscles stiffened involuntarily.

"Anywhere you say," he whispered. "Please." He lowered his head so that the secretaries and her mother would not hear him. "It could be important to your brother."

Alma stared at him and did not answer, but her eyes acknowledged him. She faced forward, hating that her body had betrayed her. Quickly she pushed her mother out the door before Merl could turn around and engage Walter. Without looking back at him, Alma said, "St. Luke's in fifteen minutes." Every nerve in her body seemed on fire.

19

Alma caught up with her mother and Aunt Joyce. Every few steps Aunt Joyce admonished Merl, "I can't believe you used me this way."

"I'm sorry, Joyce."

"You just get it into your head that you've got all the answers and you don't."

"I know, Joyce."

"Mamaw and me thought all this out. We knowed what we was doing when we got Alma to come back. Every roll of the dice you've got to put your own personal thorn in the road."

"I feel real bad, Joyce."

"I got a good mind to take you out back of the shed and wallop you a good one."

"I've learned my lesson, Joyce!"

"If they'd've put you in jail, I'd've left you there for a spell."

Merl let out a little cry and turned toward Alma as if to plead for help. Alma held open the door for them and touched her mother's arm as she passed. For all its insanity, her act had been meant to help Vernon.

Outside, the sunshine was almost warm, melting the snow. Merl pushed a cigarette from a crushed pack of Marlboros and tried to light it, but her hands shook too much. "Everybody knows I have reasons for doing the things I do," she insisted.

Alma held the lighter as her mother inhaled. Her thoughts were less on her mother's actions than on Walter's request. Why does he want to see me? she wondered. "Take Momma home, Aunt Joyce," Alma said, and turned toward her mother. "Let's just consider it a lucky break that you're not wearing handcuffs."

"That piece of squirrel dung would never call the police on me!" Her mother blew out a long stream of smoke, then stared at Alma as if she'd spoken without meaning to.

"You're getting to be too much, Mother." Alma's frustration simmered. "This isn't a funny little game! This town is coming into the twentieth century just as the world goes into the twenty-first."

Merl jerked her head to one side, looking for all the world as if she just had to explain her point of view. "Quick told me about Jefferson. I've seen that you're right, Alma Mae. All this time I thought Jefferson was on our side. Well, Quick told me Jefferson has been screwing that Ellen Farmer girl. And I didn't even know it!" She shook her head as if in disbelief that such an act could take place without her knowing it. "I thought I knew where everybody in this town slept."

Alma almost felt sorry for her. If only in her mind, her mother did believe that she might help Vernon by scaring Walter Gentry. It couldn't happen again and Alma had to see to it that her mother pulled in line with a defense strategy even if she didn't realize her part. She had to come down heavy. "Playing the cute little girl," Alma said, "and demanding your way isn't going to get you what you want."

"I only wanted to help Vernon."

"Then go home and keep your mouth shut!"

"Alma Mae," Aunt Joyce said in a warning tone, as if to stop them before both said things they could not take back.

"And pray, Mother, that this little episode doesn't end up as tomorrow's headlines, because if Charlotte Gentry does own the newspaper, she's probably got a lot she'd like to print about you."

Her mother's nose turned a cherry red and her eyes blurred with tears. "Vernon could never keep a secret from me," she squeaked. She sniffed, wiping an eye.

Secret, Alma thought. What was her mother talking about? Vernon would never have told! "Mother, not in front of Aunt Joyce."

"I did it for you, baby." Merl inhaled deeply on the cigarette, then threw it down. "Can't you see I did it for you? I knew you was the smartest kid I had. I couldn't let you stay here in this shit town. . . ." Her chest heaved. "I couldn't let you end up in the hollows. I could see you headed down that road."

"This newspaper article isn't that bad," Alma said, trying to change the subject. "It'll probably win us a change of venue." Tears began to drip slowly down her mother's cheeks. "Momma!" she said. She wished for silence—for distance—wished even for her mother's anger.

"I didn't want you to end up like me!"

Alma felt as soggy as a melting snowman on the lawn of the courthouse yard. She stared at Aunt Joyce, whose face registered a blend of confusion and sympathy. Alma prayed her mother would not reach out to touch her. A gnawing emotion was already teetering on the edge. If her mother touched her, Alma wasn't sure she could control herself any more than a melting snowman could avoid disintegration.

"I'd've done anything to get you that money. I'd do anything to get Vernon out of this mess."

"Let's just concentrate on doing what works." Alma reached into her mother's jacket, pulled out another cigarette, and placed it between Merl's fingers. "Aunt Joyce will drive you home. You just relax and get ahold of yourself. A trial takes a long time, Momma. A year sometimes. When Bob Krauss gets finished with this case, Littlefield will be the devil and Walter Gentry a hired gun. Okay?" Alma heard her voice quivering. "Take her home, Aunt Joyce."

Merl got into the Buick. She blew her nose, then opened the glove compartment and pulled out a powder compact and blue Maybelline eyeshadow. Through the closed window she looked up at Alma, her mascara running, her lipstick smeared, and mouthed, "I'm sorry."

"It's okay, Momma."

Over the hood of the car Aunt Joyce regarded Alma curiously but did not push to ask about what might better be left secret. "I'll take care of her," she said, as if anticipating a request from Alma. She nodded to Alma, then got into the car.

Alma turned away while they drove off. She shook off the infectious quiver of her mother's emotions and looked down at the newspaper, which was folded so that the name Gentry appeared in large block letters. What are they trying to do to my family? she thought. Alma stuffed the newspaper in an overfilled trash can and headed directly to St. Luke's Church.

20

St. Luke's Church. A warm breeze blew from a floor vent, and Alma stood over it to thaw her cold legs. Her chest tingled with nervousness as she waited in a small alcove. Mahogany-colored wood made the church look inviting. She hid in the shadows.

She wanted to see Walter before he saw her. Soft soprano voices of the practicing choir haunted the rafters. It was a medium-size church with a podium anchored by statues of the Madonna and child on one side and an adult, resurrected Jesus, complete with nail-scarred hands and feet, on the other.

Walnut pews with kneeling pads were walled in by six-foot-high stained glass windows depicting scenes from Jesus' life: as a child teaching in the temple, walking on water, the Sermon on the Mount, the Garden of Gethsemane, the Last Supper, the Crucifixion. All in order, except for a window showing Jesus' forty days and nights in the desert. It formed the back wall of the recessed alcove, which was draped by a curtain, almost hidden. From a rocky cliff, Jesus stared out on a brown desert and a blanket of blue sky filled with stars. One rock was drawn as a devil; sharp horns on the forehead, a mouthful of spiked teeth, a flared piglike nose. Alma was struck by how the eyebrows curved like an *s* above the slitted eyes, causing the expression to be more one of suffering and worry than of evil.

The front door tapped in its frame and a heavy-coated Walter Gentry stepped forward. His eyes looked like the devil's, slanted and equivocal. Alma stayed in the shadows and watched him enter the seating area. He removed his hat and smoothed down the sides of his head, bringing his hand forward to stroke his beard. Two fingers rested on his full lips as he looked up into the sanctuary of the church. Alma fought an urge to run out the door. He looked around, seeming satisfied that she had not yet arrived, and approached the altar rail. As he lit a candle, Alma moved behind him.

"For anyone in particular?" she asked.

A slight jerk of his shoulders suggested that he was startled, but he did not turn toward her. "For you," he said.

"I'm not Catholic." She stepped up beside him. "And neither are you." Leaning forward, she blew out the match. "So it probably won't work."

Raising one finger, he said, "But we are both attorneys."

"Boalt Hall, class of '87."

His eyebrows arched as if impressed. "University of Virginia." He dug his hands deeply into the pockets of his coat. "I'm very glad to see you've done so well. I've thought of you . . . often."

The pale quality of his voice made her distrustful. He talks like a New Age therapist, she thought.

"Is your mother okay?" A trace of angst colored his voice.

"Calmer," Alma answered, her every sense on guard. "It was generous of you not to call the police."

He hesitated, then said in a low voice, "There are some

circumstances that do not require interference from the police."

Alma couldn't figure him. He was accommodating to the point of humbleness. "You said you wanted to talk about Vernon."

"And you."

His words produced a spasm in her stomach. "The only reason I'm here is to ensure that my brother is treated fairly—"

"I need to start with you," he interrupted, fidgeting with the tail of his tie. "I never treated you fairly."

Alma sat in a pew and Walter sat in the one behind her. Maybe she'd made a mistake in meeting him. What could he do but bring those memories back to life?

"You chose a church," he said, "a place of safety, penance . . . perhaps even forgiveness." When she did not respond, he leaned forward on the knee railing. "Alma, you know, don't you, that I would never have hurt you?"

She turned toward him. "I know you're not a rapist."

The word made him cringe, and he pushed his coat off his shoulders, resting his elbows on the back of her pew and pressing his mouth into his prayer-folded hands. "I have daughters. I think of what happened to you every day of my life! I look into their sweet, little faces and I . . ." He licked his lips and sucked in a breath through his teeth.

Daughters, she thought. He has a life—a normal life—the kind of life I should have had and except for that day I might have had. Every decision, every choice, every perception was colored by her teenage reality. He must have sailed through so easily, she thought, putting his past behind him while I paid the price.

The part of her that wanted to make Walter pay for his role in her rape played tug-of-war with her curiosity.

What would those boys' joke have accomplished if it hadn't ended as it did? If they'd exposed their genitals and had a laugh, she still would have been humiliated. What did that kind of silliness do for them? Make them feel superior? Make them feel like men? *Why didn't he help me that day? He could have stopped it. He could have kept it from happening.*

"The way you look at me," he said. "You consider me just as guilty."

"You're applying that standard to Vernon. Why are you surprised that I apply it to you?"

"I wish you could understand about that day!"

Alma twisted forward so that she didn't have to look at him. "Always one standard for the hollow folk and one standard for the downtown citizens."

Walter exhaled a quivering breath as if speaking, or perhaps remembering, exhausted him. "That week my father announced to the press that he'd be running for the state assembly. My mother, of course, had bigger plans for him. If he hadn't died, I have no doubt that she would have made him governor." Walter was quiet for a few seconds, either weighing his words or choosing them carefully. "Mother and I argued that morning. No, I don't think you could call it that. No one argued with Mother. She issued the order and my father and I obeyed. Only that morning I didn't obey."

"Are you sure you want to tell me this?" As much as his explanation of that day gnawed at Alma, she was unsure whether she could endure hearing him defend himself. Now she knew how a victim felt in the courtroom when confronting an attacker. She had never wanted to see this man again and yet she couldn't keep from hanging on his every word.

"Mother could make me feel so little." Walter's voice cracked, and he cleared his throat and blew his nose before continuing. "It was the first time I'd ever stood up to her. She came into my room and told me I couldn't go to the Fourth of July picnic with Debra Halford. Her father had given money to my father's opponent. My car privileges were revoked until I came around to Mother's way of thinking. I ripped up one of Father's campaign posters in front of her. She jerked me up by my shirt collar and slapped me across the face."

Alma closed her eyes. The church seemed to be moving and the stained glass windows spun in front of her. She could see the day that had destroyed her life replaying before her eyes. "That's all so mundane . . . so ordinary."

"I stormed out of the house. I didn't care if I ever returned. Alma, I swear, before that day I never had more than a ten-word conversation with Rudy Delmar and Earl Roscoe!" He sighed heavily. "I was just a boy—an immature one at that."

"And I was just a girl."

"My mother made up for my mistake as best she could."

"You can say that to me?"

"I'm not excusing myself."

"Your mother makes my mother look like Mother Teresa." Alma stood up and looked down at him.

"Now wait a minute!" He shot up, seeming to dislike her in a position above him. "You weren't the one who spent the entire morning locked in a six-by-three-foot closet!"

"Hardly comparable!" They faced each other like boxing opponents.

He inhaled a deep breath. "Granted. Or should I say stipulated."

Alma held out her arms, palms up, in a compromising gesture. "We both have colorful mothers."

Walter looked down at the marble floor, touching one foot to the kneeling railing and pushing it up. "I am sorry for what happened to you." His voice quivered and had a softness, as if he were speaking to a hurt child. "I apologize for my part in it." He stared into her eyes, and the soft notes of "Ave Maria" floated around them. "I wish I could make it up to you."

Alma rubbed a hand back and forth on the smooth, glossy pew. She had come there hoping to prove to herself that her hate was justified. The years of humiliation kept demanding a rationalization. A price for her pain. She intended it to be an enormous cost for Walter Gentry. "It seems that the position you were in all those years ago and the position Vernon is in now are not very different. Vernon is not a murderer—not the way you're making him out to be. I want a reduced charge of involuntary manslaughter with a recommendation of probation."

"Ah, so now we are lawyers."

"I also want the newspaper articles to stop."

"I don't control the press."

"Your mother does."

"A regrettable investment."

"Are you here to spar or make peace? If it's to spar, I'll see you in court and I will win."

"I've offered second degree."

"Manslaughter."

"Voluntary."

"Involuntary."

"You're very confident."

"Let's not even talk about the dirt I have on Littlefield. There's also Johanna Littlefield's testimony."

Walter anchored all his weight on one leg. His eyes were flashing with the energy of an attorney arguing a point he knew well. "You don't have Johanna Littlefield. You may think you do, but you don't."

Alma knew enough to be quiet and let him win the point. He'd told her what she wanted to know.

"However," he said, slowing his speech and nodding his head, "I am here to make peace." He stepped out of the pew and leaned against a confession booth. "I will speak to Mother about the newspaper articles." He hesitated, rubbed a hand over his mouth and nose. "All right. I'll see what I can do about the charge. It's tricky. I can't seem wishy-washy about it." He bowed his head to her and turned toward the door. "I'll do something."

Alma caught the sleeve of his coat, and her touch seemed to surprise him, for he smiled, and Alma realized it was his almost appreciative smile that had begun her girlhood crush on him. "I don't know if I can ever forgive you, but if you do this for my brother, I'll call us even."

Walter's eyes filled with a tinge of glossiness. He pushed open the church door and left.

Alma inhaled deeply. Maybe it's over, she thought. Maybe it was *all* over. She'd won at least one small victory for her brother—almost as if she were paying him back for having saved her all those years ago. And she was even with Walter—she might even come to pity him someday. Anyone with Charlotte Gentry for a mother deserved pity.

The door of the confessional creaked and a priest stepped out. Oh, my God, Alma said to herself, he's πheard everything. The troubled expression in his eyes turned to thoughtful consideration as he folded his hands, nodded to acknowledge her, then solemnly walked in the opposite direction.

Alma stared for several seconds at the stained-glass devil. Oddly, though she'd never attended a Catholic

Mass in her life, much less been inside a confessional, she felt purged. Someone else knew, someone other than people who either blamed her, hated her, or pitied her. Someone else knew, and what he knew were simple facts—facts that no longer applied, historical facts.

Outside, she turned in a circle to look at the range of mountains surrounding the town. They seemed a little friendlier. She walked to the main street and bought a cup of hot chocolate at Lolly's drugstore. The stores were putting spring merchandise in their windows. The snow had melted throughout the town. Tomorrow was the first day of March. The weather would start to turn warm. For a moment the town began to feel like it had during her early childhood: comfortable and known. She crossed the street in front of the long, winding driveway up to the Littlefield Hotel.

The Johanna Littlefield tie-in nagged at her. Alma had set Walter up with the question about Johanna and forced him to reveal at least part of his strategy. If Johanna testified for the prosecution, they would surely argue that Vernon was a spurned lover. It was a good tactic and hard to argue against, especially considering all the gifts Johanna had showered on Vernon. Alma wished he hadn't taken them.

Maybe everything would proceed smoothly. She wanted to believe it. If something went wrong, even with a manslaughter charge, Johanna was still a wild card. But Vernon seemed to be protective of her—like a pet dog that bites you, Alma thought. Conspiracy charges flew through her mind. No doubt they'd popped into Walter's as well. It was not something Alma could afford to be wrong about. Whether Vernon wanted to or not, he was going to have to come clean with her.

21

"Do you want me to go in with you?" Jefferson asked Alma as they drove up in front of Mamaw's house. "Vernon might tell me more."

"He won't tell you or me anything." Alma scooted to the edge of the seat. "What I get out of him will be in what he doesn't say or what I trick out of him."

"Sibling subterfuge." Jefferson shook his head as if he knew it well.

Considering that he had five brothers and sisters, he probably did, Alma thought. He'd tied his hair back into a ponytail. The style showed off the attractive lantern shape of his jaw. She opened the car door and said, "Did I tell you, you look nice today?" Without waiting for an answer she added, "I'm going to want to talk to you after this."

"Sure," he said, eagerness edging into his voice.

"About Ellen." She looked away as she spoke. "Look, I cover all my bases—just in case Walter is pulling a fast one."

"Okay." Jefferson's voice was hesitant and uncertain.

"You and Ellen are an element I don't like." She glanced over, but because of his hurt expression—eyes squinted, lips parted and slightly pouted—she could not sustain eye contact. "It could be that all this is for nothing, but, unlike Bob, I'm not willing to take that risk. Do you understand what I'm saying?"

"I'm not a fool, Alma." Jefferson's hands, firmly fastened to the top of the steering wheel, twisted against the plastic. "I know you think I am, but I'm not."

She reached over and touched his arm. The muscle flexed under her touch. "Well, okay, we'll talk later." She closed the car door, feeling like she'd kicked a puppy.

As she approached the house, she saw through the window that her mother, Mamaw, Aunt Joyce, and Sue were gathered in a circle. "God's about to punish me for being mean to Jefferson," she muttered under her breath.

She opened the front door and the women looked up at her.

Sue grimaced as if she'd eaten something sour. "Well, well, the cavalry's come home from the long, hard work of saving the day."

They were quilting. A basket of small squares of multi-colored material sat in the middle of the table. Each woman held a needle and sewed the squares into what looked to be the shape of a star. "It's going to be beautiful," Alma said.

"Pull up a chair." Alma knew Sue's annoyance probably stemmed from her required presence there. Sue hated to sew. In times of stress Mamaw quilted. And whenever she needed to keep her womenfolk out of trouble, she made them quilt, too. Most likely, Alma thought, she and Aunt Joyce decided the best way to control Merl was to begin a quilt. By the time they finished it, whatever anxiety was eating at her would be lost in a pattern of thread and cross-stitching.

"I have to talk to Vernon," Alma said.

"Have I ruined everything?" her mother asked nervously as she stuck her needle into a red patch of material. "I just don't know what came over me."

Alma recognized that her mother's humbleness was sincere and figured Mamaw and Aunt Joyce had probably spent the afternoon pulling Merl in line. Alma decided to reinforce their efforts. "I won't argue with you there, Mother."

Sue let a pair of scissors drop to the floor with a thud and stared hard at Alma. "Oh, come on, Alma, if Momma gets arrested, surely you can argue one of those time-of-the-month defenses."

"Vernon's out in the barn with Albert," Aunt Joyce said, smart enough to know when to head off a sharp exchange.

"I need to talk with him alone," Alma said.

"Well, it ain't like Albert's gonna call the *New York Times*." Her mother squirmed in her seat, some of her usual sarcasm returning.

"I don't think we'll have to worry about any more of those articles." Alma draped her arm around the back of Mamaw's wheelchair. "Sometimes, things aren't as bad as they seem." She stared at her mother as she spoke, hoping to relieve some anxiety she must still be feeling after her episode with Walter. "Things have a way of working out."

"I hope . . ." Merl sniffed and her voice cracked. "I hope you're right, honey." Her mother reached for another patch of material and spread it on her knee before lining it up to the patch she'd just sewn. "It'd just kill me if something I did ended up hurting one of my kids."

"Sew, Merl," Mamaw said, not looking up as she bit a thread in two and tied a knot.

Alma circled them, then went out the back door and toward the barn. She decided to approach Vernon like a sympathetic friend. He'd try to play the jester as he did in times of trouble. She'd ease her way through that and get the information she needed, even if it meant pulling it out of him in his reactions. Whatever you do, Alma, she told herself, don't let this deteriorate into a fight.

The barn had not been functional for many years. Tattered chicken coops hung onto one side, housing only a couple of old hens. The dog lot, formed from a wooden fence attached to one wall, wobbled in the strong wind. Chicken wire led to a hole knocked into the base of the barn so that the dogs could crawl in and sleep in the shade in summer and escape the snow in winter.

Alma's thoughts flashed back to when the lot brimmed with a dozen long-legged bird dogs and scrappy beagles. Her father would carry the heavy slop bucket, her hand on top of his, letting her think she was doing all the work. As they tilted the bucket, the food emptied into the trough, always spilling on her hands. The dogs would lick them clean, even between her fingers. She'd look up at her father, who seemed taller than the trees, and he'd smile and say, "Good job, Alma Mae."

A good job—that's what she'd do this time, too. Remembering her father filled her with sadness as she approached the barn. She listened for conversation or movement from Vernon and Albert, whoever he was. Some friend she didn't know. There was only silence and the bland scrape of oak branches against the roof.

Opening the door, she expected to see two people. But Vernon sat alone in the shadows of the barn, staring down at his sleeping dogs.

22

"Good, you're alone," Alma said. She stepped inside the barn. The rueful warmth of an older sister who felt sorry for her little brother tingled in her chest. She reminded herself that for Vernon's good she'd have to interview him with the finesse of an attorney and the slyness of a sister.

Vernon smiled the quick, one-sided smile of a man who knew he was in trouble. "They started quilting, so I skedaddled out here."

"You always did have a good sense of when to leave the scene—"

"—of the crime?"

"I wasn't going to say that." She sat beside him. The ground was cold through her pants. One beagle raised its head, looked at them, then lowered it again, closing its eyes like a trusting child. "Your dogs are like children."

"I fed 'em and run 'em 'bout an hour ago, so they're pretty tuckered out. I can't let 'em out on their own no more."

"We're not that close to the road."

"I know." Vernon looked up at the rafters, where two owls perched on a cross beam.

"Is something going on that I should know about?" Alma waited until it seemed clear that he didn't want to respond. That probably meant something *was* going on.

"Let me reword it. Is something going on that I don't know about?"

"Listen." Vernon slowly snapped a twig into small pieces. "Try to answer the phone if it rings in Mamaw's house and I'm not there."

"If your girlfriends upset Mamaw, that's an easy enough problem for you to solve."

"You're a real comedian, Alma." He stood up and gently pounded his hand on the railing of an empty cow stall. "I wired an extension into my trailer. Every night Aunt Joyce and Uncle George make sure Mamaw's phone is unplugged. They're the only ones who know."

Alma stood up. "You'd better start from the beginning."

He dug his hands into his jeans pockets. "There've been phone calls—threats."

Her mind bounced between suspects, but she thought that in all likelihood the calls were from cranks.

"They said they'd gut the dogs, kill me; said they'd wipe out the whole family."

"It's crackpots, Vernon. You get them in every case, even in the city. But you're right about protecting Mamaw. I'll talk to Bob tonight. We'll put a trace on the line and a tape recorder in your trailer. If we find out who's doing it, we'll get a restraining order and pursue civil action."

"Damn it, Alma, this is more than just a law case. I should just plead guilty and have it over with."

"Why would you even think of doing that? I've as much as gotten Gentry to agree to involuntary manslaughter! Even if you're found guilty, I'll have you out on an appeal bond for at least a year." Alma circled him so that she could see his face. His nose was red and his eyes flashed like strikes of lightning. "We're further ahead in this game than you think."

"That's the difference, Alma! You act like it's a game. I caused a man to die." Vernon inhaled deeply and blew out his breath as if to expel a poison from his system. "It's not like you to walk away from something like that."

"I'm glad you're finally questioning yourself about why this happened. Question a little deeper, Vernon." She stepped up close to him. "If you do, will you find that somebody pushed you into that fight?"

"Bill Littlefield pushed me into that fight."

"So he's a slime. You've known plenty of slimes. Why did this one piss you off so much?"

"Ohhhh, Alma." Vernon punched the air and paced in a circle. "Bill Littlefield was slime like this town had never seen before. He let you know right off he thought he was better than everybody else. He didn't trust a soul, thought any hillbilly could be had for a dollar, and if he knew he could hurt you, he'd do it just to pleasure his eyes."

"Is that why he objected to you dating his daughter?"

"That had nothing to do with it. Johanna and I had stopped seeing each other. I hadn't spoken to her in over a year."

"Did she want it to end?"

"Leave Johanna out of this." Vernon rubbed both hands across his face, then held them there and blew through his fingers.

"Why would you apply for a job there?"

"Why wouldn't I take a job there? It's a free country. It was good pay. Sure beats the hell out of peddling videos."

Alma rubbed her chilled hands together and blew into them. He wasn't about to give her anything. She could sense something there, just beneath the surface. She'd have to push him in a different way—the way she'd push a hostile witness, empathize. "It's understandable to want to better yourself."

"Especially at my age?" His sideways glance seemed edged with annoyance.

"I can understand how she might end up saying or doing something to provoke a fight."

"Fish ain't bitin', Alma Mae."

She flared at the realization that her brother had seen through her ruse. "Okay, did she ask you to kill her father?"

"Quit it, Alma!"

"If she did, then she incurs a degree of guilt. Maybe more than a few degrees."

"Forever Alma—always looking for an angle."

"You tell me this, Vernon. I can use this to help you. Even if she only unwittingly instigated the fight."

"I've already said what happened. Bill Littlefield didn't like how I signed my employment application: Vernon 'Suck My Dick' Bashears. We argued, and I hit him. He hit me back, and I hit him again. That's it! Just two overgrown boys in a pissing contest! I'm sick to death of remembering it!"

Alma wanted to grab him by the collar and shake him. "No mention of a gum wrapper in your story. Why is that?"

"I guess it wasn't my flavor."

"Do I have to go to the hotel and subpoena the janitors to get information on the flavor of the gum?"

"Stay away from those people, Alma. Don't you be going anywhere near them!"

"Why? If you don't tell me, I'll get it out of Johanna on the witness stand."

"You leave her alone!" Vernon shook his finger at Alma. "That poor girl's been through enough, and I ain't gonna have you badgering her the way you do everybody around here!"

"Is that what you think I'm doing?" She kicked the side of the barn, sending a spray of dust and wood slivers into the air. A gray creature fell in front of her and squeaked, opening its mouth to bare sharp white teeth. Alma screamed and jumped as it scrambled past her feet.

"Jesus, Alma Mae!" Vernon squatted down and the furry creature jumped into his arms. "You just about scared the piss out of Albert." As he stood, the beady-eyed possum twisted its head around to look at her.

"Don't dogs kill those things?" was all she could manage.

"This possum was raised with them dogs." He stroked Albert's back and began to laugh at her. "We'll put a sock on her head and call her foolish," he said to Albert, then reached out and fanned the top of Alma's head, mussing her hair.

"Stop it!" She slapped at Vernon's hand, but he was taller and merely lifted his arm to avoid her. "You know, there are rat traps Albert's size," she said. Albert bared his sharp, pointed teeth and hissed a throaty growl.

Vernon tousled her hair again with the spite that can come only from a brother-sister exchange. "Now I know why you became a lawyer—to scare and intimidate the poor and the helpless." Vernon laughed louder. "I'm beginning to think maybe you need to go get your teeth filed."

"We'll talk later." Alma anchored her shoulder against the barn door and tripped through the pack of dogs that had been awakened by all the excitement.

"Albert's got a good vet he'd be happy to recommend!" he called after her. His laughter followed her all the way to the house.

Alma stormed up the path. She couldn't believe that

he'd unhinged her this way. She marched through the kitchen, her entry into the living room as gusty as a March wind. "Vernon thinks the world is his playground," she said. She circled the sewing women, their stitching out of sync with her tirade. "Always has to have the last word. What's wrong with him?"

"I don't know, honey," her mother replied. "Let me finish this side section and I'll think on it." She stared intently at the square of patchwork material and twisted it sideways to sew it at a different angle. Quilting obviously accomplished its purpose, Alma thought. They were in a world all their own.

"It's the way of brothers and sisters," Mamaw said philosophically.

Alma could feel the quiet of their circle and her intrusion on it. "I have to borrow somebody's car." She waited. No one responded. "Johanna Littlefield has just won the honor of being my first interview in this case's discovery."

"What did she say?" her mother asked out of the side of her mouth.

"Legal talk," Aunt Joyce whispered back. Merl nodded as if she now understood and kept sewing without missing a stitch.

"Blue Buick," Sue said in a monotone. "Keys are in the ignition." She stared at her stitching without looking up at Alma.

"Fine. Thank you. Enjoy your afternoon, ladies."

"Alma Mae," Mamaw called after her. "Wouldn't hurt for you to sit a spell and do some quilting."

23

The Littlefield Hotel and Spa clung to the side of the mountain like a medieval castle. Part stone and part red brick, it maintained its English origins with towers built at each corner. The entrance was a pioneer fortress of hewed logs and mud plaster. Each parking lot had its own name: Daniel Boone, Cherokee Way, Jack's Sack.

The spa was built in the 1930s, attracting the most prominent people in the United States and Europe. They soaked their rich bodies in the medicinal, icy cave water that fed the spa's baths. It had opened and closed a dozen times since the 1930s and had been in a state of decay since the early 1980s. Bill Littlefield had bought it and a decade later modernized the baths to heated and bubbling Jacuzzi-style comfort.

Alma rolled down the window and waved the valet away. "I have an appointment with Miss Littlefield," she lied. "She said I could park here." Vernon might not give me any direct information, she thought, getting angrier when she remembered their exchange, but his defensiveness about Johanna Littlefield clearly suggested that there was more going on than a gum wrapper.

"Yes, ma'am." The valet pointed her into a VIP parking space.

Alma felt the least bit guilty, not so much for lying to the valet but that he was so trusting. It never occurred to the boy that she would lie. He'd probably get into trouble for it. Manners and trusting natures were qualities of mountain people that sociologists too often left out of their descriptions, Alma thought as she got out of the car. It was those same qualities that allowed a man like Bill Littlefield to take advantage of them. Alma wished she'd had the opportunity to meet the slimeball. "Well, your daughter is going to have the privilege of meeting me," she muttered under her breath. "And if she's anything like you, she's going to know the meaning of a worthy opponent when I'm through with her."

Inside the lobby the air was humid and fragrant with the scent of steaming water. A caravan of tourists were trying to organize a hike to the top of the mountain. The registration desk hummed with check-ins and patrons asking questions about the effectiveness of the waters.

To the left behind floor-to-ceiling windows were the cavelike baths. A jungle sprang up around them, a variety of ferns surrounding Jacuzzi pools of various sizes. The water bubbled in several baths as people switched between the cold- and hot-water tubs. The setup was similar to the original baths Alma had seen in pictures, but the restoration had a more cosmopolitan flair. A cocktail bar, built on the Tennessee side of the hotel, was painted orange. The state line ran directly through the center of the spa and serving alcohol was legal only in Tennessee. Where the blue paint began marked Kentucky and no one was allowed to take an alcoholic beverage into blue areas.

Alma found a house phone and picked up the receiver. "Johanna Littlefield's room, please."

The phone rang. "Yes?" a woman said.

"Miss Littlefield?" Alma tried to lower her voice and muffle it as much as possible.

"No, who's calling?"

"Alma Bashears." Silence. Alma thought she might have been disconnected, but there was the noise of the phone being passed to someone.

"Vernon?" a woman's soft voice asked. "You're supposed to use the code name!"

"Miss Littlefield," Alma said quickly, "I'm Alma Bashears, Vernon's sister. I must speak with you." A click. The dial tone. Damn it! Now how was she going to find the little diva in this large resort? Alma remembered Lucy Brenner—black nail polish and pierced tongue. Just what she needed, another spoiled, rich girl.

She sat at the bar and waved to the bartender, a pumped-up boy who looked to be a few years out of high school. "A champagne cocktail," she said. She signed her credit-card receipt and tipped him five dollars cash.

"Are you sure?" he asked, looking down at the tip as if it were a lost treasure.

"I'm sure." She smiled at him and curled a strand of hair around her finger. "I'm waiting for a friend and I'm terribly bored."

"You're not from around here?" he asked, setting a tub full of glasses underneath the counter.

"San Francisco," she said.

"No kiddin'! Wow! Why'd you come here?" He smiled a goofy grin, showing straight white teeth. "Dumb of me to ask. I keep forgetting how famous this spa is." He held out his hand. "Breckinridge Cane."

She smiled. "That's a movie-star name if I've ever heard one."

"Friends call me Breck. Yeah, I've often thought of going into the movies."

"Alma," she said. "I'm visiting a friend." She leaned closer to the bar to keep an older man, who stood at the end of the bar tallying receipts, from overhearing. "Johanna Littlefield." She cupped a hand on the side of her mouth. "I figured she might need somebody to keep her company about now." Alma looked at her watch and huffed an impatient breath. "How do you think she's been holding up?"

He looked at the floor, then back at Alma. "Fine, I guess."

"Sure wish I could figure a way to help her."

"Yeah," he said, setting out a dish of cashews for her. "A lot of people wish they could help her."

"Have you ever tried?"

Breck squirmed uncomfortably. "I'd be glad to tell her you're waiting," he volunteered. "The entertainment elevator drops right down to their suites." He pointed to a boxlike service elevator behind him. "I can send her a note down in it."

"No need. I think I'll just walk there. Now . . . I get so turned around. Which way is it?"

As he was explaining the directions, the gentleman at the end of the bar quieted Breck with a wave of his hand. "Are you a reporter?" the gray-haired man asked her.

"Do I look like one?" Alma asked, sporting her most incredulous look.

He stared at her skeptically. "As a matter of fact . . ."

"Not to worry." Alma smiled. "I assure you I'm not a reporter." She slid a twenty-dollar bill across the bar and turned to leave before they could figure out what to do about her.

Alma followed the bartender's directions. The hallways twisted and zigzagged until she thought she was lost. Pale orange walls with rust-colored carpeting led to blue-carpeted corridors with blue walls. Alma knew she'd stepped from Tennessee to Kentucky. Signs on the wall emphasized it in case there was any doubt: NO ALCOHOLIC BEVERAGES IN THE BLUE AREAS. The interior decorator must have been driven nuts, she thought.

She turned a corner and stepped into a sea of orange. I'm lost, she realized, trying to figure out where she was in relation to the bar. The walls were lined with photographs of prominent Tennessee Volunteers, the University of Tennessee football team. A few feet down she entered a blue area again and the walls were plastered with photographs of University of Kentucky basketball players, the Wildcats. The color scheme followed the state line exactly.

She saw a hand-carved sign that read CUMBERLAND GAP SUITE. She wasn't sure she'd come far enough. She thought she was on the opposite side of the building, yet she couldn't have walked that distance. Hesitating, she turned the doorknob, found it open, and stepped in. Offices, drenched in blue, a reception desk, and a wall of phone sets staffed with secretaries. A well-dressed man looked as if he was waiting for her. He unfolded his arms from across his chest, showing an Yves St. Laurent monogram on his red silk tie. The smooth line of his black blazer was of equal quality.

"Our bar manager informed me there was a stranger loitering about," he said. "No doubt that is you." He was about forty, portly, dark hair, a slight olive coloring to his skin. "I was about to come and find you." He pulled out a chair from a nearby desk. "Have a seat," he offered. "The police are on their way. I'm sure they'll have many questions before they take you to the same jail where your brother is quite at home!"

24

"But I didn't come to see you," Alma said. This man didn't have the accent of a mountain-raised person. He deliberately slowed his speech as if he wanted to be certain she did not miss a word.

"Miss Littlefield does not wish to speak with anyone right now."

"You don't mind if I hear that from her, do you?"

"As a matter of fact, I do. This way, please." He indicated the door behind Alma.

She didn't move toward it. Instead she stepped forward, putting him in the position of backing away. "It's very important that I speak with her."

Several secretaries and telephone operators stared down at their desks but were obviously straining to listen. Alma surveyed the room quickly. She recognized the business office from police photographs. This was where they'd brought Littlefield for first aid. Off to the side was a door that looked as if it led into another office. PRESIDENT was carved into the wood. If Johanna is here, Alma thought, that's most likely where she is. She aimed herself in that direction and asked in passing, "I don't believe I caught your name?"

"Clark Winchell," the man said. "I'm the general manager."

"I see. I'll be wanting to speak with you as well, Mr. Winchell."

"Miss Bashears!"

"Ahhh, you do know who I am. That's the last time I'll pay by credit card."

"We have not received subpoenas, and no one from this hotel will speak with you or anyone else until we are served."

"But my brother is a good friend of Johanna's and I'm sure she'll see me." Alma stepped toward the president's door, hoping she could continue to bluff this Winchell. It was equally possible that Johanna had already warned people that a stranger was in the building trying to get to her. Yet Winchell's manner told Alma he hadn't spoken to Johanna. He was too hesitant in speaking her name. "Has she said that she wouldn't see me?"

"Your brother killed her father! You are the last person she'd want to see."

"Didn't you say you were the general manager?"

"Yes."

"Then, as an employee, I don't see how you can speak for her. I'd like to have her version of it. There are so many." Alma half sprinted at the door and flung it open. Winchell caught her by the arm and the door bounced closed. They fell into each other, sending a desk lamp shattering to the floor. The half-dozen people in the room stood up. One woman screamed. Winchell held on to Alma's wrist. She kicked him in the calf and twisted free.

"You're trespassing!" he yelled after her as she ran into the back office.

"Johanna?" she asked loudly. Someone had just left by a back door. It still swayed. Alma went through it. "Johanna!" she yelled. She ran down a private corridor. It zigzagged three times. Winchell pursued her, screaming that she was trespassing, but his hefty weight kept him from catching her. She hit the exit door and found herself in the arms of Officer Fred Walker. A red Corvette sped off behind him and disappeared onto the main road.

"Johanna!" Alma yelled. "Johanna!" She panted for breath.

"Arrest her," Winchell wheezed out as he caught up to her. "She's trespassing! She destroyed property and assaulted me!"

"What do you mean trespassing!" Alma turned on him and vented. "This is a public place. You can't trespass in the public areas of a hotel. I have business here and it's not with you." She inhaled to catch her breath and tried to ignore the amused look on Fred Walker's face. "You lay a hand on me and you'll be lucky if I don't sue."

"You got me all the way up here for this?" Walker asked the general manager. "If you call the police to arrest someone, you better have a better reason than taking a stroll."

"She nearly destroyed one of our offices," Winchell accused.

"Single-handed?" Walker asked.

Alma glared at Winchell. "That lamp would never have broken if you hadn't grabbed me. If anyone is guilty of assault with intent to do bodily harm, it's you!"

"I have witnesses!"

"That reminds me," Alma argued. "You claim to be a witness to Bill Littlefield's argument with my brother. Seems there's a whole lot of biased witnesses around this place."

Two additional policemen, including the greasy, black-haired one who Alma knew as one of the Littleafia, arrived. When they saw Officer Walker, they looked at each other with a tightness of stance as if clearly annoyed that he'd arrived first.

Clark Winchell's puffy red face began to regain its

olive tone. "I am Johanna Littlefield's fiance. She does not want anyone by the name of Bashears on this property. I would think the reasons would be evident. You will find a restraining order on file and this woman has violated it! Arrest her now!" He looked up at the two policemen and ignored Officer Walker.

"Officer Walker, arrest me. I insist." Alma held her hands out for the handcuffs.

Walker rolled his eyes. "I think I can get you to the station without having to wrestle you to the ground." He escorted Alma to his police car. Winchell and the policemen followed them. "Mr. Winchell," Walker said, pronouncing the name "wind-chill," "if you're correct about that restraining order, you'll have to come down and swear out a complaint."

Winchell nodded his head and said he'd follow them down shortly.

"And if you're not," Alma said, "I hope you have good insurance."

As they drove down the mountain, Alma leaned back in the seat beside Walker and let her muscles relax.

"Well, I'll say one thing," Walker said. "You're a mite sight easier to arrest than your brother."

"How's that?"

"You don't bite."

Alma laughed. "Don't worry, Fred. You won't even have to arrest me." She stretched her legs in the roomy police car. "I figured the commonwealth attorney would do something to try to trap Vernon into getting into more trouble before his trial, so every day we're pulling a report of all judicial orders issued."

Walker looked over at her, impressed.

"The restraining order is for Vernon. Not me. Not any other Bashears. No judge would approve an order that blankets anyone with a certain name. And as you can see,

I'm not my brother. And Vernon has been nowhere near that hotel." Alma wondered to herself if that last bit was true. There was Johanna's enthusiasm on the phone when she thought Vernon was calling her. Code name. Alma wanted to smack Vernon sideways after all his promises that he'd not seen Johanna Littlefield.

"You're a smart woman," Walker said. He bit his lip and stared intently at the road. "You must realize the kind of people you're dealing with."

"Fred," Alma said, "Vernon did not get a copy of the restraining order, but I have no doubt that you'll find his signature on the paperwork."

Walker shook his head as if disgusted by the corruption he could do nothing about. "I've seen it go this far before." He gripped the steering wheel tightly, his demeanor all at once sullen and restrained.

Before he took Alma inside the station, he slipped her a card with his home number on it. "Just in case," he said. "This could get dangerous. There's been lots of talk around. You be careful."

25

As Alma waited in a six-by-eight holding cell, her thoughts bounced between Vernon and his obviously continuing relationship with Johanna Littlefield and Fred Walker's warning: "This could get dangerous." Probably an overreaction, Alma thought. What could that foppish Clark Winchell do to her? She knew where the danger was, and she hoped that after today she'd silenced Charlotte Gentry and convinced Walter of the benefit of a reduced charge against Vernon.

It didn't make sense that Vernon would lie to her about Johanna. Bob Krauss had researched Bill Littlefield's history before coming to Kentucky and it was full of shady deals and lawsuits, several from former employees. At a janitorial company in Cincinnati, Littlefield had urinated on the floor and ordered his "goats," as he called employees, to clean it up on their hands and knees in front of him. He was not going to be a sympathetic victim. Johanna's testimony for the defense could go a long way toward helping Vernon.

"When I get my hands on you, Vernon," Alma said aloud, attracting the attention of a man in the holding cell next to hers.

"Almost trapped me one of them little grays the other night." He scratched his chin through a thick layer of gray beard.

"I'm only here 'cause it's close to the desk," Alma said, slowly scooting away from the bars that separated them. "I'll be gone in a few minutes." Her mind was racing too fast to engage in a conversation about squirrel hunting.

"See here." The man punched a finger into a blue bruise on his neck. "Transmitter. That's where they installed it. Easier to keep track of me that way."

"The police?" Alma asked, not meaning to play to him but unable to resist.

"Aliens!" he said, stamping his feet at her not understanding him.

Alma stood up. "Fred," she called out, "if Clark Winchell isn't here yet, I think you should release me."

Fred Walker stood in the hallway so that he could see her. "Jefferson is on his way over. I don't think Winchell will show, but let's give him twenty minutes, just so I can cover my butt."

"If it's any longer, I'm going to want dinner."

Walker looked over at the man's holding cell. "Onion ain't bothering you, is he?"

Alma smiled uncomfortably.

"Onion Adams," Walker said to the man. "You wouldn't be telling this lady some of your stories, would you?"

Onion grumbled something about "little grays" and turned his back on both of them.

"The best lock thief in the county," Walker told Alma. "He don't burglarize the house, he just steals all the door locks. Ain't figured him out yet."

"Sorry if I scared you, ma'am," Onion said, his face seeming less crazed and his eyes more focused.

"He did too much LSD in the sixties," Walker said. "Now and then he just has a little episode." A bell rang in the front office and he ran up to see who was there. "It's Jefferson," he called back to her. "And Mr. Winchell."

"Great," Alma said. "I have a few things to say. Let me out, please."

Onion moved over to her side of the cell. "Every now and then I'll see a bright white ball of light in the distance. I have to turn and look at other people to surmise whether or not they see it, too. If they're acting like they don't, then I just act like it's not there, too."

"I understand," Alma said, ignoring him. She heard the shuffle of papers and the snaps of briefcases, but no one was coming down the hall to get her.

"It makes no difference to me that she's an attorney," Clark Winchell said clearly. "She's still a Bashears."

"She was doing her job, Winchell. And if this is all the cooperation we can expect, then it's a simple matter to subpoena every damn person in that building." Jefferson defended Alma with more gusto than she'd ever expected.

"Don't threaten me, you small-town ambulance chaser!"

"I would like to get out!" Alma called out. "I am very much a part of this discussion." No one paid any attention to her.

"Winchell," Jefferson said in an escalating tone, "you'd like to think you're Littlefield incarnate, but even he could be brought down."

"Let's calm down, boys," Fred Walker said in his steady bass voice.

"You heard him, Officer Walker," Winchell objected. "He just threatened my life."

Alma knew things were out of control and strained against the bars of the cell but could see no farther than the edge of the desk. "I really don't like being discussed without being there," she said, growing increasingly agitated.

"Your pitiful life is the least of what I refer to," Jefferson shot back at Clark Winchell. "Littlefield was about to be investigated by a congressional subcommittee. His racketeering went too far when he demanded that his vendors cut his bills in half. Three of their businesses burned to the ground. That's a little more than suspicious. I'd bet my house that that investigation would have brought the bastard to his knees!"

Winchell was quiet.

"Look," Fred Walker said. "This restraining order is for Vernon, not Alma Bashears. Unless you are prepared to press any other charges, I'm releasing Miss Bashears."

Winchell remained quiet, as if considering carefully.

"I feel compelled to point out," Jefferson said, "that any charges you make will be your word against hers."

"You just make sure there's a subpoena next time either of you walks through our doors, Bingham!" A door slammed.

"Well, thank you very much for including me!" Alma yelled down the hallway.

"Let her sit there a minute," Jefferson said.

Alma banged her hands on the bars, then collapsed on the bench against the wall. When she sat up, Onion was staring at her shoes. "Where did you learn to steal locks?" she asked him.

"Little grays taught me. They're real good at that sort of thing."

She fought down a laugh as she saw Jefferson and Walker walking toward the holding cells. Jefferson's crooked smile seemed to say that he liked the look of Alma behind bars. "Gee, Alma," he said, "even your mother managed not to get arrested."

"I insisted Fred bring me here." She quickly defended

herself. "And tomorrow morning I want Bob to file a lawsuit against that hotel and Clark Winchell."

"Hey, Onion," Jefferson asked, "been up in any spaceships lately?"

"Good-bye, Onion," Alma said as she stepped out of the cell. "Good luck with . . . with whatever."

Outside the jail Jefferson's mood turned serious before she could reprimand him for excluding her. "I've heard from Willie George," he said, and unfolded a computer printout of tomorrow's *Contrary Gazette*.

The headline flashed across the page: LITTLEFIELD INDUSTRIES CLOSING. A smaller inset read: OVER 500 PUT OUT OF WORK BY MONTH'S END. Alma's stomach turned. "This is going to be just wonderful for Vernon's popularity."

26

"It doesn't make sense," Alma said. "That hotel was as busy as a downtown McDonald's at lunchtime. Even with Littlefield dead, why would they shut down a successful business?"

"Maybe it's not as successful as it looks." Jefferson opened the door to his office building for her. "I always suspected that Big Bill Littlefield was more bluff than substance."

"Either that or the whole thing ran around him, and without him there is no business." Alma read the article as Jefferson struggled with his office keys. "Damn that Walter," she said when she came to the part about the layoffs being a result of Littlefield's murder and recounting the details of Vernon Bashears's fight and arrest. "He promised me less than four hours ago that this would stop!"

"Why would you believe anything he says? I can't believe you even went to talk to him."

Alma suppressed resentment at Jefferson's tone. She sat at a desk and saw two phone messages from Jordan. A stir of longing shot through her and she smiled, impressed with his efforts to track her down at the office. As Jefferson watched over her shoulder, she folded the slips of paper and put them in her pocket. "It's not a matter of believing him," she said. "I didn't give him much choice."

"I can see what choices you gave him," Jefferson said, pointing at the article. "You know, these people aren't going to roll over and play dead just because you're in town."

"I am not without leverage." Alma slapped the paper onto the desk, then got up and stood in front of the window. "Jefferson, you're beginning to annoy me."

He came up behind her, his body closer to hers than it needed to be. "They towed Sue's car from the hotel." Moving to her side, he added, "It had four flats." When Alma started to back away, he blocked her path. "Sure wish I could be a fly on the wall when you tell her."

"I'll pay for Sue's tires."

He didn't move. His lips pressed tightly in an angry scowl. "Is there anything else I can do to annoy you, Miss Bashears?"

"How did you know about my mother?" Alma turned on Jefferson with the precision of a stalking cat. An intensity filled the air between them—part hostility, part a bonding that made the temptation to top each other irresistible.

"I don't know what you're talking about."

"You've been with Ellen again, haven't you?"

He didn't even bother to deny it. "Ellen did you a big favor by keeping the police away from Merl!"

"A big favor—but everybody seems to know," Alma shot back sarcastically, and clapped her hands together.

"This is not about me." He shook a finger in her face. "This is about you trusting that snake and kissing up to him."

"I don't trust anybody, Jefferson."

"Including me?"

"Including Ellen Farmer!" His face was next to hers and she could smell the mint flavor of his breath.

"You forget one thing, Alma Bashears. We've still got the same hollow dirt on our feet!" His voice broke when he said her name.

Alma caught herself from topping his response. She'd hurt him—deeply. Stepping up to him, she put her arms around his neck and pulled him close. With one hand she drew his face down next to hers and pressed her forehead into his cheek. "I get so focused sometimes. I don't realize who I'm running over."

He nodded, unable to speak.

Alma lifted her face and kissed him on the cheek. Jefferson's heart beat so rapidly, she felt the pulse in his chest. She started to pull away from him, but he held her tight, letting his lips slip over hers. She kissed him back—a friendly kiss, a kiss she'd give someone she'd grown up with. He kissed her again. Deeper, sliding his tongue into her mouth. Alma moaned unexpectedly. Before the kiss could end, he wrapped his arms around her lower back, pushing her against the wall. "I want you to quit," she said between kisses.

He bit into her neck. "I quit," he answered, then kissed her on the mouth slowly, deliberately, before he pushed himself away from her. "I'm not going to be a part of this. I'm not going to sit here and watch Walter Gentry destroy you again! He will do that, Alma. And you're helping him do it."

Jefferson reached for his coat and walked out the door, not bothering to close it.

Alma stood rooted to the floor for a few minutes, stunned. Why did I do that? she asked herself. She brushed her fingers over her lips, the scent of him still arousing her.

The phone rang, breaking her light-headedness. Bob

Krauss greeted her. "I've arranged for some outside press to take an interest in this case," he said. "We can't control what they write, but then neither can the Gentrys. Also, the *Louisville Courier Journal* is going to do an article about how the *Contrary Gazette* is handling their write-up of the case."

"Bob, you're a genius. I'm hoping that it all won't be necessary. I really believe I've convinced Walter Gentry of the rightness of Vernon's charge being dropped to manslaughter."

Bob was quiet for a few seconds. "Well, if you've pulled that off, you've done your day's work."

"Still, let's play it close to the vest. You've seen the computer copy of tomorrow's paper?"

"I certainly have," Bob answered.

"Do you have someone who can go to the county seat and check titles on Littlefield's property, especially if any changes were filed in the past week or so? Something tells me some of those properties may have already been sold."

"Hmmm. If that's the case, then all this crap about closing the business is bull."

"And if that's the case, I'm going to blow them out of the water."

"I have to think about this, Alma," Bob said. "We need to focus on a murder case, not play games with the newspapers. I'm beginning to worry about the nature of your involvement. I keep fighting the feeling that there's more going on here than I know."

"No, Bob," she reassured him. "This is about Vernon and nothing else."

Alma hung up. Late afternoon was falling into the darkness of evening. Tomorrow morning's paper had to be different from what she'd seen. Amid all the details about Littlefield Industries was prominent mention of

Vernon's part in the owner's demise. Walter had promised her there'd be no more of that. Maybe Jefferson had an earlier version of the article. Jefferson . . . A mixture of guilt and ache filled her. She dialed his home number. An answering machine picked up the call. "He's probably with Ellen Farmer," she said, banging the receiver down harder than she'd intended.

When Alma dialed Jordan's private number in California, she got another answering machine. It surprised her, and she felt a ripple of jealousy. It was his lunchtime in California, and without fail Jordan worked out on a treadmill in his office. The cellular phone was always beside him, and he always took her calls.

"Now where would he be?" she asked aloud. She hung up the phone and stared out the window at the blue-lavender sky. Stars were just beginning to peek through, and Jellico Mountain looked like a black pyramid rising out of the earth.

On the street below, people were moving in every direction to get where they were going. A couple met at the corner and hugged. The quiet of the office took on a humming sound. A wave of emotion shot through Alma as it often did when she was alone. She reached for a tissue. She was lonely. That's what kissing Jefferson had been about. And it had felt good. It had felt right.

But it was impossible, she told herself. "Impossible."

27

The sharp smack of shattering glass woke Alma the next morning. She shot up in her bed. Outside a man's voice hollered a string of unintelligible curses.

Alma stumbled down the hallway and stairs toward the living room. Mamaw held back a curtain, peering through the broken window. Without her wheelchair she looked shrunken and frail. She shouted at two men standing in the road, "You go home, Silver Jenkins! You got no claim to start trouble with us."

A brown creek rock lay in the center of the living-room floor. Shards of glass covered the couch and floor. Alma came up behind Mamaw and put her hands on her grandmother's shoulders, partly to keep the old woman from going outside and partly to see what was going on. Something cold touched her leg. Alma looked down. Mamaw clutched a small-caliber revolver. Her hand trembled.

"Mamaw, put that gun away!" Alma demanded.

Outside, a silver-haired man shook his fist in the air. "Where is that donkey's rear end? I been laid off, and it's all Vernon Bashears's fault!"

Through the side window Alma saw Vernon coming out of his trailer. He was shirtless and the top buttons of his jeans were undone. She grabbed a coat from the hall closet and struggled with a pair of boots.

Mamaw came up beside her and shoved the revolver into the coat's pocket. Alma recoiled, but Mamaw's eyes glared. "You use this if you have to. Stay behind the porch post and don't take chances, aim for the neck—that way it don't matter if you hit high or low."

Her words sent a chill through Alma, but at least she had the gun away from the old woman. "There's a card taped to the inside of my briefcase with the name Fred Walker on it," Alma said. "Call him and tell him what's happening."

At the side of the house Alma caught up with Vernon. "Be cool and play for time," she whispered. "Mamaw's calling the police." The handle of a hunting knife stuck out from Vernon's back pocket.

He spread his arms as he approached the two men. "Boys? Up awful early, ain't ye?"

The smell of liquor tainted the air around the two men. The silver-haired man struggled to keep standing without weaving. "I got two girls in junior college. The first Jenkinses to go to college. How the hell do you think I'm gonna pay for it now!"

"I'm sorry to hear you been laid off, Silver. You, too, Dan?"

A short man leaning across the hood of a silver Ford Bronco nodded his head. He scuffed one foot on the ground. "We come here to kick the shit out of you, Vernon. None of us liked ole Littlefield any better than you, but Christ! We gotta work!"

"Well, boys." Vernon spoke carefully. "Can I offer you a cup of coffee?"

"Where do you gentlemen work?" Alma asked, moving forward but staying slightly behind Vernon.

"At the utility company," Vernon answered for them.

Dan hid his hands deep inside his pockets, and Silver, still weaving, let himself lean backward until he came to rest against the truck. A rifle hung in the rear window. Silver glanced at Dan, then at the gun, but neither man made a move toward the truck's interior.

"Have you ever been laid off before?" Alma asked.

"Lots of times," Silver said, "but this time it's for good. Everything Littlefield ever owned is closing down."

Alma allowed herself an audible sigh of relief and smiled at them, hoping her casualness would draw them in. "Do you men really believe they're going to cut the electricity off in all these houses?"

Silver and Dan looked at each other and then back at her. The morning air seemed to help sober them up and they stared at their feet.

"Look at that housing project over there." She pointed at the valley below, toward rows of project houses. "Or the high school, the grade schools, the whole town. No one is going to turn the lights out in all those places. If I can suggest two things to you gentlemen, it's don't allow yourselves to be used and ask yourself who benefits by you and the other employees being all stirred up."

Vernon whispered out of the side of his mouth, "They don't understand a damn thing you're saying."

Across the street Uncle Ames and Uncle George crept from around the sides of their porches. Both carried rifles. Alma waved to show them that all was okay, but Uncle George aimed at the two men. Alma's heart beat like a drum in her chest. "Why don't you gentlemen leave, and we'll forget this ever happened?"

Dan turned around, saw George and Ames, and blurted, "Christ!"

"You want to go around busting windows," Uncle Ames called out, "then I just might bust a couple heads."

"Hey, Silver," Dan whispered. "Maybe this weren't so bright of us after all."

"You Bashears is touched in the heads," Silver slurred, looking back and forth from the uncles to Vernon and Alma.

"I can handle this," Alma called across the road. "Go back to your houses." She felt silly standing there in a silk gown, boots, and coat and realized that her appearance diminished her effectiveness.

Her uncles ignored her. Ames inched up to Uncle George's gate. "You sorry scoundrels better get the hell out of this holler before I get across this fence," he said. His eyes squinted and his jaw jutted with an immobile expression. He pointed a finger at Silver. "You ever do something like this again and your daughters'll be missing more than a Silver Jenkins's paycheck."

Alma felt time moving in slow motion. Surely he wouldn't shoot. Uncle George anchored himself against the elm tree in his front yard. The pistol in her pocket weighed down the left side of the coat. She pulled her hand from the pocket to avoid the uncomfortable feel of cold metal. "They're unarmed," she yelled across the road. "We're just going to talk a few minutes."

"Nobody comes into this holler and breaks a window in my mother's house, then stays to talk." Uncle Ames raised the rifle.

The two men got into the truck, but not before Silver threw an empty bourbon bottle toward Vernon, which shattered on a rock. "I still ain't ready to admit this ain't all your fault, Vernon Bashears," Silver yelled. He gunned the gas, slid his truck into reverse, and backed all the way out of the hollow in a drunken swerve.

The chill of the morning air mixed with the smoky exhaust. Vernon and Alma stared across the road at their uncles. Her heartbeat slowed to a trot. "I wish you had let me handle this," she said to them. "Do you know what it's going to look like if they repeat this story to the newspapers, or the police, or to anybody?" With the emergency over, her nerves let loose into her muscles. She pulled the raincoat tight around her to keep from shaking.

"What did you expect us to do, just take it?" Uncle George asked, his mouth twisting around the words.

Vernon knelt down, resting his weight on one knee. "Alma, you just don't understand. You can't be like that around here. You can't tell folks here not to fight any more than you can convince Silver not to come up here and speak his mind." The tense lines around his eyes revealed guilt at having brought this trouble on his family.

"What if one of them had pulled a gun?"

"Then he'd be dead," Uncle Ames replied in a flat tone.

"Or you'd be," Alma said.

"If I want your opinion, Alma Mae, I'll ask for it." Uncle Ames stared as hard at her as he had at Silver Jenkins.

She was caught off guard and the feeling of being a reprimanded child immediately filled her. "People are going to try to provoke us," she said, trying to regain an authoritative tone. "This is not 1930s Harlan County! You cannot take the law into your own hands."

"Stop it!" Vernon yelled, pressing a hand on each side of his head. "Don't you see what Littlefield's done? He has us turning against each other!"

"I'm not sure we were ever for each other," Alma said.

"Hush up, Alma!" Mamaw said. From the front porch she eyed her children and grandchildren, her expression one of detached guardedness Alma had never seen before. "Thank you, boys," Mamaw called out, and waved to Uncle Ames and Uncle George. "Breakfast will be at nine. I'd like some time to talk to Alma now."

Anger surged through Alma. Mamaw had not called Fred Walker. Why are they so damn obstinate? she asked herself.

Coffee cups clinked sharply as Mamaw reached along the shelf of a cabinet. When she brought down two pieces of her best china, Alma knew she was in for a serious talking-to. A cold wind blew through the house from the broken window. The coffeepot began to percolate. Alma squirmed in her chair. Mamaw hadn't said a word for the last ten minutes.

Mamaw poured the coffee and sipped from her cup. "What do you have planned for the day?" She looked directly into Alma's eyes.

Alma looked away. "Uh, Bob and I are preparing for some preliminary interviews."

"We're going to set out some rows of cabbage and lettuce and potatoes."

"Isn't it too early for that?"

"No. Head crops at the start of the ram and potatoes by the dark of the moon."

Alma noted an instructive tone in Mamaw's voice. She waited and steeled herself. She finished the cup of coffee, still waiting for Mamaw to make her point. Mamaw stared out the kitchen window for a few moments and smiled when she saw Vernon and Uncle George walking from the barn with a sheet of plywood. Within another minute hammering echoed through the house.

"I . . . think I should be getting down to the office," Alma said uncomfortably. "It's almost eight o'clock."

"Vernon's gonna help us rebuild Ely Buell's barn this week," Mamaw said. "Side of it blew down from that storm that hit the other day."

"The weather's turning warm enough for that."

"You're welcome to help."

"I really wouldn't know how to build a barn."

"Yes, I know." Mamaw sipped her coffee, then added another teaspoon of sugar. "Rodney has Sue's car at his house, fixing her tires."

"He didn't have to do that. I would have paid a garage to replace them." Alma knew she was being slowly tortured.

"Why would we do that? Everybody in this family knows how to change tires—well, everybody except you." Mamaw stood and picked up her cup and Alma's. She leaned back against the sink still holding the two pieces of china. She let one of them fall and it shattered on the floor.

Alma jumped up, not sure if Mamaw was hurt. When Mamaw stood still as a cat before it pounces, Alma realized she'd done it on purpose. "Mamaw, that's Lenox china. Why'd you drop it?"

"It's a cup, Alma." Mamaw pushed at the pieces with one foot. "A cup is only as good as its use, despite its fancy name. A cup with a fancy name breaks just as easy as one from the five-and-ten. You've journeyed a long distance from our ways and that was your path to choose. Just make sure your fancy customs don't break our family."

Alma turned away. Resentment burned in her, but she could not argue vehemently with her grandmother the way she might with her mother or brother. Mamaw's ways were as old as the mountains, passed down from generations of hollow people who had lived without the law their entire lives. "Mamaw," she said, pulling in her focus as tight as a wire. "Sometimes I get just as mad as you do. In law school they teach us that this anger must be subjugated . . ." She rethought her words. "Must be conquered. Reasonable men agree to live by reasonable laws. If one of them breaks a law, then he is brought to justice by laws that have been agreed upon, not by the feelings of an individual or a mob."

Mamaw listened quietly, her eyes as soft as a doe's. She set the other cup on the table in front of Alma, pulled her wheelchair close, and eased down into it. "We Bashearses, we don't ask for trouble, but if people do us wrong and no justice is forthcoming, then there's only one law we'll live by: the law of revenge."

28

At Jefferson's law office with Bob Krauss, Alma couldn't concentrate. Mamaw's admonishment played repeatedly in her mind. What bothered her most was that it had struck a chord. A deep chord that until this day she hadn't realized existed inside her. The law of revenge: an eye for an eye. "We're not the damn Hatfields and McCoys," she said, staring at a list of interview questions that failed to hold her concentration.

"Pardon?" Bob asked, looking at her over his glasses.

Alma picked up the newspaper. "I made a mistake in trusting Walter Gentry." The morning articles were worse than the proof she'd seen the night before. Not only was the front page dedicated to a deification of Bill Littlefield and the demise of Littlefield Industries, there was an editorial recommending that citizens write to the governor supporting Walter Gentry's appointment to the state assembly. "Our city's economy faces disaster with the impending closure of Littlefield Industries," she read aloud. "This district will need a man who can attract jobs, introduce legislation supporting stronger laws for capital offenses, and unite us as a community."

She looked up. Bob stared at her with his usual poker-faced expression. "Run your own race, Alma," he said. "Don't let what they're doing get under your skin."

"I hate making mistakes."

"Your concentration is not quite up to par. Take a break from here. Go to the library and look up the history of Littlefield in this town."

"Can't Jefferson do that?" Impatience surged through her.

"Jefferson flew to Frankfort before the crack of dawn."

"Frankf . . ." Alma remembered that she'd told Jefferson to quit the case. "Uh, Bob. There's something I need to tell you."

"He'll be back in an hour or two."

"Jefferson and I had a disagreement last night. I told him I wanted him to quit." She held her breath.

Bob threw a pen from behind his ear onto the desk. "You made two mistakes," he said, leaning back in the chair until it almost touched the wall. "Trusting Gentry was the least of them. Firing Jefferson may cost you more than you realize."

"You'd see it my way," she insisted, "if you'd think this through. We've had one leak after another, and this latest article proves it. It's got to be Ellen getting information from Jefferson, whether he's aware of it or not."

"Right now, Jefferson is petitioning the state attorney general to prosecute executives of Carfeller Oil for forcing its workers into unsafe working conditions." Bob came around the desk. "Do you know that in the years you didn't live in this town he successfully defended Grady Thompson, the United Mine Workers business agent, who was accused of bombing the headquarters of Quinntown Mines? Jefferson's spent nearly ten years fighting the execution of Richard Donahoe and will likely take that case to the Supreme Court. He also represented the local football hero against shoplifting charges. That one he lost."

"I didn't know." A flush colored Alma's cheeks.

"Jefferson Bingham is nobody's fool. He's racked up

twice your experience as a trial lawyer while you were baby-sitting empty-headed three-piece suits who can't decide how to spend their next million."

"You've made your point." Alma twisted uncomfortably under Bob's scrutiny.

"You've been spoiled in city law practice. You need to get back to basic legal work, the kind of work that's dumped on any available paralegal."

"I really resent that, Bob!"

"Why? I do it. Jefferson does it. What the hell makes you think you're such a downtown person?"

Her mouth dropped open.

Before she could recover herself and respond, he leaned over her, invading her space with the skill of an attorney against a hostile witness. "Alma, *I* am in charge of this case until my client, Vernon Bashears, discharges me. *I* will decide who works on this case and who doesn't, and *I* will decide who does what work. In the event that decisions have to be made, they will be made by me, my way."

Alma cleared her throat to try to hide the hurt she felt. "This seems to be my morning for having the facts of life explained."

"You need to decide what you want to do, Alma." Bob took off his glasses and rubbed the bridge of his nose. "You can't control everything. I tried to tell you that early on. People are going to do things."

"Okay, okay. Enough said."

Icy silence. The only sound was a secretary in the outer office tentatively opening and closing a desk drawer. Probably leaving for lunch to get away from the yelling, Alma thought. Car horns beeped from the street below. She felt like an accused suspect confronted with evidence of her own guilt. "Look, I'm going to get some lunch. Join me?"

Bob shook his head, sat down at the desk, and opened a file.

She hoped he'd argue with her, tell her she needed to stay focused on work. He did not.

At the bottom of the office steps was a newspaper boy delivering the afternoon edition. She opened it and looked at the headline. More of the same. BASHEARS LIVES AS A FREE MAN. A few columns under the front-page editorial was a smaller headline: LITTLEFIELD'S LAID OFF EMPLOYEES GO HUNGRY.

She walked to Lolly's Drugstore, fighting the certainty that people were staring at her. Identified as a Bashears, the family that had brought disaster on this peaceable community. After ordering coffee, she watched the other customers in the mirror behind the counter. Several were reading the newspaper, a few were in a lively discussion, but no one looked at her. Strangely bemused, she realized that no one recognized her. Not yet, anyway.

A younger man in a business suit explained to another that Contrary's business "was ruined."

"We got along before Littlefield," the older man answered. "We'll get along without him."

"You ain't using your brain cells," the younger man huffed, his cheeks coloring a pasty peach. "You don't kill a man 'cause he's a rascal."

"Back in my daddy's day, that was just what you did." The older man set his coffee cup down, loudly rapping it against the saucer. He dropped a handful of change on the counter. "Sometimes when I think back about it, I don't know how or why we put up with Bill Littlefield as long as we did."

The younger man scowled, slapping his folded newspaper against the counter. He watched the other man exit. The atmosphere of the drugstore collapsed into a hushed

THE LAW OF REVENGE 185

stillness. A couple of teenagers, retail workers on a coffee break, and a few other businessmen cocooned themselves from one another. Alma felt they all wanted to keep their feelings hidden.

"Yeah, I agree with you, Bo-Bo!" Behind a shelf with toothpaste and soap, the policeman who'd blocked Alma's entry into the jail when she first came stepped up to the counter. "You are absolutely right. And old Vernon's gonna fry for what he did to this town!" He moved his head just a millimeter and narrowed his eyes at Alma. He grinned, then pursed his thin lips together and kissed the air at her.

She motioned to the waitress and asked for three dollars in quarters. The coins clinked onto the counter, reminding her of the sound of this morning's shattering window glass. Alma reacted with a jerk of her shoulders. She looked up at the waitress, expecting a reaction. The dark-haired woman refilled her coffee cup and returned to washing dishes. Alma lifted the cup to her lips, but her hand shook and she set it down quickly. She realized that the Littleafia policeman had sent her fears spiraling out of control.

The policeman continued to talk loudly. In the corner of the drugstore Alma closed herself in a 1940s phone booth. Shutting out the bellowing voice of the Littleafia helped to curb her desire to slap the policeman's face. He rocked back and forth on his stool like a stalled horse, grinning and winking at Alma when he could catch her eye.

She hated the feeling of needing someone, and as she dialed Jordan's telephone number, she argued with herself. When she represented clients, she almost never thought of right or wrong, only of getting the best deal. So law school taught detachment and respect for the law, not personal vendetta and revenge. What Narly was doing to her brother, she couldn't help but take it personally. She needed Jordan right now. She needed his distance, his levelheadedness. She needed to talk to a lawyer.

"Hello, this is Jordan McFedries," she heard. "I'm not at home right now, but if you'll leave a message—" She hung up. At the lunch counter a second policeman had joined the first and both sat on either side of her stool. Their large butts hung over the seats so that their nightsticks blocked her return. She reached for the phone book, found the number, then punched the buttons with a growing rage.

Mamaw was right. She had to learn to fight like the enemy. It was stupid to forget where she was. Contrary, Kentucky, was not a playing field of equals. Who she was in San Francisco didn't matter. To the Gentrys she was just a hollow girl. She had to play on their level from now on. The phone rang. His whiny, expressionless voice came over the receiver. "Walter Gentry."

"You crossed me, you son of a bitch. Don't think I'll ever forget it."

29

When Alma returned to the law office, the blinds were pulled and the rooms were empty and dark. Bob had left her a note saying he was at city hall. The secretary's desk was locked. Without turning on the lights Alma collapsed onto an overstuffed couch where Jefferson enjoyed his afternoon naps. The fabric smelled like him—a mixture of Irish Spring soap and Old Spice. The smell was comforting, just what she needed, after the empty threat she'd made against Walter Gentry.

Alma couldn't count how often she'd seen defense attorneys playing catch-up with prosecutors. Prosecutors could and would keep opponents running in circles and biting at imaginary carrots until they lost their cases. Withholding evidence, hiding witnesses, spouting misinformation, lying—only a few tricks up a prosecutor's sleeve. That's why I hired Bob, she thought. At the same time she wondered why Jefferson stayed in the town. She closed her eyes. The turmoil of the morning had exhausted her.

A timid cough came from a dark corner. Alma shot up off the couch. Before she could switch on the light, the dark lump stood up. Alma picked up a law book, ready to throw it. She hit the overhead light switch with her shoulder. A frail, shriveled old woman wrung her hands under Alma's glare.

"I didn't mean ta scare ye." She sucked in her lips. At first glance she looked about seventy, but on closer inspection Alma placed her in her fifties. Her clothes had the gray dullness of only occasional washing, but her blue eyes twinkled with the excitement she had caused.

"Do you always bushwhack people by sitting in the dark?" Alma asked.

"Light hurts my eyes—has ever since I got cataracts. But Mr. Bingham, he just a-laughs at me an' says it's all right 'cause even Justice is blind as a bat." She had the infectious smile and all the charm of a person who approached life without caution.

"You're a client of Mr. Bingham's?" Alma dropped the law book on the desk.

"Come down ta see if'n he had any luck a-gittin' my divorce."

"Well, he's not here now. I can take your phone number and have him call."

The older woman looked at the floor. "Eh . . . No, I'll come back tamara."

Alma could have kicked herself. She recognized from the woman's accent that she was from the back hollows, where there were still no phones, water lines, electricity, or gas. Toilets were outhouses. Baths were taken in a creek or an oversize tin tub. They cooked on cast-iron coal stoves heated by wood or coal dug out of the mountainside. These people didn't often come to town, so when they did, it was usually important. Quickly Alma offered, "I could check the file and see what he's done."

"Well, Mr. Bingham, he's liable ta git mad if'n I talked 'bout it." The whites of her eyes reddened, and she looked down at the floor. "He told me not ta discuss it with anybody, 'specially my relatives."

"I'm one of his associates. I don't think he meant me.

THE LAW OF REVENGE

What's your name?" Alma's curiosity kept pace with her rising sympathy.

"Gilby is my last name. Thama is my first."

As Alma opened a file drawer, the woman sat on the edge of a chair, waiting patiently with her hands folded across her lap. "My old man, he run off last month, and h'it's 'bout time fer him ta run outta money and head back this a'way. I jest want ta be divorced 'fore then, so'n he can't cash my checks like he always does."

Alma found the divorce cases and pulled out *Gilby v. Gilby.* "Thelma," she said, pronouncing the name as it was spelled. "It appears that Jefferson has filed the motion for divorce and plans on serving your husband with the papers as soon as he's located. There's a Brenda Watson from the local Women's Aid Society scheduled to come and see you—tomorrow."

Thelma crossed her arms and inhaled a deep breath. "He said she might be a-comin'. I had me a slew of second thoughts on that."

"Mrs. Gilby, it says here that she's going to move you into a women's shelter until public housing becomes available."

Mrs. Gilby sniffed and her eyes teared. "I jest don't know if I can go through with it."

Alma sat next to her.

"I been with old Allan since I's thirteen." She spoke with a need to expunge her history, and Alma felt that in all likelihood Jefferson was the only other person to have bothered listening. Thelma managed an embarrassed smile through her sniffling.

Alma smiled back but could think of nothing to say. If she encouraged Thelma Gilby, she'd sound patronizing, and if she did nothing, how easy it would be for this woman to slide back into the cycle of victimization. "Mrs. Gilby," Alma said, "Brenda probably understands all this better than me, and Mr. Bingham, well, he wouldn't have gone to all this trouble if he didn't think it was the best thing for you."

"Ye think so?"

Alma nodded.

"Well, I think so, too." Her face lit with confidence. Alma thought it was easy to see why Thelma depended on Jefferson and how little it took to set her on a more self-sufficient path. No one had ever told her independence was possible. No one had ever offered her a way other than the one she knew.

"I'll tell Mr. Bingham that you'll expect Ms. Watson tomorrow, and he'll contact you at the women's shelter."

"I reckon that's what we'll do then." As Thelma moved toward the door, her expression returned to that of the hesitant, teary, and unsure woman who'd told the story of her abusive husband.

Alma figured if he came back before the move, the woman would never escape. It had probably taken all her courage to come there. There was probably a fifty-fifty chance that she'd even go through with the divorce. "Good luck," she said as she shook Thelma's hand.

Alma watched her walk down the stairs and said to herself, "That Jefferson." She touched the letters that spelled out his name on the door. "Full of surprises. I guess I did underestimate him." She sat at the desk and pulled out the phone messages from the day before. It would be 10 A.M. in California now, surely Jordan would be awake. She dialed the number.

"Hello?" a soft, female voice said.

For a second Alma was so stunned she couldn't speak.

"Hello?" the voice asked again, this time colored with a trace of annoyance.

"I'm not sure I dialed correctly. I'm calling Jordan McFedries."

There was a pause. "He's already left. Can I take a message?"

"Not unless you're the housekeeper," Alma said, the words flooding from her mouth.

Silence on the other end. The woman hung up. Alma slammed the receiver down.

"There could be a dozen reasons for it," she instantly rationalized. She covered her face with both hands. "What the hell is wrong with you, Alma?"

"A better question is, What the hell is right?"

She jumped up at the sound of the voice. Jefferson stood in the doorway. An open coat covered a tailored navy-blue suit. His hair was loose and hung around the collar of his coat. He threw his briefcase on the couch and stepped toward her.

A flux of heat rushed from her toes to her head. She never seemed to overcome an extreme embarrassment at being seen when she was vulnerable. "I have a headache," she said, pushing the phone away.

He dropped his coat on the desk and stepped toward her again.

Her cheeks heated up, and her eyes burned and threatened to tear.

He stepped even closer. His hand reached for hers.

She stared at his open palm. The name Jordan kept repeating in her mind, the syllables scraping like jagged glass. The trembling in her fingers was noticeable as she timidly put her hand into Jefferson's. He pulled her to him and wrapped his arms around her. "Just hold me," she whispered. "Please, just hold me."

"I'll hold you," he said. "I won't let go."

When they pulled apart, neither could look at the other. Jefferson guided them to the couch, where they sat holding hands. "Bad day?" he asked.

"Bad couple of days."

"About yesterday—"

"Yes, about yesterday," she interrupted him, and pulled back. "I never thanked you for getting me out of jail." She put a finger to his lips. "And if you'll forgive my arrogance and stupidity, then that's all we need to say about yesterday."

He looked away. If he wanted to say more, he managed to hide his feelings. "Then let's concentrate on today." He let go of her hand and reached for his briefcase. "All morning I listened for rumblings of discontent." He pulled Frankfort, Louisville, and Lexington newspapers from his briefcase. "Littlefield's ten-year plan was to open a planned community next to the hotel. He owned all the mountain ridges south of Contrary." He traced a map on the newspaper.

"That's where Mrs. Gilby lives." Alma pointed to Indian Ridge.

"Yeah." His voice softened. "I ran into her in the parking lot. Thanks for talking to her. She likes you."

Alma could feel herself blushing and stared at the map that Jefferson continued to sketch. "I . . . I admire what you've done for her."

Jefferson starred a section of his map. "Littlefield bought this flat valley where they were already working on a lake. Condos would look directly onto Cumberland Gap—that view alone is worth fifty thousand on the asking price. There's no services that far out, no electricity, no water, no phone lines, no roads, nothing."

"All those hollow people would lose their homes?"

"Yeah. Not only that, but most of the contractors would have to be hired out of Lexington or Louisville."

"Ambitious project. It could rival what the Carnegies and Rockefellers did in the 1920s."

"Littlefield couldn't have done this on his own. He had

to have investors and, more important, he had to have somebody paving the way for him in Frankfort."

"And the tentative loss of that business doesn't seem to be upsetting anyone," Alma said, catching on to his train of thought. "Not even the vendors or contractors?"

"Not a blessed word in any newspaper for the past week. I listened to conversations in every john in the state capitol. Even tried to provoke a few arguments. Nobody seems too concerned."

"I can't wait to tell Bob. Bill Littlefield would have priced Contrary residents out of their own community." Alma shook her head, thinking back to the coal barons who had taken the same advantage a generation before. "How do you think we can find out the identity of his secret partner?"

"My next brilliant idea." From a paper bag Jefferson pulled out a long brown wig. "There's a memorial service for Littlefield this afternoon. I'd bet my law degree that his silent partner will attend."

"Jefferson, I'd never get away with it." She stroked the length of the brown wig.

"No, you wouldn't," he said, a mischievous glint in his eye. "If you'll help me convince her, I know someone who will."

30

"Absolutely not," Sue said, stroking the brown wig. She glanced at her sister and Jefferson, trying to suppress a giggle.

Alma knew they almost had a sale. "You'd look great as a sultry brunette. Think of it as your debut as a professional actress. Remember when you played Lady Macbeth in the junior-senior play?"

"More likely my debut as a professional ass." Sue held the wig up to her own jet-black hair. "This is more Momma's style, not mine."

"That's what we're afraid of," Alma said, shaking her head. "If Momma hears we're doing this, you know she'll volunteer. No telling what kind of trouble she'd get herself into." Alma let a worried look cross her face. "You wouldn't want to see that, would you?"

Sue rolled her eyes. "Somehow, I think there's a little stretching the truth here." She pulled back her hair and set the wig on top of her head.

"I bought you a new suit, so you'll look like a city reporter," Alma said, pushing back the wig's bangs from Sue's forehead.

"Somebody'll recognize me."

"Nobody would ever expect this of you, my darling sister. That's why you'll get away with it."

Jefferson winked at Alma. "All you have to do is

listen, Sue. There'll be lots of reporters there, so you'll blend in. Write down all the names you hear and take a picture of anyone whose name you can't get." He handed her a camera so small, it looked like a fountain pen.

"If my boys ever find out I did this, I'll never live it down." Sue pulled out her makeup kit and went to work.

After dropping Sue off a few blocks from the Lutheran church, Jefferson and Alma drove toward the office. "Let's not go back there right now," he said as they waited for a traffic light to change.

"I'm for that," she answered, though part of her wondered if Jordan might have called. She tried putting him out of her mind, but he'd ease back in at a slow moment and it was all she could do to keep from calling him. She didn't have the strength right now to hear another woman answer his phone. Perhaps there was a reason for it. If not, she didn't want to know.

Jefferson turned onto a paved road hardly wide enough for two cars. He skirted the edge of Indian Hills, driving slowly on the hairpin turns. Alma was amazed at the size of the trees. Oak and beech trees were nearly ten feet in circumference. Tulip and hickory trees shot up over a hundred feet into the sky. A grove of winged elms spread their spiny branches across one another to form a matrix as complex as a spider's web.

The names of the individual trees came back to her as the car rounded every turn. The returning knowledge pleased her. The weather had turned warm enough to go without a coat. Alma opened her window and the fresh breeze of the coming spring filled the car and lightened her mood.

Most of the trees were still leafless, but the muted green of the pines dotted the clusters of gnarly-barked ancient forests. A budding dogwood tree on the eastern side of the mountain caught Alma's attention and she made Jefferson stop the car.

"There's always a tree like this," she said. "Blooming out of season—somehow taking root just where the morning sun feeds it like a firstborn child."

"You should have been a poet instead of a lawyer," Jefferson said. He let the car inch forward to the edge of the road. The view opened down onto a wave of mountains as vast as the sea. Strata of rock jutted out from the mountainsides and interspersed with the trees. Gray and white stone paralleled orangy-brown soil that looked muddy. The shelf of rocks rose to the tops of the mountains and down again like the pattern in a throw rug.

Alma reached out of the car and pulled a leaf from under a windshield wiper. She rolled it in the palms of her hands and breathed deeply of the grassy smell. A wave of emotion caught in her throat as the soul of the land took hold in her. "I'm glad that bastard Bill Littlefield is dead," she said with quiet firmness. She sniffed hard, inhaling the soft fragrance of soil and the crispness of budding leaves. "Anybody who'd put a planned community in these mountains deserves to be dead."

Jefferson slapped the seat between them. "Hallelujah, I believe the girl's got the spirit back in her!" He pulled the car onto the road and gunned the gas up to fifty.

"Slow down," Alma said, one hand balancing on the dashboard.

"I see that smile on your face. I ain't slowing down till I get to a creek."

"Creek?"

"When's the last time you went wading?"

"Uh . . . I don't know. Ten years ago—at the ocean."

"Ocean, smocean." Jefferson stuck out his tongue and bounced the car onto the main road, not even slowing when he passed a police car. He headed toward the hollows, then finally turned onto a side road and pulled up on a grassy bank. "Come on. Let's go wading."

She followed him down a path to a stream that meandered through a grove of locust and hazelnut trees. Patches of ferns and holly spread along part of the bank. Jefferson sat on a flat, gray rock, took off his shoes and socks and rolled up his pants. "Whoo!" he exclaimed when he stepped into the water. "Colder than it looks. Come on in, Alma."

She stepped to the edge of the water and shook her head. He looked like a tightrope walker—waving his arms to keep balance on the slippery rocks. His laughter made her smile. After what Bob had said about him earlier, she realized she was looking at Jefferson differently. He could have been a partner in a city law firm by now. Why had he come back to Contrary and dug a hole?

Jefferson pointed at the water. "Come on in and I'll officiate the baptism." He held out a hand.

"Nope," she said. "I have a lot more sinning to do before I'm ready for my soul to be saved." They walked upstream, he sloshing through the water, she balancing on the creekbank and pulling herself along by holding on to seedling trees. Neither of them spoke, as if unwilling to break the easiness that had grown between them. The quiet of the next few minutes was interrupted by a bluejay—probably the first of the season, Alma thought.

"You know, Jefferson," she said, "I've been thinking about something."

"Ummm?"

"When this is all done, I could help you get a job in the city. Lexington. Louisville. Bob would hire you in Knoxville in a minute. Even San Francisco if you wanted."

He stopped and looked at her as if she had splashed him with creek water.

"Don't get angry," she said.

Much to her surprise, he laughed. "I'm not angry, but I don't want a job in the city."

"You're too good for this town. I mean that legally and personally."

He stepped up out of the water and took his socks from his pocket. "I'm not going to give you a speech about the virtues and rewards of a small-town law practice. I don't do it because it's noble or because I harbor some deep-seated fear of success."

"I'm not trying to be snooty," she said. "The horrible fact is that even if Bill Littlefield is dead, someone else will build that planned community."

"I do it because I hate this town as much as you."

She opened her mouth to speak, thinking that she'd have to defend her opinion, when his words registered. He looked at her as though her expression amused him.

Jefferson jumped up onto a large rock and pulled his shoes out of his coat pockets. "When I beat some asshole out of the nickel he's trying to keep from my client, it makes me feel good here." He clutched his fist over his chest.

"What makes you think I feel any different when I win a case?"

As he tied his shoe, he kept smiling at her as if he knew the punchline of a joke she was about to tell. "We both know the jerks in this town. They haven't changed much in the last thirty years, and the ones who died all had children." He flipped a shoe in the air and caught it with his other hand. "Soaking them is worth more than two hundred grand in the city, litigating against people I don't have a history with."

Alma sat beside him on the rock. She felt the truth of his statement *in her bones*, as Mamaw might say. For a moment she felt ashamed that she'd never come back, never done anything for the people who lived there, most of them under some sort of tyranny that they simply accepted as life. Jefferson had set out to make a difference, even if he couldn't. But maybe he did, she thought, thinking of Thelma Gilby.

"I'll tell you what . . ." He stood up, anchored both hands on his hips, and looked down at her. "I'll offer *you* a job. If you make the grade, we could be partners in a few years." His mouth fought down a crooked grin.

She opened both hands, acknowledging that he had her. "Can't say I've had as good an offer as that this whole day."

"But?" He waited.

She stared down at the silver and black gravel surrounding the larger stones. "But my life is in California." Her voice cracked when she said it. She started to reach out for him but stopped herself.

His expression reverted to the serious Jefferson. "And someone special out there as well?" He looked up at the mountainside and laced his hands behind his head. "Let's just say it's a standing offer, should you ever change your mind."

"Jokes aside?"

"Jokes aside," he answered, looking her directly in the eyes. Then he clapped his hands, breaking the silence of the moment. "Race you up the hillside!"

She watched him sprint away. How different he now was from the boy who used to stutter when he spoke to her. She raced uphill after him.

At the top they fell against each other, panting for breath. "Where are we going?" she asked.

"Round the corner," he panted. "Then I'll jog back and get the car."

"What's around the corner?"

"Jesus Falls," he said, pulling on her hand.

"Jesus Falls?" The name went through her like a stake.

"Yeah, they've turned it into a park. Picnic tables. Swings. Paved a road into the shallow part of the pond. Sometimes the local churches have baptisms there."

"Wait." Alma stopped in the middle of the road and knelt down on one knee. She pressed her hands to her stomach. *Running . . . voices behind her. Yelling . . . pursuing. Turning back to see Rudy, Earl, and Narly chasing her.*

"I can go get the car now if you're out of breath," Jefferson said.

She stood up suddenly, then leaned down just as quickly, anchoring her hands just above her knees. *No breath . . . gulping down water . . . drowning. The eruption of sand around her. The boys would catch her again.*

"Are you okay?" Jefferson knelt and looked into her face.

She looked back at him, hoping her discomfort wouldn't make him bring up the subject of the past. His eyebrows drew inward, emphasizing his puzzled expression. He doesn't know, she thought. His knowledge of what had happened to her all those years ago was probably the same as most of her schoolmates at that time, half-tales and whispers that something more had gone on under the bridge than a practical joke. Something that the Bashears girl had probably been a party to. "I'm fine," she said, stretching upward but unable to loosen the cramping muscles in her stomach.

She walked ahead of him. It's a goddamn waterfall, she told herself. I'm not that girl anymore. I can be detached about this just like everything else.

At the curve of the road her legs began to feel weak. "Must have been that last sprint up the hill," she said as Jefferson helped her to a bench just outside the park. A gate with an adjoining open-air shelter had been built of brown creek rock. The shingled roof gave it the rustic look of a pioneer cabin. Beyond it a half-dozen young boys were playing baseball with a board and a tin can.

Alma hardly recognized the place. About three acres had been transformed into a playground. Additional shelters stood next to stone barbecues with red-stained picnic tables on either side. Beyond the shelters she saw a gated tennis court, a large plot of green grass that could double as a football or baseball field, and a concrete court with basketball hoops at each end. Strategically planted shade trees looked groomed and domestic. In the distance she heard the watery roar of the waterfall.

"We have at least an hour to kill," Jefferson said. "Come on. It's the only park on this side of the tracks." He pulled on her hand. She stood up, shook each leg, and somehow managed to follow him.

Out near the falls Jefferson guided her up a carefully designed path with rock walls on either side. It followed the creek to the falls, then veered off to a staircase, where they climbed higher. To Alma's horror she looked out and saw the bridge.

The streambed had been straightened and trees cut down. Funny, she thought, the bridge is so close. In her memory it had seemed miles away. Once the patches of forest and undergrowth were cleared, the bridge was barely two, maybe three hundred yards downstream. She stared at the underside of the bridge, both drawn to the blue darkness and filled with revulsion. The skin on her arms prickled. She turned in the opposite direction. "Who did this?" she asked.

"You'll never believe it," he said, his hands on his hips. "Gentry money paid for it. They even hired a New York landscape architect to come in and cut out the ruggedness of the area so it'd be safe for children."

"Safe for children?" Alma repeated the words more to herself than to Jefferson.

"Even Walter is capable of a good deed now and then."

More like a guilty conscience, she thought. "I have to get out of here!"

Jefferson caught her arm. She slapped it away and ran. "Alma," he called after her.

She couldn't stop running—not until she was out of this park, out of sight of that bridge and Jesus Falls. At the park entrance she fell against a sign and steadied herself, sucking in air. Jefferson ran up and stopped a few feet behind her. She looked back at him and said, "Don't come near me."

"Alma?"

She slipped around the sign, keeping it between them. "Stay over there." She huffed out breath and fought the shaking in her limbs. In front of her she saw the letters spelling the name Gentry. She stepped back from the sign and read: JESUS FALLS PARK AND RECREATION AREA. IN HONOR OF CHARLOTTE S. GENTRY AND WALTER S. GENTRY. THE TOWN OF CONTRARY THANKS YOU FROM THE BOTTOM OF ITS HEART.

Alma whipped away from the sign. Against the rock wall leaned the can and board the boys had used to play ball. She picked up the board.

"What are you doing, Alma?" Jefferson circled her but did not come close.

She smashed the board into the sign. Venom from deep within saturated her. She beat the name Gentry over and over until the board broke.

Throwing down the splintered piece that was left, she backed away from the park. She dropped onto the bench outside its boundaries. Jefferson sat beside her. He watched her but did not speak. Guilt crept through her for having kept so much from him. If he'd known what had been happening inside her ever since she left California, then Vernon's case probably would have been smoother from the beginning. At least antagonism wouldn't have colored those early days. "Jefferson?" she said hesitantly. "Don't speak. Just sit with me a few minutes more." She stared at the park.

He moved closer to her and slowly wrapped his arms around her. She let her head drop on his shoulder, and every ounce of energy drained from her. She let go, surrendering her control, letting him hold her up. "Jefferson," she said. "I have something to tell you."

31

Jefferson was quiet on the way back, and Alma wondered if she'd made a mistake. "I don't want Bob to know," she said.

He didn't answer.

"Promise me?"

Jefferson nodded. He couldn't seem to look at her.

The old, familiar embarrassment crept into Alma. She wished she hadn't told him. He parked in front of the office and turned off the ignition but did not get out. He stared at his hands on the steering wheel.

She opened her door and turned, but he caught her arm and said, "If I had known that was going to happen, I'd have never left you that day." A single tear trembled on the rim of one lower eyelid. "I ran to get Vernon. . . . He told me to stay out of it. I thought . . . I thought . . . he'd scare them away. I thought that would be the end of it. When I heard he'd beat Narly up, I thought he'd just gone too far. I didn't listen to the other rumors. I'd never have believed anything like that about you." His eyes glazed over as if he were seeing the past replaying itself like a movie clip.

She enclosed both his hands in hers. "I don't blame you." Moving next to him, she wiped the wetness that had fallen onto his cheek. "That's not why I told you. I don't blame you. Please don't think that."

"I think . . . that now I need you to hold me," Jefferson said.

They wrapped their arms around each other. The warmth of his body spread through her. Alma moved her face close enough so that their lips met. They exchanged the gentlest of kisses. "Let's go upstairs," she said. "Sue will be back soon."

On the staircase they heard Bob talking with someone in the office. When he saw them at the door he motioned them inside. "I've got a surprise for you, Alma."

She and Jefferson traded glances as if to say, Enough surprises for today. They entered the office. Jordan McFedries turned around and shook Jefferson's hand, then danced Alma into his arms for a romantic dip and a kiss that mimicked Valentino's. When he let her up, all Alma could see was the glare in Jefferson's eyes.

32

" 'Waddell Hancock, Marylou Vanderbilt Whitney,' " Sue read from a reporter's pad while Alma and Jefferson took notes. " 'James E. Bassett, III,' " she continued, the excitement of her assignment breaking through. "Let's see. 'Mary Bingham'—any relation to you, Jefferson?"

" 'Fraid not," he answered stiffly, and held up the *Louisville Courier Journal*, which the Bingham family there had owned and fought over.

Alma smiled at him, trying to ease his mood. Jordan sat beside her, one arm draped around her shoulders. She knew Jefferson was staring at him every chance he could. And Jordan did look good. His black hair had a just-cut sheen, and his angular features fit like sculpture. She could smell him, the warm cinnamon odor of his skin, and she shifted to break the hold it had on her. "I'm not getting any vibes," she said, leaning forward and looking up into Jefferson's eyes. "Anybody else?"

Bob opened his hands. "Doubtful any of those would be Littlefield's partner. Maybe the pictures will tell more."

"I dropped them at the one-hour development," Sue said, pulling out a miniature camera. "Our cousin Rodney works there. He'll get 'em done in twenty minutes," she added proudly.

Jordan's hand scratched Alma's shoulder. She knew he was impatient, wanting to leave and be alone with her. It annoyed her. He knew better than that. She would never hurry him along if he was busy with a case. She patted his knee. "Did you hire a new maid?" she whispered. The skin around Jordan's eyes tightened uncomfortably.

Rodney arrived with the pictures, and they spread them across the table. A collective sigh of frustration swept through the room. Nothing and nobody new. The usual townspeople crowded the pictures—the mayor, the police and fire chief, local business leaders. Alma felt a twinge when she saw Charlotte Gentry's face.

"There!" Jordan said, pointing at a gray-haired man with a sleek, younger beauty on his arm. "Henryk de Kwiatkowski. He could come up with the kind of money you're talking about."

"Sharp eye, Jordan," Bob said. He looked around, then again at Jordan, congratulating him. "You may have found the link that will get the press off our back— at least as far as this pseudo-economic disaster is concerned."

Alma turned to Sue and started to explain. Sue waved her off and said, "I know, he bought the Calumet Farms, home of eight Kentucky Derby winners."

"Isn't he based mainly in the Bahamas?" Jefferson asked, apparently not ready to accept Jordan's conclusion. "We need to move carefully, Bob. If it's not de Kwiatkowski, we could be asking for trouble."

"We won't do anything before we know for sure, but at least we have a direction in which to look."

"Who knows?" Alma said. "Maybe de Kwiatkowski will admit he was Littlefield's partner. Maybe he'll even take over where Littlefield left off. Look at what he did for Calumet. He could do twice that for Littlefield Industries."

"I'd be interested in knowing if the governor was there," Jefferson said, looking at Alma.

"No," Sue answered. "At least I didn't see him." Her eyes shot to one side as if she were trying to remember something.

Alma could almost read Jefferson's mind. "Looks like things are not going so well in Walter's pursuit of the assembly seat," she said. Part of her was gleeful. She'd love to see him lose that seat. "That could make him more humble."

Jefferson's expression was far more serious. "It could also make him more desperate."

Alma realized he was right, and a new level of worry opened in her mind. What would Walter do next? "Can we spend a few minutes speculating on what Walter might try now?"

Jordan yawned but did not otherwise disturb the discussion. Alma took the opportunity to slide forward in her seat, away from his touch.

"Oh, my God!" Sue exclaimed. "I almost forgot." She smacked the side of her head. "How could I be so stupid! I was so excited playing detective that I forgot the most important thing."

Alma twirled a hand to hurry her sister along.

"Guess who wasn't there?" Sue stood up, as if to hold them in suspense. "Johanna Littlefield, that's who. She didn't come to her own father's memorial service."

"She's scheduled for a deposition on Monday," Bob said.

Alma stood and said, "I wouldn't miss that for a shot at addressing the Supreme Court." She walked behind the group and touched Jefferson's back as she passed him.

"Honey," Jordan said, standing and following her. "You have a lot of time to see this man in action." He pointed to Bob. "Let's let him get to work while you and I get reacquainted." He took her hand and pulled her into his arms.

"Go on, Alma," Bob said. "Jefferson and I will work through the weekend. We'll be ready for Monday."

Alma took longer to leave the office than she ever had before. She couldn't seem to come up with a reason to speak with Jefferson privately. As she left, Jordan's arm around her shoulders, she could only stare at Jefferson and hope that he could read her thoughts in her eyes: I'm sorry. I didn't mean to hurt you.

33

Jordan had rented a cabin in Pine Mountain State Park, about twenty miles from Contrary. Not that anyone would know them in town, he reasoned to Alma, but it was better not to take chances where rules of conduct were more old-fashioned. Alma explained to him that the limousine he'd rented in Knoxville would attract just as much attention, so after taking them to Mamaw's house, the driver asked for directions to the nearest freeway and was on his way. Alma picked up some clothing and asked Uncle George if she could borrow his car. He stared at his Buick Ninety Eight, then handed her a set of keys and pointed to a locked garage. "Honda's in there," he said.

As she and Jordan drove out of Contrary, all Alma could think of was the woman who'd answered his phone that morning. But, she thought, how to bring it up? Casually she asked, "Is your brother using your apartment this weekend?" She held in a tiny breath, silently hoping he'd say yes.

"Craig's in L.A. for a week. Some kind of commercial, I believe."

"He wasn't at your place earlier today?"

"No." Jordan glanced at her, but his attention was drawn back by the tight curve of the road.

"Are you sure?"

Jordan's cheeks colored. "Yes," he said.

They sat quietly for the hour-long drive to Pine Mountain, neither seeming to notice the grand view of mountains as they neared the park. Alma struggled to let go of her suspicions. Maybe she didn't want to know. Maybe the reason he was there was that the other relationship had ended. Isn't that what he'd said to her before she left California, that he had "some things I have to handle this weekend"?

Part of her couldn't imagine another woman in Jordan's life. My fault, Alma thought, it's my fault this happened. She should have spent more time in Sacramento. At the same time she knew that if she hadn't devoted the time and effort to her practice in San Francisco, Jordan would never have been attracted to her. A man of his stature could have any woman he wanted. Her potential had been the worm on the fish hook.

She reached over and ran her fingers through his dark hair. "Jordan?"

"Alma." They spoke at the same time.

An uncomfortable pause. "You first," she said.

"Alma . . ." He whistled out a breath of air as if stalling for time. He stared straight ahead into a wall of pine trees that lined the side of a steep mountain. "We never agreed to have an exclusive relationship."

The tip of Alma's nose burned and she knew she was seconds away from tears. "I suppose that's an understanding one assumes, only to find that it gets left out by omission."

"You never seemed to want it."

"Well, I wasn't writing a contract."

"You always put up walls. I could never get close to you, not like—"

"Thank you for sharing!"

The car squeaked around a hairpin turn, and Jordan

slowed almost to a stop. "You don't understand." He massaged the side of his head with the back of a hand. "I've invested more in you than I ever have with any other woman. We take our minutes when we have them and they mean more, even if there are fewer of them. Somebody like Holly—"

"Holly Helfin?" Alma's feet pressed into the floor as if she were jamming on the brakes. "Your intern?" She turned toward him, stretching the seat belt to a looser hold.

"She's not like you." Jordan smacked the side of his head. "That's not what I mean. You can get me so flustered sometimes!"

"You're burying yourself. Why don't you shut up and take the Fifth?"

"These things are not easy for me to say. I wouldn't waste the effort for someone I didn't care about." He flipped the turn signal and entered a driveway that led up to a two-story cabin. He stopped the car and turned off the ignition.

Alma sat still. No way am I getting out of this car, she thought. She stared straight ahead, arms crossed over her stomach.

Jordan reached in the backseat and pulled a box of California raisins from his overnight case. "For you," he said, handing it to her.

"Raisins?" She took the package. "You brought me raisins?"

"Would you just open it!"

She flipped open the top and looked into the box. Raisins, golden and plump. Their tart smell wafted toward her. A blue dot caught her attention. She moved a couple of raisins. The starburst of a blue topaz—a ring, a perfect match to the earrings he'd given her in California. Pulling it out of the box, she looked over at Jordan.

He said, "I'm hoping you'll accept this as a new beginning, a beginning that starts with you and me and goes on from there."

"No one else."

"It's taken care of . . . no one else."

Alma set the raisin box on the dashboard and looked up at the cabin. The ring felt solid in her hand. Before she left California, she'd believed Jordan was her future. How stupid she'd been not to see the shaky ground on which she stood. "You're sure this is what you want?"

He nodded.

Alma put the ring on her right hand. She would not make the same mistakes again. This time he was hers, and she'd never lose him again. "Once this case is over," she said, "I'm going to want to make some plans." She waited.

"It won't be a blue topaz next time."

Alma leaned over and pressed herself against Jordan's chest. "Take me inside," she said.

Saturday, before dawn, they snuggled under a blanket in front of a warm coal fire, waiting to watch the sunrise through a window that formed most of the east wall. They opened a bottle of champagne and mixed it with fresh-squeezed orange juice. Pine trees with furry branches lined the view on the eastern horizon and their scent filled the air. A pair of squirrels scurried across the porch to peer in the window. Alma felt relaxed and, for the first time since she'd arrived, happy.

"So when do you think you'll come back to California?" Jordan placed a raisin between his lips.

"Not sure. A lot has happened." She puckered her lips and took the raisin from him in a kiss.

"I spoke with Eric before I left. He's about to start

work on a football antitrust case that would be perfect for you."

"You know better than to tempt me like that."

"I'm afraid for you way out here in the woods. You might forget how to speak Californese. You might forget how to eat quiche. You might forget the taste of sushi." He touched the tip of her nose with his. "You might forget me."

"Not likely."

He touched the lid of her left eye and traced around her face to her mouth. "I can see the toll this case has taken on you."

She leaned over and blew out a candle still burning from the night before. "Dawn is enough for me," she said, uncomfortable with his studying gaze. "Seems I remember you being the one who insisted I take my family responsibilities more seriously."

"Stupid of me." He pulled her close, and they watched the flames burn around a large castle-shaped coal. "Would you consider a few days away?"

"I can't leave, Jordan."

"A vacation. We could go to New York or the Poconos."

"I'm already in the mountains. Did Bob put you up to this?"

Jordan's sheepish grin blossomed. "Can I have a jury verdict on this one?"

"I recognize a guilty face when I see one."

"We're golf buddies." He looked down and away from her.

"Golf buddies?" Alma fought the suspicion that he was hiding something from her. The more he avoided her eyes, the more her uncertainty irritated her. She'd seen the same frozen expression on the faces of lying witnesses. "When did you play golf with Bob?"

"Two days ago, in Monterey."
"We're not talking about the same Bob."
"Bob Griffin."
"Representative Bob Griffin?"
"Yeah, he's a friend of yours."
"I've only met him one time in my life. Why would Bob Griffin be interested in having you take me on a vacation?"

Jordan sat up, looking genuinely surprised at her response. He threw another piece of coal into the fire, then slid down beside her and began kissing her neck. "Don't know, I think he likes you. Anyway, he said something and it just started me thinking. That's all." He refilled their champagne glasses and handed her one.

She didn't take the glass. Instead, she pulled away from his embrace and stood up. She stared at him and slowly rubbed one temple, refusing to look away. Jordan set her glass on the floor and raised himself onto the overstuffed couch. She couldn't help thinking about how much he looked like a guilty client trying to convince his own lawyer of his innocence.

Bob Griffin, she thought. Golf. There were too many strings. She fought the conspiracy theory jelling in her mind. "I only want to know one thing. Who asked Bob Griffin to talk to you?"

Jordan tied his robe and buried his hands in the pockets. "He's a nice man. He simply asked about you."

"You're avoiding the question."
"Don't let your imagination run away with you."
"Now you're patronizing me."
"Alma, get control of yourself."
"Who is it?"
"Nobody that I would know."
"Don't you lie to me, goddamn it!"

Jordan moved to the window and closed his eyes. His

head dropped forward until his chin almost touched his chest. "Somebody wants you out of this and they're calling in a lot of favors."

All Alma could think of was the omniscient hand of the Gentrys. Not only her family, but now Jordan had come under the shadow of Contrary's ruling family. And Jordan had been too willing a victim. Golf! He hadn't come there because he'd broken up with Holly Helfin, she realized. "You'd use me like this? You'd do this to me?"

"I did this because I was concerned about you!"

"That line might work on some stupid little intern, Jordan, but it's not going to work on me!"

The fire popped and cracked and the room turned golden with its glow. Representative Griffin intends to be the next vice president, Alma thought. If he manages that, he can certainly influence who replaces the aging Supreme Court justices when they retire. She looked over at Jordan. The intimacy of the previous night turned into a tangle of heartbreak.

Alma dressed without looking at him.

"I'm sorry, Alma. At least wait until the sun comes up." He walked around her, frustrated emotion pouring from him. "I hope you'll remember something: There's not a hell of a lot that would get me to leave California for this godforsaken place. I did this for you. You don't realize it, but you're in over your head."

"Next you're going to ask me to go back to California today."

"Yes, I am. If that's what it takes to extricate you from this mess."

They turned in different directions, enveloped in the silence that comes between two people who know they are lost to each other. "You've never really believed I could make it without you."

"Alma, I know you love me."

"When you finally see someone as a fool, you just can't love them anymore."

In her heart she knew that she lied. Part of her wanted to run into his arms. She wished with all her being that this conversation had never happened, but it had, and there were no words left to say.

34

Alma was glad she had borrowed Uncle George's Honda to drive to Pine Mountain. She hadn't exactly expected to leave at the crack of dawn, but to have stayed with Jordan any longer would have weakened her resolve. She might have forgiven what was unforgivable.

An attorney negotiates everything, he'd told her once—back in the days when she was in awe of him, the state supreme court justice who took an interest in a junior associate. They'd been the toast of San Francisco society and Sacramento political circles.

Her hands tightened on the steering wheel. It angered her to realize that if she'd never come back to Contrary, she and Jordan might be planning their wedding by now. If she'd been in California, she might have looked past Holly. She also wondered if she would have played some backstage politics to further Jordan's career. How had she let herself become so compromised? Was it the salary, the promotions, the private lunchrooms, the dinners with the rich, powerful, and social elite? Or had it been Jordan? Had she lost her integrity one kiss at a time?

Alma stared out over the mountain range—a crunched-up blanket of brown, barely visible in the fog of early morning. Had this land had a sobering effect on her or had it merely led her back to a part of herself she'd buried long ago?

Alma slowed the car, reminding herself to drive carefully down the curving mountain road. Her concentration wavered, fleeing back to the scene with Jordan, as if reliving it would change its ending. "All great loves come to bad endings," she said, sniffing back a wave of emotion. "Antony and Cleopatra. Cathy and Heathcliff. Anna and Vronsky." The tires squeaked as she rounded a narrow hairpin curve. She decreased her speed to twenty miles per hour.

Her rearview mirror caught a flash of headlights. She slowed to let the car pass. Instead it crept up behind her. Thick fog spread through the trees like smoke in the aftermath of a forest fire and it swept across the road. Her headlights could not penetrate it.

Alma pressed the brakes and turned her head. She could see the pale outline of the car behind her. It had stopped about fifteen feet back, its headlights off. A chill rushed up her spine.

She raised her foot from the brakes and inched forward. The car followed. The sun crested the mountaintop, and the glare through the fog was like staring into a furnace. The car behind her moved closer. She could see that it was red, possibly a Pontiac. She shielded her eyes with one hand, trying to watch the road and keep the car in sight at the same time. It sped up, then slammed on its brakes just before it would have crashed into her. "What an idiot!" she said.

A scenic stop ahead of her looked like the best way to lose the guy. Alma's heartbeat fluttered like a hummingbird's wings. She veered into the parking area.

The red car pulled up as far as the turn-in and idled. The glare on its windshield prevented her from seeing the driver or how many people were inside. Trouble, she thought, sickened.

Alma yanked open the glove compartment and riffled through maps and papers until her hand touched metal. Thank God! she thought. A .22 revolver. Uncle George, you didn't let me down. But the chamber was empty.

She looked around and saw a pay phone next to some vending machines. She drove up to it, and opened the car door just enough to reach the phone. She dialed Fred Walker's number. The red Pontiac revved its engine. Alma put a hand on the gun in her pocket, thinking that if the driver came for her, maybe she could fake him or her out. Just yesterday she'd chastised her family for using guns. Now she was intensely grateful to have one.

At a little past six there was probably not another soul between there and the bottom of the mountain. Her stomach churned. A ghostly memory of being pursued snaked through her thoughts. A dreamlike echo of the voices of three boys chasing her like baying hounds.

On the fourth ring Fred answered and she blurted out, "This is Alma Bashears! I'm at the overlook on Pine Mountain. A red Pontiac is following me. I don't know who it is." She gasped for air as an old, familiar panic spread through her.

"Listen to me!" His voice was deep and serious. "Drive down as fast as you can. Halfway down there's a fork in the road. Go to the left. Do you understand me?"

Alma nodded, unable to speak. Her throat burned as if it had been scalded and her nose swelled with congestion. The red car revved its engine again.

"Alma!" Fred yelled. "Do you understand!? Take the left fork. I know a shortcut. I'll meet you somewhere on that road. Are you there?"

"I understand," she managed to say, her eyes never veering from the red Pontiac. She fumbled with the gearshift and fought hyperventilation. As she drove toward the exit, the red car gunned its motor, then sped off down the road, swerving to keep from hitting her.

Alma sat for a few minutes, letting her terror fade. Farther on, the red car had disappeared. She felt silly. Teenagers, she decided, trying to scare her. Fred would probably think it was funny. She dreaded having to tell him that her pursuer had chickened out and run away. She put the .22 on the seat and pulled onto the road.

In about twenty minutes she came to the fork. The red Pontiac was parked in the middle of the road on the left, the one she had to take. Alma stopped about fifty feet short of the fork. She could see the driver of the other car. It was the black-haired policeman from the Contrary Littleafia.

An electric surge shot through her—not anger, fear, or even rage, just violent thoughts of survival. She'd felt the same, once before, when the roar of Jesus Falls was in her ears.

Alma floored the gas pedal and aimed her car directly at the red Pontiac. The policeman's mouth dropped in shock. His car swerved to evade hers as she shot past him down the left fork. Then the Pontiac chased after her. Both cars squealed around the tight hairpin curves.

As their speed pushed above the safety limit, gravel spat on all sides of them. The Pontiac bumped her rear fender. Alma screamed. She held tightly to the steering wheel, maneuvering the curves like a race-car driver.

Ahead she saw a souvenir shop at another scenic area. Spinning in, she realized too late that the shop was closed. No escape. The red Pontiac raced in behind her, scraping against her passenger side. Alma slammed on the brakes, turned her car, and hit the other on its rearside panel. The Pontiac spun around and came to rest facing her. Alma jumped out, ran to the Pontiac, and aimed the

.22 at the policeman's temple. "Get out of there!" she yelled.

His lip was bleeding from being bounced against the steering wheel. His features tightened in a mean scowl. He moved a hand toward the seat beside him.

"You do and I'll blow your brains out!" With one hand Alma jerked his car door open. "Get out!"

He raised his hands and stood. "You're interfering with the law, young lady." Alma saw a revolver on the seat.

She stepped back, refusing to let him get too close. He retreated a ways to the trunk. Alma kicked the door closed so that he couldn't get near his gun. She didn't want to chance turning her back to him by leaning in to get it herself.

"What you know about the law would fit on the tip of my finger!" she shouted. She hated this man, his disrespect, his arrogance, his assumed superiority. She backed him up toward the souvenir shop, next to a life-size carving of a Plains Indian chief. "Take out your handcuffs."

The policeman gave her a tentative look, then pulled the cuffs off his belt.

"Put one around your wrist and one around the Indian's wrist."

"Now, wait a minute—"

"Do it!" Alma pushed the gun into his ribs.

He jumped sideways, as if more afraid the .22 would go off by accident than that she would actually shoot him. His eyes narrowed and his tongue poked from one side of his mouth.

Alma knew he was measuring her. Flashes of Rudy, Earl, and Narly crowded her thoughts. Loathing gripped her stomach as the policeman slowly looked up and down her body. He stepped toward her. She thumbed

THE LAW OF REVENGE 223

back the hammer of the gun. He cuffed himself to the Indian. She ordered him to throw down the cuff's keys. He did so, and she pocketed them.

"Well, what are you going to do now?" he asked, his mouth smirking like a bad Elvis imitator.

Alma lowered the gun and pointed it at his crotch.

"No!" he yelled, covering his fly with one hand and trying to kneel behind the Indian. "Please, don't!"

"Do you know how much I hate men right now?" She felt sweat beading on her upper lip and her teeth clenched.

In the background the roar of a motor approached. A motorcycle twisted down a mountain path and jumped onto the road. It nearly passed them, then screeched to a stop and pulled into the parking lot.

The driver was clad in black, his helmet hiding his face. A rifle was slung over his shoulder.

"Fred?" she asked.

The motorcyclist lifted the mask of his helmet. Fred got off the bike and walked a circle around the policeman and the Indian. "You get engaged, Dwight?" he asked.

"Unlock me," Dwight demanded, his face coloring.

Fred took the gun from Alma. "It's empty," she whispered.

"That crazy bitch tried to kill me!" Dwight yelled. "She run me off the road and shot at me with her gun!"

Fred sniffed the .22's barrel. "Ain't been fired, Dwight." He handed the gun back to Alma. "But maybe it should have been."

"Don't give it back to her!" Dwight yelled. "She's a lesbo! She hates men!"

Alma whirled around and aimed at Dwight. A million stars burst in front of her eyes.

He howled and raised his arms to his head. "No! Don't!" His face screwed up in terror.

She pulled the trigger six times, the hammer clicking on the empty chambers.

Fred laughed aloud, waiting for Dwight to look up.

Alma went over to the Pontiac and looked inside. The car was still running.

"What are you going to do?" Fred called out to her.

Alma leaned in, twisted the steering wheel toward the mountain's edge, and put the gearshift into neutral.

"Alma, don't," Fred said. "Don't!"

She heard his feet scuffing through the gravel as he ran toward her. The Pontiac rolled forward and then disappeared over the mountainside in a clamor of twisting metal, ripping trees, and the hard grind of a disengaged engine.

Dwight looked at his car. His mouth hung open and he leaned on the Indian for support.

Fred glared at Alma. "What the hell did you do that for? He wasn't following you because he was curious about your life! Him and his friends won't forget this." He turned and put his hands on both sides of his head. "I can't believe you did that. I can't believe it."

Alma stared over the mountain's edge. The rage that had gripped her lifted and she felt giddy. "He's one of them," she said. "The Littleafia."

Fred narrowed his eyes. She saw a trace of fear, as if he was trying to tell her she'd bitten off more than she could chew. "Littlefield's dead, Alma. No tellin' who their allegiance is to now."

"There's only so many choices," she said. She motioned Fred to follow, then stood in front of Dwight, squaring her body to his. "You work for Gentry now?"

Dwight stared back at her with angry dark eyes but did not answer.

Alma stepped closer, smelling his coffee breath. She wanted to make him as uncomfortable as possible. "You check with your boss before trying anything with me." He looked down at the ground. "Mr. Gentry will tell you to give me a wide berth. And, Dwight, you'd better do it."

He looked at the clouds of dust coming up from his wrecked car. "A man's car is like his—"

"Yeah, I know what it's like," Alma said.

She inspected the scrape on Uncle George's Honda and felt like kicking Dwight. She almost wished she could turn him over to Uncle George. First Sue's tires, and now Uncle George's Honda.

Fred started his motorcycle. His forehead was lined, whether from worry or anger she couldn't tell. He didn't speak but indicated that he'd follow her down the mountain. They left Dwight cuffed to the Indian, staring after his car.

35

The hall telephone at Mamaw's house barely reached to Alma's bed, and she adjusted the pillows into a desk so that she could take notes. She dialed the number of the *Washington Post* and asked for Jill Ripley, hoping she was available on the weekend.

While on hold Alma fished through the last two issues of the *Contrary Gazette*. The editorial page lined up the candidates for the state assembly seat, showing who endorsed which candidate. The three top contenders were a nephew of a West Virginia coal baron who had moved into the state for the express purpose of entering politics; a labor attorney from Pineville who had the support of the unions and the four representatives; and Bell County's commonwealth attorney, Walter Gentry, who was endorsed by the Kentucky Bar Association, the attorney general, and both senators. The assembly seat was attached to the powerful Ways and Means Committee and was a springboard to the governorship. Whoever received the appointment would play a powerful role in the future of Kentucky politics.

The heat is on, Alma thought, realizing she meant it as much for herself as Walter Gentry. Vernon's future probably depended on how much competition Walter thought he had. It seemed foolish, but nothing could be worse for her brother than for Walter to be appointed to that assembly seat as soon as possible.

"Old Hickory," Jill Ripley admonished over the phone. "You don't call me enough!" Alma's college roommate worked as an editor for the *Post* and the two had frequently traded information and favors.

"And you only call me when you want free legal advice," Alma kidded. After a few minutes of catching up, she came to her question. "Are you familiar with Representative Robert Griffin?"

"From California. A ladies' man. Don't do it."

Alma laughed. "I'm not interested in dating him. I need to know who he hangs with—socially and politically. I'm especially looking for a Kentucky connection."

"That's easy. He's Senator McCauley's cousin."

"Sam McCauley from Kentucky?" Alma tore through the newspaper, scattering it on the floor to locate the editorial page. "Walter Gentry endorsed by both of Kentucky's U.S. senators," she read. "Jill, once again you're a fountain of the right information."

"Yeah, well, I should charge a corporate attorney's fee."

Alma hung up, wrote the names Walter Gentry and Charlotte Gentry on a piece of paper, folded it, then tore it into tiny pieces. An old superstition of her mother's to rid herself of enemies. "At least it makes me feel better," she said as she dumped the pieces into the trash can.

To say that the line had been crossed only meant that the Gentrys would stop at nothing. What Alma found more fascinating was the Gentrys' brazenness. They thought nothing of calling on a senator to call on his cousin, the representative, to call on a California State Supreme Court justice to distract his girlfriend from a court case. Alma was angered but not surprised. She wondered how much of that seventy-five thousand she'd last seen scattered on Mrs. Gentry's kitchen floor had been funneled into campaign funds. Finding out about her relationship with Jordan couldn't have been cheap.

Alma went into the bathroom and turned on the shower. She waited until the room was steamy before pulling off her clothes. The heat in the air felt like a warm, safe blanket. But Alma knew she wasn't safe right now. She didn't know who she could trust anymore. As she showered, she let the water run hot over her body. As hot as she could stand it. Concentrating on the scalding liquid was all that kept her tears over Jordan from erupting.

Saturday mornings everyone gathered at Mamaw's house for breakfast, and when Alma drained her coffee cup but declined to sit down, hardly anyone tried to dissuade her. No one had even asked why she'd come back in the wee morning hours on the back of a motorcycle. They were probably still angry with her for admonishing her uncles about their commando style of dealing with Silver Jenkins. Now she felt guilty for what she'd done to Dwight. The hot shower had calmed her nerves. She was determined not to let them find out what had happened on her way down the mountain. Why get them all stirred up?

Mamaw rolled a piece of sausage into a buttered biscuit and wrapped it in wax paper. "Eat this sometime this morning, honey," she coaxed.

"What I actually need," Alma said to everyone at the table, "is to borrow a car."

"Well, don't look at me," Sue replied, and rolled her eyes. "My automobile has done its duty for the month."

"I'll be really careful," Alma said, smarting at the remark. "It wasn't my fault they flattened your tires and I said I'd pay for them. Jack, you make sure I get the bill."

Alma hadn't told them about the scrape on Uncle

George's car yet. She had left it at a body shop in town, and hoped to have the damage repainted without anyone in the family knowing. "I wanted Uncle George's car to be clean after being on the mountain. I know I should have waited for it, but I asked for the deluxe cleaning."

"It only starts with flat tires, Alma." Uncle George spread molasses into some soft butter and mixed it together. "Next you'll get your windshield shot out."

"I don't believe anyone at the Littlefield Hotel can afford any more trouble with me." The image of Dwight handcuffed to the carved Indian came to Alma's mind. She hoped her deed wouldn't backfire.

Uncle Ames smirked. Aunt Joyce stared down at her food, then wiped a milk mustache off Larry Joe. Rodney and Jack watched their uncles as if waiting for instructions.

Merl stared tentatively at Alma, as if she wanted to offer her car but was afraid any action of hers might cause more trouble. "It's more than the hotel people, Alma. This whole town's gone nuts—all afraid they're gonna be laid off and all thinking Vernon's the cause. I've had more people tell me to kiss their butts in this one week than has cussed me out for a whole year."

Alma couldn't help but smile at her word choice. "Look at it this way, Momma. After I get the proof that Littlefield's business will continue, even if under different ownership, you can go back to all those people who told you to kiss their butts and . . . Well, I'm sure you'll come up with the right words."

Her mother let out a deep belly laugh.

"All you do is work, honey," Mamaw said. "Why don't you stay home with me today?" She touched the gold rooster pin that Alma had on her sweater.

Alma buttoned up her jacket. "Jefferson and Bob are in the office. I have to carry my load as well."

"At least let one of the boys drive you." Merl stared over at Rodney and Jack and tapped a long, red fingernail against her coffee cup.

Alma looked out the window at the hazy morning air. A bright sun burned through the morning mist. It was going to be a hot day. Vernon's trailer looked like a snail, closed up to conserve strength. "I'll use Vernon's Jeep."

As she walked to the trailer, she couldn't help thinking what poetic justice it would be if a Jeep bought with Littlefield money got its windshield shot out by a Littlefield goon. "Vernon," she called out, banging on the door at the same time.

Vernon was never an early riser and usually had the disposition of a hibernating bear when wakened, so she knew what to expect. "I need to borrow your Jeep. I have to go downtown. You can either get dressed and drive me or throw out the keys."

Some rumblings and voices inside indicated to Alma that he was not alone. Oh, great, she thought, glancing back at the house and hoping Mamaw was not looking out the window in case some half-naked, peroxided blonde opened the door. "Ooohhh, brother dearest. The woman who's going to save your skin needs a lift."

She waited. Vernon didn't answer her. "Damn it, Vernon, I'm cold out here."

The door cracked open and Vernon slid half his body outside. He wore misbuttoned blue jeans with no shirt and rubbed the left side of his neck as if he had a crick in it. "Yeah, here's the keys."

"No argument? Just here's the keys?"

"Anytime, Alma."

She studied his taut features and tried to look past him into the trailer. "Care to introduce me?" Alma couldn't help a malicious big-sister smile.

He pulled the door close to him. "Afraid Albert might get out."

Alma winked at him. "Bonnie June or Lizzy Kay?"

"Come on, Alma, give us some privacy here," he whispered.

It seemed silly that he'd try to hide his girlfriend from her. He was usually all too eager to show them off, but now he stared back at her, blank-faced and relaxed about her borrowing his prized Jeep Cherokee. Alma made a note to herself that the next time she wanted something from Vernon she should hit him up for it on the morning after.

Alma settled into the Jeep, adjusting the mirror and driver's seat. Glad to be away from the family, she turned on the radio as loud as it would go and wailed with a tune as the disc jockey announced a Patsy Cline marathon.

She was glad she'd gotten out of the house before anyone had had a chance to ask about Jordan. She decided to tell everyone that her evening with Jordan had gone wonderfully, but that she'd come back early to get a head start on some legal research. Only her mother would look at her peculiarly, perhaps intuiting the lie. Alma didn't know why she needed to lie. Partly to keep from worrying them about the seriousness of the strings the Gentrys had been able to pull. Partly because she didn't want them to see her in need. Vulnerable, hurting. It struck her that she'd kept silent about the rape for many of the same reasons. She trembled inside and sang loudly with the deep-voiced Patsy Cline in order to kill the feelings.

She breezed toward town, slowed at the cab stand, and stopped just to the left of it, looking around for police cars. Maybe the Littleafia slept late, she thought, except the ones who pulled surveillance duty. She looked at her watch. Two hours had passed since she came down from the mountain. She wondered if Dwight had been found yet.

Alma turned in at the cab stand and drove around back, where the bootlegging operation was set up. She purchased a pint of Jack Daniel's. As she sipped it, she took a picture of Jordan out of her wallet. Lake Tahoe was in the background, she and Jordan were holding hands but standing apart. How rarely they ever showed affection in public. Still, their understanding was one of the mind, one of mutual respect and complete trust. Now that was destroyed—fallen victim to the Gentrys.

As much as she tried, she couldn't seem to cry about it. It was as if her time there had been a continuation of her life as a seventeen-year-old. Her life in California had been a dream over the rainbow. She swallowed a large gulp of bourbon and coughed through the burn. Assertive, Alma thought, positioning the picture of Jordan on the dashboard so that she could look at it as she drove. "I am usually assertive."

She headed off again, then skidded to a halt, almost running a red light.

"Patsy," she said to the radio. "I used to hate it when I'd have to deal with women who tried to be assertive but ended up being ball-busting bitches." The Jeep idled and backfired. "Might be I'm going to have to be a ball-busting bitch."

The light changed to red again and Alma realized she'd sat through the green light. She turned the bourbon bottle upside down and guzzled a long drink. In her mind she saw it like a title on an office door: ALMA BASHEARS, BALL-BUSTING BITCH OF CONTRARY, KENTUCKY, ATTORNEY-AT-LAW. "Might be redundant," she said to the radio. The car behind her honked when she did not respond to the next green light. Alma leisurely rolled

THE LAW OF REVENGE 233

down her window and thrust her head out as far as she could. "Scrreew yooou!"

Then she counseled herself, "Can't go into the office like this." She turned onto a side street and cruised past two-story turn-of-the-century houses. The morning fog had burned away and bright sunlight made the community look as suburban as any in California. Alma thought of Dwight chained to the Indian and Jordan on his way back to California—to Holly. And Representative Griffin. Patsy Cline ended her song about falling to pieces, and Alma let her head lean sideways and rest on the window.

She hadn't been totally honest with Mamaw this morning. She would go to the office, eventually, when the buzz of the bourbon wore off. But first she'd pay Walter a visit. Just to let him know that his little game with Jordan hadn't worked. With satisfaction she said aloud, "Alma Bashears—still in town. What better way to start Walter's morning?"

36

Alma would have paid to have a photograph of Charlotte Gentry's frozen glare as she looked up from her coffee cup to the back door of her son's house.

"What an unexpected surprise," Alma said with her friendliest smile, and swung the screen door wide to let herself in. "I come to pay my respects to my old school chum, Walter, and find his lovely mother visiting. Guess I can kill two vultures with one stone." She pulled a chair out from the table and sat opposite Mrs. Gentry. "Good morning, Charlotte."

"Mrs. Gentry to you." She sipped from her cup, then tapped it onto a saucer. With a nod she indicated for Alma to pour herself some coffee.

"Thank you," Alma said. "You've always been an impeccable hostess."

The *Contrary Gazette* lay folded on the table. Alma picked it up and held it in front of her. Page-one stories were a hodgepodge of the annual dry- versus wet-county debate, the empty assembly seat, and the effect Bill Littlefield's death would have on Contrary's economy. A sidebar kept track of events to date. Alma counted fifteen mentions of Vernon's name. "My, my," she said. "If this press about Vernon Bashears keeps up, I'll bet his attorneys file for a change of venue. I'll bet they get it, don't you?"

"Doesn't really concern me." Mrs. Gentry pushed a breakfast plate to the side and folded her hands on the table.

"When do you think the governor is going to make a decision? I hope it's soon because I'd like to see my brother get a fair trial."

"You're impertinent."

Alma raised her eyebrows. "I always thought of myself as sassy. At least my boyfriend always thought so."

"I don't have the least bit of interest in your disgusting nocturnal prowlings. I think it's time you were on your way." With one hand Mrs. Gentry gave a Queen Elizabeth wave and stared down at the sports section in front of her.

"I bet you do. I just bet you and your son thought I'd be on my way long before this." Alma scooted back the chair and stood up. "I can't leave before saying hello to Walter." She stepped toward a door that led to the main room.

"You don't need to be going in there!" Mrs. Gentry shot up from her chair and moved to block Alma's entry.

The sharpness of her demand startled Alma. She pulled back her shoulders and with effort unclenched her teeth. "Is a hollow girl not good enough to be acknowledged in the inner sanctum, Mrs. Gentry?"

"I highly resent your coming to my son's home."

"And I highly resent what you and Walter pulled with Jordan McFedries."

"I don't know what you're talking about."

Then came the sound of footsteps down a staircase, and Mrs. Gentry twisted around, nervously clutching her hands in front of her. Walter appeared in the doorway.

"Ah, Jesus," he said, looking at his mother and Alma facing off. "Can't I get one damn day off?"

"Don't curse," his mother said. "I'll handle this. You go back to . . . what you were doing."

"What were you doing?" Alma asked pointedly. "Thinking up new schemes to get me to leave town?"

"The woman is daft," Mrs. Gentry said. "I'm beginning to believe all the female Bashearses are touched in the head."

"No," Alma responded sarcastically. "Smart in the head. Senator McCauley, Representative Griffin, Justice Jordan McFedries. Did you really think I wouldn't figure it out? Hell, for all I know, Jordan's a cousin, too!"

Walter closed his eyes briefly and opened his hands at the level of his shoulders. "What am I not getting?"

Alma reviewed his stance. His eyes and mouth were wrinkled on the left side. His palms still faced upward. He seemed genuinely confused. Mrs. Gentry on the other hand busied herself cleaning the table. Alma stepped back so that she could observe them both. "I believe it's called influence peddling—or just plain meddling. Justice McFedries and I have *terminated*"—she said the word hard and toward Mrs. Gentry—"our understanding. Any further campaign contributions will be wasted."

Mrs. Gentry let the dishes clang into the sink, then fixed her hands on her hips as she turned around. "I will not be talked to that way in my son's home."

"If you have any proof of what you're suggesting, let's hear it." Walter spoke to Alma but glared at his mother. His chest moved up and down with quick breaths and his mouth was a tightly squeezed line across his face.

"You know there's no proof." Alma looked from mother to son. Tension ballooned between them. "I'm not leaving town. No matter what. I'm seeing this through to the end." She turned and opened the screen door.

"Alma, wait," Walter called to her.

She stepped back inside. Mrs. Gentry retreated to the sink and began washing dishes, but in her reflection on the cabinets Alma saw that she was watching.

Walter said, "I've discussed the press coverage of the case with Mother and the chief editor, Richard Norville."

"Really?" Alma glanced down at the newspaper on the table, then looked back at him.

"There will have to be some coverage, you understand, but Richard agrees with me, and Mother will comply that it will be held to the highest journalistic standards . . . starting tomorrow."

Mrs. Gentry banged down a silver pot. "You don't owe her any explanation."

Alma picked up the newspaper and spread open the front page. "The damage is already done. My family can't walk down Main Street without having obscenities shouted at them."

"I told you these things take time," Walter shot back.

"And the charge against my brother?"

Walter shifted his weight to his right leg and buried his hands deeply in his robe pockets. "I have to proceed the way I see fit to carry out my responsibilities as commonwealth attorney."

"You're not running for political office in front of me, Walter. There's no need to be so politically correct."

"You're wasting your time with her, son." Mrs. Gentry turned toward Alma. Her hands gestured as if she was telling a fairy tale to a child. "She'll just hold your generosity against you."

"Mother, please." Walter motioned with his left hand in a stop gesture.

"Like all white trash, the more you try to help them, the more they resent you for it."

"I said I'll handle this, Mother."

Mrs. Gentry came face-to-face with Alma and cocked

her head to one side. "Do you feel the swamp of your heritage pulling you back into the mire?"

"Shut up, Mother!" Walter gritted his teeth so that his upper lip protruded under his mustache.

Alma stared into the old lady's steely blue eyes with the hate of a lifetime welling up inside her. She knew if she responded, Walter would have to defend his mother. She'd leave it just like this: son pissed off at mother; mother disappointed in son's lack of response. To Walter she said, "I'll see you next week when we receive the forensic evidence from your office."

"That was delivered yesterday," he replied. "Bob asked for it before the grand jury hears it on Monday. You see, I'm trying to be accommodating."

A sobering shock raced through Alma's body. "We were expecting to be heard before the grand jury in April, not March."

"Three cases were dropped for lack of evidence, so we had an opening on the final day before this grand jury is dismissed. We simply took advantage of the opportunity."

"You just want a first-degree indictment before the governor makes a decision!"

Walter was silent.

"You can't do this!" Alma shouted. "We're not ready."

"It's already done. If you hadn't gone on vacation, you would already know it. Bob Krauss and Jefferson Bingham know it."

Alma seethed, then stared at Walter's mother and said, "You could take a few lessons from your son, Mrs. Gentry."

As Alma drove away, spinning stones in the driveway, she fought the urge to floor the gas pedal. She cursed Bob and Jefferson as much as she did Walter. They knew where she was staying. They had the phone number. She stopped at the corner to get ahold of herself before driving farther. Patting the dashboard of Vernon's Jeep, she said to it, "No, I can't afford to let you get damaged just because I'm furious." Her hand brushed the picture of Jordan and knocked it to the floor. She left it there. Almost a day and a half had been wasted. "How could those two bozos do this to me?"

She looked in the rearview mirror at Walter's house. Just to the left of the driveway, behind a row of hedges, was parked the same red Corvette that had sped away from her at the Littlefield Hotel. Alma clapped her hands. "That bastard!"

Johanna Littlefield had been in the house the entire time. Alma looked at her watch. Johanna was scheduled for an interview on Monday in Jefferson's office. Unless that, too, had been changed without her knowledge.

She would bet money that the interview had been changed to today. Bob knew how much she wanted to be there. She hit her hand on the steering wheel. Lucy Brenner flashed through her mind, all studs and black leather. Alma shrugged off the unpleasant image. Two little rich girls in one month is trying my patience, she thought. "Well," she said to the Corvette in the mirror, "don't you be late, little Miss Rich Bitch, because I know where to find you!"

37

Alma popped a breath mint into her mouth as she opened the door to the law office. Inside, Bob and Jefferson looked like generals in a war room, their heads bent over a tableful of books and papers. The fluorescent light above the table cast a yellow hue, and the smell of men's sweat mixed with the metallic odor of steam heat. The television played the news at a very low volume. "So, the grand jury meets on Monday," Alma said. She used as stern a tone as she could, aware she'd slurred the word *jury*.

Bob peered over his glasses, a take-no-prisoners look in his eyes. "Nothing could change it. I decided not to call you."

She sauntered toward the table, letting the heels of her shoes tap against the tile floor. She could see how nervous it made them. "Why do I feel like you want me out of the way?"

Bob coughed and exhaled impatiently. "I don't know, Alma. Why do you feel that way?"

"I expected better from you, Bob Krauss."

He tossed a pencil onto the table. Jefferson jumped up, perhaps thinking to prevent an argument, and pulled a chair out for her. "Sit down, Alma. We can use all the help we can get."

Bob rubbed the bridge of his nose. "It is immaterial

THE LAW OF REVENGE 241

whether the grand jury hears this case now or next month. If Gentry is able to get a first-degree, the sooner we know what he has, the better. If we're going to get an indictment, I'd just as soon know the charge now."

"You mean Vernon," Alma said. "Vernon's the only one who's going to be indicted."

Bob picked up his coffee mug and sipped a long, slow drink. Anger flared in his eyes.

"I just don't want us to lose track of who we're defending here." Alma sat, kicking her shoes off underneath the table and folding her hands on a pile of papers. As much as she respected Bob's legal skills, she couldn't let herself forget that he'd earned much of his reputation by glamorizing his cases, occasionally at the expense of his client. Yet she couldn't deny his ninety percent win record.

Jefferson sniffed loudly. "You smell like a bootlegger's bed. Where the hell did Justice Jordan take you?" He smiled a smart-aleck grin. "Hey, nice ring."

"I . . . I . . ." Alma stumbled over her words. "I took some cough syrup this morning," she lied. "The shift to warmer weather gave me a chill. Why do you have the heat on so high?" She unconsciously touched the stone of the ring and twisted it off. She'd forgotten to give it back, and hearing Jordan's name pinched a nerve.

"We weren't expecting you back until Monday," Jefferson said, his tone probing for more information about her and Jordan than their itinerary.

Alma stood up and reached for the coffeepot in the center of the table. It was empty. Another on the warmer gave her a chance to put enough distance between herself and the men so that they couldn't smell the liquor on her breath. She took her time pouring the coffee, hot and black. The buzz of the bourbon disappeared, replaced by a dull ache in her stomach. "Johanna Littlefield scheduled for an interview today?"

"Sit," Bob said, his voice still formal. "I have a folder of memos to bring you up to date. And yes, Johanna will be here at eleven o'clock."

Alma felt guilty as she leafed through the memos. Bob had documented everything that had happened since she'd left. He'd kept her better informed than anyone in the San Francisco office would have done under the same circumstances. Nothing had been left to chance. A series of memos outlined possible strategies for pre-trial motions: change of venue, mistrial, replacement of judge, jury selection, and a two-page plan on Johanna Littlefield. Alma looked up at Bob after reading the first paragraph of the plan. "You're on my side about this?"

"I believe she's more involved than we know."

Alma glanced over at Jefferson. He stared at the ring she'd taken off and dropped into an empty ashtray. "Do you think this because of something Vernon said?"

"From what he didn't say," Jefferson said, grinning. He pulled out a piece of posterboard. "Here's a diagram of the office where Vernon and Littlefield fought." Jefferson pointed to a back room on the opposite side of the building from the suite of offices where Alma had been when she confronted Clark Winchell. "This is his personal office, not his business office. Their living quarters are adjacent to this office. Bill Littlefield's bedroom—here. Johanna's bedroom—here."

"Right next to her father's personal office?" Alma's mind clicked with possibilities. "That's a little strange."

Bob nodded in agreement. "Or it's the worst-laid-out architectural plan of the century."

Jefferson laughed. "My spies tell me that Littlefield was so paranoid that he believed having an office next to his daughter's bedroom would discourage anybody from trying to steal from him. The safe is in that room—here, against the wall, right next to the connecting door to her bedroom."

"I don't get it," Alma said.

"If you get arrested stealing from his safe, get ready for an attempted rape charge as well. Nothing like a father defending southern womanhood to add fifteen years to your sentence."

"He'd put his daughter in that kind of jeopardy?"

Bob tapped his fingers on the board in three different places. "There are alarms and security all over the place. No one would have gotten near her."

Alma began to see how even Vernon might have gotten twisted around this little manipulator's fingers. "Johanna would have gone along with this?"

"She already did once. Howie Cranston—doing twenty-five years in the state pen." Jefferson leaned back in his chair. His leg touched Alma's underneath the table. He sat up. "Excuse me."

Alma reached over and patted his arm. "I like these interview questions. Not too obvious. There're a dozen ways to trick the information out of her without her even knowing what she's answering." Alma continued to scan the list of about two hundred questions. "You should know, Walter Gentry has coached her."

"I don't think it matters," Jefferson said. "We had a psychologist help us. Johanna won't even realize what she's telling us half the time. About every third question is double-edged."

"What did you say?" Bob turned around from where he'd stood to look out the window.

"I said—" Jefferson began.

"Not you, her." His hands bunched in his pockets. He stared down at her like an eagle from a tall perch.

"I said I think we should be prepared about Walter coaching this witness," she said.

"No," Bob disagreed. "That's not what you said. You said that I should know that Walter *has coached her*." He rounded the table and put a hand on Alma's shoulder. "How would you know that unless you've been in touch with the commonwealth attorney again?"

"It was a . . . a figure of speech," Alma stuttered, and knew she was not believable.

"You don't make those kinds of mistakes." Bob bent over her as if intending to make her nervous. "I don't need any more shenanigans from your mother or from you."

Alma swallowed. "Johanna Littlefield's car was parked at Walter's house this morning."

"And?" Bob squeezed her shoulder until it hurt.

Alma tried to get up, but he held her down with his hand on her collarbone. "All right. I spoke to Walter for only a short time . . . to Mrs. Gentry a bit longer."

"About what?" Bob's teeth were gritted.

Alma looked down at her lap. "It's personal." Embarrassment warmed her cheeks and she couldn't look up at him.

"Since I started working on this case I've sensed more than the normal animosity between you and Herr Prosecutor."

Alma crossed her arms on her chest. "It's got nothing to do with the case." She uncrossed her arms, realizing the guilt the gesture cast on her.

Bob let go of her and smacked his fist into his hand. "Everything has to do with the case. I refuse to be half-informed."

"I hired you to defend my brother, not to snoop in my personal life."

"Let's get this one thing clear," Bob said. "I work for

your brother, not for you. I will do whatever I have to do to clear him. And if that means scrambling your personal life into a Denver omelet, then so be it."

"You two, calm down," Jefferson said. "Let's stop and get some lunch."

"I will walk out that door now if you don't tell me what is going on!" Bob said.

"Then walk out!" Alma yelled back at him.

Bob threw a file of papers onto the table and reached for his coat.

Jefferson stood up, looking at the two of them, then poked Alma on the shoulder.

She couldn't look up at him. Her insides felt like tangled hair. All she could think of was to protect the secret of her past by any means possible. "All this case is to you is a book and movie deal!"

"I'll tell you," Jefferson said to Bob. "I know the reason."

"Jefferson!" Alma stared at him, feeling the blood drain from her face.

"We need Bob, Alma. I don't think anybody else can win this case."

"I'll find somebody else." Alma pulled on Jefferson's shirtsleeve. Surely he wouldn't tell. Surely he wouldn't betray her.

"We don't have the time! You're striking out at Bob. Bob isn't the problem. Your past is the problem."

"Jefferson—don't, please!"

"Class struggle," Jefferson said.

Bob stopped buttoning his coat. "Go on."

Jefferson glanced down at Alma, then back at Bob. He bit his lower lip and then leaned on the table, pressing his palms amid a sea of paper. "I can't remember a time when the Gentry name didn't elicit curses and praise in the same breath. Until Bill Littlefield moved to town, they were royalty. They set the community standard. They contributed to the right causes. They lived in Contrary because Contrary needed them. In payment for their magnanimous gestures, whatever the Gentrys wanted, they got. They controlled the mayor's office, the police, the city council. If your brother needed a job, they'd get him one. If your cousin landed in jail, they'd get him out."

Bob nodded. "But the cost was always higher than the paycheck."

"They lorded it over you. You always had to be on their side, vote the way they ordered."

"I'm listening," Bob said, taking off his coat. "Okay, how does this concern Alma?"

"Walter Gentry, Sr., got Alma's father the job in Detroit."

Alma felt as if a train was roaring through her head.

"Your father was killed there?" Bob asked.

"That's what we believe." Alma didn't know how she got the words out. Her mouth tasted bitter.

Jefferson continued. "The Gentrys for a long time said that he'd run off, deserted his family. They accused him of taking their money and held it over the family, ridiculing them publicly in their private way."

Alma searched her memory. Was Jefferson making this story up? She'd never heard it before. No one in her family had ever mentioned any of this. Was Jefferson saying this to protect her?

He motioned for Bob to sit. "Things my father said to me makes me think they wanted Alma's father to leave. Esau Bashears was a union steward at the Gentrys' coal mine. He questioned a lot of practices. They laid him off and no company in the county would hire him."

The older adults in Alma's family had never told her any of this. Suddenly it explained the whispered conversations, the rehearsed explanations, the family meetings when the children were sent out to play. It explained the tension in the house the week her father left. He'd taken the Gentrys' money and gotten out of their hair, and it had resulted in his death in a huge, industrial city far from the mountains and the family he loved. No wonder her mother thought the Gentrys owed her.

"Walter Sr. was as much of a rattlesnake as Bill Littlefield," Jefferson said. "I've had family members have trouble with him—not as detrimental, but equally humiliating. They have a way of putting you in your place."

For the next minute a quiet hum filled the office. Not even the morning traffic outside the window disturbed their cocooned solitude. Alma's thoughts were of her father and that last day she'd seen him, waving from the car window and promising to return by Christmas Eve. She studied Jefferson and Bob and tried to imagine what they might be thinking. Jefferson was perhaps considering a task he'd set for himself long ago—to do what he could to put the citizens of the Contrary hollows on equal footing with the downtown people. Bob was perhaps thinking of the many battles he'd fought before and how little they changed from town to town. These two men were warriors, and she wasn't sure she could match the genuineness of their approach. Perhaps that was their edge, but all she could feel was an intense desire to bring the Gentrys to their knees.

Jefferson leaned over the table at Bob. "They crush you. Then they pick you up, give you a pittance, and you feel grateful. Now do you see why we hate the Gentrys so much?"

"I see," Bob said. He opened his briefcase and tossed four newspapers toward Alma: The *Knoxville Independent, Louisville Courier Journal, Philadelphia Inquirer,* and *Boston Globe.* All had articles about civil rights in small-town America and pointed liberally to Vernon's case as a sham for an aspiring politician. "Television crews should arrive today," Bob said. "Nothing like the hot glare of a television light to expose dark places. The truth has a way of standing out."

Alma looked up at Jefferson. Bob's words scared her. The truth, she thought. That's the last thing she wanted anybody to know. A sharp rap on the door startled her. Alma turned. Now she'd have her first look at Johanna Littlefield.

38

"We were expecting someone else," Jefferson said.

Vernon swaggered into the room and plopped down next to Bob. "Thought I'd come down and check out how my defense is coming along." He twisted in his position as if his back hurt him. "Just in case there's anything I need to know about the grand jury."

Bob looked swiftly at his watch and then at the door. "You won't have to do anything. The purpose of the grand jury is for the prosecutor to get his indictment. Of course, you know you won't have to testify against yourself."

"Who all do you think will testify?" Vernon's eyes were wide, and he seemed genuinely interested.

Alma wondered if Vernon finally realized the trouble he had created for himself. His temper remained his Achilles heel.

Bob pulled out a legal pad and looked through some notes. "They'll probably talk to the arresting officer, the bellboy, and Clark Winchell."

Bob deliberately seemed to not look at Vernon, and Alma wondered if that might be a strategy to make him drop his guard. "You understand, Vernon," she said. "The grand jury will issue your indictment or a no true bill, which means there will be no charges. The prosecutor has the advantage of swaying the jury with the sentiment of the moment, which right now is pretty much against you."

Vernon nodded. His left cowboy boot tapped nervously against the table leg, and he readjusted his baseball cap. "So they don't hear our side of things?"

"No," Bob answered. "We present our side at the trial in front of another jury. There'll be plenty of pretrial motions as well, and we'll start submitting them right after the indictment when the judge sets the trial date."

Vernon looked down at Bob's yellow legal pad. "Like what kind of pretrial motions?"

"The usual—a postponement, jury selection rules, change of venue."

"Change of venue? I don't want a change of venue."

"Are you nuts?" Alma asked even as Bob shushed her with the wave of a hand. "The jury pool in this community is tainted, Vernon. They all think they're going to lose their jobs because of you."

"But every one of them would've done the same thing if they'd been me!"

"Juries are emotional creatures, Vernon."

"My vote is, we stay here." Vernon stared at the floor, pressing his lips together firmly as he nodded his head.

Bob shot Alma a concerned look. "Let me ask you," he said to Vernon, "is there anyone you can think of who the prosecutor may call before the grand jury?"

Vernon continued to stare at the floor. "No, no one I can think of."

Bob looked at his watch. "Jefferson, our appointment is twenty minutes late. Why don't you have the secretary call and see if she can locate her?"

Jefferson went to the outer office. Alma wondered if Vernon knew Johanna Littlefield was scheduled for an interview. He must, she thought. Why else would he have shown up here unannounced?

"Can I have a cup of that coffee?" Vernon asked.

"Help yourself." Bob stared at Alma, acknowledging her steady gaze. The same thought swirled through their minds: Vernon was stalling. Johanna Littlefield must have some kind of story to tell—or to hide.

Jefferson stepped into the room. "No word yet. Alma, there's a call for you on line two. Justice Jordan. Are you going to need some privacy?" Jefferson's lips tightened into a smug line.

"No." Her voice wavered like a musical note. She hesitated, then picked up the phone. "Hello, Jordan."

"Alma." His voice rang with his soft, distinctive tone and created a bittersweet feeling in Alma's stomach. "Alma, I want to speak to you and Bob, but before you put Bob on, let me say that I truly regret what happened between us. No matter what you decide, I hope somehow we'll be able to remain friends."

"I understand," she said, feeling the tension of the other people in the room. She looked around. Jefferson stood in the doorway, watching her.

"I know there must be people around, so just call me if you want to talk."

"I'm putting you on the speaker phone now," she said.

"We're here, Jordan," Bob said.

"I'm here, too," Jefferson said, "right next to Alma."

Alma kicked him underneath the table. "We're listening, Jordan," she said.

"I'm in Lexington," Jordan began. "I had a close friend introduce me to friends of de Kwiatkowski's. Bob, I'm certain he's not Littlefield's partner. Littlefield offered him a partnership, but he turned it down. We spoke at length and for him, and for most people, the tax situation is just too complicated."

"What do you mean?" Alma asked.

"The hotel sits on the Kentucky and Tennessee border," Jordan said.

"Yeah, we know that," Jefferson replied, and rolled his eyes. "He built over into Tennessee so that he could have a bar. This county is a dry county. That means you can't sell alcohol, Justice."

"I know what it means," Jordan said flatly.

Alma wished Jefferson would shut up and stop sparring with Jordan.

"That information is helpful, Jordan," Bob said. "It'll save us some time that we could have wasted."

"Jordan," Alma said, "it was great of you to go to this trouble." Feelings for him stirred in her.

"Bob," Jordan said, "I know you were having trouble tracing back the shell companies that owned Littlefield Industries. If you'll authorize it, I have two contacts at the IRS in D.C. who are whiz kids at doing that sort of thing."

"Just a minute," Jefferson said. "We're going to put you on hold, Justice."

"No, we're not," Bob said. "We appreciate any help you can give us, Jordan."

"Fine." Jordan used his most professional voice. "I'll fax you the information as soon as I get it. Talk to you soon. Good-bye, Alma."

"Good-bye, Jordan." An ardent surge spread through her. She wanted to say more to him. She wanted to talk until their problems were as rationalized as law briefs. She wanted to forgive all. She wanted back what she had had before Contrary. Her dreamy-eyed state was lost on

Jefferson. She hung up. He skeptically rolled his eyes and yawned.

"Reckon you got yourself a real go-getter in that Justice Jordan," Vernon said, mimicking Jefferson's tone. "Better hold on to him, Alma. I don't know too many people who'd have you."

She looked up at the clock. Bob and Jefferson followed her gaze. Forty-five minutes late. "I'm going to call Walter," Alma said to Bob.

"Jefferson is going to call Walter." Bob quickly put a hand on the phone receiver so that Alma couldn't pick it up.

She didn't argue. Hearing Jordan's voice had produced a high in her, and as it faded, she fought a sadness. She didn't want to confront Walter again today.

"Gentry," Jefferson said after making the connection. "Johanna Littlefield hasn't shown up for her interview. I understand she's at your house." He held the phone away from his ear. The yelling and the click were unmistakably Gentry. Jefferson told the others, "He said it's his day off and she isn't there—or words to that effect." He replaced the receiver in the cradle with a gentleness that contrasted with the yelling. "Are you sure she was there, Alma?"

She watched Vernon's reaction, as did Bob. To her brother she said, "Maybe if I used a code name she'd come on the line. What do you think, Vernon?"

"You're just trying to get even 'cause of that remark I made about you and Justice Jordan." Vernon stepped toward the door as if ready to leave. "I like that name, Jefferson. Thanks for giving me something to kid Alma with."

"Just a minute," she said sternly. "I know you and Johanna call each other using code names. I got hauled off to jail to get that information. Now don't you stand there and deny it." Alma pushed him on the chest and he collapsed onto the couch.

"I don't know what the hell you're talking about." Vernon shook his head, but his wide-eyed stare gave away his nervousness.

"There're three of us here, Vernon." Alma leaned on one knee beside him and ripped off his baseball hat. "You might make a fool out of one of us. Maybe even me, your sister. Don't think all three of us will strike out."

"Okay, wait a minute." Vernon rubbed his hands over his face. His unshaven jaw made him look tired. "She wrote me a letter asking me to call her and use a code name. I never did. Everybody is making too much of her. I went out with her once or twice over a year ago."

"Your relationship with her will impact how the jury looks at you," Jefferson said.

"What relationship?"

Bob paced in front of the couch, holding his hands behind his back. "You won't be doing your case any favors by denying a sexual relationship with her. The prosecutor will bring it out and it will look like we're trying to hide it."

"But I never had sex with her," Vernon nearly yelled.

Alma fell to the side of him and burst out laughing.

"Just what do you think I am, Alma? Stud service?"

"Do you really expect me to believe that you never slept with her?"

"If that's what I tell you."

"Like you expect me to believe you and Littlefield fought because he threw a gum wrapper at you and hit you on your nose!"

"It was *my* nose." Vernon tapped the end of his nose. "His gum wrapper."

Alma clapped her hands over her ears in frustration. She stared down at the rooster pin. It reminded her of what Mamaw had said when she'd asked her about Vernon and Bill Littlefield: just two roosters in the same henhouse. Her brother was the quintessential southern man when it came to dueling: Never back down from a fight, no matter how stupid the cause.

The phone rang and Jefferson answered it. "It's Willie George," he told the others in an aside. "I called him earlier. He's at the hotel." He listened and his expression grew serious, then he paled.

Alma stood and looked down at Vernon. He stared at the floor, tapping the tips of his boots together. His joking seemed suspicious, and Alma surmised that Bob thought so, too. Bob wrote notes on his legal pad furiously, but he stopped and studied Vernon, as if documenting his every reaction.

Jefferson hung up. "Remember when Sue said that Johanna wasn't at her father's memorial service?" He scratched his head and rested his chin on his fist. "She hasn't been seen in three days. At least not at the hotel."

"Gentry!" Alma said the name as if blurting out an obscenity. "He has her and he has her for a reason." She wanted to shake the information out of Vernon, but right now she knew all she'd get was a smart-alecky one-liner.

"He might have her," Bob said, "but he can't hide her forever. And it will certainly give us a motion for a mistrial." He snickered. "I'm beginning to like this Walter Gentry," he said kiddingly to Alma. "He gives me so much to work with."

"I'd still feel better knowing what he's going to do with her," Jefferson said.

"So would I," Alma agreed. Out of the corner of an eye she studied Vernon. She couldn't help but notice that he'd been watching more than he'd been talking. That was unlike Vernon, who reveled in being the center of attention. Why wouldn't he open up about Johanna Littlefield? What was there to protect? If Gentry had her, he'd use her, and Alma had a feeling that what he had would bury Vernon.

39

Alma discovered another reason why Onion Adams's friends called him Onion. His breath could sour milk. She had managed to dress him in a suit so that when they strolled down the sidewalk, they looked like any other couple on their way to church. "Pull your hat a little lower," Alma said as a family of six crossed the street opposite them. "I don't want anyone to recognize you."

"I promise ye, ain't a soul gonna know me in this neighborhood." He smiled, showing his discolored teeth.

"And don't smile," Alma instructed. They had searched a four-block area around Walter Gentry's house and had not located the red Corvette. "I'm still convinced she's in that house."

Onion pulled out a pocket watch. "Thirty more minutes 'fore morning services start."

"Could he have hidden the Corvette in his garage?"

"Naw, he can't even get his own car in the garage. It's full of boxes of junk like you've never seen."

Alma stopped walking. "How do you know that?" She took his arm. "Never mind. I don't want to know."

"Too bad the Gentrys ain't Holiness. Their sermons go on a good hour longer than the Methodists'."

Alma counted her steps down the block. Another ten minutes and nearly every house in this neighborhood would be empty. Then she'd return to Walter's house and find Johanna Littlefield. "Let's check one more block before heading back." They turned left on Washington and walked toward Kirkland. As they neared the intersection, the roof of Charlotte Gentry's house came into view. "Let's go the other way," she said. The thought of Charlotte Gentry stirred a confusion inside her as smoky as smoldering ash.

"Red Corvette, right?" Onion's face screwed up like a bulldog's.

"Yeah," she answered, preoccupied with getting off the block before they ran into Mrs. Gentry. Either she had already left for church or the time was approaching when she would.

"Yonder it is." Onion pointed over a redwood fence that cut off the view of Charlotte Gentry's house.

The smoldering ash of Alma's confusion sparked and burned high. In the backyard, stretched out like a sunbather, the red Corvette gleamed in the morning sunlight. "Of course," she said, feeling like an idiot. "They brought Johanna here after Jefferson called Walter's house yesterday."

Alma and Onion waited another ten minutes, then checked both directions and sneaked up to the back door. Alma stood guard while Onion worked. After five minutes she nudged him. "I thought you said you could do this!"

"I'm trying to remember the words."

"Oh, great!" She was breaking into a house with a nutcase who talked locks out of their door frames.

"Here we go." He turned around, holding the entire lockset in his hand and smiling widely, showing a side of roan-colored teeth. "Told ye."

She pushed him inside. They paused in the kitchen, listening to the ticking of a cuckoo clock and the buzzing of the oven light; otherwise there was silence. Alma figured they would put Johanna somewhere comfortable, perhaps a large guest room. She wanted to find Johanna first before Onion scared the daylights out of her. "Stay behind me," she whispered back at him.

They tiptoed through the hallway, checking the library and the living room. Alma hesitated. Peering in, the scene came alive in her memory: *Her mother shouting at Mrs. Gentry, "You owe me! Damn you! You owe me!" Alma begging her mother to leave. Merl's hands clamped onto Alma's arms. Mrs. Gentry shouting in Alma's face, "You want my money, you get down on your knees and pick it up!"* Imagining the sharp sting of the bills hitting her cheeks brought Alma back to reality. She motioned for Onion to follow her upstairs.

As they ascended, a film of sweat formed on her upper lip. The enormity of breaking and entering wound through her leg muscles like the sting of a wasp. She fought to keep from trembling. That she should find herself there, breaking into Charlotte Gentry's house, flew in the face of everything she'd ever believed about the law. No choice, she thought. They left me no choice.

"Oooohhhh," Onion cooed.

She turned and found him on his knees in front of a door, peering through the keyhole. "Do you see her?"

"Skeleton key," he said, leaning back. "Hardly see them anymore. Mind if I take it?"

"No!" Alma jerked him up by the collar. "There are two more rooms to check, and she's got to be in one of them."

"I know where to find you, little one," he said to the keyhole, regarding it lovingly.

Alma opened the door to the first room. A shrine to little Walter unfolded. His framed Little League jersey hung on the wall, football helmet centered on the dresser like the Holy Grail; school pictures from every grade;

high school dance photos, each with a different cheerleader or majorette as his date.

A slow, seething burn consumed her chest. Walter Gentry's life—as normal as any small-town boy's could be. No one had ever guessed the monster that was inside him. Alma closed the door, wishing she could shut him out of her mind that easily. "She's got to be in there," Alma whispered to Onion.

She tapped on the next door. "Johanna?" No answer. Alma turned the knob. The door whined as she opened it. The bed was unmade and there was makeup spread across the dresser. Charlotte Gentry's room. Still no Johanna. "I don't understand," she said. "Could they have hidden the car here and left Johanna at Walter's house?"

An open armoire filled with photos drew Alma's attention. Grandchildren; Walter as a boy, as a young man; family picnics; graduations; Christmas and Thanksgiving portraits. A black and white wedding photo of a young Charlotte Gentry and Walter Gentry, Sr., contrasted with a color wedding photo of Walter Jr. and his wife. He had married a dark-haired woman with birdlike features and thin to the point of emaciation. Walter and his mother had the same stiff smile, as if smiling were a chore for them. Above the armoire hung a framed, yellowed marriage certificate showing that Charlotte Smith married Walter Gentry, Sr., on the 29th day of April, 1938.

Alma fought the peculiar ambivalence of seeing people she regarded as monsters in a family light. It humanized them. Doubt nagged at her; perhaps the Gentrys were protecting themselves just as surely as the Bashearses protected their family. Inequality and money gave weight to the wrong side. That's why they always won, she thought. Until now.

Onion reacted with a head twitch a second before the

sound of keys jingled in the front door downstairs. Alma jerked him into the bedroom. They listened at the door. Damn it! Alma thought. The Gentrys never missed church. "Who the devil could be downstairs?"

"Medeco, 1975 issue," Onion said, curling a finger around his ear. "From the sound of the way it scrapes the inside of the lock, the key's pretty worn down."

"Shut up, Onion!"

As the front door closed, Mrs. Gentry's and Walter's voices rose through the rooms. "I don't see why you let those kids get away with murder!" Mrs. Gentry huffed, and banged down what sounded like a heavily loaded purse.

"They're children, Mother. They can't sit through a sermon. Sunday school is enough for them."

"It certainly isn't how your father and I raised you."

"As I remember, Father sat in the side row where he could look up the organist's dress."

"Oh, don't be dirty!"

"Look." Walter's tone was conciliatory. "I'm going home to change clothes, then I'm taking Jacqueline and the kids out to the Steak House. You know you want to join us."

"And watch their weekly Sunday food fight? No, thank you."

Alma wrung her hands together. Please go with them, she prayed.

"Mother . . ." Walter's pleading tone grew stern. "You just want me to beg you. I'm going to wait here until you change your mind."

"All I'm changing is my clothes." The sound of her footsteps echoed on the stairs. "I may never go to church again. I find embarrassment exhausting!"

Alma nearly fainted. "Under the bed," she said to Onion. "Quick!"

Pressed between the floor and the dust-laden box spring, Alma realized what a huge mistake she had made. If she and Onion were caught ... The consequences made her shudder. More humiliating than jail, Mrs. Gentry and Walter would have something on her.

"Where are them little grays when you need them?" Onion licked a finger and traced a picture in the dust.

"Shhh!" Alma thought that being abducted by aliens, little grays or otherwise, was definitely preferable to being discovered by Charlotte Gentry.

She entered the room. Alma followed her feet to the closet. The dust under the bed was irritating, and she and Onion breathed as slowly as they could. Alma's mind raced, seeking an escape. She followed the frame of the bed to the wall and saw the phone jack. Gently stretching her neck so that she could see the end of the bedside table, she saw no telephone cord. Good, she thought, it's a cordless.

When Mrs. Gentry left the room, Alma pulled herself out from under the bed just enough to snatch the phone. She could hear Walter and Mrs. Gentry resuming their arguing downstairs. She punched Jefferson's number and prayed he still skipped church the way he did as a boy. The phone rang three times. "Please be there," she whispered. Onion coughed, and Alma almost gagged at the odor.

"Yep," a sleepy voice said.

"Thank God!"

"Alma?"

"No time to explain." Her voice shook. "Onion Adams and I are hiding underneath Charlotte Gentry's bed. She and Walter came home from church early. Get us out of here."

After Jefferson stopped laughing, his voice firmed

with annoyance. "I should have left the two of you in jail last week."

"I don't have time to argue! Are you going to help me, or are you too busy in bed right now?"

He sighed, then the sound of his getting out of bed followed. "Stay where you are and try not to let Onion fart."

Alma hung up the phone and wiped a tear from her cheek. She slid back underneath the bed. Onion had his eyes squeezed tight and a finger pressed to each temple. He opened one eye. "I'm trying my best to contact the little grays for help."

"Oh," Alma said, sniffing back tears of relief. "Jefferson says not to fart."

The conversation downstairs had stopped. Maybe Walter had left. Maybe they had both left. The silence steadily increased Alma's nervousness. She couldn't be sure where Mrs. Gentry was in the house. She jutted her head out from under the bed so that she could hear better. A sound on the staircase. Alma froze, then slid back underneath the bed, bumping her head on the frame. Onion farted. Oh, God, she thought. Put me out of my misery.

Mrs. Gentry's voice. Alma held still. The words didn't sound like a conversation. Mrs. Gentry was talking to herself. Footsteps. She was almost upstairs. Onion and Alma stared at each other.

A loud banging on the front door halted Mrs. Gentry's progress.

"Mrs. Gentry!" a voice yelled. "Police! Come out now! Neighbors reported a prowler in your house!"

Alma's head sank to the floor.

40

"Onion Adams! Come out now! I know you're in there! Come on now. I can smell you!" Fred Walker was doing all the shouting.

Onion squealed with delight and clapped his hands. "Little grays answered my prayer." He scooted from under the bed and signaled for Alma to stay put. "I give up!" he yelled toward the hallway.

When Alma saw his feet walk out of the door, she pulled herself from under the bed. She waited until he stepped down the first step with his hands in the air. Slowly peeking out the bedroom door, she saw Fred behind him, holding his service revolver at Onion's back.

"Wait out on the porch, Mrs. Gentry!" Fred yelled. "Sometimes Onion goes crazy."

Alma quietly stepped out into the hall. A hand clamped across her mouth and pulled her backward. Halfway down a back staircase, she twisted from the grasp and turned to see Jefferson.

"Good thing Onion didn't reinstall the back-door lock." He pointed toward the bottom of the stairs that entered the kitchen, and they slipped out of the house.

"I have to go back for Onion," she protested. "I can't let him take the blame for this."

"Just get in the car, Alma." Jefferson shoved her into the seat, locked the door, then pulled the car behind a

264

huge oak tree at the edge of Charlotte Gentry's property. Fred, Onion, and Mrs. Gentry stood on the front porch. Jefferson rolled his window down.

Mrs. Gentry wagged her hand at Fred. "Just get this fool off my porch," she said. "I don't have the time to waste on him."

"Are you sure, ma'am?" Fred asked, the model of police politeness.

"Give me back my lock!" She hit Onion's arm, knocking her rear-door lock out of his hand. With that, she returned to her house and slammed the door.

Fred walked Onion toward the squad car. They crossed in front of Jefferson's car. Fred tilted his head the slightest degree. Onion smiled like he'd never been happier. Alma was baffled by him.

Jefferson drove toward the office. He didn't speak, and Alma didn't offer any explanation though she knew she would have to soon. "I'd rather not go to the office," she said. He continued driving in that direction. "Do you think Bob's there?"

"Probably," Jefferson said coldly.

"You're not going to tell him what I did?" Alma's back was sweating. She hated making mistakes, and this was a beauty.

"No," he said in the same tone. "But you are." Jefferson slammed on the brakes and made a U-turn. He pulled into the alley behind his building and shut off the engine. "Just what the hell did you think you were doing?"

"I . . . I . . ." The stutter in her voice magnified her nervousness. She turned toward the car window so that she didn't have to look at him. "I thought I'd find Johanna Littlefield."

"Under Charlotte Gentry's bed?"

"In her house."

"Well." He waited. "Did you find her? No. You just made a damn fool of yourself and nearly ruined your career!"

"Stop yelling at me!"

"Damn!" Jefferson banged his hand on the steering wheel. "I wish I understood you."

The tip of Alma's nose burned. She continued to stare out the window at the dull red brick of the building, hoping he didn't ask her anything else.

"Fred will drop Onion off at home. You don't have to worry about him." Jefferson's voice dropped to a low, composed tone. "He also told me there's been no missing-persons report filed on Johanna, so they probably know where she is."

Alma started to speak, but her voice broke. "I knew that," she managed to say.

Jefferson touched her shoulder and she shifted farther away from him. He pulled her arm and she resisted. His grip tightened and he drew her steadily to him. Wrapping his arms around her, resting her head on his shoulder, he held her tight and waited.

Squeezing her eyes shut, she fought the heat of explosive anger inside her head. A million starburst patterns floated before her eyes as she broke, sobbing into Jefferson's chest. "I know how stupid it was to break into Charlotte Gentry's house. I've pissed off my entire family. I nearly ran Bob off this case. I talk to you like you're a schoolboy."

"College boy." Jefferson's chest shook with some amusement as he patted her back.

"I lost Jordan. I broke every ethical standard I ever believed in as a lawyer."

"Whoa, whoa," he said, pushing her away from him just enough to look at her face. "Justice Jordan is history?"

She nodded and wiped her nose with a hand.

"Things are looking up." He smiled and gave her his handkerchief.

"Oh, shut up." She smacked his chest and leaned back in her seat to straighten her hair and face.

After a few minutes Jefferson started the car. "If Bob ever found out what you did."

She put a hand on his arm. "Bob will never find out. Right?"

Jefferson stared down at the steering wheel, seeming to consider. "I don't like hiding anything from him."

"You saw how he reacted yesterday. If he finds out what I did this morning . . ." She hesitated and looked out the window. "I can't handle this case, Jefferson. This morning proved that to me. And you . . . Well, don't take this the wrong way, but both of us—by the judiciary and the jurors of this county, we're still considered hollow kids. We need Bob. Neither of us has his experience."

Jefferson looked over at her. His hazel eyes favored the green in the streams of sunlight piercing the car windows. He shook a finger at her. "If you ever . . ."

"I won't." She held up one hand as if to say, Scout's honor.

"But if you do, just make sure you call me first."

She smiled, leaned over, and kissed him on the cheek.

41

"In here, now!" Bob called out to them as they entered the office. He stood beside the fax machine, six pieces of paper in one hand. "This just came from Jordan's friends in Washington." He spread the sheets out across the table.

"Jesus Christ," Jefferson said as he traced the various companies of Littlefield Industries.

"There must be two hundred," Alma said, equally astonished, as she studied the papers.

"One hundred and sixty-five," Bob said. "So far." Another page fell out of the fax machine. It listed another twenty companies.

"I doubt we'll locate Littlefield's partner."

"That means we'll just have to live with the press." Jefferson let out a frustrated breath.

"You know what's odd?" Alma turned the sheets of paper toward her. "Littlefield Industries appears in the top half of this list, and all of the companies below it have Littlefield's name in the title: Bill Holdings, Big Bill Enterprises, William J. Company, Prince William Holdings."

Bob and Jefferson followed her hand as it moved along the page.

"Now look at the companies above Littlefield Industries: The Mirth Company, Scarlet Enterprises, Cameos

Company, Camelot Holdings, Thermostatic Incorporated, Harlot Enterprises. The naming's different."

"Perhaps somebody bought him out and let him keep the appearance of control." Bob rubbed his chin and looked through the additional papers that dropped out of the fax.

"That would explain why Littlefield seemed so unhappy the last five or six years," Jefferson said.

"What do you mean?" Alma asked.

"Everything you've ever heard about him is true. He used to rule this town like he was king, and except for the Gentrys nobody messed with him. They just seemed to tolerate him like the buckeyed fool that he was. After Walter Sr. died, even Mrs. Gentry didn't take a great deal of interest in what went on in town. But during the last few years Littlefield stopped throwing his weight around. He was still a jerk, but on a smaller level—just in his immediate area. Thinking back on it, it was as if somebody was pulling his strings."

Bob laid down one of the papers. "It says here that the parent company of Littlefield Industries was established only six years ago. I believe you may be on to something."

"Where's the page with the parent company?" Alma asked.

"Hasn't come through yet," Jefferson said, putting another three pages of companies in order. "Can't be much longer."

"Who would have the money?" Alma asked herself aloud. "Who would care enough to put up with all the tax problems?" She stared at the floor, and the names Camelot, Cameos, Harlot, Scarlet, and Thermostatic ran through her head like linked trains.

"These names," Bob said. "They have a teasing nature about them—like someone enjoyed taunting him."

"How long ago did Bill Littlefield try to change the name of the town?" Alma asked.

Jefferson thought for a minute. "Yeah," he said, agreeing with Bob. Then he answered Alma. "About six or seven years ago."

"Camelot, Cameos, Harlot, Scarlet, Thermostatic." She paced around the table. "Harlot, Scarlet, Thermostatic."

"Here it comes," Bob said, catching the page from the fax. The last three companies read: Charlie, Lottie, Smithereens. "Smithereens Incorporated, the parent company."

Alma and Jefferson looked at each other. Their gazes locked like the pieces of a jigsaw puzzle. Almost as if they were listening to the click of each other's thought processes. Jefferson spoke a second before she. "Walter Smith Gentry."

"Charlotte Smith Gentry." Alma covered her mouth with a hand. "Of course," she said. "Why didn't I see it before?"

"Are we sure about this?" Bob asked.

Jefferson scratched his head and stared out the window. "Best way to control your enemy is to keep a close eye on him." He turned toward Alma. His eyes sparkled as if to acknowledge their camaraderie, then he said to Bob, "Yeah, we're sure."

Alma reached out and held his hand. "That day at the Littlefield Hotel when the red Corvette sped away, I assumed Johanna Littlefield had run away from me." She pushed her hair back from her face and held it there, wishing she'd taken the time to track down the car rather than the woman.

Jefferson rolled his eyes. "If you'd asked, I could have told you what kind of car Mrs. Gentry drives. Might have saved you a lot of trouble." He grinned when Bob wasn't looking.

Alma stared hard at him. "So call me old-fashioned,

but I would never in a million years have guessed that Charlotte Gentry drives a red Corvette. It doesn't seem her style."

"Charlotte Gentry had much more to hide, especially from you," Bob said, nodding as if possibilities were bubbling in his mind.

"She must have busted a gut when I walked in the hotel that day and almost caught her sitting at Bill Littlefield's desk," Alma said.

Bob agreed. "She didn't dare let you see her at the hotel."

Alma didn't need to say more. Bob was already on the phone calling the television newsrooms.

42

"Very shortly," a televised, pale Charlotte Gentry said, "we were going to make all this public." Her voice sounded dry and brittle.

Alma hung on Mrs. Gentry's every word. She smiled at Mamaw and reached over and held her hand. On the couch behind her Uncle Ames, Uncle George, Aunt Joyce, and Vernon sat listening with as much attention as if they were watching the moon landing. Sue and Jack sat on the floor, while Rodney amused the two nephews in the kitchen.

"This is going to change a lot of things," Alma said.

A flustered Charlotte Gentry stared into a sea of microphones. She squinted when a television camera flashed a bright light in her face. She held up a hand to deflect the light. "I can't answer your questions," she said. "You'll have to talk to my lawyer."

"Maybe she'll hire you, Alma," Rodney yelled from the kitchen. A roar of laughter filled the room.

Mrs. Gentry's cheeks turned a fiery red as a reporter asked her to explain how she could own Littlefield Industries for six years and still let her newspaper print articles decrying the closing of all the town's companies. She shifted from side to side, pursing her lips like a schoolmarm. "Young man," she admonished the reporter, "will you get that light out of my face!"

"I love it!" Alma clapped her hands.

The news coverage switched to Walter's house, where a casually dressed Walter read a statement. " 'I have never been a part of my mother's company, nor have I been an adviser for her investments. She is more than competent to handle her affairs alone. I was unaware that she owned Littlefield Industries. This information in no way influences the attention that the commonwealth attorney's office will give to bringing William Littlefield's murderer to justice. A crime committed against one of us is a crime against us all. I will not rest until Vernon Bashears is behind bars.' "

"Reckon that says it all," Vernon said, and stood up, stiffly shaking his legs.

"Bet we ruined his day off," Alma said.

"That man's always running for office," Aunt Joyce said in a weary tone.

Uncle George clasped his hands and held them tightly in front of him. Uncle Ames stared at the television set, his eyes narrowing as if thinking angry thoughts. Vernon leaned against the wall. He shifted from one leg to the other, looking as if he wanted to run out the door. Sue sniffled, and only a tap on the shoulder from Aunt Joyce seemed to keep her from crying.

"Listen to me, everybody." Mamaw's voice crescendoed up from its usual softness. "I wish this hadn't happened to us." She turned her wheelchair around so that she faced the family. "But it has. It's not the first hard times we've seen. It might not be the last. But, by God, we're gonna do more than pray." She leaned forward, holding on to the arms of her chair. "Each of you go home tonight and start calling all the family. Every relative we have, even the ones in Georgia. We ought to be able to get twenty people here by tomorrow. You tell them I said to come and they will. Alma tells me the press will be all around, trying to catch us making a mistake. We'll have to post guards at our houses, at the mouth of the hollow, and some up on the hills. Those with jobs will have to come here in shifts. I just don't know what we're going to run into, but I don't want nothing going on in this hollow that I don't know about. I want them in the courtroom every day of the trial. I want to show Vernon he has our support."

Vernon stepped outside onto the porch, away from the family. The quiet in the room hung sickly, like a drunk who'd awakened in the early dawn hours and confronted his reflection before rising to face another day. Aunt Joyce and Uncle George left, stopping only to say a few words to Vernon. Sue and Jack gathered up the kids and drove Rodney home. Uncle Ames sat by Mamaw until she told him to push her into her bedroom.

Alma heard the front porch swing scrape the wall and looked out to see Vernon jumping off the front porch. She followed him to his trailer. "Vernon," she called out to him when he did not stop. "I need to talk to you."

He balanced on a cinder-block step that led to his trailer and hooked his thumbs in his rear pockets. "I'm kinda tired tonight, Alma."

"It'll only take a few minutes." She pointed to his trailer. A dim light glowed through the curtains. "Can we go inside?"

Vernon looked up at the dark sky and waved his arm at the millions of stars. "Nicer out here."

"But I'm cold."

"Here, take my coat."

Alma didn't take it. He hung the coat on a tree branch. She hoisted herself onto the front of the Jeep and watched him stare skyward as if counting the stars. "There's only one reason I can think of for you showing up at the office yesterday morning."

He leaned to the side, causing a wave of cracks up and down his spine. "Did I thank you for bringing the Jeep back with the windshield intact and the tires not slashed?"

She steeled herself to forge ahead. "At first I thought you wanted to run into Johanna Littlefield . . . thought maybe there was some leftover feelings there and seeing her might, oh, I don't know, revive the sparks."

"I already explained that, Alma."

"Yeah," she said. "When I think about it now, it seems more like you were trying to gauge our reactions when she didn't show up."

"See that star yonder?" He pointed upward. "It's called Alcantarus. Blinks red, then blue, then white."

"You must have been going nuts wondering what was going on in our office." Alma spoke softly yet firmly. "That's why you showed up."

"Moon's three-quarters," he said, turning his back toward her and holding both hands over his brow as he stared at the moon.

"You knew she wouldn't be there because you know where she is."

"You can see the hare in the moon. Be full in . . . what do you think, four days?"

"Is she in the trailer?"

"Hello, little bunny." He raised his voice to a squeaking pitch as if cooing to an animal. "Hello there, little fuzzywuzz."

Alma jumped off the Jeep. Vernon spun around, eyes wide and panicked. She held still. Waiting. He didn't speak. "She's in the trailer, isn't she?"

"No," he said, his hands slapping against the sides of his thighs as if he'd lost control of them. "Don't be silly. I'd never be able to get near her. You know the kind of security that's around her."

Alma stepped toward the trailer. He blocked her way. "Then let me go in and have a look," she said.

His voice rumbled in his throat without forming coherent words. He kicked at a clod of dirt and stared at the rooster pin on Alma's shirt, still unable to speak.

Alma stepped up in front of him and shook him by the shoulders. "You've got to let me see her."

His eyes teared up and he sniffed back congestion. "No." He stared down into her eyes. His deeply lined features twisted as if enduring an aching pain.

Sorrow seemed to seep from him and Alma couldn't help but feel it. "Sooner or later," she said. "I'm going to talk to her. Sooner or later."

"Later, Alma. Please." He wiped his eyes and nose with one hand. "Later."

"Tomorrow."

"Tomorrow," he said.

Alma wandered up the path toward the house. She stopped midway and looked back at the trailer. Against the dark woods and the star-filled sky, it looked like a ship afloat with no direction. Alma wrapped her arms around her stomach. It hurt. It hurt for her brother, for her family. It hurt from lack of sustenance—not food but safety. The safety that's called home. The feeling that once you're home everything will be all right. Anything could happen, and Alma didn't know in which direction to focus her energy.

She touched the rooster pin. Thank God for Mamaw. She was an anchor for them. The tip of the pin scratched her finger, and Alma turned it to examine the sharp beak. What had Mamaw said about Vernon and Bill Littlefield? *Two roosters in the same henhouse.* Alma looked back at the trailer. Vernon's shadow passed by the window, then the light went out. *Two roosters in the same henhouse.* "I wonder," she said. "I wonder."

43

The following morning Alma bought coffee at Lolly's Drugstore. Next door to the courthouse, the grill offered a perfect view of the front entrance. She sipped slowly, waiting to see Walter walk past the crowd of reporters and television cameras. A half-dozen people sitting at the counter were all engrossed in the morning paper. Alma opened her copy of the *Gazette* and smiled. The editorial page ran an apology for its nondisclosure of Littlefield Industries' true ownership. Richard Parker, Charlotte Gentry's partner, wrote that a future edition would include an interview with Mrs. Gentry explaining her role in the community's future.

A front-page article quoted the governor as saying that he expected to make his choice for the assembly seat within the week. A picture of Walter identified him as the front-runner. Alma wondered if that was just the *Contrary Gazette*'s opinion.

"I bet ye ole Vernon gets the electric chair," said a man in a booth behind her.

A younger man at the counter spun around on his stool, his newspaper rolled in one hand. "Hell, if I'd been Vernon, I'd've clobbered ole Littlefield, too. Teach him to think he's better than me or anybody else."

"I ain't saying I hope he gets the electric chair, I'm saying I bet he does."

"That's up to a jury." A woman interrupted their argument. "It's a sorry day when justice gets meted out in a drugstore."

The waitress refilled coffee cups and smiled all the way. "I personally hope the trial lasts a long time 'cause them city reporters are better tippers than the bunch of you."

A round of laughter spread through the restaurant. Alma joined in. Public opinion continued to shape up nicely. She put another teaspoon of sugar in her coffee. A reward.

Ten minutes later a black sedan pulled up in front of the courthouse. Ellen Farmer, lugging briefcase and file case, preceded Walter toward the courthouse. A town the size of Contrary had little experience with the major press and no section had been set aside for them. They mobbed Ellen and Walter, so the two could barely inch their way up the stairs.

Walter stopped to speak, as if sensing his last chance to influence the governor about the assembly seat. He held his head regally, looking over the crowd and focusing in on the television cameras. Alma left five dollars on the table and then went out, skirting the edge of the crowd. She felt this was probably her last day of anonymity and she meant to make the most of it. "I wonder why his mother hid the fact that she owned Littlefield Industries," she said behind a couple of reporters.

"Why did your mother hide that she owned Bill Littlefield?" shouted a reporter in front of Alma.

"My mother is a businesswoman. She owns companies, not people." Walter quickly looked in the other direction, facing away from the reporter who'd asked the question.

"Kinda weird that she let all those articles be published," Alma said as low as she could.

"Do you have any comment on your mother's newspaper?" another reporter shouted. The questions snowballed. Another reporter asked if Walter was an investor in his mother's many business ventures and would that affect his ability to serve fairly should he be chosen for the assembly seat. Another badgered him about his mother's influence on the governor. A third asked if his mother had advised him to seek the death penalty for Vernon Bashears. A fourth asked why he was seeking a first-degree indictment for a crime that most believed was justified.

For the first time Walter seemed rattled. He turned to go inside the courthouse. The reporters followed, shouting questions about Charlotte Gentry. "The good of this state has nothing to do with my mother!" he shouted. "Mother's mistakes are hers, not mine!"

Alma returned to Lolly's Drugstore and ordered the steak-and-egg breakfast.

Alma caught up with Jefferson on the stairs outside the office. She'd bought five bouquets of daffodils on the way over. She thrust two in his arms.

"What are you doing?" he said through the bunches of flowers.

"The first of the season," she said. "They make me feel good."

"You could have waited a month and picked 'em in your yard."

"I may decorate your whole office in daffodils," she said.

Jefferson sniffed the flowers and sneezed. "We haven't won yet."

She thought back to Walter on the steps of the courthouse, fielding questions he didn't want to answer.

"There are more ways to win than winning." She was proud of herself.

Jefferson unlocked the office and laid the flowers on the desk. "I'll get the coffee going. Why don't you tell me what you've done now?"

She dropped to the couch, kicked her shoes off, and pulled her legs up under her. "What do you think the grand jury will do?" Jefferson poured water into the coffeemaker and mouthed indistinguishable words as he ground the coffee beans. Alma threw a magazine at him. "I just hope those jurors read their morning papers before they went to work this morning."

"If we get a no true bill or manslaughter, it'll be because of your discovery."

"Jordan's discovery," she said pensively. Jefferson didn't respond and Alma knew she'd hit a nerve. "And Bob's press contacts. And your fax machine."

He smiled and brought her a coffee mug. Before he could sit, all four lines on his phone rang. "I'll get two if you get the other two," he said.

"Law office, can you hold?" Alma answered.

"No, I can't!" her mother yelled back.

"Just a minute, Mother. Law office," Alma said to the other line.

Sue screamed at her, "There are six police cars in the hollow! And twice as many policemen in Vernon's trailer!"

Alma looked over at Jefferson. He was speaking to Uncle Ames. "They're all right," he said to Alma, holding his hand over the receiver. "They don't know what's going on—the police won't let them in the trailer with Vernon."

"Sue, tell Momma I got the message," Alma said. "And don't let Uncle George and Uncle Ames near their guns!" She hung up the phone. "What should we do?" she asked Jefferson.

"Fred's probably testifying about now. Interesting timing on their part."

"Let me guess—the Littleafia."

"Let's just go to the police station and wait for them to bring Vernon in."

"I'll call Bob." Quickly Alma punched in his number. "If they're going to arrest Vernon for kidnapping, he'll want to file a wrongful arrest suit." Bob's line was busy, and she left an urgent message at his hotel.

"Kidnapping?" Jefferson asked after she hung up.

"Jefferson," Alma said, not sure how he'd react, "I think Johanna Littlefield was in Vernon's trailer."

Jefferson whistled a long, low note. "Even if they arrest him on a kidnapping charge that they can't prove, the damage will still be done."

By the time they were out of the building, the crowd of reporters in front of the courthouse had doubled. Now Alma wasn't sure if that would be good or bad. They sprinted toward the police station, slowing to a walk only when a few reporters turned toward them. In front of the station four police cars were parked partially on the sidewalk. They were all empty. Several policemen joked and laughed as they loitered around their patrol units.

"I don't see Vernon," Alma whispered.

One officer saw Jefferson and alerted the others to his presence. Their talk stopped and they stared at him but looked away quickly. "This is bad," Jefferson said. "Something big has happened."

"How bad? How big?" Alma held her breath.

"You're staring at the executive committee of the Littleafia. By now I'm sure they're all Gentry's henchmen. They'll spy for him, intimidate for him, even commit illegal acts for him."

"And nobody ever complains, I'll bet."

"Did you report your slashed tires?"

"I get your point," she said, "more than you know." She looked around for Dwight but didn't see him.

Four policemen went into the station, while the other two deliberately walked past Jefferson and Alma, slowing as they approached, then crossed the street and entered Lolly's Drugstore.

"It's too calm here," Alma said. She grabbed Jefferson's hand. Touching him soothed her nervousness.

"Let's go back to the office," he said. "They don't have Vernon."

His voice trembled and Alma knew he was worried. They turned and faced Dwight. He stood at the end of the block, staring at them, focusing on Alma. His nightstick was drawn and he twirled it in his hands. His toothy grin seemed just as evil to Alma as when she'd first seen it. "Let's cross the street," she said.

They walked quickly back to the office, but Alma felt as if they were moving through water. "They took Johanna," Alma said as they neared the building. "That's why a missing-person report was never filed. They always knew where she was."

Jefferson held the door open for her. "And you know what that means."

"They had a plan. A plan we didn't prepare for." Alma started up the stairs, hoping Bob would be in the office. She needed to feel the security of him right now. The sound of footsteps pacing in the hallway above signaled that security was not what she was about to get.

Vernon waited at the door. He had a swollen lip and the skin around his bruised eye would soon be black. "You told them!" he yelled at Alma. "You told them she was there!"

Alma could barely get the word "No" from her lips.

"Just what the hell did you think you were doing?" He pounded his fists on the stair railing.

"Vernon, I'm taking you to the hospital!" She knew Dwight had beaten Vernon. It was his revenge for what she'd done to him. "That bastard," she said under her breath. "Is the family all right?"

"Yeah, no thanks to you! Luckily, I'm the only one stupid enough to try to fight the great and mighty Contrary po-lice." Vernon stomped down the stairs. He stopped halfway down and looked up at Alma. The blood in the corner of his mouth had cracked and dried. "I can't believe you told them," he shouted.

"She didn't tell." Jefferson raised his voice to match Vernon's.

"I may have fallen off the turnip truck, but I didn't fall off yesterday!" Vernon yelled back. He made a fist and punched the wall. The plaster cracked and spilt onto the floor. "Go back to California," he snapped at Alma. "Get out of here before you get somebody killed!"

Alma cringed. The front door slammed. She looked at Jefferson, who started to speak, but she put her finger to his lips. "Yes, I would appreciate it if you'd explain to him."

"Consider it done. Just give me a few minutes." Jefferson unlocked the door. The aroma of coffee filled the office. "She's got to be testifying before the grand jury," he said. "They let her have the illusion of a safety net until they needed her and then . . . bam!"

"If she didn't want to testify and was forced into it, that must mean she knows something damaging to Vernon."

"But what?" Jefferson leaned his head back and cracked his neck.

Alma dropped to the couch. Her stomach felt full of lead. "Johanna knows why they fought." She whispered the words. "She knows why they *really* fought."

44

Alma left Bob and Jefferson formulating strategy with a psychiatrist hired to testify that Vernon's aggressive tendency was a product of his culture. She feigned a need for a walk but knew she would head for the courthouse. Alma had never represented a client indicted by a grand jury, but in her fledgling years she had assisted with a tax-evasion and money-laundering case. Her job had been to hang around the courthouse hallways. Listening often paid off, because eventually someone—a bailiff, a juror, a lawyer, a witness—said something, and small clues were better than none.

The goons of the Littleafia were milling about on the front steps of the courthouse. She didn't see Dwight, which made her suspicious that he'd be lying in wait where she least expected him. Alma circled the block and came up behind the courthouse. Two police cars were parked on a side street. Probably how they brought Johanna in, she thought. A policeman sat in the rear of one car. His head rested on the back of the seat, mouth open, expelling an intermittent snore loud enough to be heard through the cracked car window.

No wonder they didn't arrest Vernon for kidnapping, she thought as she sneaked past the car and into the courthouse. Walter was happy to keep tabs on Johanna by letting her think she was safe with Vernon, then whisking her to the grand jury before she had a chance to run. Alma wondered if Vernon had been planning to run away with her. He might have been more desperate than she ever realized. That he'd been forced to this point angered her. A surge of hatred rose in her. Hatred for Walter Gentry.

In a back alcove a janitor mopped the floor and a young man napped on a long wooden bench. She didn't see any police or reporters. She wanted to avoid the press for as long as she could. They had yet to find the hollow where her family lived. But that wouldn't last long. By tomorrow they would discover the location of Jefferson's office and pounce on all of them with the tenacity of feeding seagulls. She thought it better that they didn't recognize her as a defense attorney slinking around the courthouse on grand jury day.

She removed her high heels and sprinted up three floors. Outside the grand jury room Fred had stretched his body lengthwise on a bench. When he saw her, he held up a newspaper to hide his face.

"Lying around courthouse hallways has been labeled by the surgeon general as dangerous to your health," she said, sliding his legs off the bench and sitting next to him.

"I already testified," he said. "They wanted me to wait in case something else came up. You know I ain't gonna say nothing, so don't ask."

Alma pulled the newspaper down so that she could see his face. "All the standard stuff, I presume?"

Fred folded the newspaper and slapped it against his leg. He looked down the hall to ensure no one was watching. "Yeah, I downplayed the part where Vernon bit me while resisting arrest."

"Thanks," Alma said. Fred put the newspaper up to his face again, though she was sure he wasn't reading it. "I guess I owe you another thank you for the Sunday snafu."

He dropped the paper and looked at the toes of his boots. His lips pressed together as if he were willing himself not to speak.

"Jefferson rode me pretty hard about how stupid I was. I just want you to know, I had good intentions."

"Yeah," he said, folding his arms and resting them across his knees. He shifted his weight forward so that he wouldn't have to face her.

Something is wrong, she thought. She sensed more than the usual cynicism between them. Alma followed his gaze to the floor, trying to intuit his increased aversion. The toes of his boots were scuffed and the hem of one leg of his blue jeans hung loose on the left side. "You're not in uniform?" she asked.

"The last thing I want to do is make a good impression."

Her thoughts clicked like a computer. "The prosecutor would have insisted you be in uniform unless . . ." She leaned over and touched Fred's shoulder, dipping her head so that she could look up into his eyes.

"Yeah." He puffed out the word. "I've been fired."

"Oh, no." She knew without his saying that it had to do with her.

Fred shrugged as if he didn't care. "They been looking for something on me for a long time, since I wouldn't pull in line with that gang of Littlefield's—now Gentry's."

"Look, I didn't press charges against that Dwight goon, but it can be easily arranged."

"And then he can sue you for destruction of property." Fred sighed and rolled his eyes. "Let's just stop it. Enough. Anyway, that's not why they fired me."

Alma tried to see through the controlled exterior he

insisted on presenting. She didn't believe for a minute that his work skills had been at fault. "Oh, no." She dropped her face into her hands. "You didn't fill out any paperwork on Onion and Charlotte Gentry mentioned what had happened in her house to her son." Alma sank against the wall. That had to be it. "Walter inquired and found out you'd let Onion go, and Mrs. G. lied about not wanting to press charges. I'm amazed at how well I can predict them these days." Guilt welled up inside her. "Is there anything I can do? I'll work free on a wrongful-termination suit."

Fred chuckled and shook his head. "Listen to you, you sound like you're gonna stay in this town. That'd be the last thing I need." He rolled his eyes again.

"I'll take total responsibility."

He turned his full body toward her. "You better never let the Gentrys know you were in that house. You just forget you ever were. If you're too silly to do it for yourself, then do it for Jefferson. You made him an accessory, you know."

"What will you do?" Alma could barely look him in the eye. He'd been fired and it was her fault. She had to at least help him get another job.

"Ahhh," he said, waving his hand to dismiss the importance of what had happened to him. "I got a cousin who's a sheriff in Claiborne County. He's offered to hire me."

Alma thought for a minute. "You know ..." She squeezed her eyes closed, trying to concentrate. "My mother has a slew of second cousins in Claiborne County. One of them works in law enforcement. I've only met him once or twice when I was a kid going to family reunions. Randy ... Randy Sparks. That's it, Randy Sparks."

"Who?" Fred asked.

"Randy Sparks. Yes, we didn't keep real close touch with that part of the family, but I'm sure my mother would make a phone call."

"Who?" Fred's voice wavered through three notes.

"Is something wrong?" she asked.

"Randy Sparks is my first cousin."

Both were quiet for a few seconds, absorbing the information and its implication.

Fred buried his face in his hands. "Oh, Christ, Elly May, we're related."

She giggled.

Fred scooted away from her. "This just makes a totally crappy end to my totally crappy day."

"Don't worry, Fred. I'll never ask to borrow money."

He sneered and crossed his legs, purposely checking the time on his wristwatch. He looked over at her, his head cocked sideways, and his mouth trying its best not to break into a grin. "Better not."

They watched as several press photographers got out of the elevator and slinked toward the men's room. In about a minute a bailiff ran them out and told them to get off the floor. One photographer argued about First Amendment rights but to no avail. When the bailiff said, "Sue me," and the photographer responded, "I will," Alma realized that Contrary was in for a shot in the arm like it'd never had before. "Contrary's not so far away from the outside world anymore, Fred."

"Not like when we grew up."

"I think that's good, in the long run."

"Don't look for me to be nostalgic."

The bailiff stared hard at Alma, but seeing she was sitting quietly beside Fred, he must have assumed she was another witness. He reentered the foyer to the grand jury room and locked the door behind him.

"How long have they had Johanna Littlefield in there?" she asked.

"About two hours now."

"What do you think of her?"

Fred thought a minute, then said, "A sad little girl."

"I can't help worrying that that sad little girl might get my brother a first-degree indictment."

"Alma," Fred said in a lecturing tone. "Vernon has helped as much with that as Johanna Littlefield."

Alma shook her head in reluctant agreement. "I just wish I could find out why."

"Vernon still clamming up?"

"Yep," she said. "Vernon is Vernon when it comes to being helpful."

Alma waited another half hour. Her imagination ran circles around her, worrying about what Johanna might be saying, but Alma was determined to stay until she came out. If Johanna was surrounded by the Littleafia, Alma thought that at least she'd be able to see her, perhaps read her face, her reactions. She reminded herself that it was only a matter of time before the defense team could question Johanna, but still Alma couldn't shake the feeling of danger when she thought of that "sad little girl."

As time passed, her impatience grew. "How long has it been?" she asked.

"Three hours," Fred answered.

She stood up and paced. "I've got to see her. Damn it, I got to talk to her."

Fred let out a huff. One arm crossed his stomach as if indigestion had set in, and his other hand rubbed his mouth as if hoping to keep himself from speaking. "I ain't ever seen anybody testify before the grand jury for three solid hours without taking a whiz."

Alma stopped pacing and looked at him. "You're a fricking genius, Fred."

She meandered down the hall, checked that no one was watching her, and ducked into the ladies' room. She splashed her face with cold water. A vending machine in the outer lounge had coffee, sandwiches, and candy. She dug in her pocket for change. Juicy Fruit gum—thirty-five cents. Alma stared at it. If it hadn't been for a gum wrapper, Vernon wouldn't be in all this trouble. *When Littlefield threw that gum wrapper at Vernon, what did it mean?* The question tumbled through Alma's thoughts.

A half hour passed before she heard a commotion in the hall. A petite woman rushed in and darted into a stall. She moved so quickly that Alma barely saw the flash of her rust-colored blouse. Sounds of regurgitation followed by flushing. Water splashed in a sink. A bone-thin young woman came around the corner, wiping her face with a wet paper towel. She studied Alma, then sat on a couch, facing away from her.

Alma moved to the vending machine, inserted three coins, and bought the gum. "Here," she said to the young woman. "Take a piece. It'll calm your stomach."

The woman pushed evenly cut bangs from her forehead. Her hair was the color of clover honey and shaped in a pixie cut that framed a long, lean face. She stared at the gum and touched the edge of the package but did not look up at Alma.

Alma sat next to her and pulled out a stick of gum, offering it to her again, then said, "You look at it like it means something to you."

The woman's large blue eyes flashed up and instantly down again as if she had trouble looking into Alma's face, then she licked her lips with a quick stroke and took the stick of gum but did not open it. "A voice from the grave," she said, looking up at Alma to see if she would respond. When Alma sat quietly, the woman flashed a quick smile that disappeared as fast as it had appeared. "I didn't mean to scare you," she said, her eyes darting from her lap to Alma a dozen times in about twenty seconds.

"You didn't scare me," Alma said, and smiled. "Are you feeling better?"

"No." The woman leaned back on the couch. "I've got ten minutes to pull myself together. I don't think I could do it in ten years."

Alma looked at the door. Through the slats she could see the outline of someone pacing outside. A bailiff, she thought. She'd have to be quiet. If she got caught talking to a grand jury witness, she could draw a contempt of court charge. She'd have to approach this carefully. "Is there anything I can do to help you?" She studied the thin face, the pallid skin with ruddy acne on her forehead. Not Vernon's type of woman. There was much more to this story than Alma had ever realized.

The woman twirled the still-wrapped piece of gum through her fingers. "Help? If I screamed 'Help' at the top of my lungs, twenty people would come running and none of them would be able to help me."

"I can tell you're troubled," Alma said, taking the woman's hand to steady her. "I'm a good listener if you care to talk."

"Are you a reporter?" the woman asked.

The woman's limp hand was moist with perspiration. She seemed aware of it and pulled it back, wiping it on her pants. Alma opened another piece of gum and watched her reaction. She slowly raised it to her lips and bit off half. "No. I'm a lawyer."

The woman's facial muscles briefly constricted as she regarded Alma suspiciously. "A lawyer?"

"This is a courthouse, I'm a lawyer."

"Yeah." The woman relaxed a half portion. "I guess

there are a lot of them in this building." She seemed relieved and let her body relax into the couch. "I'm supposed to stay away from the reporters."

Alma carefully wadded up the gum wrapper, aware that attention was focused on it like a pinpoint. She tossed it up and down in her hand. The woman's features froze. Alma took in the dark circles under her eyes and the haggardness of her appearance: slouched posture, nails bitten to the quick, wan cheeks that had lost their firmness and hung below her jaw bone. "Sounds like you could use a friend."

"I hate gum." She handed back the piece of gum Alma had given her. "And any friend of mine isn't a friend for long."

Alma tossed her gum wrapper toward a trash receptacle on the side of the couch, purposely aiming toward the woman. It hit her cheek and bounced off. The woman's face contracted reflexively as if she were reliving a nightmare. Then her arms flew up to shield her face. "Forgive me, Father, for I have sinned," she said. She seemed disoriented, living a memory in another place. Her words were automatic: she spit them out like the praying of the rosary. She dropped to her knees as if in prayer.

Alma froze. What had she done? The woman struggled to regain her composure—her head revolving in a semicircle as though looking for a tyrant above, her hand clutching the couch as if afraid she'd be dragged away, her breathing heavy and fast. All Alma could think of was how much the vacant, immobile eyes resembled her own after she had been raped. Alma started to touch her but pulled back. The woman repeated, "Forgive me, Father, for I have sinned." She spoke the words like a recitation she'd already said a thousand times.

No wonder Vernon was so protective of her, Alma

thought, and was stirred with similar feelings of protection. She touched the young woman's shoulder and she seemed to come to herself. "I'm sorry," Alma said. "I aimed for the trash can."

The woman's eyes followed the line of the furniture to the floor and focused on the wrapper beside the trash can. She seemed unconscious of having said anything.

"What were you saying about reporters?" Alma asked innocently.

The woman rubbed her temple. "Uh, I'm not to talk to them."

Alma smiled and casually smoothed back her hair. "If you did, what do you think is the worst that would happen?"

"They would tear out my heart."

"You know, I once heard it said that we are defined by our secrets. I've always wondered if we never kept secrets—if everyone knew all about us—if maybe we'd be happier. At least the people who knew our secrets couldn't use them against us."

"I'm too tired to talk right now."

"Ah, you prove my point. You're tired of keeping secrets, I'll bet."

"I'm tired . . . of everything."

"I understand how you feel." Alma moved closer to her. She pointed a finger at her chest. "Once some people hurt me—very badly. So badly I thought I'd die." A pasty taste in her mouth caused her to stop and swallow. She had to choose her words as carefully as she did when addressing a jury. "I'd been violated. I was never the same person again."

The thin young woman focused her whole attention on Alma. Her eyes narrowed as if trying to judge whether to trust her. She interlaced her fingers, squeezing her hands so tight that her knuckles turned white. "Why are you telling me this?"

"My brother saved me. If it hadn't been for that one person, no one would ever have known. Now I wish more people had known back then. Maybe my life would have been different. Maybe the people who hurt me would have paid for it. Instead, all the wrong people paid for it."

The woman looked away, staring at her distorted reflection in the chrome of an ashtray.

"Just remember that the press is outside the courthouse. Nobody could tell your story better." Alma waited to see if the woman would respond. Her eyes were closed and she seemed to be concentrating on some deep recess in herself that gave her strength. "Just think about it," Alma said.

The woman nodded. A knock on the door startled them both. The bailiff grumbled unintelligible words. Alma reached out and held the woman's hand. "Just think about this: Who told you not to talk to the reporters and why would they tell you that? The press is in front of the courthouse. If you left in that direction, you could wash all those secrets away, once and for all."

"My name's—"

"Your friend." Alma pointed quickly to the door, where the bailiff waited. She didn't want Johanna to tell her her name because if their meeting ever came to light, she could claim that she had not known the identity of the woman she had spoken to.

Johanna blinked several times, as if Alma's words were a jump rope through which she had maneuvered. "It's been nice to know you." She walked toward the door, turning to look back before she opened it. "Some secrets are just too godly to be understood."

Alma waited a few minutes before going out. She

stared at the gum wrapper on the floor. Then she picked it up and threw it in the trash. "Too godly"? What the hell had she meant by that?

Back in the hallway, Alma sat beside Fred, who nervously studied her face. He seemed to want to know and not want to know what had happened. "I told the bailiff I thought the bathroom was empty," he said. He crossed his arms behind his back and stretched his legs out in front of him, finally crossing them at his ankles, but he kept looking over at her as if he were about to burst with questions.

"You did the godly thing," Alma said, still reflecting on Johanna's last statement.

"I don't know why I do the things I do when you're around. I'll be glad when you leave town."

Alma patted his hand. "You were right—a sad little girl."

"Don't be cagey, Elly May. I can tell there's more."

Alma nodded and exhaled deeply. "Let's just say I'm glad Bill Littlefield hailed from Ohio. If he'd been from the south, it would have been too much of a cliche."

Fred stared at her, then jerked his head forward and stared straight ahead. His lips parted and he uttered a single word: "Incest."

Alma stood and looked at him. He not only suspected, he'd probably known! Jesus, that meant the whole town knew about it.

45

Back at the law office Vernon sat surrounded by Alma, Bob, and Jefferson as if he were an inquisition witness about to be interrogated. The psychiatrist, Kyle Muncy, sat in a chair well away from the others, as though a therapist should give Vernon some distance.

When Vernon spoke, anger and disgust twisted his features. "Throwing the gum wrapper meant that he'd had her." His face and neck were flushed crimson, and the color deepened and looked hot when he spoke. "I had her out of there. About a year ago. I had her convinced to leave. I was all set to meet her that night."

"She changed her mind?" Kyle Muncy asked with a slight nod, as if implying he already knew the story.

Vernon shook his head. He stared at a portable television set up on a file cabinet. The sound had been turned down completely on a Donald Duck cartoon. "When I got there—Falcon Rock, that's where we were gonna meet—Littlefield and his mafia were there. I thought I was gonna get the crap beat out of me." Vernon rubbed his hand over the side of his face that wasn't bruised.

He leaned forward, staring at the floor. "They didn't touch me. Littlefield comes up to me and smiles. He takes out a piece of gum and talks as he chews. Then, wadding the wrapper up in a ball, he says, 'When I throw a piece of gum paper at trash like you, it means two things. Means I want you to pick it up, and for you—especially for you, ole Vernon boy—it means I just fucked your girlfriend.' "

Vernon touched the edge of his swollen eye. "Then the bastard starts crying. Crying! He says to me that he loves his daughter more than anything and I'd have to understand that he'd never let anybody take her away. He says that just because I don't understand, don't mean it don't make sense and that it ain't right. He says that theirs is more than father and daughter—that they're spiritually connected. He taps his chest and says, 'My little girl is in here, in my heart.' He was like two different people."

The silence in Jefferson's office felt as uncomfortable as a hot, sticky day. Muncy cleared his throat as if he felt he had to bring some understanding to the situation. "From what you've told me, Vernon, I suspect her father had been abusing her since childhood. Most likely, he brought her up to believe that this was her duty to her father."

"I wanted to kill him," Vernon said. "I wanted to kill him right then and there."

Muncy cleared his throat again. "It would be consistent with his actions that he had entered a lifestyle that in his mind got out of control. He probably hated his behavior but couldn't stop himself."

"Why did you help her?" Alma asked Vernon. "Why did you get yourself involved in such a situation?"

Vernon sputtered a half-laugh. "Tell you the truth, she reminded me a little bit of you, Alma."

Her steely resolve melted. She looked at her brother and no longer saw the arrogant hayseed that she'd judged him to be. His beaten face was swollen and blue; his large hands, the knuckles bruised, held to each other with a quiet determination. Alma realized that he'd been right to do what he did—even if he was the only one who understood it. "How could Littlefield get away with doing such a thing for so many years?" She looked directly at Jefferson as if to blame him for living in this town.

"Money," Vernon answered. "You ain't in San Francisco, Sis. In the mountains, money buys a whole lot of looking the other way." He stood and reached his arms up, touching the ceiling. "It ain't nobody's fault. There wasn't nothing we could do about it."

"It's not so much money," Jefferson said. "It's power, control. He had it. I don't know what gives it to a man like him, but he just had it."

Alma shook her head, disgusted with what she was hearing.

"Think back, Alma," Vernon said. "There ain't nothing you can do about it in a town like this. There ain't enough Jefferson Binghams to go around. The Fred Walkers get stomped until they don't care, and the smart ones like you—they leave."

"It's not enough," Alma said. "It's not enough to clear my conscience. If I lived in this town and I knew about it, I'd make it my business to do something about it."

"Johanna is an adult, Alma," Bob said. "She would be held responsible for what happened to her, even blamed for it."

Jefferson folded his arms across his chest, looking as if he was feeling his conscience and blaming himself for his own inaction. "She had no way out."

"Except for Vernon," Alma said. "Why didn't she leave?"

Another tightly wound piece of silence filled the office. None of them could look at one another for long. Kyle Muncy cleared his throat once more, usually a sure indication that he was about to speak, but even he remained silent.

"Vernon," Bob said. "Were you applying for a job at the hotel to be near Johanna, perhaps watch over her?"

"I wasn't applying for a job at all," Vernon said. "I never figured why they made all that up. Johanna called me and, for the first time in a year, sounded like a normal person." He sucked in a deep breath and wiped the edge of his bruised eye. "After she hung up, I went to the hotel and sneaked into her room. Thought if I could just talk to her one more time, then maybe . . ." Vernon licked his chapped lips and continued. "She wasn't there. I heard noises in Littlefield's office, and when I listened at the door, I heard, 'Forgive me, Father, for I have sinned.' He made her say that when he . . . when he . . ."

"How sick!" Alma expelled the words as if she were spitting out soured milk.

"Littlefield pulled up his pants and that was where we fought," Vernon said. "I don't know how he ended up in the business office. Somebody must have dressed him and carried him."

"That's where the hotel doctor's office is," Jefferson said. "The police report stated that Winchell thought he might still be alive, but of course, it was too late."

Bob sighed and patted Vernon on the back. "I admire what you tried to do, Vernon, but Johanna's testimony will give you a motive for killing Littlefield, and unfortunately, if Walter twists the facts the way I think he will, he may convince the grand jury of unimpeachable grounds for returning a first-degree indictment."

"Is this prosecutor really that twisted?" Muncy asked.

Alma caught an involuntary laugh. "After all you've heard today, do you really have to ask that?" She looked over at Vernon and stroked the back of his shoulder. "I encouraged Johanna to talk to the press afterwards. Do you think she will?"

"I don't know what good it would do," Jefferson

said. "Walter will try to get the sexual abuse ruled inadmissible."

"Which will prevent us from using a diminished-capacity defense," Bob said.

"It'll get her story out her way," Alma said, "and Vernon's story. The grand jury will have heard it from Walter's point of view. I have no doubt that he packed that jury like sardines in a can. Who better to get the real story out than the victim's daughter telling everyone that her father's death was deserved? Vernon saved her life." Alma stood, waving her hands animatedly. "He did, he saved her life by killing that scum."

"Johanna can't handle the press." Vernon sat up. "She gets too nervous, closes down. I don't know if she'll even make it through the grand jury. Alma, you've got to promise me you won't let her go in front of the press."

"Vernon, it may happen whether any of us likes it or not."

Bob turned up the television. "It may be too late." A special news bulletin was about to come on. While they waited, the anchor replayed Walter denouncing his mother repeatedly. A pale and shaken Charlotte responded that she didn't know what had gotten into her son. Clearly, she was stunned. Alma smiled as she watched.

The coverage went live and a picture of the Contrary Courthouse flashed onto the screen. A pale and shivering Johanna Littlefield crouched in a corner on the front steps. "Get away from me!" she shrieked at the top of her lungs. "Don't touch me!" The camera lights flashed on her and reporters shouted questions. She covered her face with her hands and sank to the ground, shivering and crying. The reporters hovered like vultures.

"I can't watch anymore." Alma turned away.

Vernon grabbed her arm and slung her back so hard

she hit the desk. "This is your fault! This is your fault! You talked her into this! I told you!" He sped from the room, slamming the door so hard, the window cracked down the middle and a piece of glass shattered to the floor.

Alma stared at the television set and saw the pathetic, crouched figure of Johanna Littlefield clawing at the concrete corners that boxed her in. Vernon had been right. Johanna couldn't handle it. It had been wrong to suggest she try. This was a woman who should have been protected. Alma had sent her into a lion's den.

The television picture blurred as people broke through the crowd. Johanna howled like a wild animal. Clark Winchell pulled at her, trying to force her into a limousine. The police roughly pushed back the reporters and camera crews, all eagerly filming and daring the cops to push more. Vernon crashed through toward Johanna. She screamed his name as the limousine door shut and the car sped away.

The reporters turned on Vernon. His face—stark under the glare of television lights—looked like that of an animal caught in a hunter's gun sight. His facial bruises and cuts looked more animated, more painful. Reporters shouted questions at him. He broke through the crowd and ran. The television camera followed his sprint until he was just a dot far down the street, then it rose upward, focusing on the front of the courthouse, on a stone statue of a blindfolded Justice.

By midafternoon the grand jury had returned an indictment against Vernon Esau Bashears: murder in the first degree.

46

Alma spent the rest of the day with Mamaw. She wasn't as upset about the first-degree indictment as Alma had feared. The rest of the family was a different story. One at a time they'd wander into the house, peek in and say hello to Mamaw, and regard Alma with a chilly air as if she were the quarterback who'd fumbled the ball on the winning pass. Only Alma's mother sat down for fifteen minutes, wanting to talk about anything other than the case. "'Member that Millie Jackson who married Denny Barnwell?" She leaned in toward Alma and Mamaw to speak in a half-whisper. "She up and left him for Denny's boss."

Alma nodded, vaguely recalling the names.

"His boss was the head of the Democratic Party, and Denny got so mad he went down and registered as a Republican!" Merl slapped a hand against her thigh before standing up, as if to indicate that she'd had enough of sitting. "I got to get to the A&P. Lets me and you go out sometime, Alma."

Alma appreciated her mother's efforts to get along but knew it was more than that. Merl's invitation, however genuine, was laced with the guilt of a mother who felt she hadn't done quite enough for her daughter. Only now, at the time of Alma's greatest failure, could her mother reach out to her. It made Alma uncomfortable, and she hoped her mother would not pursue the invitation. "Yeah, Momma," she said, "we'll do that real soon."

At midafternoon some of the relatives began to arrive. First and second cousins mostly, a sister of Mamaw's and a brother of Uncle George's. They spread themselves through the houses. All offered support, the women cooking endlessly, the men talking about the best way to fortify and protect the hollow. It surprised Alma that so many had responded—dropping their lives and agreeing to visit in shifts until the trial ended.

Vernon had locked himself in his trailer, not even coming out for dinner. Alma supposed the jesterlike front he had kept up for the family's sake was finally too much even for him.

Around five o'clock Alma knew that she, too, needed some time alone. She could think of only one place where no one would look for her. "I'm going to ride out to Jesus Falls, Mamaw," she said. "I won't be gone long. No need to mention to anyone where I'm going."

Mamaw nodded, working on the edging of the finished quilt. "I want you to take this home with you when you go. Something to remind you of us."

Alma's eyes burned as she drove away in Vernon's Jeep. Someday soon she would be gone and whatever happened to him would have happened. It would all be like a dream to her. Or would it? Could she force this place and these people back into her memory again? Could she forget them again as surely as she had the first time? Insecurity and dread welled up inside her. She held back feeling anything. She couldn't afford to be emotional now. "There has to be a way. There has to be a way out of this," she kept repeating to herself as she turned into the park at Jesus Falls.

The unseasonably warm weather had brought out a

church group. They were conducting a baptism in the pool below the falls, where the water was still and quiet. Several people wore wet clothing, so Alma figured the service wouldn't last much longer.

She avoided the group and climbed the path to the top of the falls. The flow was light, a gentle cascade rather than the thundering water mass that the falls could sometimes be. She lay down on a huge rock. The church group had brought torches, and as dusk approached they lit up the area like a circus. A gentle mist blew off the falls, moistening Alma's skin. She turned over on her stomach and watched as a girl of about fourteen was lowered under the water by a minister.

The girl came up with her arms raised and shouted hallelujahs. "Praise the Lord!" called out her pastor. She walked out of the pool into the arms of her waiting family, who hugged her and welcomed her into the family of God. Alma felt so empty and so alone. The sight of Johanna crouched in a corner trying to escape the press haunted her like an apparition. She squeezed her eyes closed, wishing she could shake it from her thoughts.

The group sang a hymn.

> "Blest be the tie that binds
> Our hearts in Christian love.
> The fellowship of kindred minds
> is like to that above."

Alma turned over on her back. The inky-colored sky, pierced by stars whose twinkling seemed painful, was streaked with red on the western horizon. The group sang the verse again as they walked to their cars, and in a few minutes only the tickling sound of the waterfall remained. "The tie that binds," she said to herself as she looked out over the park that Walter Gentry and his mother had built.

The evening air began to turn cool. Alma was glad they had left the torches, which created a circle of heat. She walked down to the pond and took off her shoes, shirt, and jeans. She gasped as she stepped in. The icy water spread a chill through her. She went in deeper and the water covered her ankles.

The baptismal pond had been cemented to about four feet in depth, and the sand from the larger stream softened the coarseness against her feet. Her heart beat fast. She struggled to contain the panic of memory: thrashing, swallowing gulp after gulp of metallic-tasting water. She stared into the darkness of the pool, the flames from the torches reflecting her shape in a twisted collage of colors as she stepped even deeper, the water covering her knees. She could almost see herself falling from the top of the falls, feel the stinging impact of the water, then the soft, sandy bottom erupting around her.

Alma sat down. The cold no longer bothered her. She inched herself forward until she floated. Ducking under the water, she swam until her feet touched the rocks of the main stream. She dove, touching the bottom and then soaring up to the surface, breaking it with a splash. She gasped for air, staring back at land and the burning torches. Seconds of panic passed as she forced herself to dog-paddle in the deeper water.

Leaning back, she floated and willed the angry struggle inside her to cease. Her ears picked up the rhythms of underwater: the splash of the falls hitting the stream, a thumping of watery life, squeaks and thuds belonging to creatures she could only imagine. Then a steady whine interrupted and the sounds of night life ceased. She lifted her head and faced two glaring headlights.

A string of breaststrokes toward shore and she was waist deep. The headlights went out and a figure stood just beyond the light of the torches.

"I couldn't believe it when Mamaw said you'd come out here." Jefferson stepped into the light. The leather of his black jacket picked up glimmers of reflected torchlight. His jeans were ripped at the knees, and the shadow of a beard curved around his jaw.

"There's a blanket in the back of the Jeep," she called out. "Would you get it for me?"

He retrieved the blanket and wrapped her in it as they sat at a picnic table. His eyes were full of questions that he didn't ask. He pushed back a strand of wet hair from her forehead. "Wait a minute." Taking one of the torches, he lit a fire in the barbecue pit. Within a few minutes Alma was warm and drying out.

"You didn't have to come out here," she said. "I'm fine, really."

He looked away from her, staring into the fire, then bit his lower lip and sucked in a deep breath.

She could tell he hadn't come there for her. "Jefferson?"

"Johanna Littlefield tried to kill herself," he said. He exhaled a shivering breath. "Hung a rope from a ceiling beam in her father's office, wound it around her neck, and jumped off her father's desk."

Alma was too stunned to speak.

"The rope broke before she strangled. They've got her in a hospital in Louisville. She won't be coming back . . . not for a long time."

"She was our best hope," Alma managed to say.

"A couple of bailiffs spilled their guts about the grand jury. You know they listen through an air duct outside the jury room. Walter really tore Johanna up. She tried to protect Vernon, and he twisted everything she said, got her all confused. Vernon ended up looking like a co-conspirator in the incest."

"But we know just the opposite is true."

"When are you going to tell Vernon?"

Alma thought, dreading it. She wasn't sure how Vernon would react. "Tomorrow morning," she said. "Let him get a night's rest first."

"There's something else." Jefferson inhaled a deep breath. "The bailiffs—some female reporters got them drunk at the Holiday Inn. Johanna's testimony is going to be in every news report by tomorrow morning."

"Think we can get a dismissal?"

"Not a chance. The grand jury's already ruled. It just spills some of the prosecution's case, and they probably don't consider it that critical now that she's not available to testify."

"A crazy woman can't clarify herself." Alma huffed out a frustrated breath. "Is that *Headlines* producer still interested in a show?"

"According to Bob, the show's producer wants to do it tomorrow. They're afraid the judge will issue a gag order at the preliminary trial on Wednesday. I believe they're waiting on Walter to decide."

"He'll agree," Alma said confidently.

"How do you know?"

"The governor's going to make his decision this week. After all the damage Mrs. Gentry did to Walter's chances, what better way to make him look like his own man? Walter wouldn't miss that show for a hundred convictions."

"Alma, I wish the governor would appoint him. Maybe sending Walter to the state capital is the best thing for all of us."

"No," she said. "Walter's crossed the line. He's hurt too many people. There's only one choice that is best for every one of us. It's time to enforce a little-known law that Mamaw taught me."

"Alma?"

"The law of revenge."

"You make me nervous when you talk like that."

"I'm the only one who can enforce it. I'm the only one in this town with the moral right."

"Slow down, Alma. Look at all the trouble you've gotten into here. You don't need any more trouble."

"Just like Vernon was the only one with the moral right to kill Bill Littlefield."

"And you see what it got Vernon."

"I have to go home now. I need to think."

"Think well, Alma. You're a lawyer. You know the right decision. You're a lawyer. Just remember that."

Sitting alone between the cold sheets on her bed, Alma thought and thought and thought. She stared at the faces of her family, the old black and white photos seeming stern and forbidding. She stared out the window at the potato field. Recently tilled, the black mounds of earth looked like giant anthills. She thought of Mamaw and Papaw, working the land as young people—starting out their lives with no certainty of their future. And her father, so full of dreams that were never to be, and her mother, living those dreams vicariously through her children.

Vernon had told her to get off the case before someone got killed. Now Johanna had tried to kill herself, and Alma couldn't help feeling some responsibility. "The choices that people make," she said, surprised at the calmness in her voice. She was sorry for Johanna, as sorry as a person could be. But her own family—the Bashearses were not going to end up with the guilt of murder on them. "It is not going to happen that way."

47

When dawn broke, she went outside and knocked on Vernon's trailer.

"It's open," he called out.

She stepped inside. Vernon sat at his kitchen table, staring out the window at the mountainside. The trailer was sparser than she'd imagined—a few knickknacks she recognized from Mamaw's house, a king-size waterbed that took up the entire living area, boxes of cereal lining a kitchen counter. Scattered snapshots were taped to the walls. Mostly of Vernon and various girlfriends. Some of the family. None of Johanna Littlefield. "You been up all night?" she asked.

He pointed to his swollen eye, where the surrounding skin was beginning to turn blue. "Kept me awake."

Alma sat opposite him, moving a salt shaker and a jar of jam so that nothing was between them.

"What's wrong?" he asked.

She turned toward an oversize window that looked custom-made. Outside, knee-deep fog hid the trunks of the trees. The remains of an old treehouse looked as if they held together the branches of two intertwining oaks. She touched his hand, which was wrapped around a mug of coffee. He winced, and she realized that his knuckles were badly bruised. Alma looked into his eyes, which continued a steady gaze into hers. "It's Johanna."

"Yes?"

"She tried to kill herself."

Vernon pushed back his chair and stood up. Facing the window, he shoved his hands deeply into his pockets. If the bruising stung, he did not show it.

"She's in a mental institution in Louisville." Alma rubbed her hands over her face. A minute of silence passed. She didn't know what to say.

He stepped away and sat on the edge of the waterbed. The sloshing of the water added to the awkward silence.

"Vernon?"

"You're always so damn cool."

She had expected anger from him, perhaps grief. Vernon sloughed down onto his bed, curled into a fetal position, and stared at the wall.

"Vernon?" She went to the edge of the bed. He didn't respond when she touched his shoulder. "I take responsibility for this, Vernon. I'm sorry."

For all her trying, she couldn't get him to speak. Finally she pulled a blanket over him and closed the curtains across the window so that when the sun began to cut through the fog, it wouldn't disturb him. "Just sleep, baby," she said. "I'll take care of this."

48

"We're not doing the *Headlines* show," Bob announced to Alma and Jefferson.

"We have to do *Headlines*," Alma said, stunned by the announcement. "Their ratings equal *Larry King*'s and *Nightline*'s. The exposure we'll get will knock Walter on his ass."

Bob shook his head. "It's in bad taste."

"What about this case is in good taste?" Alma stood, one hand anchored on her hip. She knew her challenge would make him defensive, but she had to do that television show.

"Freelancers for *Hard Copy* and *A Current Affair* showed up this morning," Bob said. "I'm sure *Inside Edition* is right behind them. Anything we do on television will look like we're trying to sensationalize the trial, our client, and this case."

Jefferson sat quietly, watching Alma. "Potential jurors will get a bad taste in their mouths and blame Vernon," he agreed.

"They will do the stories anyway," Alma said, a growing anger rippling through her voice.

"Let them," Bob said. "Let them focus on Walter. That way our case will have the flavor of the underdog. I want to manipulate the press, Alma, not look like I'm manipulating them. We'll have the advantage."

"Not if the governor appoints Assemblyman Gentry this week. That appointment will make him look right. It'll make him look moral, a . . . a reformer . . . a hero." Alma was nearly shouting. "I'm doing that show!"

"No, Alma!" Bob shouted back. "That's the end of it. The less we engage the commonwealth attorney publicly, the better."

49

Alma waited in the seating area of a midsize studio. WCON—"the contrary voice of Contrary," the local cable station billed itself. An interview stage had been arranged to match the set of the *Headlines* show, which originated from Washington, D.C. Alma saw the anchor, Ross McGuire, inspecting it for inconsistencies. He looked up, saw Alma, then motioned for an assistant to introduce them.

Alma stepped forward and shook Ross McGuire's hand. After the introductions, she commented, "It was ambitious for the show to come all the way down here. I'm sure the Knoxville stations could have set up a feed."

"I wanted to beat *60 Minutes* to the draw," he said, a directness in his tone. "I hear Larry King's producers are also leaving messages for you all over town."

"Pity I haven't been home much."

McGuire stared at her, seeming to wait and watch. "You've been offered money for your story, surely?"

Alma touched his arm. "No amount of money can compensate justice, and that's the only reward I'm aiming for."

"Interesting response."

"You know that Bob Krauss will not be here?" Alma asked, hoping this would not endanger the interview.

"It's unfortunate not hearing his side of the story."

"He always considers the legal ramifications and felt the judge may view his involvement with this interview harshly."

"You expect a gag order to be issued in tomorrow's hearing?"

"I expect so," Alma said. Behind McGuire, the door opened. She could see Walter and Ellen Farmer greeting the producers. "I'm sure that expectation won't stop the prosecutor from showing up."

A producer named Jim pulled Ross away to introduce him to Walter, who deliberately kept his back to Alma. Ellen, once again lugging Walter's briefcase, frowned when she saw Alma. Setting the briefcase beside a couch, Ellen sauntered to the water fountain. As Ellen sipped from a paper cup, she circled to face Alma and said, "Jefferson tells me Krauss is really scrambling." She slowly lowered herself on the couch, crossed her legs in an artificially sexy pose, and cocked her head sideways. "This suicide attempt looks like it's connected to the father. You know, Johanna was real upset by his murder."

Alma bit the inside of her cheek and smiled her most insincere smile. She leaned forward and looked into Ellen's eyes. "Jefferson didn't tell you pig shit."

Ellen's face registered a wide-eyed shock. "I . . ." she stuttered, trying to speak. "I . . . you . . ."

Alma walked away. She stood in front of a makeup mirror and adjusted her jacket, all the while watching Walter's reflection.

The group of producers waved their hands and gestured frantically. Walter walked over to where Ellen sat and crossed his arms over his chest.

The producers talked among themselves, then a thin, blond-haired man was sent in Alma's direction. "There's a slight problem," he said to her. "Seems Mr. Gentry was expecting to be on the show with Bob Krauss. He's concerned about appearing with you since you're related to the man he's prosecuting."

"He's not concerned," Alma said, loud enough for Walter to hear. "He's terrified."

Walter's head jerked around and he glared at her.

Alma glared back. Her posture straightened and she pulled her shoulders back like a cat confronting an invasion of territory. "Fine," she said to the producer, still speaking loud enough for Walter to hear. "I'm more than happy to do the show alone."

The young producer excused himself and hurried back to his flock. Alma thought they obviously had their own ideas of what this case was about. She'd have to break that perception wide open. In all likelihood, Ellen had spent the entire afternoon compiling information for them. Alma hoped they were smart enough to see through it.

Ross McGuire came out of a dressing room and the producer approached him. As they spoke, McGuire's expression became agitated. He took Walter aside. Alma would have given just about anything to hear their conversation. She prayed that she'd made a good impression on Ross earlier.

In a few seconds the blond-haired producer returned to Alma. "We'll do the show with both of you," he said. "Mr. Gentry has agreed."

The stage manager explained the procedures to them and positioned them next to each other, facing Ross. Walter sat without looking at Alma. She could feel the intensity of his anger coming off him in waves. His fruity cologne flavored the air. Alma purposely sneezed. The show was live, and the excitement of the cameras, moving and jostling offstage, became nerve-racking. Even Walter held his hands together on his lap to still a slight tremble.

The director gave a signal and the stage became quiet.

A monitor showed a reporter assessing the background of Contrary, Kentucky, and the case of Vernon Bashears. Alma was thrilled that he reported as much on Bill Littlefield's shady life as on his good works in Kentucky. Next came the news reports showing Walter denouncing his mother and Mrs. Gentry responding to her son. Alma felt Walter tighten up as he shifted in his seat several times.

The tape continued with Johanna's breakdown in front of the courthouse and Vernon running from the reporters. Then Ross McGuire spoke, reporting the sad news of Johanna Littlefield's attempted suicide after her grand jury testimony and her confinement to a mental hospital. The show broke for a commercial. During a second uncomfortable wait, Walter peered over at Alma with an eyebrow raised, as if trying to intimidate her.

Ross McGuire introduced his interview guests and opened the questioning with Alma. "In that last clip, Miss Bashears, why is your brother running?"

"Why is he running?" Alma repeated the one question she wasn't prepared to answer. She inhaled a deep breath. "I can't speak for my brother. I can only imagine what I would do in his position. The hostile environment in this town created by the commonwealth attorney's office has branded my brother a murderer despite the fact that he has not had a trial. He cannot walk down the streets of his hometown without being spat on. He cannot obtain employment, visit friends, do all the daily errands that you and I take for granted. It's like the old church tradition of being shunned. As a matter of fact, these attacks have been focused toward my entire family, and I lay the blame for them at Walter Gentry's door."

"Mr. Gentry, any response?"

"Certainly," Walter said, his voice clear and deep. "A heinous crime has been committed in our town. It has permeated the entire fabric of our community. Now we do not sleep so soundly in our beds at night, knowing that Vernon Bashears is in our midst. Any animosity toward the Bashears family is unfortunate, and I do not condone it, but it should not surprise them. We are a small town, an intimate town. Life is slower here, and perhaps a little more precious."

Alma fought the urge to interrupt, but she didn't want to sound like she was attacking the town. Ross McGuire stared into the television camera and said, "The focus of our report tonight: small-town justice. You brought up the point of being found guilty without benefit of a trial, Miss Bashears. Run with it."

"A quick survey of our local press coverage will paint the picture of a martyred savior in Bill Littlefield," Alma said. "How could any Kentuckian read this and not hate the man who killed him? Reportage glossed over the complexity of this case. It's easy to gild the truth when the victim is an individual of uncommon morals. And by 'victim' I refer to my brother, not Bill Littlefield."

Walter raised a hand, shaking his index finger for emphasis. "That is not our goal," he stated. "A free press is fundamental to our society. However, the prosecutor's office does not control it."

"Yes, but your mother does," Ross McGuire pointed out.

Alma hopped in before Walter had a chance to speak. "And Mr. Gentry makes great use of that connection. What is the one obsession this prosecutor has had since my brother's arrest? It's not truth or justice. His one concern has been to get himself appointed to the state assembly—"

"I resent that," Walter interrupted.

"It's not the first time this accusation has been made, Mr. Gentry." Ross McGuire waited.

Walter hesitated before responding. "It's a typical criticism. One to be expected. I cannot stop doing my job just because I also want to serve my state."

Alma sailed in the direction she wanted to go. "You're so busy wanting to serve your state, why didn't you simply serve your community, Mr. Gentry? Why did no one protect Johanna Littlefield from her father?"

"I'll let the question ride," Ross interjected in an obvious effort to wrestle back control of the interview. He glanced once at Alma before speaking again. "It seems to be out that Miss Littlefield's grand jury testimony included certain charges. Mr. Gentry?"

Walter shifted from side to side. He looked straight at Ross and spoke firmly. "I can't speak of grand jury testimony."

"Why?" Alma asked. "Because it protects you?" She crossed her fingers and sensed Walter fighting to keep from responding.

"Let's approach it another way, Mr. Gentry," Ross said. He slowed his speech, seeming to listen to his ear set. "You said it yourself, Contrary is a small town. Certain allegations are known in the community. To be direct, incest."

Walter's left cheek pulsed and the blood vessels in his neck stood out. His hands gripped each other under the table. "There you have it, Mr. McGuire," he said. "Vernon Bashears's motive." He leaned forward, casting a glance of conquest toward Alma. "Everyone knew it was going on for years. We will prove that this abuse is why Vernon Bashears killed Bill Littlefield."

"What did you say?" Alma pounced. He did it, she thought. He made a mistake.

Walter glanced at her, a perplexed look on his face.

"You knew of the abuse," she said. "You knew about it for years."

"I ... I ..." he stammered. "No, that's not what I

mean. You can't charge someone without evidence. The girl would never testify. We had only heard—"

"It's your job to get that evidence, is it not? And you let it go for years without even trying to get the evidence."

"Her mental state was always precarious. I repeat, the girl would not testify."

"Well, she did yesterday, didn't she?"

Walter looked at Ross, almost imploring his help. Ross's eaglelike visage remained implacable as he asked, "Do you believe Miss Littlefield attempted suicide because you forced her testimony?"

"Of course not," Walter retorted. "She's always been a disturbed young woman. Vernon Bashears did not help her mental state."

Alma felt a rush of energy spread through her veins. "Vernon Bashears seemed to be the only person she trusted enough with the secret of her life. He was the only person she believed would protect her since she couldn't get that protection from the local authorities or from the commonwealth attorney's office."

Walter sneered, not trying to hide it. "It's easy to say that from the outside, Miss Bashears. Maybe you do that in a big city like San Francisco, but in this town you don't just walk into Bill Littlefield's office and make accusations without evidence."

"Why not? Did you think Bill Littlefield was above the law?"

"We did what we could."

"Well, let's look at what you've done."

A nervous expression crept onto Walter's features.

Alma counted on her fingers. "You never investigated Bill Littlefield, who was your mother's business partner. You allowed your mother to convict my brother in the newspaper that she owns. You forced a mentally unstable girl before the grand jury and so traumatized her that she attempted suicide. This child, whom you knew was an incest victim, was denied the protection of you and your prestigious office."

"I don't have to listen to this!" Walter started to stand as if he might walk off the set, then looked out toward the television cameras and reseated himself. "My record of service speaks for itself."

Alma focused on him. "And does that service include driving young girls to attempt suicide?"

"I won't dignify that with a response." Walter glared at her.

"Of course you won't," Alma said, attacking with all the hostility of an enraged animal. "Silence is too often golden, but in this case the silence was about incest. How many young women will suffer because of your ineptness?"

"That's evidence that will be presented in the trial."

"How many bodies of young women will you pile up to form your staircase to the capitol?"

Ross McGuire leaned toward a camera and said, "We'll be right back after a commercial break. In our final seconds you will hear the commonwealth attorney's response." Alma knew, and the panicked expression on Walter's face said that he knew as well: it was too late.

After the show a young producer came running after Alma. "Miss Bashears, you have a call." Alma took the phone.

Without introduction Bob Krauss snarled at her, "How do you say it in the mountains—I could skin you alive!" She could feel Bob's anger coming through the receiver. "You are off this case!" he continued. "You will not be in court for a single session. And I, personally, will buy you a plane ticket back to California. Your involvement is at an end. Do you understand?"

"I'm sorry, Bob. I had to do it." Alma handed the phone back to the producer. She looked up as stagehands and technicians scurried around, breaking down the set. Walter stood by himself in a corner. His eyes were fixed on her but didn't focus on any one part of her body. He seemed to stare through her. His expression was drained; his forehead was wrinkled and bags drooped under his eyes. Only his beard hid what might have been an enraged grimace. Alma fought the urge to run as he walked toward her. His steps were slow and methodical, like a professor approaching an errant student.

Her heartbeat sped, a race car going around a track. Her throat felt parched, and she held on to the back of a chair to steady herself. She was afraid of what he would do.

He stopped a few steps short of her. His eyes were wide, the whites visible all around the dark pupils. His lower lip trembled, and his cheeks and the tip of his nose flushed a cherry red. A shaky breath spilled from his mouth.

"I saw the park," she said before he had a chance to speak. She folded her arms across her chest, now shaking and unable to stop. "I . . ." Her voice trembled and barely came through her throat. She felt as if she and Walter were in a vortex with the rest of the world disappearing in the whirl. "I saw the park." Alma had memorized the words on the park's sign and she repeated them to him in a clear, unshaken voice. " 'Jesus Falls Park and Recreation Area. In honor of Charlotte S. Gentry and Walter S. Gentry. The town of Contrary thanks you from the bottom of its heart.' "

"Alma," he said, his voice unnaturally low. Tears brimmed his lower eyelids and spilled over, disappearing into his beard. Ellen came to his side and touched his arm. "Alma," he said, his teeth chattering as he spoke vehemently, "I will bury your brother."

50

Alma woke before the alarm clock rang. She gazed upward to a pool of pale lavender—a lightning-shaped crack jagged diagonally across the ceiling. The sounds of movement from the kitchen told her the family had come in for breakfast. She listened to the somber inflection of their voices—the tone of a serious morning. It was almost as if she were a child again, waiting for her mother to tiptoe into the room and wake her and Sue for school. Her father would check her homework before breakfast and kiss her on top of the head before she left the house. Alma curled into a ball, wishing she could close her eyes and wake up during those years again. She lay there remembering until she heard them getting ready to leave.

The noise of the front door closing and someone jiggling the doorknob brought her suddenly back to the present. *Johanna Littlefield had tried to hang herself from the rafters of her father's office.* Alma sat up in bed. Walter's voice in her head: *Alma, I will bury your brother.* The grind of a car starting and its wheels spinning on the gravel driveway as it pulled onto the paved road. "How did things get so out of control?" she asked herself. "How did I let this happen?"

The sounds disappeared down the road like a chugging train in the distance. Alma lay back and stared at the ceiling again. When she looked at the clock again, nearly an hour had passed. Court would be called into session in forty-five minutes. She rubbed the sleep from her eyes, then superstitiously crossed and uncrossed her fingers as if it might send Vernon luck. In her gut, the uncertainty of his future churned like a child's toy caught in an eddy.

Another ten minutes passed. She watched the minute hand on the clock click around to a quarter past the hour. The family pictures on the walls seemed to lord their presence over her. Mamaw's look of longing, as if imagining a pinnacle she knew she'd never reach. Uncle George, Aunt Joyce, and Uncle Ames—in their eyes Alma saw that they knew the limits of their lives and accepted them without complaint. Such glee lit her mother's face at seventeen. No hint of knowing what life had in store for her. Her father, smiling as if nothing had happened, and for him it hadn't. For him, life was still in the warm summer days of the 1970s, Vernon an infant and she and Sue his little princesses. Their youthful faces, trapped in time, seemed to pass judgment on Alma. I should have done better, she told herself. I could have done more. She was their future, and what a mess she'd made of it.

She flung back the blankets and jumped out of bed, stretching her arms above her head until her spine cracked several times. In the dresser mirror her pallid skin and puffy eyes reflected her sleepless night. I am beginning to look like Momma, Alma thought. She sat in front of the mirror, studying her face. Her imagination kept envisioning Johanna dangling from a rope. She rubbed her eyes and tried to stop thinking about it. Angrily she said, "God, how you deserved to be brought low, Walter Gentry. You deserved it so much."

Downstairs, she drank the last of the lukewarm coffee directly from the pot. Mamaw had spread out the morning paper for her, a large circle drawn around the lead article: GOVERNOR APPOINTS EDWARD STOCKTON TO THE STATE ASSEMBLY. Alma let out a deep, satisfying belly laugh. "Oh, God, Vernon," she said to the empty kitchen. "What have I done to you?" She continued to laugh, knowing the dire consequences this appointment had. Walter would enter that courtroom determined to get every drop of Vernon's blood. She'd have given her career to be there.

Alma heard a loud burp from the direction of the back porch. She circled around the table and peered out the door. Her mother, legs dangling off the porch, stared out at the countryside, a six-pack of Budweiser beside her. One can had already been emptied and crushed. Albert sunned himself in a long strip of sunlight. His beige paws, jutting out from his round, fleshy body, made him look like a rug.

Alma stepped gingerly over Albert. He lifted his pink opossum snout, sniffed at her, then lazily threw his head back and covered his eyes with a paw. She sat next to her mother and let her legs swing over the side of the porch. One by one her shoes dropped off and landed on the ground beside her mother's loafers. "A little early in the day, isn't it?" Alma asked.

"I'm depressed." Her mother handed her the beer she was drinking. "Bet you never thought you'd be sent to the back porch again."

Alma snickered. "Never thought I'd be out here for the same reasons as you, Mother."

"Ahhhh." Her mother took back the beer and raised the can as if to toast the mountains. "Story of my life, banished to the back porch." She swigged a drink. "These damn Bashearses—isolationist, every one of 'em. 'Cept your daddy. He was a hellraiser."

"Oh, Momma. Daddy was never a hellraiser."

"That's what caught my eye."

"Daddy was more the noble-savage type."

Her mother spat a spray of beer. "You remember him the way a little girl remembers her daddy." She wiped her mouth with the back of a hand. "I was there, honey, and Esau Bashears was the kind of hellraiser that'd make you, me, and Vernon look like angelettes. He didn't take crap from nobody."

Alma popped open a beer and sipped from it. She couldn't remember the last time she'd drunk beer—college probably. It tasted milder than she remembered. Memories, she thought vaguely. Maybe she remembered everything wrong or at least askew. "Daddy was the reason . . ." Alma hesitated and swallowed a guzzle of beer. "The reason Charlotte Gentry gave me that college money."

"Well, hell." Her mother flipped a middle finger in the air as if gesturing to Mrs. Gentry. "That's the least she could do. Her damn husband was the reason Esau left. Esau couldn't get a job in the whole damn state 'cause of him."

"Funny," Alma said, reflecting. "Her money sent me to law school and eventually led me back here into direct conflict with her son."

"On a little more equal terms than the first time."

Alma looked over at her mother, unable to tell what she meant by "than the first time." Alma was still fairly sure that Vernon had never told Merl about the rape, but perhaps he had hinted of some schoolkid humiliation by Narly. Alma swallowed more beer.

Merl stared at the giant acorn tree that bore the carved initials of every Bashears born in this century. "We, uh," she said, "we never wanted you children to know about all them troubles." She drained the beer, reached for another one, then looked at her watch and cursed. "I called the damn cab stand over an hour ago and them lazy codgers ain't here yet."

"Another six-pack?" Alma asked.

"Albert drank two of them," she answered matter-of-factly. "He chews up the cans, so he don't leave no evidence."

Alma didn't feel like putting up an argument or a front. Her mother could drink all the beer she wanted to, at whatever time of day she wanted. It didn't really bother her, she thought, realizing she was almost through the beer she'd opened. Alma reached for her mother's wrist and turned it so she could see her watch. "Court is in session," she announced. She banged her can on the porch, mimicking a judicial gavel.

"I know how much you want to be there, honey."

Alma shook her head after gulping a long swallow. "Bob was right, Momma. I don't belong on this case anymore. I stepped over the line."

"You called an asshole an asshole."

"Believe me, it was very satisfying, but it may have ended up hurting Vernon's case."

"Vernon's case, Vernon's case," Merl said as if sick of hearing the words. "So how long do you think these pre-trial motions stuff will take?"

"The judge will probably rule by next week and set a court date at that time."

"Here." Her mother popped open the last beer can and set it between them. "I'll split this one with you."

Alma crushed the beer can she'd emptied and swallowed a long drink of the one her mother offered to share. "Trial'll probably start in a month. Don't be surprised if the judge issues a gag order at today's session."

"Only thing that surprises me anymore is the damn cab company can't get their deliveries done on time!" Merl glared at the road and shook her head impatiently.

Alma laughed, feeling warm from the beer. "Maybe it'd be faster if you ordered room service from the Littlefield Hotel."

"You know, about six years ago, before he turned that hotel into that la-di-da place, he used to run it as a high-priced whorehouse."

"No," Alma said incredulously. Then she remembered that Charlotte Gentry's involvement had begun about six years ago, so it made sense.

"Yes," Merl said, nodding. "It was the best-kept secret this town never kept. Entertained contractors, politicians, half the police force, anybody he wanted something from . . ."

Alma giggled. "You know, they have a little elevator by the bar and the bartender puts the drinks in it and drops it right down into Bill Littlefield's personal office."

Her mother howled. "I can just see Bill Littlefield calling upstairs and asking to have one of the whores sent down in his little drinks elevator."

Alma laughed so hard, she had to hold her side. "All the bartender would have to ask is blonde, brunette, or redhead?"

"And fold her properly!" Her mother cackled. "Oh, lord, I have to pee. Help your old ma up."

"So do I." Alma stood, weaving from the rush of the beer. She held out her hand for her mother to take, then had a sudden thought and turned away from Merl. Think, Alma, think! she said to herself. With both hands, she pulled her hair at the roots to help her focus. What is wrong with this picture? Bill Littlefield having his folded-up whores in a drinks elevator and sending them down to his office. His personal office. Sending the drinks down to his personal office. "Oh, my God! Mother! Oh, my God!"

Merl had stumbled backward, slipped off the porch,

and landed on her butt. She stared up at Alma with the wide, annoyed eyes of a drunk who knew she'd been dropped. "Yeeessss," her mother said, holding out her hand and still expecting to be helped up.

"We have to get to the courthouse, now!"

"Honey, are you crazy?"

"Yes!" Alma yelled, near hysteria. "Now!"

51

All Alma could manage was a half run–half walk through the halls of the courthouse while her mother clung to her arm doing her best not to fall. "Hurry, Mother!" she urged Merl.

"I can't believe you figured a way to save Vernon and all I can think of is how bad I have to pee."

"You can do that afterward. We have to get to that courtroom."

Her mother's loafers slid on the slick marble floor and Alma caught her. "Go ahead without me," Merl wheezed. "I'll catch up."

Alma ran toward Judge Dulaney's courtroom. She nearly fell as she caught the door handle and swung it open. A backdraft from the door spread a whiff of beer. She panicked, thinking she might appear drunk. About seventy-five heads turned and looked at her. Walter and Bob faced each other in front of the judge's bench, appearing to be in an argument. Both wore expressions of anger and weariness.

Judge Dulaney tapped her gavel. "Order," she said to the courtroom. Alma saw Sue, Jack, Aunt Joyce, Uncle Ames, George, Rodney, and several cousins scattered throughout the room. Their eyes were wide and expectant, as if waiting for a bomb to rip open the court. Alma slipped up the side aisle. The people in the front row scowled at her but grudgingly let her pass. She knelt behind the defense table and tapped Jefferson's arm.

Vernon turned around at the same time that Merl crashed through the door. The noise of her pushing into the last row of people and forcing them to make room for her caused the judge to tap her gavel again. Alma looked around. Her mother had managed to squeeze between Charlotte Gentry and Clark Winchell. Merl smiled maliciously at each of them, then elbowed for more room. Vernon turned forward and hid his face in his hands.

Jefferson watched the spectacle in the back row, then looked hard at Alma. She tried not to lean too close to him so he wouldn't smell the beer on her breath. "I have to talk to Bob," she whispered.

"Wait, Alma." Jefferson closed his hand tightly on her arm. "Either get out of here or go sit down. Above all, don't get in Bob's way."

"I have to address the court."

"You got lucky the first time. We no longer have the advantage."

"I can get the case dismissed."

Jefferson breathed through clenched teeth and narrowed his eyes. "All you're going to do is get yourself thrown in the can on a contempt charge."

She stood up.

"Alma, no!" he gruffly whispered as loud as he dared.

Alma stepped over the legs of the front-row spectators until she reached the center entrance. "Your Honor," she said. "Forgive my interruption. I must address this court."

Bob and Walter turned around. Their facial muscles were cramped so tight, their expressions appeared the same—like men who'd just discovered their Porsches had been repossessed.

"I must object, Your Honor," Walter began. "We've agreed to no further hysterics or grandstanding."

"In this case I agree," Bob said. "I object to Miss Bashears addressing the court as well."

Judge Dulaney looked at Alma over her glasses. She ignored the objections of the two lawyers but at the same time did not seem amused by the interruption. "I hadn't intended on hearing any motions today other than from the attorneys of record."

"I'm here to request that Your Honor dismiss this case."

Walter threw the papers in his hand up into the air. "Your Honor, please! Remove that woman from this courtroom."

"Your Honor may ignore me," Alma pleaded, "but I appeal to you as an *amicus curiae*. I am prepared to present the reason why you should dismiss this case."

"Your Honor," Walter said, stepping in front of her. "This woman is no more a *friend of the court* than a Bengal tiger is a friend to Bambi."

Judge Dulaney perked up. She motioned Alma to the bench. "I read somewhere that friendship is a responsibility, not an opportunity." She took off her glasses and studied her. "I have to ask myself, Is this Bengal tiger here for food or sport?"

Alma stood quietly, sensing that she should not challenge her.

"How long will you take to show this court your sincerity of *amicus curiae*?" the judge asked.

"Less than ten minutes," she replied.

"You've whet my curiosity, Miss Bashears."

Alma thought that Judge Dulaney must have seen her on last night's *Headlines* show. She'd have to be quick, thorough, and to the point.

"I strongly object to this," Bob Krauss said. Alma

figured he was reacting in the way he believed to be in the best interest of his case. "I hope," Krauss went on, "that the court will recognize that Miss Bashears is no longer associated with Mr. Bashears's defense."

"Please, Your Honor," Alma begged. "Please."

Judge Dulaney looked at her watch. "I'm timing you. If you don't make a significant point in seven minutes, I'll lock you in jail on a contempt charge."

"Thank you, Your Honor."

Alma pulled a chalkboard from the side of the room and made a quick sketch. She looked into the audience, then asked Fred Walker to come forward. "Officer Walker," she said, admiring the deputy uniform of Claiborne County. "Congratulations on your new job."

"Six minutes, forty-five seconds, Miss Bashears," the judge reminded her.

"You were the first officer on the scene when the call came in on Bill Littlefield's death?"

"Yes," Fred answered.

"This is a brief sketch of the basement of the hotel. Show me where you found him."

Fred pointed to the room.

"This is the main business office, I believe."

"Yes, I think so," Fred said.

"Your Honor," Walter objected, "I will cover all this when the state presents its case. The woman is wasting your time."

"And you're wasting my seven minutes, Mr. Gentry, so shut up!"

"Sustained," Judge Dulaney said, looking over her glasses at Walter.

"Mr. Winchell." Alma pointed to Clark Winchell, who was sitting in the back row beside her mother. "Will you stand?"

He looked over at Mrs. Gentry. A nervous expression crept onto his face, and slowly he rose.

"Mr. Winchell, at what time did you find Mr. Littlefield's body?"

"About six P.M.—give or take a few minutes."

"At what time did you hear my brother arguing with Mr. Littlefield?"

"About noon. Again, give or take a few minutes."

"Thank you. Do not sit down," she ordered with the authority of a judge, speaking as quickly as she could. "Mr. Bingham, will you please read for me the official time of death on the coroner's report?"

Jefferson flipped through papers. Alma prayed for him to hurry. "Twelve noon to three P.M.," he said.

"Mr. Winchell," she shouted. "Will you confirm that your statement to the police says—and I'm summarizing to save time—that the fight between Vernon Bashears and Bill Littlefield took place in his personal office, and that you and several porters carried him to the business office? It's called the Cumberland Gap Suite, I believe."

"We didn't disturb the crime scene," Winchell said defensively. "We knew what a heinous crime had been committed. I thought Bill Littlefield needed medical attention. The first-aid kit and all that doctor equipment was stored in the business office."

"Yes or no, Mr. Winchell?" Alma knew her minutes were running out.

"We didn't know he was dead. We had to save his life if we could." Winchell's tone boasted of his efficiency. "When we realized he was dead, that side passage out of the building was the most reasonable! Otherwise, you would have had to tramp right through the main lobby with him all beaten like he was. Mr. Littlefield wouldn't have wanted his hotel guests upset by having to view a dead body—even if it was his."

"Yes or no, Mr. Winchell!"

"Well, yes. We did carry him from his personal office."

"Now this is very important, Mr. Winchell. In what position did you find Bill Littlefield's body?"

"All beat up, of course." He gave Vernon a disgusted look.

"Where in the room, for God's sake!"

"Draped over his desk." Winchell looked around, as confused as the rest of the spectators.

Only Charlotte Gentry reacted. Her head dropped until her chin almost rested on her chest. She covered her eyes with one hand.

She knows, Alma thought. She knows just like I know.

"Sit down, you fool!" Mrs. Gentry said to Winchell.

"Your Honor," Alma said. "I make a motion that you dismiss this case on the grounds that you do not have jurisdiction over it. Bill Littlefield died in Tennessee."

A stir in the crowd brought an immediate rap of the judge's gavel. "Turn that chalkboard toward me," she ordered.

Alma drew a thick line to represent the Tennessee state line. "The basement of the hotel is an optical illusion, built this way so that Mr. Littlefield could enjoy alcohol in his living quarters. From the front it appears that these living quarters are in Kentucky, but if you look at the floor above it," she said, quickly making a second sketch, "you can see that the bar is directly over the living quarters. The state-line demarcation in the bar is drawn precisely, as Mr. Winchell can tell you. The same line runs through the personal office just in front of the desk. A small drinks elevator behind the bar drops into the office behind the desk, where Bill Littlefield died—in Tennessee."

Judge Dulaney studied the chalkboard, read over the

police report and the statements of hotel employees, then looked up at Fred Walker and Clark Winchell. "If I put you two under oath," she asked, "will your testimony change?"

"No, sir," Fred said.

Winchell looked over at Mrs. Gentry. The scowl on her face seemed to shriek the words "You're fired." Merl had twisted toward Mrs. Gentry with a wide, mocking smile. Winchell turned ineptly toward the judge. "No, ma'am," he replied. "What I said is . . . what happened."

Judge Mary Dulaney instructed her clerk to locate the county assessor, then announced to the courtroom, "I'm going to call the sheriff, the prosecutor, and the coroner of Claiborne County. If the county assessor confirms that the state line is where Miss Bashears has marked it, then I will turn this case over to Claiborne County officials. Court is adjourned for one hour."

Alma ran over and hugged Vernon. The stir in the courtroom seemed like a whirlpool around them. "Claiborne County," she whispered in his ear. "Claiborne County is a great place for a trial."

"Why is that?" Vernon asked.

Alma hugged him again and looked over his shoulder to Fred Walker, making sure she caught his gaze, and winked at him. "Because we have kin in that county."

52

After the case was moved to Tennessee's jurisdiction, the many relatives Mamaw and Aunt Joyce had called to Contrary for support got together for a party. The kitchen table was covered with food: homemade cakes, fried chicken, banana pudding, okra and rhubarb, fried green tomatoes, squirrel gravy, and baked rabbit. Every side table in the living room had plates of dips and candies and colas and cakes. Alma was introduced to so many people, she stopped trying to remember their names.

Jefferson drew her aside just when she thought she'd drop. He made her take off her high heels and sit back in a chair, then massaged the arches of her feet. "I spoke to Richard Finn in Claiborne County," he said. "They'll get the paperwork by the end of this week and reinvestigate."

"Hard to believe we have to start all over again." Alma wiped her forehead as if drying sweat.

"I didn't get the impression from him that we could expect any surprises. He'll issue a manslaughter charge, if that."

"Any chance he'll recognize the so-far-ignored issue of self-defense? After all, there was no intent in that fight. Littlefield could have just as easily killed Vernon."

"Well." Jefferson narrowed his eyes, seeming to think critically. "Maybe Finn would if he knew he'd have to face you in the courtroom."

Alma smacked Jefferson's shoulder.

"Alma," he said seriously, "Vernon will never do time on this charge. Even if he's convicted on the manslaughter charge, which I doubt, under the circumstances he'll get probation. It's crazy in Tennessee, but it's not like what we faced with Walter Gentry." Jefferson was quiet for a moment and let his hand slip up the calf of Alma's leg. "Not like what *you* faced with Walter Gentry."

She reached down and squeezed his hand. "I hope you're right."

"If I were a betting man," he said, "I'd say it's a ninety-nine-point-five percent probability."

Sue entered from the kitchen carrying a large tray of fried chicken. Everyone reached for a piece and she promised to make more. A knock on the door brought in more neighbors—friendly, conciliatory, offering their support in the times ahead. Most brought food: deviled eggs, potato salad, and Jell-O fruit salad. A line of young blond women with sad, soulful eyes and too much makeup followed Vernon around as if he were a lost pup in need of comfort. He spent time with each of them, then scooped up Larry Joe and Eddie, turning them upside down on his shoulders as they gleefully screamed.

Vernon settled in the big chair, the one Grandpa Bashears had built. He balanced each boy on a knee and pointed at pictures in one of a dozen family albums. "And this is your Aunt Alma as a little girl," Vernon said to his nephews. "As she grew older, she eventually earned her living as a desperado, robbing banks from here to California."

"I knew that!" Larry Joe yelled at the top of his lungs.

"What's a desperado, Uncle Vernon?" Eddie slurred in baby talk.

"Well," Vernon replied, and peered through the crowd

of people, his gaze connecting with Alma's. "It's a person who starts a barroom brawl and also ends it. It's a person who fights off a stalking wildcat, who calls Superman when a bullet's headed your way, and no matter what, never gives up on you." His mouth curved into a smile and a sparkling moisture glistened in his eyes. "Even if you're dying and almost dead."

Alma smiled back at him, feeling a connectedness that she'd never felt before in her adult life. She looked around. In the corner of the room Mamaw and Bob Krauss took turns teaching each other Yiddish and the mountain version of old English. Her mother primped in front of the hall mirror, teasing the top of her hair. Her uncles dozed and awoke a dozen times. Her many actual, distant, and claimed cousins compared photos of children. Aunt Joyce and Sue danced through the crowds, making sure everyone had all that they needed. It might as well be Christmas, Alma thought. She felt the warm assurance of early childhood blossoming in her like the first day of spring.

Jefferson handed her a piece of peanut butter fudge. "My new office window hasn't been painted yet," he said. "There's still time. Bingham and Bashears, Attorneys-at-Law."

Above the racket of family and friends—each telling his or her own version of the courtroom scene, the crashing static of the television set turned on too loud, the crackle of newspapers being passed back and forth, and the clanking of dishes—she could hear Larry Joe and Eddie squealing with delight.

"That's what I want to be—a desperado!"

"I want to be just like Aunt Alma!"

Alma knew her decision was made.

AUTHORS GUILD BACKINPRINT.COM EDITIONS are fiction and nonfiction works that were originally brought to the reading public by established United States publishers but have fallen out of print. The economics of traditional publishing methods force tens of thousands of works out of print each year, eventually claiming many, if not most, award-winning and one-time best-selling titles. With improvements in print-on-demand technology, authors and their estates, in cooperation with the Authors Guild, are making some of these works available again to readers in quality paperback editions. Authors Guild Backinprint.com Editions may be found at nearly all online bookstores and are also available from traditional booksellers. For further information or to purchase any Backinprint.com title please visit www.backinprint.com.

Except as noted on their copyright pages, Authors Guild Backinprint.com Editions are presented in their original form. Some authors have chosen to revise or update their works with new information. The Authors Guild is not the editor or publisher of these works and is not responsible for any of the content of these editions.

THE AUTHORS GUILD is the nation's largest society of published book authors. Since 1912 it has been the leading writers' advocate for fair compensation, effective copyright protection, and free expression. Further information is available at www.authorsguild.org.

Please direct inquiries about the Authors Guild and Backinprint.com Editions to the Authors Guild offices in New York City, or e-mail staff@backinprint.com.

978-0-595-36711-5
0-595-36711-9

the United States
00008B/29